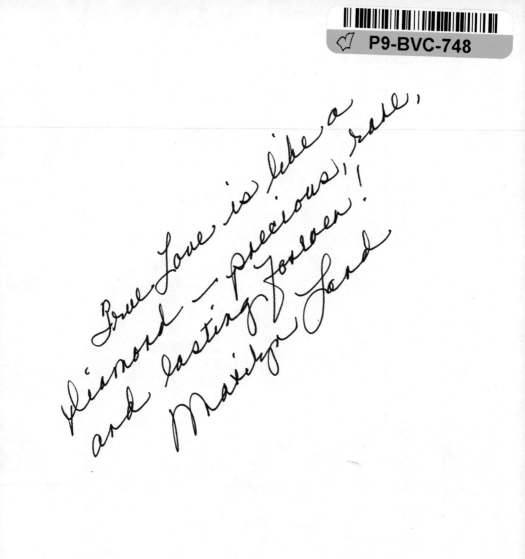

True Love is like a
diamond — precious, rare,
and lasting forever!

Marilyn Ford

A DIAMOND IN THE ROUGH

A DIAMOND IN THE ROUGH

A NOVEL

MARILYN LAND

A DIAMOND IN THE ROUGH
A NOVEL

iUniverse books may be ordered through booksellers or by contacting:

iUniverse
1663 Liberty Drive
Bloomington, IN 47403
www.iuniverse.com
1-800-Authors (1-800-288-4677)

ISBN: 978-1-5320-2140-4 (sc)
ISBN: 978-1-5320-2142-8 (hc)
ISBN: 978-1-5320-2141-1 (e)

Library of Congress Control Number: 2017908037

Print information available on the last page.

iUniverse rev. date: 06/28/2017

A Diamond in the Rough:

Someone (or something) that has hidden exceptional characteristics and/or future potential, but currently lacks the final touches that would make them (or it) truly stand out from the crowd.

The phrase is metaphorical and relates to the fact that naturally occurring diamonds are quite ordinary at first glance, and that their true beauty as jewels is only realized through the cutting and polishing process.

To Jack—my Diamond in the Rough!

This one is for you—I love you and miss you
every single minute of every single day.

Other books by Marilyn Land

Clattering Sparrows

The Dollmaker

Us

Us—a word so small
Two letters when separated mean nothing at all
When put back together encompass a world

A world where two hearts beat as one
A world of love, of promise to come
A world where dreams yearn to come true
A world that's ours—just us two

Us—a word so small
Two letters when separated mean nothing at all
When put back together define happiness untold

I believed in Us from the very start
The moment you captured my heart
From that day on we were no longer you and me
Just Us—eternally.

PROLOGUE

TEL AVIV, ISRAEL—2016

The Grand Ballroom at the David InterContinental Hotel was decked out in its finest. Festive posters and pictures along the walls, beautiful flowers on each table set with the finest china and crystal, and the multitude of wait staff, all indicated to the guests that dinner would be nothing less than superb. Ongoing preparations for this event had been in the works for months, and as the hotel's banquet manager stepped back and surveyed the room, he was quite pleased with the results of his team's efforts.

Security throughout the interior and surrounding the outside of the building was at its highest level.

The one thousand people in attendance—by invitation only—were neither there for the food nor for the decorations. They had come to honor Jacob Aaron Lyons.

At last, everyone was seated, and as Zoe Handler stepped to the podium, a hush fell over the crowd. There was no introduction nor did she introduce herself. Looking into the faces of the audience, she began speaking.

"What was once thought to be the largest diamond heist in history was never recorded; was never reported to the authorities; and to this very day some seventy-five plus years after it is believed to have occurred, it is uncertain who stole the diamonds or from whom and from where they were taken—100,000 carats of meticulously cut and polished diamonds in various shapes and weights that on today's market are estimated to be valued at over half a billion dollars.

"It is highly unlikely that the truth will ever surface since it is highly unlikely that anyone who was involved is still alive today. One might even question if there was a heist, but then one would have to question where such a cache came from and why no one ever sought to lay claim to it.

"Jacob Lyons was my father. He is known for the impact his innovations and skill have had on the diamond industry worldwide, and for his undaunted and exceedingly generous philanthropy, all of which he accomplished after his discharge as a highly decorated RAF Ace Pilot at the end of WWII.

"What you will learn from my novel is how he became the recipient of the spoils, but because he was unable to uncover the story behind the diamonds and discover who placed them in his care for safekeeping, he never thought of himself as the rightful owner of the jewels or that they had been given to him personally.

"He came into this world the son of immigrants who left Russia shortly after they were married in Minsk for a better life in England. He grew up overnight when the horror of WWII landed on London's doorstep. *The Blitz* began in September 1940 and lasted until May 1941. It didn't break the British people as the Nazis had hoped nor did it break my father; it only made them both stronger.

"My mother encouraged him to write the Lyons story for our family, and it was in fulfilling that promise to her that my brothers and I urged him to release it to the public. It was a work in progress when he passed away last year at the age of ninety-one. After his death, more determined than ever to finish my novel by the deadline I had set, I fervently returned to my notes and recordings.

"This is the Jacob Aaron Lyons story, and as you learn his story, you will come to realize as I did that he was truly *A Diamond in the Rough.*

"My father was not a religious man, but his faith was eternal. He lived his life thankful for every blessing and endured every loss with acceptance and dignity attributing them to God's plan for him. The spiritual afterlife is referred to in Hebrew as *Olam Ha-Ba* (the World to come)—it is a higher state of being. In the *Mishnah,* Jewish oral scholarship teaches us *This World is like a lobby before the Olam Ha-Ba—prepare yourself in the lobby so that you may enter the banquet hall.* Jacob Aaron Lyons has entered the hall.

"Following dinner, I invite you to view the diamonds on display that we have set up in the adjoining room. I have chosen a sampling of my father's work, which includes several rings and various other items that he crafted when he was a young boy under his father's tutelage.

"At the center of the Exhibit is the precisely carved wooden chest that held the diamonds when they came into my father's possession. For the remainder of his life, he never waivered in his efforts to learn the rightful owner of the diamonds, exhausting the sole clue he felt he had been given—the obvious significance of the precise carvings on the chest—carvings he equated to the precise cuttings of the diamonds it held.

"The room is not large enough to accommodate all of us at one time, so we ask that you form a line. One hundred people at a time will view the Exhibit entering the room by one door, working through the displays, and leaving by the door on the far side.

"In order to accommodate everyone here this evening in a timely manner, we are suggesting that your cursory viewing of the Exhibit be brief; however, we encourage you and welcome you to return as many times as you wish in the months to come.

"The Exhibit will be on display here in Tel Aviv for six months, at which time it will be moved to Jerusalem for an additional six months.

"I now invite Rabbi Levi Shuman to the podium to recite the blessing over our meal."

"Baruch atah A-donay Elo-heinu Melech Ha'Olem Hamotzi lechem min haaretz."

"Blessed are You Lord our God, King of the Universe Who brings forth bread from the earth."

PART ONE

CHAPTER ONE

Harry nervously paced back and forth, head bowed, praying as he had never prayed before that he would soon hear the cry of his first-born child, and that his beloved Ada and the baby were just fine. She had been in labor for hours, and outside of the midwife hurrying in and out of the room, he was told nothing, so all he could do was wait and pace and pace and wait.

At long last, Harry heard the lusty cry he had been hoping for, and Hannah, the midwife, opened the door just long enough to say, "Mazel Tov Harry; you and Ada have a fine son. Give me a few minutes to get Ada and the baby ready to see you."

Henry bowed his head and thanked God; a son, he and Ada had a son. God had blessed them. At last, Hannah opened the door. "Come, come in Harry and meet your son."

Four years had passed since Harry and Ada Lyons were married in Minsk, Russia, and left to pursue a better life in England, far from the persecution of Tsarist pogroms that their families had endured for decades. As a wedding gift, family and friends managed to come up with enough to pay their passage and tide them over until they found employment and a place to live. One bag held a pair of gold candlesticks, her mother's diamond earrings, and their few belongings.

The young couple travelled across Europe to the main departure point—Hamburg—as it was the least expensive route to London. Sixteen shillings per head for adults and half price for children, but the steerage conditions were appalling. It was a long journey, and Ada, who was a small, slightly built young woman of eighteen, spent most of the time aboard ship curled up in a fetal position suffering from seasickness in the small space that Harry had managed to secure for them.

When they arrived in London, and her feet were once again on solid ground, she quickly became her old self. They spent their first few weeks at the Jewish Temporary Shelter at 84 Leaman Street, as they explored London, weighed their options, and looked for employment.

The area known as the East End was made up of many hamlets adjoining the old City of London. They settled in the part of the East End, known as the Jewish Quarter; the area that had become a magnet for the thousands of Jewish immigrants fleeing Europe searching for a better life in cosmopolitan London.

They crowded into the two square miles of Whitechapel and Stepney, not far from where their ship had docked. It was the beginning of the 20th Century, home to an estimated 300,000 Jews and more than 100 synagogues. Although they had no family in England, they felt at home among their own people, and set out to begin building for the future.

Harry was a diamond cutter; taught by his grandfather and father. His grandfather often told him that he had that *special* eye for perfection that was critical in cutting precious stones. He was also a fine jeweler who could craft rings, earrings, necklaces, broaches, and various other items in gold. With tools in hand, he went looking for employment and secured a job with Max Lerner, an elderly jeweler who had no sons of his own. Max took an immediate liking to the young man, and although he couldn't offer much in the way of earnings, he suggested that he accept the position while continuing to seek other opportunities. Harry jumped at the chance.

Ada found employment at Ida Kaplan's dress shop as a seamstress. She was also very adept at embroidery, and brought samples of the collars and scarves she had made. Ida welcomed the pretty young girl into her shop and into her heart.

Their next priority was to look for a place to live. The Shelter was crowded and lacked privacy, and they were uncomfortable under the prying eyes of many who had been living there for months. Upon the recommendation of Max Lerner, Harry rented an apartment in a newly constructed tenement on Vallence Road. Hughes Mansions, a tenement of three blocks, offered reasonable rents, were well cared for, and strictly supervised to avoid overcrowding and unhygienic conditions.

Ada loved the Jewish Quarter. From the merchants shouting out prices in Yiddish as they pushed their wooden carts in the old markets and narrow streets of Petticoat and Brick Lane, to the tailors, shoesmiths, cabinetmakers, cigarette makers, jewelers, and thriving community of actors continuing the great tradition of Yiddish theater, she felt this was as close to heaven as she had ever been. She felt free and unafraid, and looked forward to each tomorrow.

The East End offered much more than merchants and a place to worship; it also offered security and social services. The Grand Order Sons of Jacob was one of many lodges in the East End. Members paid a shilling a week, which entitled them to medical attention and burial rights.

Next door to the Lodge stood a grand Victorian building, which was the Victorian Boys Club—a club established to counter hooliganism. The Jewish community also created the Brady Club, which gave youngsters the opportunity and a meeting place for sports, hobbies, and games, as well as the option of going to the seaside camp in summertime. The community offered not only services that they needed, but also for the family they looked forward to having.

The area between Brady Street and Vallance Road, known as the waste market, had a wide pavement reputed to be the widest in London. It served as a promenade especially on the Sabbath and Festivals when young Jewish boys and girls paraded up and down eyeing one another. Many a shiddach (match) was made here!

Both Harry and Ada spoke enough English to get by, but when they learned that classes were available in the evening, they enrolled. They attended three nights a week to perfect their speaking and writing of the King's English. On Sundays, Ada and Harry often spent the day getting to know the East End and beyond. Their dreams included a family, a house outside the City, and a Jewelry Emporium aptly named *Lyons and Sons*.

Four years had passed since they had arrived in London, and Harry and Ada were quite pleased with what they had accomplished. They were both employed; they had a nice apartment; and they were saving for a family.

In January 1924, God blessed them with the birth of a son; they named him Jacob Aaron Lyons.

CHAPTER TWO

By the time Jacob was a year old, both of Harry's parents had passed away in Minsk. His two brothers decided to leave Russia and pursue a life elsewhere as Harry and Ada had done a few years earlier. Neither was married. Unable to immigrate to the United States without a sponsor, they opted to go their separate ways. Sidney chose Cuba, optimistic that he could eventually make it to America. Benjamin chose South Africa where he felt his diamond background would enable him to secure a position and carry on in the family tradition.

It was 1925, and with most of Europe still recovering from the Great War, the brothers felt Europe was not an option. Times in Russia had only worsened, and with Communism rapidly spreading throughout the Country, they sought to try their luck elsewhere. They assured Harry that they would each send word as soon as they were settled.

Before they were married and sailed for London, Ada's parents had been killed in a Pogrom. She was an only child, and Harry's parents welcomed her into their home. As Ada approached her eighteenth birthday, there was no need to seek the customary arranged marriage for her; Harry and Ada had fallen in love. At the urging of Harry's parents and brothers, they decided to leave Minsk—leaving only distant cousins scattered among the many small shtetls (towns)—some they had not seen in years as well as others they had never met. By the time Sidney and Benjamin left, the void had only deepened.

The early years of Jacob's life saw little change in the Lyons household. When he was an infant, Ada often took him with her to work. He slept in the small bed in the back of Ida's shop between feedings. As he grew older, Ada found ways to amuse him, but once he mastered walking and talking, there was no way he was going to be content tagging along after Ada.

He was a happy baby who grew into a rambunctious little boy with an unquenchable thirst for knowledge. He questioned anything; he questioned everything. It was always: *Why? How? When? What?* But mostly it was a combination of all four.

She enrolled him in the day care program at their synagogue where he could be with children his own age, and he thrived. It wasn't long before he started school. He became a member of the Brady Club where he participated in sports, excelling at soccer, his favorite. He was tall for his age, with blond hair and piercing, deep blue eyes; he resembled a young Greek God!

As the years passed, he did exceedingly well with his studies, but the mandatory religious classes were not to his liking. Rabbi Levin, his Hebrew teacher, was a stern taskmaster and accepted no excuses. Jacob, who was often late because of a myriad of reasons, was continually reprimanded with the eternal promise of punishment.

Although they had wanted more children, year after year went by without Ada conceiving. When Jacob was seven years old, Ada became pregnant; and three months after his eighth birthday, the twins were born—Rose and Rachel weighed in at exactly five pounds each. After a difficult pregnancy and hours of another hard labor, Dr. Rosen told them there would be no more children.

Harry and Ada viewed the girls' arrival as true blessings that completed their family. Like Jacob, they were both fair-haired, but only time would tell if their eyes remained that same deep blue. Jacob adored his little sisters, and helped in any way he could. He now had a new reason to dodge his religious classes—he was needed at home to help his mother.

When the school semester ended in June, Rabbi Levin summoned Harry to his office for a conference.

"Shalom Rabbi Levin. It's good to see you."

"Please take a seat Harry. I have put off speaking with you about Jacob because I hoped beyond hope that the situation would right itself. However, at this point, I no longer believe that will happen without a little intervention.

"Since Jacob has been a student in my Hebrew class, he has rebelled time and again. He's either late or misses class entirely; and his studying is inconsistent and disappointing.

"I know that he is a good scholastic student, and that he is quite capable of doing much better. He simply doesn't assert himself, and seems to have no interest whatsoever in preparing for his Bar Mitzvah.

"Although a little over four years seems a long way off, I have been remiss in speaking with you about this sooner, hoping that he would come around and apply himself. I have been thinking that perhaps another teacher could get through to him."

Harry sat stunned at what the Rabbi had conveyed to him. Never had any of his teachers had anything adverse to say about Jacob. Whether it was his schoolwork, sports, or how any of their many friends and neighbors felt about him, he was always spoken of with praise and adoration. He was kind and always ready and available to help anyone he could.

Ada had never mentioned anything to the contrary either, and Harry was certain she would have if there had been a problem. Where was this coming from? Was it possible that he and Ada did not know their own son?

"Rabbi, I had no idea that our Jacob has been so difficult for you to deal with. There is no need to retain another teacher. You may rest assured, when the new semester begins in the fall, he will become your best student."

As he walked home, Harry's thoughts were all over the place, as he slowly formed a plan in his mind of how he would handle the situation with Jacob. He concluded he did indeed know his son, and he knew his son well; he also knew that the offer he was about to make him would not be turned down.

If one looked at his plan as a bribe, so be it! He knew in his heart it would all work out.

The Father's love for his son knew no bounds; the Son's love for his Father was mutual, but the love, the respect, and the admiration the son felt for his

Father, went far beyond that. To the Son, his Father was his Champion; his Idol; his Hero; you could almost say that he worshipped him.

To the Father, leaving Russia meant he could give his Son the freedom and opportunities that he never had. That did not leave the Son free of responsibility. He was Jewish. Becoming a Bar Mitzvah was not his choice it was his undeniable responsibility.

As they were finishing dinner, Harry put his arm around Jacob. "Son, after we clear the table, and help Mama put everything away, I'd like you to take a walk with me. Are you up to it?"

Jacob was delighted. "Yes, Papa, where shall we walk?"

"Not far, but it's a beautiful evening, and there is something I wish to discuss with you."

With Harry taking the lead, they left Hughes Mansions walking at a brisk pace. They turned onto Charing Cross; at Trafalgar Square they made a left onto Fetter Lane then a slight left onto Holborn Circus towards Hatton Garden. Jacob had no idea where they were headed.

As they walked, Harry began speaking. "Jacob, Mama and I have told you many times the story of our coming to London for a better life; a life free of persecution; a life where you can worship the God of your choice; and a life in a community you are a part of and where you are treated with respect and appreciation even at your young age.

"Our lives in Russia were nothing even close to what we have here. To be blunt, living in Russia was not living.

"When Mama and I decided to come to a new country where we knew no one, leaving what little family we had far behind, it was a big decision. We knew in our hearts, we would in all probability never see our parents and other relatives again, but we felt it was worth it because it offered us the opportunity to live a better life and give any children we had a better life.

"I was very fortunate to get a job immediately with Max Lerner, doing what I do best. Diamonds have been my family background for generations, and now you—the next generation—are ready to follow in my footsteps."

At last, Harry stopped walking. Raising his hand upward and waving it around, he said, "Jacob, this is Hatton Garden, better known as London's

Jewelry Quarter and the center of England's diamond trade. This is what I aspire to and where I aspire to be. When the time is right, this is where I want to open my own, or shall I say, *our* own Jewelry Emporium.

"I see in you what my grandfather and father saw in me. You have a *special* eye for diamonds, and that my son, pleases me to no end."

Jacob listened and absorbed all that Harry said, and as soon as he paused to catch his breath, he hugged his father and said, "Papa, I love you. Thank you, I only want to be like you. Cutting a dull stone and making it into a beautiful and shiny jewel is what I love best. I am amazed each and every time I watch you pick up a stone that resembles broken glass, and then I see what it becomes when you have cut and polished it."

Harry smiled, "I love you too, and although you are quite young, I know you are speaking from your heart. You seem to have caught *diamond fever* from your Papa. Diamonds are not everything; they are only one part of our lives."

Harry paused and then began speaking again, "Jacob, I had a meeting with Rabbi Levin the other day."

Suddenly, Jacob grew quiet.

"He tells me that you are not doing too well with your Hebrew lessons, and he's afraid you will not be prepared to become a Bar Mitzvah."

"Papa, I just don't like Hebrew. It's not really hard, but I find it boring and repetitive, and Rabbi Levin is mean. He doesn't think we should have any other interests but learning Hebrew."

Harry tried hard not to laugh. He had felt the same way when he was growing up. "I understand all that you say, but you are Jewish and you will become a Bar Mitzvah. So, I have come up with a plan that will hopefully make all of us happy—Rabbi Levin, you, your Mama, and me.

"Starting tomorrow and all through the summer, you will come to work with me each and every day. Max has agreed to it. I will teach you everything I know about diamonds. I will get you the tools that you need to learn to cut and polish a stone. I'll even teach you how to work with gold.

"In return, your part will be to diligently return to your Hebrew lessons in the fall and make us proud of you. I know you can do it. Do we have a deal?"

Jacob did not hesitate. "Oh Yes, Papa, yes we have a deal."

On the walk back to the apartment, Jacob talked and talked. He was so excited. Harry was excited too. He couldn't wait to start teaching his son all about diamonds and the art of diamond cutting.

Jacob readily gave up his annual trip to the seaside camp that had occupied his previous summers for the chance to work with his father.

The very day after their walk to Hatton Garden, Jacob arose early and accompanied Harry to work. It became their routine. Each morning they would have breakfast; Ada would prepare their lunch; and for the remainder of June, July, and August, Jacob was at his father's side eagerly absorbing everything and anything Harry taught him.

Max Lerner welcomed the young boy. "Shalom, Jacob. So your Papa is putting you to work. We can always use a smart young man in the business."

"Thank you, Mr. Lerner. I want to learn as much as I can about diamonds. My father says that I'm a quick learner, so I'm ready to get started.

"Did you know he was my age when his father and grandfather began teaching him how to cut diamonds?"

The summer flew by quickly. Both Harry and Jacob were true to their promises. Much to Rabbi Levin's surprise, when religious lessons began in the fall, Jacob became his best student, by far. When the Rabbi asked if he had studied during the summer, Jacob's reply was simply *no* without any further explanation.

The winds of war were blowing stronger with each passing day. At their synagogue after Sabbath Services, congregants compared notes about Germany's actions that were relayed by their relatives all over Europe. Many were seeking help to leave and come to England or go to America.

Others did not fully believe the stories. They felt, with the 1936 Olympics in Berlin a little over a year away, the eyes of the world would be on Germany.

How could they be persecuting and displacing so many, while managing to avoid anyone taking notice of what was actually happening? How was that even a possibility?

Harry listened with concern. He did not have any relatives in Europe, however, it brought back disturbing memories of life in Russia, and he prayed that war would not come to pass.

CHAPTER THREE

At times, the days flew by melding into weeks, months, and years; but, when time seemed to stand still, it was frustrating. Harry never found the need nor the time to seek employment elsewhere. He liked working with Max, and over the years, his skill, expertise, and growing reputation brought many new and repeat customers to the small shop. Accordingly, Max was able to increase his wages consistently.

Harry never put a time limit on the goals he hoped to achieve. On one hand, he was quite pleased with all that he and Ada had accomplished since coming to London over fifteen years before, but each passing day showed him how quickly Jacob and the girls were growing up, and he was still working for Max Lerner. His dream of opening his own Emporium was still not imminent, and his dream to move his family into a house outside of London seemed also to lie in the distant future.

On a beautiful spring morning in April 1935, a distinguished, well-dressed gentleman entered Max Lerner's shop and asked to speak to Harry Lyons. Max went into the back of the shop where Harry was working.

"Harry, there is a gentleman here to see you."

Harry was puzzled. "I don't have an appointment with anyone. Who is he? Did he give you his name?"

"I'm sorry Harry, I didn't think to ask his name. When he asked for you, I just assumed you were expecting him."

He put down his tools, washed his hands, and went to meet the person who came to see him.

As Harry approached, the man extended his hand and introduced himself.

"Good morning. My name is Marcus Hirsch, and I wonder if I might have a few minutes of your time."

For a brief moment, Harry was speechless.

Max handed Harry his jacket. "Why don't you take a break and head over to the Café where you and Mr. Hirsch can enjoy a cup of tea and freshly baked scones?"

Acting on Max's suggestion, they crossed the street to the Café and were soon seated. After placing their order, Marcus Hirsch handed his business card to Harry, who looked at the card and saw that he represented the De Beers Diamond Companies. Harry, as everyone else in every aspect of the diamond industry, knew the De Beers name and what it stood for. The words *diamonds* and *De Beers* were synonymous and had been for years.

For almost an hour, they spoke of diamonds. Marcus relayed De Beers' position of supplying the world with the finest finished product.

"Although a diamond in the rough is very valuable, it is the end piece of diamond jewelry, the highly sought after perfect stone which is worth much more. At De Beers, we are involved in every step of the diamond supply chain that begins with the mining of deposits to sorting to cutting and polishing to jewelry creation, and finally to the selling of the finest product attainable.

"We are opening a facility in Hatton Garden here in London under the name of The Diamond Trading Company to control supply, secure demand, and tighten our grip on the market. At this facility, we are introducing auction rooms for potential buyers of rough diamonds. The auctions will be advertised as London Sales Meetings and those in attendance will be by invitation only to buyers who have expressed a desire to do business with De Beers.

"We have scheduled our first London sales meeting to take place in mid-May, and I am here to offer you a position that I feel you are very qualified to fill. Should you accept our offer, we will work with you prior to the opening and show you what we hope to accomplish and the part you will play.

"Although in the beginning, we will only be selling rough diamonds, we plan to move forward in the not too distant future with retail establishments that will sell the final product to our customers directly.

"I don't expect your answer today; go home and talk it over with your wife and family, and if you have any questions, please do not hesitate to contact me. Let me know your decision, shall we say by the end of the week?"

Harry was amazed, and he did indeed have questions—a million of them. How did this man know so much about him? How did he know that he had a wife and family? Why did he think he was so qualified for the position? Why did he assume he was even interested in working for De Beers?

Marcus continued. "Of course, if you accept the position, I think you will be pleased not only with the salary we are offering, but even more so with the opportunities that are endless. I am not at liberty to disclose that salary until you accept our offer, but I assure you, it is considerably more than you are now earning."

Again, Harry couldn't believe he knew so much about him, including what he was earning.

At last, Harry found his voice. "Mr. Hirsch, as you can probably sense from my demeanor, you have caught me completely off guard. As you can probably also sense from my reaction to your offer, I have many questions. How is it that you know so much about me, and I knew nothing of De Beers' interest in hiring me?"

Marcus laughed and sat back in his chair. "A couple of months ago, a gentleman came into our corporate office in London inquiring about the new auction house and what type of positions would be available. He was an elderly man, and at first, the person he made contact with was reluctant to speak with him at all. But he was quite sincere and persistent, and that person decided to put him in touch with the man that was chosen to manage the daily overall operations of our new facility, Albert Werner.

"Albert met with the elderly gentleman several times and learned that he was not inquiring about a position for himself, but for you. He filled him in on your expertise in sorting and rating diamonds, and your inherent talent for cutting and polishing diamonds, as well. He supplied samples of your work, and when all was said and done, your qualifications exceeded what we originally planned for this position. So with an eye on future growth and expansion, we decided to make you an offer to become a part of our team.

"Who was this elderly man? Do I know him? Why didn't he say anything to me?"

"He is Max Lerner, the man you have worked for since coming to London. He feels that your talents and abilities should have the opportunity to grow and expand allowing you to better provide for your family.

"I hope you won't be angry with Mr. Lerner for going behind your back, but he really has your best interests at heart. He told Albert that he loves you like a son, and although he gave you a job when you needed it, he feels that he got the better end of the bargain when you came into his life."

Harry's thoughts were beginning to see the light. "I love Max and Reba Lerner like parents. In fact, after leaving my parents behind when my wife and I came here from Russia, they became surrogate parents to us, and ultimately surrogate grandparents to our children.

"Honestly, I could never bring myself to leave Max. He is getting up in years, and he has had several health issues recently, as has his wife. From time to time, Max has alluded to my looking elsewhere, but I never took him seriously."

Their meeting over, they shook hands. "Please give me your decision by week's end. I hope you will accept. I think it will be a good fit for both you and The Diamond Trading Company, and I look forward to working with you. We've had a slight change in plans; Albert Werner will soon be leaving for South Africa, and for the foreseeable future, I will be replacing him as overseer of daily operations."

Marcus left the Café and walked up the street to the right. Harry left the Café, literally flew across the street, bounding into the store embracing Max in a big bear hug.

When they finally broke apart, Max saw that Harry was crying.

At supper, no one ate. Everyone was so excited at Harry's news of the offer from De Beers. He insisted that Max and Reba come to dinner and be a part of the discussion and any decision that was made. At last, Ada said, "Please eat something. We can continue to talk while we eat, and after dinner when the girls are in bed, we can have tea and dessert and come to some conclusions."

Harry agreed. "Ada is right. She has prepared a wonderful meal, and it shouldn't go to waste."

Jacob was so excited. He helped clear the table and did the dishes while Ada put the twins to bed. At last, things had calmed down somewhat. Ada put the kettle on for tea and brought the honey cake she had made that very afternoon to the table. Now each of them would express their feelings and discuss the offer.

Max began by relating how his mission got started.

"Just after the holiday season, one evening when I came home from the shop, Reba told me that De Beers was building a new facility in Hatton Garden. We had noticed the construction going on for months, but no one seemed to know who the occupants would be. When Reba met her friends for lunch that day, a new sign had been erected announcing that it would be a De Beers entity.

"A few days later, I decided to visit their corporate offices just up the street from the construction site. I inquired about the positions that would be available, and if they were hiring to fill those positions from outside the Company. I was put in touch with Albert Werner who worked with me to get all the information he needed about you. They also interviewed other people, and evidently came to the decision to offer you one of the available positions. When Marcus Hirsch walked into the store, I had no idea who he was, as I had never met him. I also had no idea that they had decided to make you an offer."

Harry was still somewhat amazed and in awe at everything that had happened that day.

"Max and Reba—there are no words to express my gratitude to both of you for all you have done for all of us. As I told Mr. Hirsch, you are parents to Ada and me, and grandparents to our children, and we love you unconditionally. Before I can consider accepting the offer, I have to know what your plans are for the both of you. Can you continue to run the shop without help, or do you plan to sell it and retire?"

Max gathered his thoughts for a moment.

"Reba and I have been slowing down lately, and we certainly know we are not getting any younger. The business has been good to us, and we are quite comfortable financially. We have you to thank for all you brought to the business, not to mention the many new customers from outside the East End.

"Our needs are not great, and for whatever time we have left, we will be fine. We have no family other than all of you, and when you came into our lives all those years ago, we couldn't believe our good fortune. We intend to keep the shop open for the near future, and Jacob can continue to work with me. He's quite capable even though he is so young, and I love having him around. And, you are welcome to use the workshop if the need arises apart from your new job. That said, Reba and I think you should accept the offer.

"We look forward to spending many happy occasions together as a family while watching the children grow up and become fine young adults. Keeping the shop will keep me busy with something I love to do, and Reba has her women's clubs and luncheons to keep her busy.

"As I have already said, it would please us greatly if you accepted the position. Allowing us to take the journey with you is all we ask."

Ada had always felt in her heart that Harry was destined to achieve far more than working for Max Lerner. She too loved Max and Reba, but at times she was frustrated by Harry's reluctance to seek employment elsewhere. It bothered her that he put his dreams and goals aside so he wouldn't risk disappointing the Lerners. She now realized that he would not have disappointed them at all. She and Harry had both underestimated Max and Reba's love and devotion.

"I agree with Harry wholeheartedly that no words can express our gratitude to you both for all that you have done for us, but you have gone far beyond what we could have ever imagined when you contacted De Beers on Harry's behalf.

"I am certain there are many details to work out, questions to ask, and considerations to be given to any doubts we may have, but I'm seeing this as a once in a lifetime opportunity, a very good thing; and I think above all, Harry should accept this offer for himself. I sense that this will give him a chance to fulfill his dreams and attain the goals he set for himself all those years ago when we left Minsk and came to London."

Jacob, who sat and listened with all the reserve he could muster, was about to burst at the seams. He remembered the walk he and his father had taken to Hatton Garden. That night, Harry had proclaimed he envisioned his own Jewelry Emporium on that very site. Jacob never forgot that conversation.

"Papa, I know I am young and not yet a man—I won't be a Bar Mitzvah for two more years, but if I have a vote, I think you should accept. I think De Beers is pretty smart to want you, because you're the best!"

Ada rose from the table and went to the cabinet and retrieved five wine glasses and a bottle of wine. She poured the wine and handed each of them a glass, including Jacob. It was, after all, a very special occasion.

She raised her glass: "To all of us, L'Chaim—To Life; may God always be with us to guide us and bless us. Amen"

CHAPTER FOUR

I t took fifteen years, but Harry believed good things come to those who wait, and he definitely considered his offer from De Beers a *good thing*! The new facility opened a month after his initial meeting with Marcus, and during that month, Harry learned more about diamonds and the diamond industry than he could have ever imagined he did not know.

The building was state-of-the-art for the 1930s, and the rooms where the sales meetings/auctions were to be held were beautifully furnished and conducive to making their clients feel *right at home* while offering their bids.

Marcus introduced Harry to his tailor and saw that he was outfitted with suits, shirts, and all the accessories needed to deal with their distinguished clients.

———〰———

The first meeting held in May 1935 was a huge success, and Harry was quite pleased with his efforts in helping achieve that success. Not only was he charged with seeing that the bidders were welcomed and made to feel at home, it was his job to answer any and all questions they had, and in order to do that, he acquainted himself with their backgrounds and the companies they represented in advance of the meetings.

Although he was busier than he had ever been, each night when he arrived home for supper, his family eagerly awaited to hear about his day. Each nightly conversation began with Harry's detailed explanation of what he had learned, what he had accomplished, and what was in the works for the future, if anything new had been introduced. On days when there had been an auction, the excitement in his voice spoke volumes as he told of bidding wars, mergers, and concessions that the bidders negotiated among themselves. Of course, all of this was relayed with total anonymity, and Harry never mentioned the companies or individuals with whom they did business.

As supper wound down, the conversation always ended with the children and what was happening at school. Jacob, Rose, and Rachel were all doing well; Jacob was also keeping up with his Hebrew lessons. There had been no more summons from Rabbi Levin to speak with Harry, and when he inquired about Jacob's progress when he was at Shabbat Services, the Rabbi smiled and winked his approval. In just eighteen months, Jacob's Bar Mitzvah would take place.

Many of his friends had already had theirs, and there were quite a few coming up in the months leading up to his. He didn't particularly look forward to the services on Saturday morning, but eagerly attended the evening parties. They generally included the boys and girls from his synagogue, but many of the families had relatives that lived in the East End that belonged to any one of the numerous other synagogues, and it was always fun to meet new friends that you didn't see everyday.

On the last Saturday in September 1936, Jake and his two best friends, Henry Rosen and Sid Golden, set off to attend the party for Ivan Portman.

The party was in full swing when they arrived at the social hall, and when the boys walked in, they immediately spotted many of their other friends. These parties were just for the young people, and it was a good way to meet boys and girls their age that didn't attend their school or belong to their synagogue. Most of the time, these new faces were cousins or friends of the family of the Bar Mitzvah boy.

Jacob looked around the familiar room where in a few months his party would be held and his eyes came to rest on the most beautiful girl he had ever seen. Her flaming red hair came to her shoulders, framing her face and accenting her blue-gray eyes that seemed to be looking directly at him. He wanted to look away; he tried to look away; but he was mesmerized.

He had never had a *girlfriend* and was often chided by his friends who told him he was too serious and spent too much time working at Max Lerner's shop. However, that hadn't deterred the many young girls who tried to gain his favor but failed to do so.

It seemed like forever, as he stood caught in her gaze, but when Ivan suddenly appeared beside her, Jacob seized the moment and decided to congratulate his friend and get an introduction.

His eyes still on the beautiful redhead, Jacob offered his hand to Ivan and said, "Mazel Tov my friend. You did good."

Ivan took Jacob's hand. "Thank you. It won't be long before I'll be extending my congratulations to you."

Noticing that his friend's attentions were not solely directed to him, he stepped back and said, "Jacob Lyons, I'd like you to meet my cousin Alexandra Portman."

Jacob smiled and nodded, "Pleased to meet you."

Just then, Ivan excused himself and went to greet a group of friends who had just arrived.

Alexandra seemed to be under the same spell as Jacob. Although Ivan had excused himself and left, neither made a move to do the same. Not willing to give her the chance to walk away, he suggested they get some punch and something to eat.

They spent the better part of the evening getting to know each other.

"As you know, my name is Alexandra Portman—Ivan's first cousin— our fathers are brothers. My father is a physician and my family lives on the outskirts of London. I have two older brothers, one who is in medical school, and the other who will soon follow in his footsteps. You could say I plan to do the same—that is enter the medical field—I want to be a nurse and help as many people as I can. And please call me Lexi; no one calls me Alexandra except my parents when they're unhappy with me."

Jacob laughed. "OK, Lexi it is." He told her all about his family and the twins; his father working for De Beers; how he idolized his father who taught him to cut and polish diamonds; how he loved working at Max Lerner's shop in his spare time; how he hated his religious lessons but looked forward to becoming a Bar Mitzvah next January; and last but not least, that diamonds were his future—taking a rough rock and turning it into a thing of beauty was a special talent that he intended to put to good use.

When the party ended, they said their reluctant goodbyes.

"Thank you for a great evening; I really enjoyed the time we spent talking. Most of my friends think I'm too serious for someone who is only twelve. Just the fact that I know what I want to do with my life blows their minds. If I invite you to my Bar Mitzvah party, will you come?"

Lexi smiled, and again Jacob thought how beautiful she is. "Of course, I will come. And one more thing, I'm going to call you Jake; it's less formal and now that you are about to become a man in a few months, I think it suits you."

There was no question that Jacob was absolutely and totally taken with Lexi Portman.

———⦚———

Although unsettling reports continued to pour out of Germany, many still did not believe them, while others who had relatives involved and did believe them were unable to be of help.

In August 1936, the Summer Olympic games were held in Berlin. Hitler managed to somewhat fool the world by putting on a good *show*. But as he watched, Jesse Owens became the first American track and field athlete to win four gold medals in one Olympiad. Jesse Owens' success offered a strong rebuttal to Adolph Hitler's theory of Aryan supremacy; he was not only an American—he was a black American—which was especially significant, since he had chosen the games to show the world the revival of Germany and white supremacy under the Third Reich.

On the evening of 11 December 1936, a radio address shocked the UK. After ruling for less than one year, Edward VIII became the first English Monarch to voluntarily abdicate.

The royal family's disapproval of Edward's married mistress, Wallis Warfield Simpson, did not deter his intent on marrying her. However, before he could discuss his intentions with his father, King George V died in January 1936, and thus Edward ascended to the throne.

On 12 December 1936, his younger brother, the Duke of York, was proclaimed King George VI. In less than one year, three Kings sat on the English throne.

Four months passed quickly, and the day of Jacob's Bar Mitzvah arrived. Londoners in January 1937 had seen an extremely wet but milder winter with cloud-free days sandwiched in between drenching rainstorms about once a week until the very end of the month when snow finally arrived.

Saturday, 16 January 1937, was one of those cloud-free days with sunshine to spare. The Great Central Synagogue on Rotary Square was packed with friends and congregants all there for the Lyons family. For a brief moment, Harry wished that his parents and his brothers could be there, but he and Ada were very proud of Jacob and nothing could possibly take away from their happiness and blessings of the special day.

How different this day was compared to his own meager Bar Mitzvah in Russia, where everyone was watching and waiting for something bad to happen.

As Jacob chanted his Haftarah, Rabbi Levin sat on the Bimah with a smug smile upon his face—how could he have ever doubted Jacob's ability or his own, for that matter, to teach him?

As the services came to an end, and the many guests began filtering into the adjourning room where tables of food and drink had been set up, two men came forward and approached Harry and Ada as they were accepting the good wishes and congratulations from the many congregants.

At first Harry stood stunned, not believing who stood before him. Then in an instant, he was hugging Benjamin and Sydney, his brothers. He had no idea they were coming; no idea when they had arrived, but he simply didn't care.

Sidney left Cuba years before and both of the brothers were now together in South Africa. They had decided to travel to London to see the brother they had not seen for seventeen years. What better time would there be than to see their nephew become a Bar Mitzvah? They had arrived the day before, but thought it best to keep a low profile and not take anything away from Jacob. They were planning to be in London for a week, and there would be time enough to catch up on all the years they had not seen each other.

What a day? From the sunshine on a winter's day to meeting his uncles for the first time to making his parents, sisters, Max and Reba Lerner, and, of course, Rabbi Levin, proud of him. Lexi had come to the services and was coming to his party later that evening. Jacob could hardly contain his excitement.

As he stood with his family, Lexi came up to him. "Jake, you were truly perfect. Mazel Tov." Jacob introduced her to his parents, and then she walked over to see other friends.

Harry and Ada looked at one another, and Ada whispered to Harry, "I guess our Jacob or should I say *Jake* is growing up."

As they continued to welcome their guests, Ada wondered. Who is this beautiful young lady, Lexi? What kind of a name was *Lexi?* She had never heard the name before. Jacob seemed quite pleased to see her, to say the least, and since she didn't recall having seen her before at their synagogue or anywhere else, was quite certain she didn't live in the East End. Yes, Jacob was growing up.

The party that evening at the social hall was packed. Jacob had a lot of friends, and it seemed that each and every one had come. Aside from accepting congratulations throughout the evening, and spending a brief few minutes with his parents when they brought his uncles by to see the hall and the setup for the young people, he never left Lexi's side.

All too soon, as the evening was coming to an end, he realized that since Lexi had come into his life, he had changed a great deal. Although it had only been a few months since they met, there was no denying she was his first love, and truth be told, his feelings for her ran deep; he adored her.

When he walked her out to meet her father who was waiting to pick her up, she stopped shy of the door, turned to him and kissed him full on the lips. "Great day; wonderful party; but best of all, I got to share it with you. Goodnight Jake."

"Goodnight Lexi; thank you. You made this day extra special for me."

He dreamt about Lexi that night and their first kiss—hoping fervently that she felt the same way about him as he felt about her.

CHAPTER FIVE

With his Bar Mitzvah behind him, Jacob abandoned his Hebrew lessons with Rabbi Levin as many others had before him. The Lyons family was not Orthodox, and felt it was more important for him to concentrate on his scholastic studies going forward, so they did not try to convince him otherwise. As always, his grades were exemplary, although he continued to spend a good deal of his time playing sports, socializing with friends, and working with Max.

And then there was Lexi. Although they lived a distance apart, they saw one another as frequently as possible. Jacob was unrelenting in urging Ivan to invite his cousin to the various activities sponsored by the Great Central Synagogue that took place each weekend following the Sabbath, as well as various holiday Festivals.

On certain occasions when there was a special celebration or festival held at their synagogue, Lexi stayed over with her cousin Ivan's family, and attended the parties all weekend. Jacob was delighted; Harry and Ada observed with interest.

On 9 November 1938, in an incident known as *Kristallnacht*, Nazi Germany torched synagogues, vandalized Jewish homes, schools, and businesses and killed almost 100 Jews. In the aftermath of what became known as the *Night of Broken Glass*, some 35,000 Jewish men were arrested and sent to Nazi concentration camps. No longer was it whispered and debated what the Nazis were up to—it was fact. After *Kristallnacht* conditions

for German Jews continued to grow worse by the day, as the world stood by and watched.

———ɷ———

Life was good for the Lyons family. Harry's position with De Beers became all that he hoped it would, and they began looking toward making some of their goals for the future a reality. Harry purchased a secondhand Ford V-8 from a De Beers employee who was relocating abroad, and most Sundays found them driving to nearby towns outside of London looking for a house. They always made it a *family* excursion, and the children were as excited as Harry and Ada at the prospect.

The years since Harry had gone to work at De Beers had proven lucrative. They were able to breathe a little easier financially and even managed to save towards buying a place of their own.

During the 1930s, there was a boom in homebuilding on the outskirts of towns and cities all over England, all of which were fairly uniform in style and all of which were considered the most modern for that time. This boom created what became known as the *suburbs* or *suburban housing*.

On one particular outing in the spring of 1939, Harry and Ada came upon Orpington Gardens located in Edgware, Middlesex, a new suburban housing development in the London suburbs. Orpington Gardens featured rows of semi-detached houses in blocks of two, which were mirror images of each other, with a side entrance in between, and both front and back gardens.

The homes were moderate in size and space. The front door opened into a hall from which there were stairs to the upper floors, two doors to the living area, and at the end of the hall, a door to the kitchen.

On the upper floor was a landing, two bedrooms above the sitting room, another bedroom above the front part of the hall, and a bathroom above the kitchen. On the third level, there was a sizeable loft with floor space equal to that of the upper floor.

Some houses had chalet-style roofs that translated to smaller loft areas and in some cases, one less bedroom. Windows varied with rounded bays, square bays, and some had no bay, but all were single glazed in wooden frames and consisted of several door windows with smaller fanlight windows above.

To Harry and Ada, it was nothing short of a palace. Everything was so new and shiny and absolutely beyond their wildest imagination. To even think that this could be their home was almost beyond belief. The children were also in awe. There were so many rooms—Jacob could have his own room, the twins could have their own room, and the sitting room and big dining room were large enough to create an open feeling—and three floors.

The cost of the home they all fell in love with was 835 pounds. Abbey Road Building Society offered a twenty-year mortgage, with a down payment of 200 pounds, and a monthly payment of 4 pounds.

Weeks turned into months as Harry and Ada agonized over taking on too much by going for home ownership. Tying themselves to some 20 years of mortgage payments weighed heavily on their minds along with the fact that if anything went wrong and needed repair, it would have to be paid for out of their own pocket. In addition, they didn't want to become *house poor* where most of their income went into the house.

The world was in disarray. Horrific stories out of Germany continued and increased, and many lost contact with relatives who seemed to have disappeared into thin air.

All through the summer of 1939, they went back and forth trying to justify becoming homeowners and what they would have to give up in the process. They looked at other new housing communities, but they kept returning to their original choice—Orpington Gardens. Some of the other developments were less costly, but they didn't feel they were getting as much for their money. In the end, they chose to wait a while longer.

Only days later, their decision would take on new meaning.

On 1 September 1939, the Nazis invaded Poland. Under a Mutual

Assistance Treaty Great Britain signed in August 1939, they were committed to defend the Poles.

On Sunday, 3 September 1939, Neville Chamberlain issued an ultimatum to Germany demanding the immediate withdrawal of German Troops from Poland.

The ultimatum, issued at 9:00 a.m. was due to expire just two hours later at 11:00 a.m. Expire it did. Mr. Chamberlain took to the airwaves broadcasting to the nation via the radio that Britain had declared war on Germany.

Before the year would end, France, Australia, New Zealand, and Canada would also declare war on Germany, with the United States declaring neutrality. The Soviets invaded Poland and attacked Finland. The Soviet invasion of Poland resulted in Germany and Russia dividing up the country.

What had been whispered, discussed, and even refuted had come to pass.

As 1940 dawned, rationing began in Britain. An air of apprehension was everywhere. Most Londoners tried to remain in *normal* mode, but it was not always an easy thing to do.

The Lyons family held a subdued birthday celebration for Jacob's 16th Birthday, which included Max and Reba Lerner. For the most part, everyone seemed unusually quiet during dinner. Max asked Harry what the talk was at De Beers.

"For the most part, it's business as usual. They keep me pretty busy so I probably don't hear a lot of what is said."

When everyone finished eating, Harry stood and raised his water glass. "Here, here, this is a celebration of Jacob's 16th Birthday. So let us dispense with the worries of the world for tonight and wish our Jacob a very Happy Birthday!

"As you know, we didn't ask what you wanted for a gift this year, because your mother and I had something in mind. I hope that didn't make you think that we had forgotten and weren't getting you anything."

Seeing everyone amused as his expense, he replied, "I did notice that, but I knew you would come up with something."

"Indeed we have. We have decided that it's time for you to learn to drive the car, so we are giving you driving lessons"

"Wow" was all Jacob could say, and he repeated it, "Wow! I have the best family in the world. When do I start?"

Again, everyone laughed, and Harry said, "I've arranged with a driver for De Beers to teach you, and you can work it out between the two of you taking both of your schedules into account. I have no doubt that it won't take you long to get the hang of it, and you can apply for your driving license as soon as you are confident that you can pass the test."

Jacob hugged and kissed his parents and thanked them profusely asking to be excused so he could tell his friends.

For the time being, although the Country was at war, life went on as usual. Harry continued working at De Beers, Jacob and the girls continued to do well in school; and an apprehensive atmosphere continued to consume the Nation. Spring arrived without fanfare and eased into summer.

CHAPTER SIX

The War brought many changes and hardships, and no city was more susceptible to its effects than London.

After the fall of France in June 1940, Nazi Germany had one major enemy left in Western Europe—Great Britain. Hitler's strategy expected Germany to quickly conquer their enemy by first gaining dominance over airspace and then by sending in ground troops across the English Channel.

The Germans began their attack on Great Britain in July 1940. At first they targeted airfields, but soon switched to bombing general strategic targets, hoping to crush British morale. Unfortunately for the Nazis, Britain's morale was steadfast, and the reprieve given to British airfields gave the Royal Air Force the break it so desperately needed.

The Germans continued to bomb London for months, but as the fall of 1940 approached, it was clear that the British had won, and that the Germans were forced to indefinitely postpone their sea invasion across the English Channel. With overconfidence and meager planning on Hitler's part, the Battle of Britain was a decisive victory for the British and was the first time the Germans faced defeat since the War began.

However, Britain's troubles were just beginning.

Their setback in the Battle of Britain did not contain the Germans; and the appearance of German bombers in the skies over London during the afternoon of 7 September 1940, heralded a shift in Hitler's attempt to overtake Great Britain.

By abandoning his airstrikes on British airfields, Hitler's new targets became manufacturing facilities and the harbor. As the Battle of Britain was being put to rest, Germany embarked on a new assault on England—The

Blitz. For the next 57 consecutive days, London sustained intense bombing both day and night—ending in May 1941, when Hitler called off the raids to move his bombers in preparation for Germany's invasion of Russia.

Ada was beside herself. Each time the sirens started to wail, she became frantic. If the raids occurred during the day while Harry was at work and the children were in school, she feared she would never see them again. When the raids were at night, even though Harry was home, and they fled their flat together to seek shelter, her nerves were so on edge, she acted like a person gone mad until they were all secure in one of the designated underground shelters. The girls were scared, but Jacob was strong and helped his father calm his mother and sisters time and again.

Harry and Ada tried their best to allow the children freedom to continue with sports and social activities. Of course, the children attended school; Harry went to work; they attended services at their synagogue as a family; but that didn't deter from the fact that each time Ada left the flat alone to buy food and supplies, she didn't totally relax until she was once again home. Home had become her sanctuary; the only place she felt truly safe.

By the end of October, although the raids had not stopped, they abated somewhat and were not a day after day occurrence. De Beers suspended their auctions, but Marcus assured Harry that it was temporary, and that his expertise would be used in other ways. Harry was greatly relieved, as was Ada when he conveyed the news to her. She viewed it as one less thing to worry about.

In early November, Jacob approached his parents with a request. "I'd like to invite Lexi to the Cinema in London to see the new American film *Strike Up the Band*. It opens this coming weekend, and it really looks good. I'll need the car to pick her up."

Harry and Ada were aware that she lived near Middlesex, just a couple of miles from Orpington Gardens. The first thing that came to Ada's mind was the air raids. Though they had abated, they were definitely not over. Harry on the other hand quickly replied, "Of course, you may have the car. As you know, we don't use it much since petrol rationing, but I always keep enough on hand for special occasions."

"Thank you, thank you. Now I can make my plans. There's a matinee Sunday afternoon."

Harry and Ada not wanting to upset Jacob by reminding him to be alert and extra vigilant for their safety, simply told him, "Have a good time and enjoy the show."

What a wonderful afternoon they had—just the two of them. The film starring Mickey Rooney and Judy Garland was a great diversion. Sitting inside the theatre, they were propelled into a different world, a world far away from the bombed out buildings and destruction one saw all around London.

Jake put his arm around Lexi and pulled her close. The music and the love story portrayed on the screen were wonderful. The stars, Mickey Rooney and Judy Garland, were students in high school about their same ages, and it was easy for them to equate with the story.

When the show ended, they stopped at a nearby teashop for sandwiches and tea. Not wanting their afternoon to end, they opted to walk around London in the immediate area of the theatre before heading home. Even though they were talking about the film and the actors as they walked, the destruction all around them left by the bombings continued to distract them. They decided to head home after all.

When they arrived at Lexi's house, he insisted on seeing her safely inside, but not before pulling her close and kissing her goodnight just as Dr. Portman opened the door.

—m—

Harry and Ada felt remorse that they had not moved out of London to the suburbs. Although seeing the destruction grow so widespread was unnerving, the worst was knowing that shortly after hearing the sirens wail, you would hear the German planes grinding in the distance as you waited to hear the boom, boom, boom of the bombs tearing buildings apart while knowing they were not too far away from where you were, praying that they would turn back before reaching you.

In mid-December, the agent that had shown them the houses in Orpington Gardens contacted Harry to see if they were still interested in the house they previously wanted. A young couple had purchased the home but had never moved in. Unfortunately, the husband was killed in the Battle of Britain, and his widow was anxious to sell before returning to America. The house was partially furnished; and her asking price including the furniture was the outstanding mortgage—a sum of 500 pounds, almost half of the original asking price. Since the transaction would be a transfer of the existing mortgage, no down payment was required.

When Harry told Ada, it was the first time he had seen her smile in months. She put her arms around him and kissed him.

"Oh yes, Harry, let's buy the house. It will be safer for all of us, and possibly far enough away that the air raids won't impact us as much, if at all; it will be good news for the children too. We can still come to our synagogue for services, and Jake can continue his sports at the Brady Club. With graduation only months away, I am certain Jake will opt to stay in school here; you can drop him off on your way to work. I will certainly feel better knowing the girls are in primary school outside the city limits."

Harry pondered his thoughts not knowing whether to consider their good fortune a blessing or an omen of bad things to come. When he thought about the young couple who had purchased the house, but never lived in it, he couldn't shake the bad feeling that came over him. The young man had been killed, and his widow was returning to her family in America. He could only imagine what their hopes and dreams had been when they purchased the house. Had they been as excited and loved it as much as he and Ada had? Or more?

In the end, he put his thoughts aside and said, "Then it's settled. I will contact the agent tomorrow and make arrangements for us to see the house as soon as possible. If all goes well, we can move forward with the paperwork to transfer the mortgage to us, and our new address will be 11 Brook Avenue, Edgware, Middlesex."

Because of the holiday season, the appointment to meet with the agent to walk through the house was set for early January 1941. It was a cold winter day when Harry and Ada met him at the property. It was even more beautiful than she remembered. All the old feelings of how much she loved the house came flooding back to her. Ada hadn't realized until now how disappointed she had actually been when they decided to postpone their plans to become homeowners.

The furniture, all new and purchased before the War, was a real bonus. With rationing and all manufacturing geared toward the war effort, it was certain that very little if any furnishings were currently available and probably wouldn't be until the War was over. The only furniture the house lacked was bedroom furniture for the children; and they could bring what they had for the time being, or perhaps try to purchase a few pieces secondhand.

Ada was happier than she had been in months. After telling the agent they would take the house, they went home to tell the children. Now it was just a matter of time for the paperwork to be processed, and they could move into their new home.

With Jacob's Birthday just days away, they decided to wait until then to tell the children, Max, and Reba. However, this was not an easy thing for Ada to do. Her upbeat mood did not go unnoticed. The children had not witnessed her cheerful demeanor in a long time. Although there were no air raids leading up to his birthday, Ada showed no signs whatsoever of fearful anticipation as she had in the past.

Jacob's 17th Birthday finally came. Ada busied herself all day preparing dinner, baking a cake, and setting the table complete with glasses for wine. When the girls came home from school, she shooed them out of the way, and told them to keep busy until they were told to wash up for dinner.

Harry, Max, and Reba arrived simultaneously, and when Jacob walked in a few minutes later, the party began. Unlike the previous year, the banter around the table was lighter, and there was definitely more laughter. Everyone agreed that dinner was delicious.

When Harry stood and clinked his fork against his glass to get everyone's attention, it was assumed he would make his announcement of Jacob's gift pretty much as he had done the previous year when they had given him driving lessons.

This was not so.

"Ada and I have something to tell you; we made a decision several days ago, but decided to wait until tonight to tell everyone. We are buying the house we all fell in love with in Orpington Gardens last year. It was purchased by another family, but recently came back on the market. When the agent contacted me, we went to see it, and we agreed to make it our own. It is partially furnished, and since it is being sold with the furniture, we will be in good shape. We are waiting for the papers to be drawn up for our signatures, and we will soon learn when we can move in. So tonight we celebrate Jacob's Birthday and our new home.

"I know you children may have a lot of questions; school, our synagogue, all will be worked out to everyone's satisfaction. First and foremost, we hope it will get us out of the city limits of London and further away from the air raids."

At first everyone was quiet and just sat there. Then realizing what their father had just said, Jacob, Rose, and Rachel began jumping for joy. A new home, their own rooms, an upstairs, a downstairs, a garden front and back— this was truly the best day ever.

Max and Reba congratulated them, truly happy that they were moving out of the City. Max pulled Harry aside, "You can fill me in on all the details in the days to come. Tonight, we just celebrate."

Harry poured the wine, while Ada served the cake and tea. There were many toasts—to Jacob, to moving to the new house, to good health, to staying safe, and to the end of the War. It seemed like old times—before the air raids—before the bombs falling too close for comfort—just a normal family dinner celebration.

Ada slipped out of the room and returned with a leather jacket for Jacob. Harry had pulled more than a few strings to get it.

"Happy Birthday Jacob; come and try it on."

All too soon January became February and February became March. The Nazis continued their assault on London as the air raids increased and then lessened, but not before dropping their payloads on schools, churches, and residential areas.

In mid-March, Harry and Ada were notified by the bank manager that at long last, the papers for the sale of the house were ready for their signatures. Harry wore a blue suit and his favorite tie; Ada wore her favorite dress that was usually reserved for the Sabbath. This was a very *special day* in their lives, and Ada wanted it to be just right.

Now that the day had arrived, Ada was a bit nervous, but elated nonetheless; she once again had her eye on tomorrow and hoped the War would soon end. Their very own home was a dream come true. Though it was part of the plan all along, she couldn't deny the sense of accomplishment and pride that engulfed her as they prepared to leave for their appointment at the bank.

Harry was excited, as well. Having put his bad feelings about the house aside, he felt perhaps 11 Brook Avenue was destined to be theirs all along.

Before leaving their flat, Harry pulled Ada into his arms and kissed her. "I love you Ada Lyons with all my heart. All I have ever wanted and imagined was to spend all of my days with you, and provide you and our children with some of the finer things in life along the way. I see our new home as only the beginning of many good things to come."

"I love you too Harry, and I too truly believe that it is only the beginning for the Lyons family."

When they arrived at the bank, they were surprised to see Max and Reba waiting for them. "I hope you don't mind our being here. Reba and I wanted to share this important occasion in your lives."

Harry felt terrible. Although he was surprised that they hadn't mentioned their wish to come with them, Max and Reba were the only family they had, and Harry and Ada's remiss in including them could only be attributed to the fact that they were so caught up in their own excitement, they simply had given it no thought.

"Of course, we don't mind at all; we should have asked you to be a part of this day and join us. Please accept our apology."

"No need for any apologies, Harry. We just want you to know Reba and I are here for both of you."

They were shown to a small room at the end of the hall. Mr. Westin, the bank manager, introduced himself and asked that everyone be seated. Harry and Ada having never previously purchased property had no idea of the process or paperwork involved.

Mr. Westin placed the first document to be signed in front of them. There was a bank draft in the amount of 500 pounds made out to the Abbey Road Building Society attached. He instructed them to sign and date above their names where indicated. He further explained that it was the Bill of Sale paying off the mortgage held by the previous owners.

Next he produced the Deed to 11 Brook Avenue, Edgware, Middlesex, indicating Harry and Ada Lyons as the new owners. Sliding the Deed into an envelope, he handed it to Harry; he then stood and extended his hand indicating that the transaction was complete.

Harry was a bit confused. "Where are the papers outlining the mortgage agreement, and the process for repayment?"

Mr. Westin sat back down. "There is no mortgage. Mr. and Mrs. Lerner have paid off the mortgage on your behalf. The house is yours free and clear of any encumbrance. Congratulations! I wish you well; enjoy your new home. Now, if you will please excuse me, I must be off to my next appointment."

Once again, the Lerners were truly their guardian angels. Harry and Ada had no idea what they had done to deserve them, but they were genuinely grateful regardless, knowing they could never repay them.

Max and Reba did not want or expect repayment. As they had said many times before, they were both up in years, and for whatever time they had left, they were secure in the knowledge that they had more than enough for their needs. They had recently revised their Wills and left everything to Harry, Ada, and the children anyway.

They left the bank, walking arm in arm; Harry and Ada were walking on air. When they reached the Corner Pub, Max and Reba ushered them inside before they knew what was happening. For the next hour, they laughed and cried and toasted to the future again and again and again.

To Harry and Ada Lyons, owning their own home was the dream of a lifetime; an investment in their future, an act both permanent and profound.

HOME—where Love resides, Memories are created,
Friends are always welcome, and Laughter never ends.

CHAPTER SEVEN

For the remainder of March, Harry and Ada, with the children pitching in, packed their things and steadily moved them to the new house. They felt that in doing so, when the day came for the final move, the majority of their belongings would be in place and ready to receive them. It was also an opportunity to give to others; there was clothing that the children had outgrown, and items that they no longer needed. Rationing had hit everyone pretty hard, and children's clothing and shoes were in constant demand.

Since Passover was approaching in early April; they would remain in their flat through the week of observance at which time they would pack up the Passover dishes, and the remainder of their belongings, and be in their new home before the end of the month. This proved to be a great family experience. The children excited about the move were more than eager to help, and in the long run made the move easier than having to unpack everything at once.

Spring had arrived, and Ada looked forward to planting a few flowers, and possibly even putting in a vegetable garden. The many bombings had left their toll. In and around London, there was devastation wherever one looked, and each time Ada passed a bombed-out building, it tugged at her heart.

It was also the twins 9th Birthday; Max and Reba would be joining them for the Seder and their final celebration in the place they had called home for twenty years. During the day, as she prepared for dinner, she recalled coming to London as a bride and falling in love with the East End. After all these years, she still felt the same way; but times change. It was time for them to move on. Empowered with fulfilling their dream of home ownership came the ability to put some distance between them and the German air raids.

Jacob had been working on a surprise for Rose and Rachael for weeks. He spent as much time as he could in the back of Max's shop crafting matching rings for his sisters. The rings were identical—each with a diamond centered in a gold heart; he had cut and polished the diamonds himself. His secret was his alone; he hadn't told his parents nor confided in Max. He also had a surprise for his parents. He had taken a key to their new house and attached a gold plate engraved with the date April 1941—the date they would move permanently to Orpington Gardens.

There had been no air raids for over a week, and Ada had taken advantage of the time by planning as elaborate a Seder as she could by adjusting her recipes and stretching her ration coupons that included several Reba had given her. The table was set; Harry was home; Rose and Rachael were looking forward to celebrating their 9th Birthday; and Max and Reba had just arrived. Ada excused herself and went to check on dinner. As soon as Jacob came home, the Seder would begin.

With the key and the two small boxes containing the rings in his pocket, Jacob left Max's shop and locked the door behind him. He was running a little late; he just couldn't resist one last swipe of the polishing cloth on the rings before heading home. Picking up the pace, he smiled, quite pleased with himself as he walked. He felt certain the twins would love the rings; certain that his mother would equally love the key to their new home; and he hoped his father would be proud of his skill and ingenuity.

On Friday, 11 April 1941, 153 Luftwaffe Aircraft bombed Bristol, England.

The City's docks, St. Philip's Bridge, and widespread residential areas were damaged. In addition, the bombs that hit St. Philip's Bridge destroyed the tramway power supply line. The damage was too severe to repair, and all the tramcars were soon scrapped for the war effort; none of which were preserved for historical purposes.

As the planes began their retreat, one lone stray bomber, short of fuel, veered off course and accidently released its load over the East End, resulting in a direct hit on Hughes Mansions—more precisely on the very building where the Lyons family lived—until month's end.

There was no warning. As Jews in the East End were sitting down to their Seders, the bombs fell. Not only was it the first night of Passover, it was Good Friday with Easter Sunday approaching. Ultimately, it would become known as *The Good Friday Raid*.

There were 159 fatalities in the East End; all in the building that took the direct hit—many were guests for the evening. There was collateral damage to nearby buildings, and hundreds suffered injuries, but none were life threatening.

Jacob was two blocks from home. The blast knocked him to the ground, but he was unhurt. He stood and began running towards Vallence Road. The sirens were deafening; everyone was running in the opposite direction.

When he arrived at his building, his heart stopped. It was gone. In its place was a massive pile of smoldering rubble. The screaming was horrifying; he looked around and saw no one he knew. It was then that he realized that the screams he heard were his own.

Rescue equipment was everywhere. The wail of the sirens was deafening as vehicle after vehicle arrived. Medics were treating people in the street as ambulances pulled away with the badly injured inside. Jacob stood back in the shadows across the street from where the building had once stood. He was in shock. He watched and waited and waited and watched. He searched for a familiar face, but there was none. That meant only one thing—everyone was already in the building when the bombs hit. He pictured them seated at the table, waiting for him; but he wasn't there because he had gone by Max's shop to pick up the rings for the twins' birthday.

It was well after midnight, and rescue workers were still attending to the injured that remained. The crowds were thinning, but emergency lights glared in the dark night and sirens continued to wail as ambulances, time and again, left only to return to the scene. The pile of rubble that had once been the building where he lived remained untouched as he kept staring at it willing someone to rise from the ashes.

Jacob did not know what to do. He was alone; he lost everyone he loved in the building; he could think of no one that he could turn to. It was mid-April and the evening had turned cold. Realizing that he was shivering, and that he hadn't eaten in hours, he walked away from the pile of rubble that buried all—his family, the Lerners, his seventeen years of life as he knew and lived it.

He set out towards the only place that came to mind—Max Lerner's shop. As he arrived at his destination, the sounds faded in the distance. Fumbling for the key in his pocket, he found it and unlocked the door. Without turning on the lights, he headed straight to the back of the shop.

When Max and Reba launched their business, they invested all of their savings to purchase the store; it was big enough, however, for them to create a small living area in the back. For three years, it was there home. By the time Reba became pregnant, Max had established himself and the business afforded them enough income to rent a flat with two bedrooms—one would serve as the nursery.

Their daughter, Erica, was born two months after moving into their new flat. She was a beautiful child who fulfilled their every dream, but unfortunately they lost her to an outbreak of Meningitis two months shy of her fifth birthday. They desperately longed for another child, but it wasn't to be. Harry and Ada had no way of knowing that when they came into Max and Reba's lives, they were filling a void that had engulfed them for over thirty years.

Although they no longer lived back of the store, the only change made to the living area was to relocate the workbench and tools out of their customers' sight, thus allowing a bigger showroom area. The new small refrigerator, the stove, and the loo came in quite handy through the years, and they were pleased that they had the foresight to preserve the space pretty much in tact.

After making his way to the back area of the shop, Jacob collapsed on the small sofa, sobs wracking his entire body. At last, thoroughly exhausted, he fell into a deep and troubled sleep.

Marcus Hirsch woke the next morning to the news of the bombing in the East End. He immediately dressed and set off to see if Harry and his family were safe, and if he could help in any way.

His worst fears were realized when he stood in front of the rubble that had once been the building where they lived. There were still several emergency vehicles and medics on the scene, and he approached them seeking information.

He was so visibly shaken at being told that there were no survivors in the building that had taken the direct hit, he almost collapsed. Two of the men guided him over to the First Aid area that had been set up, and there he stayed until he once again regained his composure and assured them that he was okay.

Marcus was confident that he knew everything there was to know about Harry. For almost six years, they had worked side-by-side, and prior to that, he had been the person who vetted him and offered him the position at De Beers. On several occasions, Harry had even sought his advice.

The one thing that remained certain in his mind was the fact that on the first night of Passover, ALL of the Lyons family had been seated around the Seder table in their apartment. He knew they had no relatives in London, but the two people that were close enough to be considered family were Max and Reba Lerner. He had no idea where they lived, but he knew the location of Max's shop.

Twenty minutes later, he stood in front of the darkened store. Realizing that it was Saturday, a day when businesses in the East End would normally be closed for the Sabbath, he started to walk away. On second thought, he turned, putting his face up against the glass of the front door, and looked in; he soon realized it was too dark to see anything. As he stepped back to leave, he stumbled and grabbed hold of the doorknob; to his surprise, he found the door unlocked, and it opened.

Carefully, he entered the shop and made his way to the back. There on the sofa lay Jacob fast asleep. Not wanting to startle the boy, he decided to wait for him to awaken. When Jacob finally began to stir, Marcus approached him and gently calling his name gathered him into his arms. Together they sobbed holding on to one another for dear life.

Finally letting go, Jacob went to wash up and refresh himself. While he washed up, Marcus went into the kitchen area and finding only tea and an unopened box of matzo, put the kettle on. He reached into the cabinet for two cups and set them on the small table. When Jacob returned, he asked him, "How long has it been since you've eaten? There's not much here, but I'm making tea and you should at least eat a little matzo."

"Thank you Mr. Hirsch. I haven't eaten since lunch yesterday."

Marcus poured the tea and sat down at the table. Jacob hungrily ate three large pieces of matzo and drank the cup of tea. Not wanting to press him about the previous night, he rose and put the kettle back on to make more tea.

When he returned to the table, Jacob began relating his story of the night before. He started with coming by the shop to pick up the rings he had made for his sisters and the key to their new home ending with waiting in the shadows until well past midnight when reality finally set in, making him realize that he had lost them all.

"I was so excited about the surprise for Rachael and Rose, the key for my parents, and moving to our new home. The fact is, stopping by the shop is what made me late, and being late is what saved my life. But I don't feel grateful for being alive; I feel guilty. Why would God want me all alone? I should have been with them; I have no one left. My father's two brothers who live in South Africa are the only remaining blood relatives I have, and I only met them once at my Bar Mitzvah."

Marcus was overwhelmed at Jacob's revelations, but he was quite impressed with the young man who, though he had recently turned seventeen and forced to grown up overnight, appeared smart, extremely strong under the terrible circumstances he found himself in, and displayed more common sense than many people Marcus knew that were two and three times his age.

"Jacob, I worked side-by-side with your father for six years. I was proud to call him my friend, and fervently hope he felt the same way about me. He often told me I taught him more about diamonds than he knew there was to learn, but he taught me a lot too. We were a good pair, and I was grateful to Max Lerner many times over for putting us together.

"I want to help you in anyway I can. Please come home with me; stay as long as you wish, and take your time making any plans."

Jacob sat quietly thinking. "Thank you. I need help; I need to make some serious decisions. I accept your offer; I will come with you, but I need a favor. If it's not out of the way, I would like to go by the house in Middlesex and pick up some clothes. I don't want to stay there; I'm not ready for that just yet. We were only days away from moving in."

"That's sounds like a good idea; it's not out of the way at all."

Jacob spent only one night with Marcus and Elena Hirsch. He gratefully appreciated their kindness and concern, but at breakfast, he told them he had made up his mind. "I can't thank you enough for all you have done for me. I've decided to go back and stay at Max's shop alone. I must think things through, determine what my options are, and come up with a plan that will work best for me.

Marcus and Elena's hearts broke at the mere thought of what Jacob was going through; however, they understood and respected his wishes. Having learned that there was very little if anything to eat at the shop, Elena insisted on giving him some food to take with him.

As he wrestled with his thoughts and options over and over again, an emotion he had never before experienced emerged. That emotion was *hate*. His entire life, he had been wrapped in love and kindness. His parents and his religious teachings instilled in him to do unto others as you would have them do unto you.

When the Nazi bombs ended all of that, to Jacob, it became personal. He had to do more than just return to school—he would graduate in less than two months anyway. Legally, he was considered a minor, and he didn't want to think about what that meant.

He knew above all else that he had to do something to purge the hate from his mind and spirit while trying to make any sense whatsoever of what had happened. He went to bed with a clearer mind, satisfied with his decisions, but only the future would tell if he had chosen well. Time no longer stood still; he was no longer in limbo; the crying stopped; he slept soundly.

Monday morning, Jacob rose early. Bathed and dressed, he set off for the house in Middlesex. He went to the closet in his parents' bedroom and retrieved the box that held the papers he needed. At first, he thought only of removing the ones he sought, but decided to take the box intact.

In the small desk in the hallway, he removed a sheet of writing paper, an envelope, and a pen. He sat down at the kitchen table and wrote a letter to Lexi—the only person left that he loved with all his heart. He knew exactly what he wanted to say even though it broke his heart to say it. He slipped the paper into the envelope, sealed, and addressed it. He placed it in the box.

He walked through the entire house, room by room, floor after floor. It was so beautiful, but what once held such high hopes for the future was now tarnished beyond repair. He knew at that very moment that he could never live there—alone.

He bowed his head, and repeated the mourner's Kaddish. Wiping tears from his eyes; with box in hand, he locked and closed the door behind him.

His next destination was De Beers, to see Marcus Hirsch.

Although Marcus did not know that Jacob was coming to see him, he was not surprised to look up and find him standing before him. He had not heard from him since dropping him off at Max's shop.

"Good morning Jacob; please have a seat. How are you doing? Can I get you something to drink, hot or cold?"

Jacob sat down across from him, placing the box on the desk.

"No thank you. I'm okay. I'm doing much better. I've spent my time giving thought to my situation, and good or bad, right or wrong, I have made my decisions. I have no desire to return to school for the next two months; and the thought of moving to Middlesex alone is not what I want or need just now. I have decided to enlist in the RAF, as soon as possible.

"I'm here to take you up on your generous offer to help me. I need your assistance in tying up the many loose ends that I'm leaving behind. This box contains many papers you may need—the Deed to the house in Middlesex; a copy of Max and Reba Lerner's Last Will and Testament, contact information for my uncles, and other papers that you probably won't need, but I just brought the entire box.

"I know that I am the sole heir left in the Lerners' Will, which includes the shop, its contents, and the contents of their flat. The house in Middlesex and its contents also passes to me. As I grew older, my parents always explained these things extensively, but honestly I never paid too much attention.

"First and foremost, a wire must be sent to South Africa immediately, notifying my uncles of the tragedy, my plans to join the RAF, and naming you as their means to contact me.

"I don't want to sell anything at this point—the house, the shop, or any of the contents of both. I am sure it will be some time before all this legal stuff gets sorted out, and I'm not waiting around. I can't.

"My biggest responsibility is to see that my family and the Lerners get a proper Jewish burial when their remains are finally retrieved from the rubble. Since we all worshipped at the Great Central Synagogue on Rectory Square, services can be held there; burial will be in the Brady Street Cemetery. In the meantime, I would appreciate your contacting Rabbi Levin at the synagogue and arranging for a memorial service. I think this coming Friday's services would be an appropriate time.

"My one last request is that you see that this letter is delivered to Alexandra Portman. I don't want to post it; I would prefer to have it hand delivered."

Once again, Marcus could not believe that he was sitting across from a seventeen-year old boy—he had surely become a man in just three short days.

"Of course, I will do everything and anything you ask. Your parents would be so proud of you, and I am proud of you too. The one thing I must insist on is that I know how to get in touch with you at all times. I willingly accept the responsibility of being caretaker of your assets, but should a problem arise that needs your approval, I must be able to reach you. Your safety and wellbeing in the choices you have made are paramount."

Jacob stood and offered his hand to Marcus. "Absolutely, I will keep you up to date on my every move. Again, I can't thank you enough for all you have done, and all that I have landed on you today. Give my best to Mrs. Hirsch, and tell her the food she gave me was delicious and very much appreciated."

Marcus came from behind his desk and hugging Jacob he said, "Take care of yourself and God Bless—until we meet again."

Jacob's entrusting Marcus with everything gave food for thought. While his offer to help him was genuine and sincere, he felt an air of finality on Jacob's part. It made him consider that perhaps Jacob's thinking was that he would not return from the War. He hoped that this was not the case.

He couldn't have been more wrong. Jacob had every intention of doing his best to come back safely and alive.

By the end of the day, Marcus had sent a wire to the Lyons brothers in South Africa. After going through the papers in the box that Jacob left with him, he made a reference list of the documents and prioritized those he felt needed immediate attention. After making a mental note to pay a visit to Rabbi Levin the next day to arrange a memorial service, he decided to leave the office and head home.

On his way home, he delivered Jacob's letter to Alexandra Portman. He had no idea who this person was, but it was obvious she meant a great deal to him. The fact that she was the only person he sought to contact other than his two uncles, and his insistence that his letter to her be hand delivered, convinced Marcus to take care of this request as soon as possible.

He drove down the street looking for the address on the envelope and came to a stop in front of a modest Tudor style house. He walked up to the front door and lifting the brass knocker, rapped it twice. Introducing himself to the woman who answered the door, he inquired if this was the home of Alexandra Portman. Having given no thought to the age of the letter's recipient, for a brief moment he felt perhaps she was Alexandra.

When the woman, replied, "Yes it is, but exactly why do you wish to see my daughter?" He knew that his initial instincts that told him she was Jacob's age had been right.

Lexi was not at home. Elise Portman invited Marcus in and over tea she learned that Jake had survived. "My brother-in-law and his family live in the East End, and we learned Friday night about the bombing. When my husband went to inquire about his family, he learned that the building where Jake and his family lived took a direct hit and that there were no survivors. We assumed that since it was the first night of Passover, everyone was already seated around the Seder table when the bombs fell.

"No one had seen him, not any of his friends, not the Rabbi, not anyone that my husband spoke with. Our nephew is one of his closest friends, and he could find no one who had seen or heard from him either.

"Our daughter Lexi and Jake are quite close and have been for some time. My husband and I care a great deal for him. They are two of a kind—mature beyond their years, excellent scholastic students, and both with an eye on their futures. We know they are young, but if their fate is to have a life together, we embrace it."

Not wanting to relay too much about Jacob's situation, Marcus briefly told Elise Portman that his late arrival home had saved his life, but left him with the dilemma of making some serious decisions; and joining the RAF was one of them.

Marcus handed the letter to Elise. "Thank you for your hospitality. I have no idea what is in the letter, but I suggest that you let her read it before telling her what I have related to you. I'm guessing a good deal of it she will learn from Jacob. You can fill her in on the rest from what I have told you.

"Tomorrow, I'm planning to meet with Rabbi Levin to arrange a memorial service for Friday evening. Maybe you can tell your nephew to tell his friends so they will have a head's up if they wish to attend."

Marcus drove home slowly. It had been quite a day.

Elise Portman waited for Lexi to come home; and while she waited, she gave great thought to what she would tell her daughter. She had no way of knowing what was in the letter, but she was certain that learning that Jake was alive would be exhilarating. When Lexi learned of the bombing and that there were no survivors from the building, she became quite despondent.

Elise thought about calling her husband to discuss the situation, but decided against it, mainly because she knew in her heart he would definitely not sanction what she was thinking of doing.

She thought about what she had said to Marcus—that she and her husband felt that if Jake and Lexi were fated to have a life together, they embraced it. Why was she now rethinking those words?

The world was at war; everything seemed so uncertain; and Lexi was due to start nursing school in a few months. Marcus Hirsch said that Jake had joined the RAF and was going off to fight the Germans. That meant that even though Jake had survived, he would no longer be a part of her life until the War was over, and who knew when that might be, or if he would return at all.

She tried to rationalize what would be best for her daughter; or was she thinking what would be best in the long run for her family. She wanted a good life for Lexi, not a life of waiting—waiting to hear, waiting for someone, waiting to be disappointed.

By the time Lexi came home, the letter had been put away, and Elise greeted her with the wonderful news that Jake was alive, and that he had left to join the RAF.

CHAPTER EIGHT

O
n 14 April 1941, Jacob Aaron Lyons joined the Royal Air Force. After passing tests and a medical exam; receiving a myriad of inoculations and vaccinations; receiving the compulsory haircut which was *neither a comb nor scissors* affair; and having been kitted out, he was enlisted as Pilot U/T (under training) and posted to Lords Cricket Ground for basic training. From there he was sent to Stratford-upon-Avon for navigation, signaling, and arms drill. At the conclusion of the course, the instructor congratulated the group of fifty and told them they were being shipped overseas to the United States for flight training.

Jacob fit in quite well with the group of fifty young men, not all of who wished to pilot the planes. Tommy Butler and Andy Barbour were aiming to be navigators. They struck up a friendship during basic training that continued at Stratford-upon-Avon. Any free time they had, the three spent together taking in the local sights and offerings.

Having introduced himself as *Jake* from the beginning, he turned when he heard Tommy's voice. "Hey Jake, get a move on and come with us. We're going into town to hit a couple of the pubs, play some darts, and dance a little with the local *lassies*."

Jake really liked both Tommy and Andy. They were all about the same age, but it was evident they had each lived vastly different lives.

Tommy was a scrappy kid who grew up on the streets of London. He never knew his father, and his mother went from job to job trying to support the both of them between drying out from her alcohol binges; unfortunately, her last binge killed her. She was buried in the local potters cemetery with money that their neighbors collected. The very next day, Tommy joined the RAF.

Andy was totally at the other end of the spectrum—his father was a Barrister. Although he was a product of the finest prep schools, he was not in the least affected by his upper class upbringing. When his older brother was killed in the Battle of Britain, he too made up his mind to join the RAF.

They were both pretty cool guys who like Jake wanted to kill as many Nazis as possible. The friendship they offered was genuine, and they were fun and carefree and that was just what Jake needed; the truth was, it was just what each of them needed. They introduced him to beer and cigarettes, both of which he had managed to avoid for seventeen years. In fact, to the best of his knowledge, none of his friends in the East End had ever expressed a desire to smoke or have a pint of beer, at least to him.

Grabbing his jacket, he said, "Sounds good to me. I'm in."

The first time Tommy and Andy asked Jake to join them they took him to O'Hara's Pub. It was a local favorite, and since it was the weekend, the place was really jumping.

Although Jake was not legally old enough to drink alcohol, in reality he wasn't old enough to join the RAF without parental consent either, but after telling the recruitment officer that he had lost everything including his entire family in the air raid, they accepted him without question even though he admitted to them he was seventeen. They were at war; all things change and all rules bend in wartime.

O'Hara's Pub was crowded and the smoke was so thick, Tommy joked, "Save your smokes; you don't need one in here—just inhale."

They were having fun mingling with the crowd, and Jake was in a serious Dart Game competition when the fight broke out. At first, no one paid much attention, but when glasses started crashing to the ground, and they heard the wail of Police sirens growing closer, one of the local girls steered them out the back door into the alley where they took off running.

They discussed dropping in at another pub up the street, but decided instead to head back to the base, laughing and joking all the way. Although he didn't show it, Jake was more than a little shaken up. He had never outrun the law. In fact, he had never found himself in a situation where he had to—before this night.

———✷———

Since September 1939, when Neville Chamberlain had announced Britain's declaration of war, trained pilots were urgently needed if the RAF was to meet its operational commitments. The struggle and success in achieving the required number of pilots turned out to be one of the biggest battles of the War.

Time was of the essence and initially the focus was on revising the training programs by shortening the courses and increasing the capacity of pupils at the training schools. This, however, proved unsuccessful. Faced with a limited amount of equipment available and a shortage of instructors, Great Britain turned to its allies for help.

During WWII, the majority of men training to become RAF aircrew were taught overseas. By war's end, there were a total of 333 flight training schools all over the world. Although other training was available throughout the United States at many flight schools operated under contract to the RAF, in early 1941, under President Roosevelt's approval, seven British Flying Training Schools were set up in short order to satisfy the demand.

Two days after their night on the town, their group of fifty was shipped from Liverpool to St. Johns, Newfoundland, and on to Toronto for a brief stay. They were kitted out with grey suits so they could travel to the States as civilian Aeronautical Students since America at the time had not yet entered the War.

Jake, Tommy, and Andy took time out to hitchhike to Niagara Falls where they found the sights awesome, but were more impressed with the food that was not only good but plentiful.

From Toronto, they embarked on the long train ride to Georgia. It was a slow journey of about five days, but at each stop they were welcomed with fruit and cookies and endless enquiries about how the British were holding up—so much for their disguise as civilians in grey suits.

They arrived at Darr Aero Tech in Albany, Georgia, a civilian flying school taken over by the U.S. Army Air Corps on a beautiful but hot summer day in mid July 1941. They were required to repeat basic training, and although they were looked after very well, they weren't allowed off base for six weeks.

When the six weeks were up, and they were given a weekend pass, Jake, Tommy, and Andy set out to sample some of the southern cooking and southern hospitality that they had been hearing about. On base, they wore khaki shirts and slacks, but on excursions into town, they once again wore their civilian clothes, and it almost made it seem as though they were on holiday.

Jake was having the time of his life, as he waited impatiently to fly. His first flight made on 5 September 1941 was an experience that he would never forget. Dressed in overalls, helmet, and goggles, he sat in the rear seat and bumped across the grass until the aircraft suddenly stopped bumping and he realized they had left the ground below. It was 40 minutes of sheer ecstasy until they touched down. A feeling of euphoria came over him and at that moment, he realized he had made the right decision to join the RAF.

After ten hours of dual instruction, Jake flew solo and passed with flying colors. He almost drove his instructor crazy by constantly urging him to test him further and further. It worked. He passed the Flight Commander 20-hour and 40- hour checks with no problem whatsoever, and also the Army 60-hour.

Both the flying instructors and flight instructions at Darr were first class. All flying was done without airspeed indicators—in other words—*by the seat of your pants*. The *feel* and *flicks* of loops, rolls, slow rolls, and aerobatics were used to make the pilot feel as *one* with the aircraft they were flying, and their ability was judged accordingly.

Two incidents occurred in September. The first was the sole fatality during Jake's time at Darr. A solo student took off and climbed too fast causing him to collide with a dual aircraft ahead of him. The instructor and the pupil in the dual aircraft survived without serious injury, but the solo student crashed, and the plane caught fire killing him. The group attended its first Military Funeral held at St. Paul's Church in Albany, but it cast a shadow over the group of young men forcing them to face reality.

The second was the hurricane that hit Darr. Gil Carson their meteorology instructor was in his element when word reached him that a hurricane was coming. His ability to forecast the hurricane's precise arrival greatly impressed the group. Most had never experienced such a phenomena before and were at first amused by the apparent panic to get the aircraft into the hangers and everything movable tied down and secured. It was while watching from the comfort and safety of their barracks, and seeing the ferocity of the wind, the deluge of the rain, and the sudden calm in the eye of the hurricane as it passed directly overhead, that they soon realized the seriousness of the situation.

Thanksgiving Day in November was yet another new experience. The group enjoyed a traditional turkey dinner with all the trimmings. In the evening, there was a dance arranged and busloads of local *Georgia Peaches* were imported to supplement the women who worked on the base. By American standards, the group's dancing abilities were staid.

A pretty young girl with blond, curly hair approached Jake, and with her pronounced southern drawl said, "Hi, my name is Sally. Would you care to *cut a rug*?"

Jake didn't have a clue what she was suggesting. "Hi to you too. I'm Jake, and what is it exactly you want me to do?"

Sally laughed. "I didn't know you were British. I asked if you would like to dance—jitterbug, that is."

Jake laughed too, although she had cleared up one thing, he now wasn't too sure about another. "If jitterbug is an American dance, I'm afraid I'm not your guy."

As the band started playing *In the Mood*, Sally grabbed Jake's hand and in a manner of seconds, she had him *in the groove.*

All too soon the dance floor was cleared, and Jake and Sally were the only couple dancing—to the hoots and hollers of his friends as they cheered him on.

On 7 December 1941, several cadets came up with the idea of staging a British Rugby Football Match. The two teams of cadets impressed the locals not only with the physical game that ensued, but the fact that they wore no helmets or protective padding. At the conclusion of the game, the public address system brought the news of the Japanese attack on Pearl Harbor.

This brought America into the War, and immediate changes to the routine at Darr. Security was increased; the tempo of their training was significantly put on a faster track, and the wearing of civilian clothing was banned.

Less than a week later, the students that had completed their 60 hours flying in the Stearman Aircraft left Darr to start the next stage of their flight training at Cochran Field Macon. The excitement and anticipation was tinged with regret at leaving the town that had introduced them to southern hospitality, not to mention, bubble gum, Coke Cola, peanut butter, southern fried chicken, French fries, pumpkin pie, peaches and pecans, and the best iced tea ever—and, of course, the jitterbug!

With his Primary Training behind him, at Cochran Field Macon, Jake looked forward to starting his service flying with U. S. Army instructors on the Vultee BT13A Aircraft. Having learned how to fly, he now had to apply his skill and knowledge to service requirements. The Vultee was a monoplane with fixed undercarriage and two-speed propeller. It also had some flying instruments—airspeed indicator, altimeter, compass, needle, and ball indicator.

Blind flying, night flying, formation flying, and day and night cross-countries, all helped make the course extremely intensive. Twelve-hour days with only Christmas Day off and only one weekend leave, which Jake spent in Atlanta with his friends, took him to completion of the course on 12 February 1942. And while no one was watching, Jake's 18th Birthday came and went in mid-January. He did not allow himself to become sad or morose or recall old memories of happier times and birthday celebrations. He didn't share with anybody that it was his birthday. He looked forward to the day when he would shoot the Germans out of the sky.

Jake left Georgia a week later. He was moved to Napier Field, Dothan, Alabama, where he learned to fly AT6A Harvard Aircraft, a much more advanced aircraft with retractable undercarriage, variable speed propeller, a full set of blind flying instruments, and capable of flying much faster than any plane he had flown to-date. Two days after dual flying with Lieutenant Billings, Jake went solo. Formation flying took place day and night; tactical flying consisted of a *Rat Race*—chasing the instructor and trying to keep on his tail. Now that he was flying so much, time seemed to pass quicker.

On 17 April 1942, Jake graduated, and received his American Wings. He became an honorary 2nd Lieutenant in the U.S. Army Air Corps. He declined an RAF Commission, as it meant staying in the United States and instructing future RAF Cadets. By May 1942, Jake was back in England—with five days of leave.

He arrived in London and booked himself into the Savoy Hotel. Located just off the River Thames near Hyde Park, the hotel had been bombed repeatedly during the Blitz, but was never forced to close. Facing a manpower shortage, food rationing, and a decline in the number of foreign visitors following the barrage of German air raids, business reversed itself once America entered the War.

It again became a favorite meeting place for American officers, diplomats, journalists, and world leaders. Winston Churchill often took his cabinet to lunch at the hotel, and Lord Mountbatten, Charles de Gaulle, and high-ranking British and American military were regular Grill Room diners. The Savoy management cooperated fully with the government's wartime restrictions helping to draw up an order imposing a five-shilling limit on the price of a restaurant meal. In addition, the hotel's air raid shelters were known to be *the smartest in London.*

After a shower and a change of clothes, he headed off to De Beers to see Marcus Hirsch.

When he walked into his office, Marcus let out a big whoop. "Jake, you are a sight for sore eyes! You look fantastic."

He rose from his desk and pulled him into a bit bear hug. "Do you have any plans? Come home with me. I'll call Elena and tell her we're having company for dinner, but I won't tell her it's you. We'll surprise her."

Jake smiled. It sure was good to be home even if it was just for five days. "No, but I do now. Dinner with you and Elena sounds like a good plan to me."

They spent the evening catching up, but Jake did most of the talking. He told them all about the numerous flight schools, about his friends Tommy and Andy, about America, about southern hospitality, about all the good food he had sampled, and about learning to dance the jitterbug. Now the time had come for him to get down to business and do what he was trained to do. After his five days of leave, he would learn where he would be posted.

Jake spent a day at the office with Marcus going over all his personal affairs that he had entrusted to him. Marcus showed him his reference list of documents and noted the dates when each item had been executed. When the victims' remains were finally removed from the rubble, identified, and officially declared dead, all of his parents' assets were transferred to him. In addition the Lerners' assets were transferred to him as their sole heir, as well. All cash was placed in a bank account bearing the name Jacob Aaron Lyons. When all was said and done, Jake was financially quite well off—especially for someone who had just turned eighteen.

The next day, he visited Rabbi Levin who was more than pleased to see him. He rightfully observed that the boy he once taught was gone and in his place was a tall, good looking young man with an air of confidence about him. As Marcus had surmised, so too did Rabbi Levin that this air of confidence was unprecedented for someone so young. Jake thanked Rabbi Levin for the Memorial Service he had asked Marcus to arrange for him.

"It was quite a service. Never in all my years, has there been such an overflow crowd at the Great Central Synagogue on Rectory Square—no Bar Mitzvah, no wedding, no Sabbath Service—other than on that Friday night. Mr. Hirsch who worked with your father generously insisted on arranging and paying for the food and wine for the Kiddush following the service. Not only was it a miracle we didn't run out of food and drink considering all those who attended, but that he even managed to secure the provisions since rationing was imposed.

The Rabbi accompanied Jake to the Brady Street Cemetery, to the graves of his parents, his sisters, and the Lerners. They recited the mourners Kaddish together, and then Jake continued, *"Baruch Dayan ha'Emet—M*ay they rest in peace."* Rabbi Levin thought to himself—Harry and Ada would be so proud. He bid farewell to the Rabbi, promising to stop by to see him again when he was in London. The Rabbi promised to pray for his safe return.

At first he didn't intend to go by Valance Road, but he changed his mind and began walking through his old neighborhood. When he reached where their building had stood, a great sadness washed over him. Most of the rubble was gone but a fence had been erected around the site, and it was locked. He stared into space for a few minutes and then made his way to Max's shop. He unlocked the door and saw that it was emptied of its contents, just as Marcus had told him—only the showcases and worktable remained. Marcus had taken the jewelry, the supplies, and all the tools and stored everything securely in the basement of the house in Middlesex.

He spent the last day of his leave at the house on 11 Brook Avenue. Once again, he walked through the rooms, up and down the floors, all the while fighting the demons in his thoughts, just as he had done before he left to join the RAF. His feelings hadn't changed; he could never live in the house. For now, he had no plans to sell it; that could wait until the War was over, and he came home.

He wanted so desperately to contact Lexi, but he had conveyed to her his heartfelt thoughts in his letter and felt it best to leave things as they were. Seeing her would also have to wait until the War was over—until he could offer her a life, a secure future.

He had dinner once again with Marcus and Elena, but this time, he took them to dinner in London at the Savoy Hotel where he was staying. The rules had recently changed, and hotels no longer had to contend with rationing thus allowing them to secure ample supplies of food and wine to serve their guests. What a wonderful dinner they had. They laughed and talked about the past, but it didn't make Jake sad. Instead, he was glad that however short his father's life had been, he had realized so many of his goals and dreams—first and foremost was the family he had.

As they said their goodbyes, Jake told Marcus that he would let him know when he got his orders where he would be posted. "By the way, did you get to deliver the letter I left with you?"

Marcus thought for a moment. "Why, yes I did. I delivered it personally that very day on my way home. The young lady was not at home, but I had a very nice visit with her mother, and I left the letter with her."

"Thank you. I appreciate the fact that you delivered it immediately. It didn't require a response, so I was just checking to make sure she received it."

Marcus could not understand why but he had a gut feeling that something was not right with the letter. He had hoped he would see Elise Portman, her husband, and daughter at the Memorial Service, and get to meet Jacob's young lady; but despite the crowd, he was quite certain they had not been there.

—◦◦◦—

Indeed, Manny and Elise Portman were not at the Memorial Service. They did not know Harry and Ada Lyons having never met them. However, Lexi had been there with her cousin Ivan, but she did not know Marcus Hirsch nor of him, and he did not know her.

CHAPTER NINE

At the end of his leave, Jake discovered that due to the excellent training he had received in America, and because he had declined a commission to remain and instruct future pilots, he was promoted to Flight Lieutenant and assigned to RAF Winkleigh in Devon.

RAF Winkleigh was home to an incredible array of international combatants and their support units, including the IX USAF Service Command, the crack RAF 161 Black Squadron, the RCAF Swordfish Squadron, and the Free Polish Air Force.

The brand new, purpose built RAF base at Winkleigh was just five minutes flying time to the north Atlantic coastline of Britain and less than an hour from the battlefronts of France. Therefore, it played an incredibly important and strategic role to the war in Europe, both as a tactical support unit for Coastal Command and an offensive battering ram against the rapidly approaching Germans.

The Winkleigh family of squadrons resembled a flock of protective hawks in the skies over Britain's southern cities. Their fearless pilots like stealthy black panthers in the night destroying the transport and communication systems of the enemy. Meanwhile behind closed doors, new developments in radar technology were being undertaken; munitions development and enhanced communications were being nurtured; secret operations planned; and deadly airstrikes begun.

The Quarters on base were Nissan huts, constructed of corrugated steel, which formed the roof and sides in a half circle design. They were erected over a cement base with an access door at each flat vertical end. The huts were not heated but they did have a small cast iron stove in the center of the room.

The ration of coke for the stove was one full scuttle per week. Scrounging for additional fuel was out of the question as the coke storage compound had excellent security, and anyone even found walking in the area was considered a potential thief.

Single cots were provided with felt mattresses, a pillow or bolster, and two gray blankets, but no sheets or pillowcases. Jake found himself thinking more and more about that good old southern hospitality.

A wide variety of operational aircraft flew out of RAF Winkleigh during the war years, including many flown *by the seat of your pants* super heroes in Spitfires, Hurricanes, Mosquitos, B26 Marauders, Albacores, and Dakotas, to name a few.

As Jake and several others newly posted to Winkleigh were ushered around as an overview of the facility and the various aircraft, he eyed the Spitfires and Hurricanes longingly. He had never flown either plane, but that didn't stop him from hoping that one day soon, he would be in the cockpit of one or both. He had heard a good deal about the planes, and the parts they played during the Battle of Britain.

The Hurricane was paralleled in many ways to the Spitfire in with which it was destined to form a legendary partnership. While the Spitfire was an entirely new concept based on specialized experience, the Hurricane was the logical outcome of a long line of fighting aircraft. Although the two fighter planes met the same requirements, they represented entirely different approaches to the same problem.

The two approaches were reflected to an interesting degree in their respective appearances—the Hurricane workmanlike, rugged, and sturdy; the Spitfire slender and sleek as a thoroughbred. One was the studied application of experience, the other a stroke of genius. The fact that both the Spitfire and the Hurricane were developed and appeared on the scene at roughly the same time was purely coincidental.

During the Battle of Britain, the Luftwaffe had tried to destroy the RAF Fighter Command and had conspicuously failed. At the time, the RAF had 33 Squadrons of Hurricanes compared to 19 Squadrons of Spitfires. Although they were lauded as the victor of the battle having been responsible for destroying more enemy aircraft than the Spitfires, the Hurricanes outnumbered the Spitfires, and many RAF pilots felt neither could have won without the other.

Jake and nineteen others comprised the group of 20 who were selected to fly the newly equipped Spitfires.

For the next two months, Jake and the others in his group were briefed on the Spitfire's characteristics that were considerably different from other types of aircraft anyone in the group had flown. The instructors, who were fighter pilots themselves on break, led them on formation exercises and critiqued their every move while sharing their experiences with the aircraft in battle.

After two weeks had passed, Jake's group got a new instructor. On his very first day, the new instructor chose Billy Webster as the first to take a *Spit* up and fly it around a bit. Of all the others in their group, Billy did not stand out as being up to the task, and there was no way the new instructor could have known anyone's potential his first day on the job. In fact, Billy was quite shy and laid back, and Jake couldn't understand why the instructor had chosen him as the first to fly or chosen anyone to fly until he became more acquainted with them.

Sadly, the instructor's decision proved fatal. Billy was so visibly nervous, that in all probability, it severely hampered his ability to think clearly. His coarse take off caused him to clip the top of a hangar and crash into a storage building killing him instantly. For Jake, this brought back memories of the chap who had been killed in the States, once again forcing him to question his immortality.

Three days later and yet another instructor, Jake was called up to fly. Putting Billy out of his mind, he concentrated on what he had been taught. The Spitfire was beautiful in appearance, graceful to handle, and deadly in combat. It's clean lines and rounded wings were both aerodynamic and elegant. This was exactly what Jake had been hoping for, waiting for, and his excitement in finally getting to fly a Spitfire not only dispelled any nervousness he might have had, but actually boosted his confidence.

With these thoughts in mind, he taxied the plane to the far end of the field. At the holding point on the grass, he did his run up and instruments check, winding on full right rudder trim. Having moved up to the *ready* spot on the grass, he lined up with the hangar on the far side of the field, and waited for a green, one eye on the rapidly rising coolant temperature, the other on the tower. On getting the green light, he released the brakes, and glided the stick back gradually opening the throttle to takeoff power, then carefully brought the stick forward to neutral. Immediately, the tail was up to flying attitude; an almost full right rudder was needed to keep straight. A few seconds later, with some light bouncing on the grass, the plane flew itself off.

Sitting in that snug cockpit, almost on the trailing edge, and with that beautiful wing in his field of vision, it was hard for Jake to believe he was really flying a *Spitfire*. With speed building up, he retracted the undercarriage, closed the canopy and climbed to a safe height over the training area.

After getting a feel for the sensitivity of the controls, he ran through a series of exercises he had been taught, including stalls and spins; and then executed a simple loop. For a brief moment he seemed to lose control of the plane, but without any input on his part, the aircraft righted itself, and he was back in business.

Having been out for over an hour, he headed back to the field and landed. He was still on *cloud nine* and could not recall one aspect of his first Spitfire landing, as he taxied back across the field to the hangar where his instructor awaited him. Climbing down from the cockpit, he noticed the scowl on his instructor's face. "Lyons, you came in too fast and too straight, causing you to float halfway across the field; good job otherwise."

In the days following his initial flight, he perfected his landings. All Spitfires were known to float a fair distance, even when brought in at the correct speed; this made landing easy. He learned to hold it level as it floated, and when it started to sink, raising the nose progressively, until, with the stick back in his lap, it settled down like a feather. Once mastered not only was it efficient, but it felt good. With the landing field in full sight, slipping the turn would cause the loss of any excess height.

At the end of two months, Jake finished the course with 37 hours on Spits, and was posted to 1111 RAF Squadron, newly formed at Peterhead on the North Sea coast of Scotland, 30 miles north of Aberdeen. A week later he flew with his squadron for the first time, and for the first time from a paved runway.

Although Scotland is second only to the Aleutians for bad flying weather, especially in winter, 1111 Squadron flew hit-and-run raids, and convoy patrols over the North Sea the entire winter of 1942, while the locals claimed that it was the worst winter in living memory. When the runways were not snowed in, it was routine to be scrambled into ceilings as low as 300' depending solely on your gut to get back down out of the clouds, preferably over the sea.

The Spitfires were modified many times as the War progressed; they were given larger engines, more spacious cockpits, and 20mm cannons. When RAF pilots starting bombing Germany in 1943, the bombers needed fighter planes to escort them all the way into the heart of Germany, and Jake's Squadron was called up. During most of that year, Bomber Command's priority was attacking Germany's U-boat ports as part of Britain's effort to win the Battle of the Atlantic.

Month after month, 1111 Squadron flew escort to the British bombers whose attacks had done considerable damage to industrial cities throughout Germany. The Battle of Berlin was launched, along with attacks on other cities aimed at preventing the Germans from concentrating on their defense of Berlin.

In mid-December, escorted by fighter planes for the first time both to and from their targets, 710 bombers took part in the largest daylight raid to date over Kiel, Germany. Although the attack resulted in the loss of 5 Allied bombers, 15 Nazi fighter planes were destroyed at the hands of Jake's Squadron.

The Spitfire was significantly faster, more nimble, and had a higher rate of climb, and many pilots felt they were so well balanced, they could practically fly themselves. The brave pilots who flew them proved they could do it all; they could fly all the way to Berlin and back, and out dogfight the German fighters time and again.

To be proclaimed an *Ace*, a pilot had to have five confirmed victories. Jake actually made *Ace in a day* and was well on his way to becoming one of the top scoring RAF fighter pilots of the War. He had 18 kills, and was credited with destroying 18 enemy aircraft, five probable, and five damaged. Across

A Diamond in the Rough

the chest of his uniform were displayed a Bomber Command Campaign Metal, a War Metal with bronze oak leaf, an Air Crew Europe Star, and the Distinguished Flying Medal. His recent promotion to Squadron Leader was his latest achievement.

RAF 1111 Squadron was selected to join in the combat missions scheduled to begin in early 1944, and leading up to Operation Overlord. With the Squadron's recent return to Winkleigh, Jake felt as though he had come home.

The last two years had been stressful and intense. He had flown over 60 missions, lost fellow pilots who had become good friends, and had 18 kills to his credit. Although his fellow pilots marveled at his ability to out maneuver the enemy by dubbing him *Jitterbug Jake*, he found himself in several precarious situations that resulted in his bailing out over the English Channel in one incident, and a crash landing back at the base in another. Fortunately, his injuries were of little concern.

It was almost Christmas, and with a ten-day leave in hand, he was officially off duty until the New Year. He eagerly boarded the train to London with a fellow pilot and checked into the Savoy.

Now, he simply wanted to unwind, see Marcus and Elena, and not have to get out of bed at the crack of dawn each and every day. He also wanted to go to the cemetery and pay a visit to Rabbi Levin. It had been almost two years since he had been in London, or even been on leave, other than a day here and there requiring him to stay near the base.

Because of the blackouts, the streets of London were quite subdued, but inside the hotel, holiday decorations were plentiful and festive; and when he checked in, there was a notice on the desk inviting all service personnel to a New Year's Eve Gala in the Grand Ballroom sponsored by the Red Cross Club in conjunction with the American USO. Handing him the key to his room, the desk clerk pointed this fact out to Jake. "I hope you will join us New Year's Eve. The staff has been working quite handily to make sure that it's a glorious event."

"Thank you, sir. I will certainly consider it."

His first call was always to Marcus—simply because he considered Marcus and Elena family, his only family. This time, he insisted they join him at the Savoy for dinner his first night in town. After a brief rest, a shave, and a shower, Jake left his room to go downstairs to meet them in the Grille Room for dinner. He was early, but decided to hang out in the Lobby. The Savoy was a favorite of both British and American servicemen alike whenever they found themselves in London, if they were lucky enough to secure a room.

To his utter delight and surprise, when the lift opened on his floor, there stood Tommy Butler. "*Wow*! Is that really you? It is so great to see you."

Filled to capacity the lift became an express to the Lobby. They hugged and just stared at one another. They hadn't seen each other since they parted ways after arriving in London from the States, and neither knew where the other was ultimately posted. Jake spoke first. "I know I keep saying *Wow*, but I just can't believe we're both here. How could we have been so stupid not keeping in touch? I've really missed you and Andy too."

Tommy laughed. "Well, you can say *Wow* again, when I tell you I'm meeting Andy in the bar here at the hotel. Have a drink with us."

"I have dinner plans, but hey, please join us. The people I'm meeting are the closest to family I have, and it will be so good to share stories and catch up. I promise you, Marcus and Elena Hirsch will enjoy meeting you and Andy and hearing every single detail of any time we spent together."

"I would love to have dinner with you, and I accept your generous offer, but Andy is meeting his parents here for dinner too, so I can't speak for him. Why don't we go to the bar, grab a quick ale, wait for him, and see what we can work out."

Merging the two dinner reservations allowed Andy Barbour, his parents, Tommy Butler, Marcus, Elena, and Jake to spend a delightful evening together over a sumptuous meal where laughter was the entrée and friendship the dessert—removed from the raging War that overshadowed all of their lives. It was a night they hadn't experienced in far too long, and they embraced it.

After dinner, everyone said their goodbyes and Andy's parents and Marcus and Elena left. Tommy, Andy, and Jake headed back to the bar.

After ordering a round of drinks, Tommy asked, "What do you guys say we make plans to attend the New Year's Eve Gala here at the hotel? It sounds like fun and the desk clerk said there will be plenty ladies to check out and maybe have a dance or two. Hey Jake, you do remember how to jitterbug don't you?"

"I think I do although I haven't had a chance to do much dancing since we left the States. I know we can't really talk about what's waiting for us at the end of our leave, but with the recent victories the Allies have racked up, I sure hope we're heading towards the end of this War. I've seen some pretty bad things happen to too many chaps that I cared about.

"After spending such a great evening with friends and family, I really look forward to returning to a normal life and making plans for the future. You can count me in. It looks like the perfect way to begin the New Year."

Andy thoroughly agreed. "Count me in, as well. At least for the evening, we can forget about the fighting for one night."

Andy left for home; Tommy and Jake took the lift to their rooms.

CHAPTER TEN

As Marcus Hirsch drove away from the Portman house in one direction, Lexi arrived home from the other. Elise greeted her with the good news that she had learned that Jake was alive and had not yet arrived home when the bombs fell on their building. As Lexi sobbed with relief in her mother's arms, she asked a million questions—none of which was answered. Instead, Elise comforted her daughter with soothing and reassuring words and offered to make tea and something to eat. When Manny Portman came home, he found them in the sitting room.

To both of them Elise related the story of Jake's survival without once mentioning Marcus Hirsch or Jake's letter—which she had quietly tucked away in one of two small drawers in the bottom of her jewelry case before Lexi arrived home. Neither questioned how she learned of Jake's survival; both assuming that she heard the news during the day while she was out running errands.

Although Lexi learned that Jake was alive, she couldn't dispel the sadness and abandonment that she felt. She could not come to grips with the fact that he had not contacted her direct to tell her the decisions he made, or what his immediate plans were. She only knew he was joining the RAF; and that meant he could be anywhere. Most of all, she had no way to contact him or find out how he was faring. She could only imagine how terrible it was to lose one's entire family, but she knew he loved her as much as she loved him, and leaving without a word was not Jake's way of doing things; it was the opposite. Her only conjecture being that his loss was so great, he knew of no other way to cope.

Lexi attended the Memorial Service the following Friday night at the

Great Central Synagogue in the East End alone. The multitude of people who attended was overwhelming. In the weeks and months following the service, she would inquire if her cousin Ivan had heard any news about Jake; his answer was always the same, "No, not a word." Finally, she stopped asking, realizing that if Ivan heard anything, he would surely tell her. A month after her graduation from high school Lexi enrolled in nursing classes.

Elise Portman wrestled with her conscience on a daily basis. Had she done the right thing by keeping the letter from Lexi? If she reconsidered and changed her mind, how could she possibly produce the letter months later without a valid explanation? She had no one to confide in; she had never mentioned the letter to Manny. With each passing day, her guilt continued to consume her.

She threw herself into volunteering at the hospital; chairing luncheons and various events for the war effort, and working with the newly opened USO in London and the Red Cross to open clubs throughout the City for both British and American military personnel on leave.

———✠———

At her father's suggestion, Lexi applied to a newly built hospital on the outskirts of Birmingham and was accepted for the four-year training course to become a registered nurse. It was a teaching hospital adjacent to the University of Birmingham and its Medical School, and at the time was rated as the most modern and state-of-the-art hospital in the United Kingdom.

Because of the War and the desperate and immediate need for medically trained personnel, nurses in particular, her classes started in July following her graduation from high school, in lieu of commencing in the fall. Classes were no longer suspended during the summer months, and the new nursing students were further encouraged to take extra credits, allowing them to complete the four-year course in two and one-half to three years. Lexi welcomed this new opportunity and looked forward to becoming an RN in the shortest possible time.

On a beautiful summer weekend in late June, Elise and Manny Portman drove Lexi the 162 km to Birmingham to begin her nursing studies. This was what Lexi had talked about since she was five years old—often hosting a *get-well* tea party for her dolls in a makeshift hospital in their backyard garden. She wanted to be a nurse and help sick people get well.

"Why are you so quiet Lexi? Aren't you excited about starting your classes? You seemed quite pleased when we came to visit the school a few weeks ago."

"I'm fine Mum. I'm just thinking about all that I have ahead of me, and I want to do it all as fast as I can. I'm totally looking forward to the accelerated program being offered."

Lexi couldn't tell her that all she thought about most days was Jake. Where was he? What was he doing? Did he think about her? She hated this War; she yearned for the way things were what seemed a lifetime ago, but in reality were just months ago.

The Queen Mother had declared the new hospital open in 1939, and graciously consented to give it her own name. It became known as the Queen Elizabeth Hospital. All nursing students were required to live in, and at no time were allowed to wear their uniform away from the hospital. Very strict rules were observed including that which forbade marriage during the period of training, which was a difficult decision for many a young girl whose fiancé was due to ship out for overseas combat. Each student was required to pay 20 pounds for their uniforms and textbooks; however, they did not have to pay for board and lodging.

The medical profession was male-dominated at the time, and female medical students were noticeable by their absence. On the other hand, the nursing profession was all female and no training existed for males to become nurses.

Lexi threw herself wholeheartedly into her studies and moved forward quickly. After six months of her initial training, she was called upon to carry out the tasks generally assigned to porters and orderlies who consistently fell short of demand. One Ward Sister took a particular liking to her and often requested that she accompany her during rounds. This allowed Lexi good experience in dealing with the many patients who were coming into the hospital on a daily basis.

As air raids and military campaigns intensified, their nursing duties and experiences expanded. The hospital received many air raid casualties from surrounding areas, including those from city hospitals. The center of Birmingham was attacked relentlessly, and at times, the casualties admitted exceeded their capacity. After one particularly vicious bombardment, they were forced to put the wounded on stretchers in the corridors due to lack of beds.

As they viewed the glow of fires burning in the City, the Queen Elizabeth Hospital was subjected to attack after attack by incendiary bombs. Medical students took turns manning the rooftops of the hospital in fire-watching duties. It eventually became necessary to evacuate hospital patients from some of the wards in order to make room for air raid victims. Emergency units were set up in small cottage hospitals and convalescent homes throughout the surrounding area to accommodate the evacuated patients.

Some of the injuries sustained by air raid victims were devastating and made an everlasting impression on the young student nurses involved in their treatment. The memory of these tragic cases remained with Lexi long after they died or were discharged. At times like these, she instinctively thought of Jake.

However, there were many lighter moments, as well. Some of the army personnel who ended up as patients were injured during training exercises. One young man who shot himself in the foot while on such an exercise was visibly embarrassed by his predicament when asked by the Ward Sister what had happened. His explanation didn't help the situation any when nearby patients who heard his every word roared with laughter.

All too soon, she had been at Birmingham for over two years, and aside from several visits home, her life was pretty much centered on her studies. On the occasions when she went home, she travelled by train, and her father picked her up at the Charing Cross Station. For the most part, these visits were strained, and she bristled under her mother's constant questions. Although she had always been *Pops' Girl*, growing up she had a good relationship with her Mum. They only began drifting apart when for some reason she disagreed with Lexi's reaction to Jake not having contacted her before leaving to join the RAF. This continued to puzzle her.

She became friendly with two of the student nurses—Betsy Bromwell and Lily Martin. Whenever they had some free time, they went into the surrounding towns and had dinner or just relaxed and talked about some of the patients they had encountered.

Both Betsy and Lily grew up on the outskirts of London, so the girls often talked about celebrating in the City when they finished their studies and became full fledged nurses.

One Friday evening as she was looking forward to having both Saturday and Sunday off, she arrived home after classes and was surprised to see her father standing beside his car waiting for her.

She quickened her pace and gave him a big hug. "Hi Pops. What are you doing here? Where's Mum?"

"Your mother is home. I was up this way on business, and I thought I'd have dinner with you. I hope I'm not upsetting any plans you may have.

"Well, I do have plans, but Betsy and Lily will understand. Give me a few minutes to change out of my uniform and freshen up a bit, and we can be on our way. I know of several good places to eat that I'm sure you'll just love."

Lexi raced up the steps, told her friends that she was having dinner with her father, and decided to take a quick shower. The hot water felt good on her aching back, but her Pops was waiting, and she didn't want to keep him any longer than necessary.

He left the car parked outside her building. It was a nice evening, and they opted to take the twenty-minute walk to City Centre. "What are you up for Pops? Are you hungry, want a few beers, or what?

"I just want to enjoy a nice quiet dinner with you; nothing too noisy like a pub, but it doesn't have to be too fancy either."

"Fine, I know just the place—Oak Hill. I know the couple that owns it; their daughter is one of the nursing students. She started her studies a couple of months ago."

They were seated at a small table in the back away from the noise coming from the bar, which allowed them to speak without shouting. They took the waitress' suggestion and ordered the day's Special—Fish and Chips. It was perfect. They talked about school; her father caught her up to speed on her brothers who were attending Cambridge Medical School. They chose to share a dessert, and the waitress served their tea, and left the pot on the table.

Suddenly, her father grew quiet. "I'm afraid I haven't been too truthful with you about my visit. I had no business to attend to up this way; I specifically came to see you. I'm afraid I'm the bearer of bad news; Mum is very ill— she's been diagnosed with lung cancer. For weeks, she has undergone every test imaginable. We've consulted with doctors who referred us to specialists, seeking in earnest the best possible treatment available. This has all taken quite a toll on both of us.

"Yesterday, we had an appointment to meet with the doctors and consider our options to proceed. All our hopes were dashed when we were told that the doctors concluded in agreement that because the cancer is advanced and has begun to spread throughout her body, we have no options. They've given her a month or two at the most, and advised us to set up a hospice in our home to keep her as comfortable and pain free as possible for whatever time she has left."

Lexi sat quietly in disbelief at what her father told her. A wave of guilt washed over her as she thought of her recent relationship with her dear Mum as totally her fault. "I'm speechless. I had no idea she was not feeling well. How long has this been going on? When I saw her a couple of months ago, she was her usual bubbly self, and in speaking with her from school, she kept me up-to-date on the many luncheons and committees and volunteering for so many events, all for the war effort. Meanwhile, she was neglecting her own needs."

"It does sound quite unbelievable. The worst part is that I'm a physician, and I can't help her. My dear, sweet Elise has always been strong and very healthy. The first sign was a severe pain in her chest. At first, the doctors thought it was her heart, but after a series of tests, they realized the pain was caused by a large mass in her lungs. Ultimately they diagnosed her with lung cancer. By that time, the cancer had already spread."

"How is she taking all of this? She must be so scared. Oh Pops, I have to take a leave of absence from my studies. I'll come home with you and spend what little time we have left, together. Actually, I've come far enough in my nursing studies to be of help in taking care of her. I want to help any way I can."

Manny Portman never loved his daughter more than at that moment. He drove to Birmingham with such a heavy heart not knowing exactly how he was going to tell Lexi about her Mum. It was without question the hardest thing he had ever had to do. But then, as a physician, he had been the bearer of bad news to many over the years he had been in practice, just not to his family.

They left the restaurant and walked briskly back to the Queen Elizabeth Hospital. After a few calls, they were seated opposite Lexi's Ward Sister and an administrative representative requesting a leave of absence.

She left notes for Betsy and Lily stating that she would call them and explain, gathered a few of her things, and in less than an hour, they were driving back to London, each lost in their own thoughts. Manny pondered the future without Elise by his side; Lexi returned to the past. Once again, her thoughts were of Jake. She was losing her beloved Mum, but she would be able to spend time with her, however brief that might be, and they could say their goodbyes. Jake lost everyone without having that chance.

Elise was asleep when they arrived home. Manny made arrangements for nurses around the clock—three nurses each day on eight-hour shifts. In the morning, a hospital bed would be delivered and set up in one of the guest bedrooms, along with any medical equipment that may be needed. Her brothers were close enough to visit on a regular basis, and Lexi was home. For the first time since this nightmare began, Manny felt at peace; he had done everything he could.

Elise was elated to see her daughter. She missed the closeness they once shared and hoped that Lexi did also. She had a mission to accomplish before she grew too ill; she had to set things right with her daughter before she died, and to beg her forgiveness. In retrospect, she could never come up with why she had reacted the way she had to Jake's letter on that fateful day, and why she thought she had to protect Lexi from its contents which were unknown and remained unknown to her to this very day.

The first weeks Lexi was home were filled with laughter, lunches, and visitors. Except for times when Elise was too tired to take part in these activities, it was fun and lighthearted. They spent time outside in the beautiful garden that Elise had nurtured through the years starting when the children were little and the only free time she had was when they were napping.

Her brothers stopped by often and joined them for dinner during which they told and retold childhood stories, many of which Manny and Elise had never heard. It had been a long time since their family spent so much time together and aside from their terrible circumstances, they realized how much they missed one another.

September began with typical autumn weather of sunny warm days and cool nights. Elise was beginning to slip away. They were having lunch outside, relaxing and enjoying the beautiful fall flowers even though the leaves had begun to fall, when Elise decided that the time had come. "Lexi, please go to my room and bring me my jewelry box."

"Oh Mum, what's so important in that box. Let's just enjoy the afternoon. The weather will change soon enough."

"Please, do as I ask and go get the box. This nice weather isn't going anywhere."

Lexi carried the lunch dishes into the house and went upstairs to her parents' room. There sat the beautiful ornate jewelry box that her Pops had bought for her Mum on their trip to a Medical Convention in Paris soon after they were married. Through the years, Elise placed items in the box other than jewelry, just as she had done with Jake's letter.

When Lexi came back to the garden, Elise was staring into space unaware that she had returned. "Mum, Mum here's the box. Are you okay?"

Elise turned, "I'm fine. Please help me move to the chaise, and I think I could use a light blanket. The breeze is beginning to pick up."

When Elise was comfortably settled on the lounge with the blanket covering her legs, Lexi handed her the jewelry box. She smiled broadly. "You know of all the gifts my darling Manny gave me, this box was always my favorite. We had such a wonderful time on that trip to Paris. We were so young and so poor, and we couldn't believe we were actually in Paris, France—Elise and Manny Portman from London's Jewish Quarter, no less.

"To me, this box represented far more than a place to keep jewelry. At the time, I had no other jewelry than my wedding ring that I wore and never removed even to wash my hands, and the diamond earrings that were my grandmother's given to me when we got married. I never questioned his choice because I loved the box the minute I laid eyes on it."

There were two drawers at the bottom of the box; opening one of the drawers, Elise withdrew several small folded pieces of paper. She opened one and laughed. "This is the first picture you drew for me; flowers that you saw right here in my garden. And this one is our family, only you left yourself out." There were other drawings by her and her brothers, as well.

Opening the other drawer, Elise withdrew Jake's letter. For several long moments, she said nothing; she had waited far too long to do the right thing.

"Lexi, again and again and again for over two years, I have imagined this scene, and how I could possibly explain to you my actions on the day I learned that Jake had survived the air raid bombing in the East End."

Although she was listening to her Mum all along, the mere mention of Jake's name suddenly and dramatically changed her casual mood of fondly reminiscing happy memories to the loss she had not yet been able to accept or put in the past.

Elise did not look at Lexi; she stared off into the distance and continued. "I never told anyone, not you, not your father, no one about the visitor I had that day. In reality, he came to see you to deliver a letter from Jake. His name was Marcus Hirsch, and although I only met him that one time, I never forgot his name. He was a gentle soul, and I sensed immediately how much he genuinely cared for Jake, and mourned the loss of his father along with him.

"He was employed by De Beers and worked with Jake's father. When he heard of the bombing in the East End, he came looking for Harry Lyons to assure that he and his family were safe and unharmed. When he saw with his own eyes the total destruction of the building where they lived, he was devastated. He went in search of the only people that he knew had ties to the Lyons family, only to learn that they too had perished in the air raid. It was, however, at their shop where Jake's father had previously worked that he discovered Jake had survived.

"Jake was in shock, unable to process the terrible tragedy that had befallen him, and the loss of his entire family. He had no one. Mr. Hirsch took him home and offered to help him. Over the weekend following the air raid, Jake decided against returning to school; he opted to join the RAF instead. He accepted Mr. Hirsch's offer to handle his affairs while he was gone, with one last request—deliver a note to you which Jake entrusted to him, and he in turn entrusted to me.

"He did not know anything about the contents of the letter, nor do I to this day. I never opened it. When Mr. Hirsch left shortly before you came home, I don't know what came over me, or why I felt threatened by a letter from a young man I genuinely liked. Though you were quite young, the deep feelings you had for each other were so evident, your father and I often compared the two of you to our courtship when he went off to medical school, and we faced years before we could marry.

"All I could think of was Jake asking you to wait for him, and what a burden that would be—constant worrying and wondering while facing the possibility of injury or perhaps not returning from the War at all. You were due to leave for nursing classes after graduation, and I wanted you to become the nurse you've wanted to be since you were a small child.

"I regretted my decision to keep Jake's letter from you almost immediately, but with each passing day, it became harder and harder for me to undo what I had done. Lexi, when I learned I was ill with only weeks to live, I knew the time had come for me to tell you the truth. I beg you to forgive me, but if you can't, I truly understand.

"As I told Mr. Hirsch, your father and I felt that if you were fated to have a life together, we embraced it, and we still do.

"There were times when the urge to contact Mr. Hirsch to inquire about Jake was so compelling that I could hardly live with it. The only thing that stopped me was the possibility of his learning that I never gave you the letter. I was too ashamed to admit that I had made such a terribly important decision for you; I had no right to do that. The decision was yours to make, not mine."

Elise handed the letter to Lexi. She was visibly crying as she placed the small drawings back in the box. "I'm really tired and would like to go in now."

For some reason, Lexi made no move to embrace her Mum or offer any words of comfort. Instead, without saying a word, she took the letter, stood, and walked into the house.

She sent the nurse on duty to get her Mum.

Lexi went slowly up to her room tightly caressing the letter to her breast. She knew, always knew deep in her heart that Jake would not leave without a word. By the time she reached the top of the stairs, she was sobbing, utterly overwhelmed by her Mum's revelation.

She closed the door, sat down on the bed, and withdrew Jake's letter from the envelope. With tears streaming down her face, she began to read.

My Dear Lexi,

By now, you have learned that I have lost everyone I have ever loved—except you. I do love you with all my heart as I have since I first laid eyes on you at Ivan's Bar Mitzvah.

Since Friday night, I have had many more questions than answers; and finding myself forced to face the urgency of my situation alone, I felt the decisions were mine alone to make. The best way for me to honor my parents and go forward is to join the RAF and fight for Britain—the Country where they were free to live the life and have the family they dreamt of. I trust you will understand this feels like the best decision for me at this time.

I do not have the right to ask you to wait for me. No telling how long the War will last. I want you to go to school and become a nurse. It's what you always wanted and talked about, and it's one of the many things I love about you. You will be the best nurse ever, of that I'm certain.

Above all, I don't want you to worry about me—I survived for whatever reasons God has planned for me, and I have no doubt that He is watching over me as he always has and always will.

God Bless you Lexi. Meeting you, loving you, and you loving me back were the best things that ever happened to me.

I'm hoping against all hope that when the fighting has ended, and Britain is victorious, we can return to a normal life with our eyes on the future once again.

Wherever I may go, I will carry you in my heart. Until we meet again.

I will always Love you,
Jake

In recent days, Elise had been too weak to join them for dinner. It was evident they were losing her. Her pain had escalated to the point that most days she slept more than she was awake due to the increased dosage of morphine. Their last day in the garden turned out to be her last good day.

Ironically, Jake's letter had not asked Lexi to wait for him, as Elise has thought. Regardless of that fact, there was nothing that could be said or done to stop Lexi from worrying about him or waiting for him—she loved him every bit as much as he loved her.

Three days later Elise Portman passed away quietly in her sleep. Lexi had taken to spending her last days and nights at her bedside. She talked to her; read to her; told her she loved her, and repeated again and again, "I forgive you. I forgive you." To her Pops and brothers, her continued, "I forgive you.

I forgive you." was puzzling to say the least, but she knew that although she remained unresponsive, her Mum heard her every word.

Elise Portman was laid to rest on the first day of autumn.

Marcus Hirsch sat drinking coffee before leaving for work. Skipping the front section of the paper that contained mostly news about the War, he came to the Obituary Page. There his eyes rested on the announcement of Elise Portman's passing. Her picture was exactly as he remembered her.

The article gave a brief history of her origins and praised her community involvement on behalf of the war effort. Her survivors included her husband Dr. Emanuel Portman, two sons, Mark and Samuel, and a daughter, Alexandra. Noting the time and place of the service, he called and left word at the office that he would be in around noon, allowing him to attend.

There for the first time he laid eyes on Alexandra Portman who even in mourning was nothing less than stunning. His thoughts wandered back to the letter, and he hoped for both their sakes that after the War, these two beautiful, young people found their way back to each other.

At the family's request, a book was placed on a small table in the lobby for visitors to leave condolences and/or simply sign denoting they had attended the service. He thought about signing the book, but decided against it. No one would know the name *Marcus Hirsch* or who he was anyway.

To himself he said, "May you rest in Peace, Elise Portman." As he walked to his car, his thoughts were of Jake.

CHAPTER ELEVEN

Lexi returned to Birmingham and resumed her studies. Betsy and Lily were wonderful and hovered over her like two mother hens until she convinced them she was just fine. Reminding them she had a bit of catching up to do to allow her to graduate with her class next year, did the trick. They finally gave her some space.

The following weekend, Lexi took the train to London to spend Rosh Hashanah with her Pops and brothers. After attending services at their synagogue, they had dinner at the house. Manny turned down an invitation from his brother to join his family, but accepted an invitation the following week for Yom Kippur.

Lexi prepared a simple meal of roast chicken, potatoes, and green beans; she picked up a challah and a honey cake from a bakery near the train station. It was somewhat of a solemn day with Elise's passing still fresh on their minds, and a far cry from the many lavish holiday meals Elise had prepared for their family and their many guests over the years. But, they were all together, and they were in agreement that's what she would have wanted.

It was back to Birmingham for a week, and then once again she took the train to London for Yom Kippur. They were having dinner with Ivan's family on Saturday. Lexi hadn't seen or really had a heart-to-heart talk with him in two years; he was away when Elise died. She looked forward to seeing Ivan who had joined the Royal Navy and was due to be home on leave before shipping out.

Since attending the Memorial Service for Jake's family, Lexi had not been to the East End. Although Ivan lived a few blocks over from where Jake had lived, the bombed out buildings were hard to look at; devastation was everywhere. Just as in London and Birmingham, where the damage was even more extensive, the effected areas were blocked off and cleared of as much rubble as possible awaiting war's end.

Dinner was quite nice; it was good to see Ivan who looked so handsome in his uniform. He always was a charmer, and this night was no exception as he tried to lift everyone's mood.

On Sunday, Lexi took the train back to school once again. She doubled down on her studies; she still had some catching up to do. Her next trip home would be over the Christmas Holidays when she would be on school break until after the New Year.

The girls were eternally busy with their studies, and spent endless hours at the Queen Elizabeth Hospital that was now receiving military patients from all over England. British air attacks against Germany, having reached an all time high in recent months, measurably increased the number of patients who were RAF pilots with severe spinal injures in need of specialized care.

In short order, a Spinal Injuries Clinic was set up in a nearby building to accept these patients under the auspices of Stoke Mandeville Hospital located in Aylesbury, Buckinghamshire. The Hospital, whose specialty was spinal cord injury, continued to draw wide attention from the medical world for their new treatments and rehabilitation programs.

At first Lexi found working at the Clinic depressing, but she was soon won over by the brave young patients, as well as the physicians and nurses brought on board to implement the new treatments and rehab programs, all of which had been developed at Stoke Mandeville. She found herself spending time with pilots and listening to their stories; always thinking about Jake and hoping perhaps one would mention his name.

Time passed quickly and with the holidays approaching, the girls decided to make plans for their break. They were all going to be in the London area, and decided that they would definitely meet up and spend some fun time together.

Although Betsy and Lily were going home to family, Lexi would be staying at the house alone. Her Pops was on a special mission to Jerusalem with a group sponsored by the British Government. He felt terrible telling her he wouldn't be around when she came home, but she knew that her Mum's passing had hit him hard, and she accepted the fact that his way of coping was to keep busy.

Betsy invited her to join her family for Christmas Day Dinner, and she accepted. She had never celebrated or attended a Christmas Dinner, but why not? It was better than spending the day home alone, and she appreciated Betsy and her family including her.

She was glad she did; she hadn't had as much fun in a long time. There were five siblings including Betsy—she had two older sisters and two younger brothers. Her parents were friendly and welcoming, and there was even a present for her under the overly decorated tree that stood in the corner. Betsy pointed out the many ornaments and their special meanings; including some that she and her siblings had made when they were children.

It was a warm, wonderful day. She had never met Betsy's family prior, but now felt as though she had always known them. Lexi returned home exhausted, and fell asleep with a contented smile on her face. As she often did, she dreamt of Jake. It was a beautiful, sunny day, and they were having a picnic. They were near water and children could be heard playing in the background. Was the War over? Were she and Jake married? Were the children she heard theirs?

Although her dreams were vastly different, her questions were always the same and remained unanswered.

Lexi spent time going through some of her Mum's things. Her Pops had gently suggested that he would appreciate her help. She wasn't in the mood to go shopping; there was nothing she needed and rationing was still a factor. She did pick up some food for breakfast and lunch, and had dinner with her brothers, her aunt and uncle, and cousins who were around.

As the final weekend of their break approached, the girls made plans to meet for dinner at Archie's Pub near Lily's house. After ordering, Betsy offered a suggestion. "With New Year's Eve only two days away, we need to get serious and make some plans—time's a wasting. The Red Cross Club and USO are sponsoring a Gala in the Grand Ballroom at the Savoy."

Feigning a *swoon,* she continued, "Brits and Americans, oh so handsome in their uniforms—just waiting to meet some young ladies such as ourselves to make some beautiful memories together to carry with them into battle. My sisters and their friends are going, because, as they put it—with entertainment, live band music, food, and drink, it can't be anything less than fabulous."

Laughing at Betsy's performance, they too agreed that it sounded great. Their plans set, they bid one another good night. "See you at the Savoy Friday, 9:00 p.m. sharp; let's meet in the Lobby."

She finished going through her Mum's clothes, keeping more items for herself than she had intended. One was a bright blue, backless sheath that had been one of her Mum's favorites. She held the dress in front of her and peered into the mirror, noting how the color of the dress brought out the blue in her blue-gray eyes. She decided it would be just right for New Year's Eve.

At present, her wardrobe consisted mainly of casual clothes worn only when she was not wearing her uniform. She couldn't recall the last time she had the need for dressier evening attire. There were a few items she put in a box to give away, but most of Elise's beautiful dresses fit her perfectly, and she decided to keep them, along with several pairs of shoes that matched.

After a late lunch, Lexi fell asleep reading. When she awoke, she realized she had to get a move on or she would be late meeting her friends. She took a hot shower letting the water thoroughly relax her.

Blessed with a peaches and cream complexion and long full eyelashes, the only makeup she wore was lipstick. Her alluring red hair was shoulder length and required little more than a brushing to fall in natural waves. Five feet, six inches tall, a shapely woman's body, and long legs left no doubt, the gangly girl had become a real beauty.

She sat at her dressing table staring at herself, wondering what she was doing. She had no desire to *meet* a nice young man and send him off to battle with any memories whatsoever; or spend an evening dancing with one or more awkward young men stepping on her toes and attempting to make boring conversation.

Jake was still first and foremost in her thoughts; not a day went by without her wondering where he was, recalling a fond memory, or picturing the two of them together.

She stood and slipped on the dress, once again questioning herself why she had agree to attend the party. She was pleased with the reflection in the mirror. She never gave much thought to her looks, even though her entire life she had been told how beautiful she was—and that red hair! The comments never affected her; she was still the same Lexi.

Suddenly, it felt good to be dressed for a night out and not wearing her compulsory uniform or casual attire. Before she could change her mind, she grabbed her coat and purse and set off for the Savoy.

She longed to be meeting up with Jake for a night to remember instead of meeting up with friends to attend the New Year's Eve Gala.

Chapter Twelve

British spirit remained undaunted on New Year's Eve 1943, in London, England. Foot traffic was brisk as Londoners and visitors alike set out for a respite from four long years of war. They hurried past the bombed out areas, heading to gatherings both large and small, that had been planned on a high note based on news of the Allies' recent victories. For months, there had been no further air raids, and many were predicting the possibility of an end to the War in the New Year.

Although Jake, Tommy, and Andy had not yet learned the part that each of their Squadrons would play, rampant rumors at their posts led them to believe it was *something big* and that, if successful, would finally bring an end to the fighting. The fact that they were given ten days of leave further enforced their belief that the rumors were indeed true.

Jake was in a good mood as he dressed to go down to the Gala which was scheduled to begin at 9:00 p.m. He had spent the week as he usually did when he was in London—with a visit to the cemetery, and stopping by to see Rabbi Levin. This time, he did not go to Valence Road; nor did he go to Max's shop that had been emptied of its contents for some time. He had come a long way in putting the past behind him, and had only recently been able to recall happier times without revisiting the horror of that awful night. Returning to where it all happened served no purpose whatsoever.

Studying his reflection in the mirror, he saw a man. Technically he was still a teenager, being two weeks shy of his 20th Birthday. He wore his RAF uniform with an air of pride to be serving his Country; he felt secure but never cocky. His personal losses and the War had matured him far beyond his years, but the boyish grin remained. He stood six feet, four inches tall, and had put on just enough weight. There was no denying his blond hair and deep blue eyes revealed a stark resemblance to his Mother, and for a brief moment, he grew sad.

He longed to be meeting up with Lexi for a night to remember instead of meeting up with friends to attend a New Year's Eve Gala.

Setting his thoughts aside, he returned to the present. He had three days of leave remaining, and he knew that once he returned to his post, his next leave would be a long time coming if any of the rumors proved true. Although Marcus and Elise had said their goodbyes, before leaving to spend the holidays with their daughter and her family in Manchester, north of London, Jake promised to stop by De Beers on Monday before catching the train back to Devon.

The clock showed a little past eight when Jake left to meet his friends in the bar for a quick drink until it was time for the festivities to begin. Running in to Tommy and Andy had been an unexpected bonus, and the three of them agreed that they couldn't have planned it better.

They were seated at a small table when he arrived. As he approached, he noticed their eyes glued to the bars and metals that adorned his uniform. Andy exclaimed, "I don't know if you're able to discuss the particulars, but you seem to have been quite busy since we last saw one another. I didn't want to bring it up the other night, but I'm impressed, really impressed. In fact, there's been a little bit of a buzz about Britain's RAF heroes in the military community. Looks like you're on your way to be up there with *the Best of the Best*."

"I haven't heard about any buzz; I just do what I set out to do when I joined the RAF. It hasn't been easy, but then it's never easy losing flying buddies, no matter what the circumstances."

For the next hour, they revealed all the good and the bad they felt they could divulge. Andy and Tommy were both bomber navigators, but they were posted to different squadrons and had different stories to tell. Neither had seen each other since coming back from the States, but connected earlier in the week by a chance meeting on the streets of London.

Noticing that it was past nine, Jake urged, "Let's go have some fun and bring in 1944 in style."

———⟨𝔪⟩———

Lexi came out of the Underground Station at Hyde Park Corner and walked the half block to the Savoy. A light snow was falling as she made her way up the street. Putting her earlier doubts aside had reversed her mood, and there was a spring in her step as she approached the hotel. For the first time since her Mum died, she looked forward to a carefree evening with her friends before returning to Birmingham. Anticipating a full schedule the next few months leading up to her graduation, she fully intended to make the most of the three days she had left on break.

Since arriving in London, she had managed to sort through her Mum's things, seen family members that were in town, and had dinner with her brothers on two occasions. Her older brother was spending New Year's weekend with his fiancé and her family; her younger brother was set for a weekend of partying with his pre-med pals. She assured them that she was fine, and that she too had plans. Above all, she hoped tonight would be an omen for good things to come in 1944.

It was a little past nine o'clock, and when she entered the hotel lobby, they were eagerly awaiting her.

Betsy spied her immediately and prodded, "Come on Lexi; we've been watching some handsome chaps, both Brits and Americans, mind you, go into the party, and we need to get in there so we can stake them out."

Lily backed her up. "We've also been watching some pretty young ladies go in, and we don't want them to get too far ahead of us. What I'm saying is we don't want to miss a thing."

"Okay, okay you two, I get the message. Where do we check our coats?"

The Grand Ballroom was beautifully decorated for the season, as was the large Christmas tree that stood next to the bandstand. Along the walls were tables of food and drink manned with volunteers ready and waiting to serve. The band was playing, and there were a few couples on the dance floor.

As the girls surveyed the room, almost immediately, Betsy and Lily were no longer standing beside her. As they headed to the far side of the room, Lexi found herself alone. Feeling uneasy and a little insecure, she walked over to one of the tables. The woman volunteer said, "May I offer you a drink dear? We have ale and beer, and I highly recommend the punch; it's spiked, but rather refreshing."

Lexi smiled. "Yes, thank you; the punch sounds good."

She handed her the glass saying, "You look familiar. Have we met before?"

Lexi was certain she had never seen the woman. "No, not that I recall. I haven't lived in London for years, and any time I've spent here recently has been on school breaks; I've been attending nursing school at the University of Birmingham. I graduate in a few months."

Suddenly, the woman realized why her face seemed familiar to her. "My dear, I think I knew your mother, that is if she was Elise Portman."

Lexi nodded, and the woman continued. "She often showed us pictures of you and your brothers. She was so proud of the three of you. You might not be aware, but your mother was instrumental in putting evenings like this together for all our young lads in service, and not just on special occasions mind you. She wanted to make sure that anyone away from home would have somewhere warm and inviting to go. I am so sorry for your loss; all of us who volunteered with her miss her."

Lexi was touched by the woman's kind words. She thanked her, turned and spotting Betsy and Lily, started walking towards them.

Suddenly—her heart stopped. There he was. There she was. Their eyes locked across the room. The years melted away. It was exactly like that very first time at her cousin Ivan's party when they were twelve years old. Neither was certain what they were seeing was the real thing, as they made their way towards one another, brushing past and through the crowd that continued to grow. Time stood still for both of them.

Neither spoke a word. Jake pulled her into his arms and kissed her with all the pent up longing in his heart. For years, each had dreamt that this moment would actually happen, and now here they stood unable and unwilling to let go of one another, fearing that if they did, it would prove to be a dream and evaporate.

———〰———

Their surprise and utter joy of having found one another caused them to both start speaking at once, and the questions flew.

"My God, you are more beautiful than ever. You're beautiful and wonderful and best of all you're here! How are you? Are you alone? Are you staying here at the Savoy? Are you living at home?"

There it was that Lexi smile. "You're pretty beautiful yourself and looking so sharp in that RAF uniform with all those ribbons and metals, I might add. How are you? Are you alone? What are you doing in London? Are you posted here or nearby?"

Out of the corner of her eye, Lexi noticed Betsy and Lily staring curiously at her, as a few feet away to Jake's surprise stood Tommy and Andy staring curiously at him. Jake never spoke of Lexi to his friends—it hurt too much. Lexi never spoke of Jake to her friends—she simply didn't know what to say.

To the four friends, however, it was evident that Jake and Lexi cared deeply for one another—it was plainly written all over their faces.

Taking Lexi by the hand, Jake walked over to his friends. I'd like you to meet the two lads I went through flight training with. My two best buddies—Tommy Butler and Andy Barbour, this is Lexi Portman."

Andy nodded. "How nice to meet you."

Tommy reached for and kissed her hand. "Leave it to Jake to just happen to know the prettiest girl in the room."

His charm was not wasted on Lexi. "Thank you, but from what I've observed, there are dozens of pretty girls here tonight."

Observing that her friends had moved closer and were itching to get into the conversation, Lexi introduced Jake, "I'd like you to meet the gals that I'm in nursing school with and soon to be two of the best nurses ever. Betsy Bromwell and Lily Martin, meet Jake Lyons."

"The pleasure is all mine."

Of course, Betsy couldn't leave it at that. "We've been friends for a long time; why haven't we ever heard you mention the name *Jake Lyons* before?"

At hearing this, Tommy piped up, "Ditto, we've been friends for a long time too; why haven't we ever heard you mention the name *Lexi Portman* before?"

Turning to Lexi, Jake said, "I think we're being ambushed." He introduced his friends to her friends. "Have a great evening; we'll catch up with you later." Taking her hand, he led her to the dance floor where once again he could hold her in his arms, close to his heart. When the song ended, they quietly slipped out of the ballroom.

Jake retrieved her coat, and without saying a word guided her to the Lobby, where they took the lift to his room.

By midnight, they hadn't been seen for most of the evening, and their friends stopped looking for them. They were having quite an evening themselves.

Barely inside the room, and unable to keep their hands off one another, a trail of shed clothing led to the bed. At first, Jake just wanted to hold her and never let her go. She was more beautiful than he ever imagined—his Lexi. His love for her encompassed his whole being, and he couldn't imagine his world without her.

They made love slowly and deliberately willing it to last forever. They explored every inch of one another, wanting only to etch in their hearts and minds their first time.

As Lexi slept in his arms, Jake held her close, still not quite believing that they were in his room at the Savoy. He knew all too well they had precious little time before reality would once again part them. He could barely remember the last time they were together; it seemed longer ago than it actually was. They were so young and naïve when the War changed the course of their lives, but not the course of their love.

It was undeniable that their love for one another had not only endured, but their time apart had drawn them closer, made them stronger, and deepened their connection.

Lexi woke, and they realized they hadn't eaten; they were starving. It was too late for room service, but the woman who answered the call told Jake to come down to the kitchen, and she would put together some nibbles and a pot of tea.

While Jake was gone, Lexi freshened up and found one of his shirts to wear. She sat cross-legged on the bed waiting.

He returned with an odd array of food, some of which may have been left over from the party. There was an assortment of cheeses, crackers, scones, slices of cold meat that didn't look too appetizing, and a big pot of hot tea. They ate hungrily and savored every bite. Playfully, they fed one another and teased one another as they had when they were in school; all the while, thanking their lucky stars that had brought them together.

As light snow continued to fall on London, 1944 arrived. They made love again and yet again; they fell asleep, their bodies entwined, just as dawn was breaking.

Jake woke and slipped quietly out of bed. He showered and dressed while Lexi slept through it all. Sitting on the edge of the bed, he watched her for a while; not only had she matured into a beautiful woman, but she was about to become the nurse she aspired to be since she was a child. He briefly thought about the letter he had written her, hoping that in some way he had encouraged her to pursue her dream and not worry about him. He was so proud of her.

As he leaned over and kissed her, she opened her eyes. "Am I dreaming or was last night really the best night of my life?"

"No, my Love, you are not dreaming, and it was the best night of my life too. I'm showered and dressed, and since we didn't spend any time talking last night, we need to do so. I'll order breakfast from Room Service while you rise and shine, shower and dress, and then we can have our little chat."

Over breakfast they learned that each was due to leave London on the same day—Monday; it was Saturday. Lexi wanted to go home where she could change into something more casual.

Without explanation, she said, "I'm staying at the house alone, so we can have our little chat there and decide how to spend the next two days. Do you have any plans? I don't. Other than meeting Betsy and Lily at the train station Monday afternoon to head back to Birmingham—I'm all yours."

Jake grinned broadly. "Those are the best three words you could have said, second only to "I love you. Don't ever stop saying them. I have no plans, so let's make some."

Grabbing a change of clothes, they headed for the lift down to the lobby and out the door to the street.

Arriving at the Portman house, Jake recalled the night they had gone to the Cinema in London to see the American film *Strike Up the Band*. It was actually one of only a handful of dates they had. The majority of the time they spent together was attending youth events at the synagogue. He remembered kissing her goodnight at the door. He also remembered their first kiss—when she kissed him at his Bar Mitzvah party. For Jake, that had been the best part of the evening.

Lexi opened the door, and Jake followed her inside. Nothing had changed from what he could remember. She turned to him, "I'll just be a minute. I want to change into something more comfortable."

When she returned she asked, "Do you want something to drink? I do have a little food in the house if you're hungry. My father left me his ration books in case I needed them, and I did pick up some basics when I got here."

Jake reached for her and led her to the sofa. "I'm fine. If you care for something I'll wait, but we must have our talk. I have so much I want to tell you, so many blanks to fill in. I want to account for every minute of the years we've spent apart; but most of all, I want you to understand the decisions I made and how I made them.

They sat on the sofa; Lexi cradled in Jake's arms. Slowly he returned to that awful night; the night that changed everything. "It was Rose and Rachael's 9th Birthday and I had been working on a surprise for them—two rings with diamonds that I myself cut and polished. It was my surprise, and I had not shared it with anyone. It was as much a surprise for my father because they were diamonds that I cut and polished without his guidance. It was the surprise that made me late and being late saved my life."

He related his waiting and watching in the shadows of the destruction left by the air raid; to realizing he was alone with no family left; to Marcus Hirsch finding him at Max's shop and extending him a life line. The next three days passed in a blur, leaving him with immediate decisions to make; decisions that would impact the rest of his life.

Jake stopped speaking, and she felt him shutter. She realized he was crying. Trying to turn towards him, she couldn't. He held her tightly, rocking her against his chest.

After a few minutes, he began speaking again. "I had turned seventeen only months earlier and technically, I was a minor. That fact alone convinced me that my choices were limited, and I opted to join the RAF. Marcus offered to take care of everything for me, including arranging the memorial service, and later seeing that they were properly buried.

"I went to the house in Middlesex, and although I knew at that time that I could never live there, I decided that I would keep it until I returned home after the War. Knowing we were due to move by month's end and how happy my parents and sisters were, was very hard for me to deal with. All I could think about was if we had moved before Passover, everyone would be alive.

"After walking through the house, packing some clothes, and gathering the papers and documents I wanted to leave with Marcus, I sat down to the hardest task—writing a note to you. I couldn't face you for if I did, I could never have left you. I loved you with all my heart, yet I had nothing to offer you, and above all else, I didn't want to alter your plans for the future. As I wrote you out of my life that day, I sat there crying for my latest loss—you."

Again, Jake paused. Lexi offered to make tea again, but he declined. As he began anew, his story became light and his voice upbeat as he recounted becoming a Pilot Under Training posted to Stratford-upon-Avon, meeting Tommy and Andy and becoming fast friends, and how the three of them as part of a group of fifty traveled to Canada and down the east coast of the

United States to the State of Georgia where he spent a year training to fly the latest aircraft available.

He even chuckled as he told her about southern hospitality, foods he had never heard of let alone eaten, and learning how to jitterbug. "You were never out of my thoughts, and each time I returned to London, I ached to get in touch with you, but hesitated not knowing if you had moved on, and had someone new in your life. If I had discovered that there was someone, it would have destroyed me. So I took the coward's way out.

"Since returning from the States, I've been posted at Winkleigh in Devon, except for several months I spent in Scotland. With the War ongoing, and my squadron actively engaged on a daily basis—we're consistently on call. There haven't been many extended leaves, and with a one or two-day pass, I stay close to the base."

He released her so she could turn and face him. With a devilish grin on his face, he said, "Lexi, I don't know how to tell you, but I do have another *Love* in my life, but it's not a person. It's my Spitfire Aircraft, and she's a beauty. The first time I flew in a plane, I was exhilarated, but there was no comparison to the elation I felt when I flew solo for the first time. It was at that moment that I realized I had made the right decision by joining the RAF.

"The hardest part is when we lose aircraft and fellow pilots. When Andy's brother was killed in the Battle of Britain, he postponed his studies and joined up. His father is a barrister, and he has plans to go to Cambridge when the fighting is over and ultimately join his father's firm. It seems as though this War has changed things for so many.

"The past few months, the Allies have scored some resounding victories, and I so look forward to the War ending; it can't be soon enough for me. I am so very sorry, I pushed you out of my life; it was the one decision I truly regret. Until I saw you yesterday, I didn't realize how much I need you and how empty my life has been without you. I don't ever want to feel that way again." He pulled her close and kissed her.

When they drew apart, he joked, "Let's see what you have to eat around here; if you have eggs, I can whip us up a little something."

"I do have eggs, just three though. Is that enough? I also have cheese, scones and jam, and I have some soup. It sounds terrible all together."

For the next hour, they had such fun. They made an omelet with the eggs to share, accompanied with scones and jam, and hot tea. They didn't talk about anything that Jake had told her; their banter was light, funny, and so natural.

———————

When they returned to the parlor, Lexi urged him to sit beside her. It was her turn to fill in the blanks.

"I was totally devastated when I learned of the bombing in the East End. Told that it was your building that took a direct hit and that there were no survivors took my breath away; and for the entire weekend, I never left my room. I cried and cried. I wouldn't eat; I was a mess. My parents were beside themselves. They didn't know what to do or how to help me.

"On Monday, I woke early and decided to go to Ivan's to see if I could learn anything. While I was out, Mr. Hirsch delivered your letter, and when I returned home, my Mum told me you were alive, but you had lost everyone, adding that you left to join the RAF.

"Of course, I was thankful, relieved that you had been spared, but I was also terribly hurt that you didn't come to see me in person. I realized we were young, but we had professed our love for one another, and seeing you alive and unhurt would have meant the world to me.

"What I have to tell you now will upset you, but please hear me out before you say anything. When Mr. Hirsch left, my Mum having seen my reaction to the bombing and having learned you left to enlist had second thoughts about giving me your letter. Before I returned home, she put the letter away. She had no knowledge of its contents, and wanted to spare me the heartache of waiting and worrying about you, not knowing how long the War would last. She wanted me to go forward with my dream of becoming a nurse.

"I know deep in my heart that she did what she thought was best for me, but the ache I have carried in my heart, coupled with the inability to reconcile the fact that you left without a word to me were far more damaging than the actual contents of the letter or what she surmised the contents to be. My gut feeling was that something was awry, but I could never identify it. As a result, my relationship with my Mum grew strained, and I came home from school as infrequently as possible.

"Last summer, my dear, sweet Mum was diagnosed with lung cancer. She died in September. I took a leave of absence from school, and I spent the last two months of her life by her side. It was shortly before her death that she told me of Mr. Hirsch's visit that afternoon, gave me your letter, and begged me over and over to forgive her.

"At first, I felt utterly betrayed, by my own Mum no less, but then as I read and reread your letter, I realized I had been right all along. My Jake would never leave me without a word, and it proved to me that although you didn't feel you had the right to ask me to wait for you, I felt your love surround me. There is no one for me but you, and there never will be."

Jake was stunned to learn not only that Elise Portman had not given Lexi his letter when it was delivered, but that she had died the previous September. He wondered if Marcus knew about her mother's passing. Probably not, or he would have certainly told him.

"I'm so sorry to hear about your Mum. I didn't know. And I certainly have no right to judge a mother looking out for her child's best interests. Sadly, I've learned that war has a tendency to bring out the worst in all of us."

"Thank you. I miss her terribly, but my Pops is having a really hard time coping without her. They were together since they were children, like us. He left for Palestine with a group of other medical personnel two weeks ago, and he plans to spend three months at the Hadassah Hospital in Jerusalem. He'll be back for my graduation."

They both sat quietly for a while, each lost in their own thoughts. They had been through a lot during their separation, albeit in different ways.

"I'm glad we spent the day making peace with the past and catching up. We're far different today than when we parted—we've grown up overnight. "Robbed of our youth, we have to look to tomorrow. Never have I felt indispensible, but my initial guilt of having survived that awful night weighed heavily on my mind as I struggled to make the hardest decisions of my life. Then my thoughts turned to the possibility that God had plans for me. It's hard to explain, but whenever I fly on a mission, I know that He is watching over me, and I feel safe. I can't believe, I refuse to believe that I survived only to be killed in the War.

"I promise you Lexi, I will come home when the War is over, and my life's goal will be to love you forever and make all your dreams, our dreams a reality. I want to have a family again; live a normal life again; all with you by my side."

Jake stood and pulled Lexi to her feet to face him. "For now, I have some suggestions for the rest of today and tomorrow; Monday will come sooner than we both want. I hereby proclaim today *ours*, and *ours alone*. Let's ring up our friends and make plans for the six of us to spend tomorrow together in and around London ending with dinner at the Savoy or a local pub. Then on Monday, I can go to the train station with you, see you off with Betsy and Lily, and catch my train to Devon. What do you think?"

"I think you're wonderful. But what shall we do today?"

"My plans are to make love to you for the rest of the day. Have dinner in the City, and go to the hotel, or come back here and make love to you all night.'

Lexi answered with her kiss of approval.

CHAPTER THIRTEEN

Their Saturday couldn't have been better. Although they ate at a small local pub within walking distance of the house, they spent the night at the Savoy. They rang up their friends before leaving for the City, and after reaching everyone, it was agreed they would meet in the hotel lobby for breakfast before setting out on foot for an impromptu day. Jake asked Lexi to tell her friends to dress casually, wear a warm coat, bring a scarf and gloves, and wear comfortable shoes for walking. He had a few ideas in mind with the thought of keeping their last day, before returning to the real world, upbeat and fun."

The London Underground known simply as the Underground or the Tube connects the London suburbs to Central London and forms a network linking major railway stations throughout England. The Underground serves North London much more extensively than South London as a result of a combination of unfavorable geology. Since the 1930s, the Underground has been London's primary public transportation system.

When the friends met up in the Lobby of the hotel, they were anxious to get going and spend a memorable day together.

Jake took the lead. "After giving thought to what we could do today, I wasn't able to come up with anything novel that we could do. Then, the thought occurred to me, why stay in the City? We can hop on the Underground, get off wherever we choose, explore that particular town, and hop back on and move on to the next town. It will be a no stress, no have-to-be-anywhere day, and it will be great just being together. Then we can wind down over a nice quiet dinner.

"I don't want to be a party pooper, but we all have to leave sometime tomorrow, so I think we should make it an early evening."

Tommy with a mischievous grin on his face said, "Andy and I have been doing some thinking too. Why don't we go to Piccadilly Circus? There is a lot to do there—Leicester Square, London Pavilion, and neighboring Soho—shopping, restaurants, pubs, cinema, and theatre. There are nightclubs featuring risqué Paris style shows, but I don't know if they're open during the day; maybe we'll get lucky.

"The best part is we can walk. It's only half a kilometer, and although it's cold, we're dressed for it, and it'll be fun. Why don't we forego breakfast here at the hotel and grab something to eat when we get there?"

All agreed. They made their way out the door and headed up the street towards Piccadilly Circus.

Piccadilly Circus is a road junction and public space of London's West End in the City of Westminster, built in 1819 to connect Regent Street with the many shopping streets of Piccadilly. In this context, a *circus*, from the Latin meaning word *circle* forms a round open space at a street junction.

The Circus, from its inception, became a major tourist attraction with its offerings of shopping, theatre, entertainment, restaurants, pubs, private clubs and nightclubs. It particularly became known for its video display and neon signs, after the intersection's first electric advertisements appeared in 1910, with electric billboards set up on the façade of the London Pavilion.

In peace or in war, Piccadilly Circus became known as *the Hub of the World!*

What a day they had. It was as close to perfect as one could get. By the time they chose a small quiet restaurant in Soho to have dinner, they were exhausted but happy, and pleased that above all else, they had fun. As they perused their menus, each was lost in their own thoughts knowing the day was drawing to an end.

Jake and Lexi held hands under the table. Neither had ever been to Piccadilly Circus, but since no one asked, decided not to divulge that fact. Both had their beginnings in the East End, and even though Lexi no longer lived there when they met, they were two Jewish kids who were born and rooted in a Jewish world. The War had changed all that.

They ordered, and as they waited for their food to be served, Tommy attempted to return to the earlier upbeat mood of the day by relating the saga of the Piccadilly Commandos—due to become one of the great unsung elite units in history.

Leaning back in his chair, he cleared his throat. "Listen up; I'm about to convey some wartime info I think you should know about. I myself only learned of the situation as recently as days before my leave began.

"Soon after America entered the War in December 1941, the presence of GIs here in wartime Britain was everywhere, but nowhere more prominent than in London and its surrounding areas.

"Although we know the Yanks are on our side and here to help us defeat the Nazis, almost immediately the GIs inspired envy in us Brits. Less than a year after arriving on our shores, many began judging our overseas guests to be guilty of three heinous offences—being over-paid, over-sexed, and over here.

"Prostitution is pretty widespread in this area, and word is that in addition to the regular practitioners of the oldest profession, many of the female munitions workers and other women are being drawn to Piccadilly by the promise of young men in well-cut uniforms more than willing to share disposable cash.

"The prostitutes around Piccadilly Circus and Coventry Street are of a lower type, quite indiscriminate in their choice of clients and reportedly thieves, as well. They have a tendency to congregate in drunken groups and are openly brazen with the American GIs accosting them in public and touching them in inappropriate places. All this has resulted in a *sticky* situation between the two countries.

"It's become quite a problem with both the American military and the

Metropolitan Police. The newspapers in London haven't covered the story much, but from what a friend tells me, American newspapers report that letters sent home by American GIs have created a serious and unfortunate impression on both sides of the Atlantic for them to deal with.

"I don't rightly know who dubbed them *The Piccadilly Commandos,* but the name sure fits and has stuck like glue. I might add, that this remains an ongoing problem with no end in sight.

"This brings an end to my story; I'll have to update you at a later time, that is, if and when I learn anything new. Before you start with the questions, I'll add one more thing. An American chap posted to my base relayed the story to me, and in turn, I have passed it on to you. In other words, I'm not speaking from experience; the Piccadilly Commandos aren't interested in Brits anyway. I'm fairly certain they see us as—being underpaid, undersexed and always here."

They were still laughing when their food was served, and the conversation turned to other subjects. Tommy had accomplished what he set out to do. For the remainder of their evening, they were just six young people having a good time.

When they left the restaurant, there were hugs all around. Emotionally, Jake pulled Andy aside and wished him Godspeed. "Take care of yourself. When this is all over, we'll meet up without time limits."

Andy, Betsy, and Lily went to the Underground each heading home.

Jake, Lexi, and Tommy opted to walk back to the Savoy. Once in the lobby, Tommy turned to them and said, "I don't think I have to tell you how lucky you are to have each other. You're two beautiful and extra special people who I feel truly blessed to know.

"Take care *Jitterbug Jake* until we meet again when this damn War is finally over. I don't know about you, but I can't wait to celebrate a victorious Britain."

They hugged, and when they parted both had tears in their eyes.

Tommy pulled Lexi to him and hugged her too, kissing her on both cheeks. "Goodbye for now pretty lady. I'm sure we'll met again because in case you couldn't tell, I'm a little sweet on your friend Betsy. I hope to keep in touch as best I can."

Tommy went into the bar alone; Jake and Lexi took the lift to his room.

Spending the night at the hotel, they made love as the hours ticked by, and fell asleep holding onto each other until the last possible moment.

Jake woke first. He shaved, showered, and dressed. Walking over to the bed, he leaned down and kissed her. "Hey sleepyhead, it's time to get up. We have a lot to do before catching our trains."

"Five more minutes, please."

"Okay, as long as you don't ask for five more."

"In that case, I might as well just get up now. You think you know me pretty well, don't you? When I was little, I always wanted to stay up five more minutes, now I want to spend those five more minutes sleeping."

Lexi had brought a change of clothes to wear back to school. While she showered and changed, Jake packed his bag and checked to see that he wasn't leaving anything behind.

They took the lift to the lobby and Jake checked out. Hand in hand, they walked to the Underground and caught the train to Hendon Central. They were quiet as they walked to the Portman house.

It only took a few minutes to pack. Any food she had brought into the house was long gone and everything put away in the kitchen. Once again they were on their way.

"Where to now? It's far too early to meet the girls at the railway station."

Until now, Jake hadn't told her what he planned to do. "I want to go to the house in Edgware. Are you okay with that? If you'd rather not, I'll go alone and come back for you."

"Of course, I'll go with you. I'm just surprised that you didn't mention it."

Once again, they took the Underground, three stops past Hendon to Edgware. Until now, Lexi hadn't realized the close proximity of the two houses. She was aware that both were in Middlesex but had never been in the Edgware area. As they came up from the station to the street, she saw that even in the dead of winter, how pretty the neighborhood was. Briefly, images of the destruction left by the air raid bombings throughout London flashed before her.

At the corner, they turned onto Brook Avenue and came to a stop in front of #11. Jake unlocked the door, and stood back to allow Lexi to enter in front of him.

He dropped their bags inside the door.

"I'm going down to the basement to get what I came for, but I won't be long. Make yourself at home. Before we leave, I'll take you through the house, if you like."

"I would like that very much."

Most of the furniture was covered, and one could easily tell that no one currently resided there; nonetheless the first level exuded an inviting and warm feeling. There were curtains on the windows, paintings on the walls, and family photographs along with various personal objects on display in each room. The love that went into making the house a *home* was evident throughout.

As she gazed intently at a family photo that had obviously been taken not too long before that awful night, Lexi suddenly felt Jake's pain. She knew they were due to move by month's end following Passover, but what she hadn't realized was that their new home was so ready to welcome them.

Jake returned, took her in his arms and kissed her. "Come, I'll show you around. The upstairs is not fully furnished; only my parents' bedroom is complete. The other rooms are mostly finished, lacking only our beds which were to be moved from our flat."

As he guided her through the house, the raw pain he once felt seemed to have eased with the passing of time. However, he remained resolute in his decision to sell the house at war's end. On each level, in each room, he showed Lexi his parents' dream with pride, pointing out objects in his sisters' room, and ending with a lone photograph of her sitting on his desk.

Taking her hand, he led her down the stairs to the sitting room where he partially peeled back the cover on the sofa, and bade her to sit down.

He knelt before her. "My darling Lexi, I love you from the depths of my being, as I have since the very moment I laid eyes on you, and *you and I* became *us*. The past three days have not only been the best days of my life, but have shown me that without you, I have no life. We just found our way back to one another yet in mere hours, we must once again part. This time, I'm not pushing you away; I'm asking you to wait for me. When I come home, I want to live the life we dreamt of as children."

Pulling her to her feet, he kissed her. He wanted to just hold her and never let her go; that was not possible.

Releasing her, he looked directly into her eyes. "What do say, Lexi Portman, will you wait for me and marry me?"

"Yes, yes, yes I will wait for you and I will absolutely and most definitely marry you. I love you more than life itself."

He kissed her again. Reaching into his pocket, he extracted a beautiful gold ring with two equal sized diamonds mounted on angle side by side. "I made this ring for you with plans to seek your parents' blessing and give it to you when we graduated. My father cut and polished one of the diamonds; I cut and polished the other with his help and guidance. When we finished, he told me I did such a good job that he couldn't tell which stone either of us had cut. They were identical.

"I had no way of knowing your ring size, and I can tell just by looking, that it's too big for your finger." Again reaching in his pocket, he produced a gold chain. "Wear it on the chain next to your heart; I think I like that better for now."

Putting the chain around her neck, he stood back and surveyed how very beautiful she looked. She had a glow about her that had only appeared three days ago; a glow emanating total happiness and contentment. She was in love, and had just promised to marry the *Love of her life*.

"You take my breath away Jake Lyons. I promise the chain with your ring will not be removed by me. I will wear it around my neck until you come home and put it on my finger where it will stay until eternity."

Again they kissed and held one another close.

Asking her to wait for him in the sitting room, he went to the small desk in the hallway where he had penned his letter to her. He removed two sheets of writing paper. On one, he wrote Lexi's home address and contact information in Birmingham. On the other sheet of paper, he wrote what was actually an informal Will. Stating simply, in case of his demise in the War, his entire net worth was to be transferred to Alexandra Portman. Placing each note in an individual envelope, he addressed them both to Marcus Hirsch.

Once again they took the Underground to the City. Jake said they had one more stop to make before leaving London. As before, Lexi had no idea where they were headed.

They arrived at De Beers precisely at noon, and found Marcus in his office. The delight on his face at seeing Jake and Lexi standing before him was undeniable. He came around his desk, and Jake introduced them.

"Marcus, I'd like you to meet Lexi Portman." To Lexi he said, "I want you to meet the man without whose help, I probably wouldn't be standing here right now. This is the one and only Marcus Hirsch."

Marcus was so pleased to meet Jake's young lady, but he was elated at seeing them together. He had no idea how they had met up and knew that he would have to wait to find out—but seeing the obvious written all over their faces would do for now.

"We can't stay long; we have trains to catch. I trust you and Elena had a good visit with your daughter and family?"

"Yes, we sure did. The grandchildren are growing up so fast."

Jake handed him the first envelope and said, "I've given you contact information for Lexi at home and Birmingham where she is in nurses training."

Trying to underplay what lay ahead of him when he returned to Winkleigh, he said, "I have no idea if I will be able to write to her or keep in touch on a regular basis. However, since you are my official contact, from time to time, I'd appreciate your letting her know that I'm okay."

"I certainly will." Turning to Lexi, he said, "I might add, that it was our agreement from the beginning that I would be informed at all times where Jake was and how he was doing. Outside of never knowing when I might look up and see him standing in front of me, it has worked just fine."

"I know you must have a lot of questions, but they will have to wait. It will be quite a conversation over dinner with Elena, of course. We're in a bit of a rush to catch our trains."

Out of Lexi's view, he handed Marcus the second envelope on which he had printed: To Be Opened Only Upon My Demise. At first, Marcus was taken aback, but managed to place the envelope face down on his desk, and bid the young couple goodbye.

They arrived at Charing Cross Railway Station and found Betsy and Lily waiting for them. The train to Birmingham was due in twenty minutes and was expected on time. As they waited on the platform, the girls stood aside, and allowed Jake and Lexi a bit of privacy in a very public place. All too soon, their final *kiss*, their final *I love you*, and she was on board—seated at the window waving to him with one hand and holding the ring on its chain with the other, as the train slowly pulled away.

One half hour later, Jake boarded his train to Devon. He had a long ride ahead of him—three hours plus. Over and over in his mind he recalled the last three days. It felt good to be *us* again—Jake and Lexi—Lexi and Jake. He had missed her, but didn't realize how much until she came back into his life. They were one now; as good as married as far as he was concerned. He agreed with Tommy. If this damn War would just end, everything would be great.

CHAPTER FOURTEEN

Three weeks after returning to Winkleigh, Operation Steinbock, a nocturnal Luftwaffe bombing offensive, chiefly targeting the greater London area, began in earnest. In Britain it was known as the Baby Blitz, due to the smaller scale of operations compared to The Blitz in 1940-41. These attacks resulted in few aircraft reaching their targets, with virtually no achievement by the Germans. The Allies, however, successfully destroyed 70% of the aircraft assembled by the Luftwaffe, and ultimately brought an end to the heavy air raids on London.

In January 1944, planning for D-Day took on greater urgency, as Allied Commanders began revising draft plans, and fine-tuning precise preparations. Midget submarines secretly visited the Normandy beaches to take sand samples needed to confirm that the sand on sections of the chosen landing beaches would support the weight of the tanks and other heavy equipment planned for use in the offensive.

Across many parts of Europe, British and US aircraft began dropping weapons and supplies to the Resistance to enable them to flight back against the occupying Germans.

In the UK, the first amphibious exercise for American troops took place at Slapton Sands, Devon. The exercise involved thousands of assault troops, and was a rehearsal of the techniques that were to be used on D-Day itself.

Jake's last contact with Lexi was in late January. He rang her up at school and through the efforts of a clerk in the Administrations Office managed to arrange to have her await his call at 7:00 p.m. that evening. At precisely that time, he called, and she was put on the phone.

At the sound of her "Hello" he melted, and then she added, "Happy Birthday." "Hello to you my Love and thank you for the birthday wishes. I'm due to be pretty busy moving around the next few months, and I asked for and received permission to call you. I needed to hear your voice; I miss you so much, but I love you more."

He could tell she was crying. "You probably can't say where you're going, so I won't ask. I love you and miss you too. Take care of yourself; be safe; come back to me soon; I'll be here waiting."

Their simultaneous "I love you!" ended the call.

The very next day, Jake's squadron moved to RAF Coltishall in Norfolk. The base became operational in May 1940 and was initially conceived as a bomber base. It was later pressed into service as a fighter airfield as battles in the air increased in intensity. The first to operate from the base was a Spitfire Squadron.

At Coltishall, they were engaged in various exercises in preparation of joining the offensive operations over occupied Europe. They took part in their first Ramrod, escorting American Marauders to Paris and back. The operation took one hour and fifty minutes. They also took part in *Rodeos*—ground attack operations. These sorties were routed close to the enemy airfields along the coast of France aimed at catching enemy aircraft at a disadvantage in their landing or start circuit.

In February, the *Big Week* heavy bomber offensive led by American Major General Jimmy Doolittle absolved earlier setbacks by winning air superiority in daylight. Doolittle's implementation of major changes in fighter formations was credited with bolstering the confidence of the crews under his command. Until that time, allied bombers avoided contact with the Luftwaffe. Following the offensive's success, they began using any method that would force the Luftwaffe into combat.

British bombing was chiefly waged by night with large numbers of heavy bombers escorted by Spitfire and Hurricane Squadrons. Together they made up a round-the-clock bombing effort as the Allies looked toward Berlin and raiding the German capital. Their goal was to destroy as much of the German air force as possible, rendering them too weak to oppose the allied landings in France.

In March, the Allies launched the first of several attacks against Berlin. Fierce battles raged and resulted in heavy losses for both sides; though the Allies lost 69 aircraft, the German Luftwaffe lost 160. The Allies replaced their losses; the Luftwaffe could not. The last week in March, the RAF made one last large raid on Berlin.

Jake's squadron, along with numerous others, took to the skies night after night laying the groundwork for the landing of troops in Europe.

Supreme Headquarters Allied Expeditionary Force (SHAEF) moved from Norfolk House in central London, to Bushey Park, on the western outskirts of the capital. It had grown too large for Norfolk House, and Supreme Allied Commander General Dwight D. Eisenhower felt it necessary to move away from the distractions of London.

As part of the Transportation Plan, allied forces began carrying out raids on the French railway network. This part of the plan aimed to reduce the Germans' ability to use the French railways to transport troops and military supplies.

At the start of April, a 10-mile strip along much of Britain's coastline became a *Restricted Zone*. Civilians living outside the Zone were forbidden from entering it, and those inside could not leave.

Marcus lost direct contact with Jake in January, as did Lexi. He searched for news in the papers every day, but grew to accept *no news* as *good news*.

He had spoken with Lexi two or three times, having told her to ring him up whenever she felt the need to do so. Although it was generally easier for her to reach him, he assured her he would call immediately upon hearing any news whatsoever.

Over and over in his mind, he returned to the last time they spoke. Her usual light and friendly voice appeared strained and brisk, not even inquiring how he was. She said she had written to Jake, but had not received an answer. Marcus had no idea how long it took those in the military to receive mail, and not knowing if Jake was even still in England, had no response.

Before ending the call, she told him she was graduating in April: her oldest brother was getting married in May; and that although her father was back in England for her graduation and the wedding, his plans were to return to Jerusalem soon after; she added that he was urging her to go with him.

For some reason, Marcus sensed that she hadn't told her father about meeting up with Jake. He himself had not learned how it happened, but the fact that Jake made no mention of Lexi when they met for dinner at the Savoy, reinforced his belief that it had been just as much a chance meeting as his running into Tommy and Andy.

This posed another question? Why wouldn't she tell her father? He recalled Elise having made it a point to say when he delivered the letter that although they were young, she and her husband both liked and approved of Jake.

May 1944 is a busy month. The date for D-Day is moved forward. Two periods in June are identified as suitable, based on the tides and the amount of moonlight: 5-7 June and 18-20 June.

Exercise Fabius, the largest series of training exercises to date and the last before D-Day, begins at several sites along the coast of Southern England.

On 15 May, the final briefing for allied senior officers takes place at St. Paul's School, London. Both King George VI and Prime Minister Winston Churchill are in attendance.

On 1 June, Eisenhower moves his Headquarters to Southwick House, just north of Portsmouth. England, veiled in secrecy, tightened security, and on guard, waits; and as She waits, a security scare emerges when, for the fifth time in a month, one of the D-Day code names appears as a crossword clue in the Daily Telegraph. It turns out to be a bizarre coincidence; a Surrey School Headmaster having compiled the crosswords months earlier.

On 2 June, Jake and two of his pilots are called upon to fly escort for an unmarked aircraft headed to France in close proximity to the planned invasion. Although the chief allied weather forecaster predicts bad weather, their plans remain in tact.

Under the cover of night, with low clouds, strong winds behind them, and rough seas below, the planes take off and reach their destination without incident. As the three Spits head home, they find themselves flying into the strong winds causing their planes to separate, becoming lost in the heavy clouds, and rendering them out of one another's view. As he struggles to stabilize his aircraft, and remain on course back to the base, Jake finds himself in a tailspin.

With no time to spare, he reaches for the lever opening the hatch. Almost immediately, the wind blows the canopy off, and as his Spit continues to spin out of control, Jake literally falls out of the plane. Pulling the ripcord on his parachute, he drifts downward into the dark, choppy waters of the English Channel, as he watches his beloved Spitfire dive into the water below.

Only two of the three Spitfires return to Coltishall. Upon learning that Jake's plane is not one of them, a quiet pall falls over his squadron who refuses to believe that their beloved Squadron Leader *Jitterbug Jake* is not alive—somewhere.

By the time Marcus is notified that Jake is officially listed as missing, Lexi, who is five months pregnant, and her father have set sail on the long journey to Palestine.

CHAPTER FIFTEEN

S ituated off the coast of France within the English Channel, the Channel Islands, although fiercely independent, are dependents of the British Crown. Considered remnants of the Duchy of Normandy and not part of the United Kingdom, the Islands include two separate bailiwicks—Guernsey and Jersey—each administered separately.

Adolph Hitler's ambition to invade Britain during World War II got no further than the Nazi occupation of the tiny Channel Islands off the coast of France. He viewed the Islands as a valuable landing stage for his invasion of mainland France, as Jersey lay just fifteen miles off the French coast. Guernsey was his ace in the hole; while 30 miles from the French coast, the Island lay just 70 miles south of the UK. Churchill was of the mindset that the Islands held no strategic importance for Britain and demilitarized them, leaving them undefended.

Prior to the German army storming through France in June 1940, 30,000 Channel Islanders were evacuated, primarily children, teachers, and young men leaving to serve in the military. German reconnaissance flights failed to reveal the British evacuation, and on 28 June, as Luftwaffe bombers struck the harbors of Guernsey and Jersey, they mistook lines of trucks at St. Peter Port for troop carriers. The trucks were actually lined up to unload tomatoes for shipment to England. Forty-four people were killed in the attack.

It was not until two days later, when the Germans took control of the Guernsey airfield, that they learned the Islands were undefended. Telephone lines to England were disconnected immediately, as German forces moved quickly to consolidate their positions and firmly establish themselves. They stationed a substantial garrison of infantry troops and set up communications facilities and anti-aircraft defenses, rendering resistance by the Islanders almost impossible. Villages and towns were given German names; clocks were set to Central European time; and vehicles were switched to right lane driving on all roadways.

Their wide range of strict regulations began with issuing Identity papers, requiring that they be carried at all times. All Jewish owned businesses were confiscated and turned over to non-Jews to run. Strict curfews were enforced. All vehicles and petrol were confiscated, forcing the Islanders to walk, ride bikes or travel on horses. All weapons and radios had to be turned in; occupation authorities took over the newspaper; and over 2,200 civilians who were Jewish or not native to the Islands were deported to Nazi internment camps.

As time passed, resentment grew, and more and more Islanders opposed the Nazi occupation. The occupiers had taken control of the minimal media outlets—primarily newspapers and radio. This caused illegal news sheets to be printed and circulated. The most famous was the Guernsey Underground News Sheet (GUNS), copies of which were frequently thrown into the backs of Nazi cars or posted in the village squares.

A series of aborted raids on Guernsey by British commandos were considered counter productive by the majority of Islanders who felt vulnerable to all sorts of reprisals these raids might bring. Most attempts to escape did not succeed. For every Islander who was successful, there were numerous others who were not. A number of youths drowned and many were arrested and sent to German concentration camps—never to return.

Nevertheless, many Islanders successfully hid their radios or replaced them with homemade crystal sets, and continued listening to the BBC despite the risk of being discovered by the Germans or being informed on by neighbors. These hidden radios also allowed them to keep in touch with the young children evacuated to the British mainland, and to learn firsthand news about the War.

At first, the German soldiers were an intriguing spectacle. Tall, blond, and handsome, and fortunate to be staying on a sun-drenched island, their time was often spent on the beaches and at swimming pools. Although the

Islanders considered them the enemy, their Aryan good looks and debonair behavior continued to fascinate them.

Women from all classes risked the wrath of their families and the majority of Islanders by becoming romantically involved with the young men. Inevitably this was to have devastating consequences—more than one-third of all recorded births on the Island of Guernsey alone were illegitimate.

Jake's parachute brought him down into the icy waters of the Channel causing a cold shock to overcome him and momentarily disorient him. Fighting to get his bearings, he did a cursory check of his surroundings. His observations indicated that the fierce winds and clouds he had struggled with in the upper altitudes were gone, and visibility was good. In the distance, he took the sprinkling of lights as an indication that land was close by.

Shedding his parachute, he began swimming towards shore.

On the far side of Guernsey, opposite of St. Peter Port, stood the largest dairy farm on the Island, wholly owned by the Walsh family; the majority of both agricultural and dairy farms on the Island were tenant farms. Bill, and his twin sisters Lulu and Lila, as the only surviving members of the Walsh family, ran the farm without outside help since the evacuation.

British by birth to an English father and German mother in the UK, the Walsh siblings took over the farm upon the death of their grandfather. When the Germans came calling at the onset of the occupation, the German Commandant was quite impressed when Lulu spoke to him in fluent German, and he took an immediate liking to her. A liking that would leave the Walsh family virtually free of German restrictions imposed on the Island.

In the four years since the occupation began, the Walsh Farm had remained the same as it had always been. Visits by German officials were virtually non-existent. The remote location and the long winding road leading to the farm kept it out of sight and out of mind.

In the early hours of 3 June 1944, Bill found Jake unconscious on a grazing field not far from the water's edge. Observing immediately that he was an RAF pilot, he moved quickly. Securing a small cart, he gently lifted Jake onto the bed and pulled it up to the house.

Lulu and Lila were both in the kitchen when Bill came through the door urging them to help bring Jake into the house.

Assessing his condition, they noted nothing appeared broken; he was unconscious, and their attempts to waken him brought no response. Lila had some nursing experience, and after taking his temperature, her initial thoughts were confirmed; he was experiencing hypothermia. They began at once—removing his wet clothing, wrapping him in blanket after blanket, filling hot water bottle after hot water bottle, and placing him on a cot in front of the fireplace, where although it was June, Bill started a fire.

He remained unconscious for two days. On the third day, as Lulu sat at his side, Jake opened his eyes. "My, my, what beautiful blue eyes you have!"

It evoked no response whatsoever as he took time to assess his surroundings. His eyes wandered about the unfamiliar room; he had no idea where he was; he had no idea how he came to be in the care of the person who had just spoken to him. However, the sound of a British voice seemed familiar to him.

"Where am I? Who are you? What's wrong with me?"

Lulu was happy he had finally regained consciousness. "Whoa. Slow down, and I'll answer all your questions, but I prefer to take them just one at a time.

"You're on Guernsey Island on a dairy farm owned and run by my family, and I am Lulu Walsh. Nothing is broken; we were just waiting for you to wake up.

"Now I get to ask you a few questions. Who are you? Do you recall what happened or how you could have possibly come to our Island's shores?"

Jake could not. "I seem to be a bit confused. How did I get here to the farm?"

Lulu hoped his memory loss was only temporary. "My brother Bill found you unconscious on a grazing field near the water's edge of the Channel. When he brought you up to the house, you were experiencing hypothermia.

My sister Lila, Bill, and I have been taking turns caring for you. When your temperature finally returned to normal last evening, we hoped that would be an indication that you would soon awaken. Now that you are awake, we have to get some food into you and build up your strength. Your memory will return soon enough.

"When Bill found you, you were wearing the uniform of an RAF pilot and your dog tags prove that. Your surname is Lyons if that helps any. Now just rest a bit while I heat up some soup for you."

Lulu left the room as Jake struggled to remember—RAF pilot, the name Lyons, reaching instinctively for his dog tags which were not there—he suddenly recalled an icy cold engulfing his body and swimming towards lights. He recalled nothing before and now here he was learning what came after.

Lulu returned with a large bowl of soup. She helped him up from the bed they had moved before the fireplace and guided him to a chair in the sitting area. Covering him with a blanket, she placed a small tray holding the soup on his lap. Jake ate hungrily and asked for more.

Although she was pleased to see him eat, she didn't want him to overdo. "I'm glad you like the soup; I made it myself with veggies all grown here on our farm; all of which we grow for our own consumption. Our farm is a dairy farm producing only dairy products for market."

It is 6 June, D-Day. After an air assault during the night, over 160,000 Allied troops land along the Normandy coast. Operation Overlord is the largest amphibious invasion of all time. D-Day marks the Anglo-American invasion of Europe, and continues for two days.

As part of the invasion, the Allies decide to bypass the Channel Islands, prolonging the occupation. The Islands are amongst the most heavily fortified part of Hitler's Atlantic Wall; Germany has managed to turn them into an *impregnable fortress.*

As a result of the invasion, German supply lines for food and medical supplies through France are completely severed. The Islanders' food supplies having consistently dwindled for four years head towards an all time low.

———⟋⟋⟋⟍———

When Bill and Lila returned to the farm, Lulu told them their patient was awake, and introduced them to Jake. They decided to call him *Lyons* since his surname was the only name they learned from his dog tags, hoping it would trigger his memory to recall.

Bill Walsh was a WWI veteran who considered himself fortunate to have recovered from a severe leg injury with only a slight limp. For four years of German occupation of the Channel Islands, he had bided his time, searching desperately for a way to aid the war effort on Britain's behalf. Resistance had been passive mainly due to the separation of the Islands (21 miles between Jersey and Guernsey), and the density of German troops, roughly one to every three civilians.

A large barn housed the Guernsey cows that produced the dairy products for the Walsh Farm. The weather vane made by their grandfather sat atop a small room built atop the roof of the barn—the room from which one could survey the entire farm down to the grazing fields along the waters of the Channel. The room was accessible only by the release of a stairway that tucked up into the room when unoccupied.

It was in that room that Bill had set up his short wave radio; surrendering instead a smaller radio at the onset of the occupation. This had been his one effort of resistance. He had kept the radio risking everything if caught, based solely on Lulu's having gained the good graces of the German Commandant, which thus far had resulted in relatively few demands and restrictions upon them and their farm.

His broadcasts over the four years of occupation allowed him to keep in contact with other operators along the southern coast of England. On rare occasions, he broadcasted the situation on Guernsey, but his main goal was to learn of news of the War. Being cut off from all communication, Islanders were forced to rely on German propaganda, having no way to learn the truth.

On the day following Jake's awakening, over dinner they discussed the War, the German occupation of the Islands, and family. Bill took it further. "At any time, if anyone from the occupying forces is approaching the farm, we are going to have to hide you. You have no papers, and we have no explanation for your presence here. The good news is there are a number of hiding places where you will be safe and undetectable."

Talk of the War had sparked some food for thought, but Jake did not reveal this. Instead, he relayed concern. "I owe you my life, and I don't want to compromise your safety and freedom. I also intend to carry my weight and help any way I can around the farm; that is, if you will teach me about farming—something I am quite certain I know absolutely nothing about."

As Bill, Lulu, and Lila laughed at his professed statement, they realized how much they had taken a liking to this young man and were thankful he landed on the shores of their farm and not in enemy hands.

They continued their discussion and decided that Bill would contact an operator in Portsmouth and relay the information on Jake's dog tags in an attempt to learn his identity, as well as to advise that he was alive and safe on Guernsey.

The signal plans (call signs, frequencies, and times of transmission) and procedures used by these clandestine operators during the War were for the most part of utmost simplicity, making one service easily distinguishable from another by their different characteristics. The random contact times and frequent changes in wavelength considered so essential were represented by uncomplicated regular patterns simple to reconstruct. They were given a reasonably good range of operating frequencies to help protect them from detection and arrest. Thus far, Bill had successfully sustained regular contact with several operators in the UK.

After dinner, Bill retreated to the room atop the barn to transmit information on Jake's dog tags and to relay that he was safe. In return, he learned of the D-Day invasion and the Allies' success to begin the liberation of France.

Now that he was awake and on the mend, Jake was given a guest bedroom.

Bill's clothing was a close enough fit to replace his uniform, which they buried in a box along with his dog tags in the yard beneath Lulu's flowerbed.

Jake spent a restless night dominated by thoughts of their conversation over dinner. Bits and pieces began to emerge, but the pieces didn't fit. He dreamt of a family seated around a dinner table—there were three children—a boy and twin girls. Was it his family? Was it the Walsh family? He dreamt of an RAF pilot flying a plane, a plane in distress—was he the pilot? Was it his plane that was in distress? As he continued to drift in and out of sleep and dreams, he suddenly bolted upright in bed and uttered but one word, *Lexi*.

After D-Day, and in fear of commando raids, the Germans adopted a more strict approach to controlling the Islanders. All the beaches were mined and put out-of-bounds to civilians.

The Islands became a base for treating German soldiers injured in the battles in northern France after the Allies had broken out of their beachheads on D-Day. As more and more of France was freed from Nazi control, more and more Channel Islanders tried to get there to escape the occupation they had endured for four years.

Because the Islands were not a part of the Normandy landings, they remained under German occupation, severed from the rest of Europe. As food and fuel supplies dried up, life became steadily worse with both the occupying forces and Islanders suffering from starvation.

Farms on the Islands were stripped of their meager remaining resources, as the Germans confiscated all remaining cattle and crops from civilians. Having managed to virtually escape the hardships of the occupation, Bill, Lulu, and Lila considered their situation extremely fortunate. They, however, did not allow themselves to become passive and overconfident and continually planned ahead and kept their eye on what the future might bring.

They stockpiled crops and butchered the two sheep they had raised as pets. The two remaining cows not previously confiscated by the Germans were solely to provide milk and dairy products and were never considered for meat consumption. Once again, the German Commandant paid a visit to the farm; he took one of the remaining two Guernsey cows and left the other for Lulu.

It was the Commandant's last visit to the Walsh Farm, and the only occasion there was a need to hide Jake. All went well.

By August, the food situation was dire—the Islanders and German forces alike were on the point of starvation. In September, a ship sailed from France to Guernsey under a white flag. The Americans on board asked the Germans if they were aware of their hopeless position. The Germans refused to discuss terms and the ship sailed away. The cold winter of 1944 made life even more unbearable.

Bill began broadcasting each and every night about the plight of the Islanders, and the desperate need for food and supplies before it was too late. They shared what little they had with the few nearby neighbors that remained.

After months of protracted negotiations before the International Committee of the Red Cross, the SS Vega was permitted to bring relief to the starving Islanders in December 1944, carrying Red Cross parcels, salt and soap, as well as medical and surgical supplies. The SS Vega made five additional trips to the Islands.

The Walsh Farm remained safe and secure. Jake's memory returned over time during the long winter months triggered by information Bill received about his identity and military status. Although they spoke of family and London and the War and how it had affected them, Jake kept his thoughts of Lexi to himself.

His sleep was troubled, and he often woke in a cold sweat. Jake recalled over and over again the three days he and Lexi spent together in London; he lived for the day they would be reunited. He had made her a promise that he would return, and he intended to keep that promise.

They celebrated his 21st Birthday with as good a meal as possible under the circumstances prepared by Lulu and Lila. Jake regaled them with stories of past celebrations and gifts; he thanked them for the best gift of all—having saved his life and hidden him from the Germans.

Bill spent more and more time broadcasting the dire situation on the

Island. In return, news about the War was exhilarating as the Allies basked in victory after victory. Winter passed and spring arrived.

On 12 April 1945, Bill learns on his evening broadcast that Franklin D. Roosevelt has died of a massive cerebral hemorrhage. Harry S. Truman has been sworn in as the thirty-third President of the United States of America in charge of a country still fighting WWII; and unbeknown to the world in possession of a weapon of unprecedented and terrifying power.

Less than a month later on 9 May 1945, the German Commandant, who had taken such a liking to Lulu Walsh, surrendered and the first British Troops landed in St. Peter Port from HMS Bulldog. The occupation of the Channel Islands, the only British soil occupied by German troops during WWII, was at long last over.

Jake bid farewell to the Walsh Farm—to Bill, Lulu, and Lila. It was a bittersweet farewell, and he promised to return to Guernsey.

CHAPTER SIXTEEN

W hen the HMS Bulldog docked at Portsmouth, Marcus and Elena were there to welcome Jake home. Although they knew he was not free to leave with them, they wanted to see for themselves that he was truly okay. They wanted to be there for him as the only family that he had. As they watched him walk down the gangplank of the ship, they saw that except for appearing thinner, he was a welcome sight.

They called to him waving frantically. "Jake, Jake, over here."

As he waved back and approached them, he was visibly crying. By the time he reached them, they too were crying—tears of love, joy, and relief. The three of them stood hugging one another; it had been a long time. He was home, and he was safe. The War in Europe was finally over.

Painfully noticeable was Lexi's absence. Not knowing what else to say, Marcus assured him that she was fine; that she was in Jerusalem with her father.

They only had a precious few minutes together before Jake was whisked away.

The last time Marcus had spoken with Lexi was in late March 1944. On that call, she told him that she was due to graduate in April; her brother Mark was getting married in May; and her father was returning to Jerusalem in June, urging her to go with him. It wasn't until months later that Marcus received word that Jake was missing.

He rang up the number at the house; there was no answer. He even went to the house on several occasions, but no one answered the door. He contacted her school hoping they had a forwarding address; they did not.

After continuing to use any and all resources he could muster, he learned that Jake was in safe hands and unhurt on Guernsey Island. He was given this information in strictest confidence indicating it was not to be shared, but he would have shared it with Lexi if he had been able to get in touch with her.

When the War ended in Europe and the Channel Islands were liberated, Marcus received word that Jake would be coming home by week's end on the HMS Bulldog docking in Portsmouth. He rang up Elena immediately.

"Jake is coming home. I want to meet him when his ship arrives in Portsmouth. I know he will not be free to come home, but I want to see him; I want to hug him; I want to know that he's okay."

Elena shared his elation. "Oh Marcus, that is such wonderful news. Of course, we will be there; don't even think about going without me."

On his way home, he went by the Portman house to give it one more try. He walked up and lifted the knocker. The door opened, and there stood a pretty young woman about Jake's age.

"Good afternoon. I hope I am not disturbing you. My name is Marcus Hirsch, and I would like to inquire about someone who used to live here."

Since he was an older gentleman, she assumed he was inquiring about her father-in-law; Lexi never entered her mind. "Hello, I'm Rosalie Portman. I'm married to Dr. Portman's eldest son Mark. Won't you please come in?"

She showed him into the sitting room—the very same sitting room where he and Elise had sat discussing Jake's plight. He noticed that very little had changed, but this was not unusual due to shortages of everything during five long years of war.

"If you have time, I'll make some tea and hopefully, I can answer your questions. Things always seem to work out better over tea, don't you agree?"

Marcus smiled. "That will be fine."

As he waited for her to return, he walked about the room looking at the many photographs that were recent. There were wedding photographs of Rosalie and Mark, a family photograph at the wedding with Lexi, her father, younger brother Sam, and the bride and groom. And then suddenly, there it was, a photograph of Lexi holding a beautiful newborn baby girl—with the same red hair as her mother's.

Rosalie returned and placed the tea on the table. Pouring them each a cup, she said, "So what do you wish to ask me about my father-in-law?"

At first Marcus was speechless. Why would she assume he was inquiring about her father-in-law? After seeing the photo of Lexi, he decided it best to take the opening she had given him and do just that—inquire about Manny Portman. "I heard he was leaving for Palestine well over a year ago. Is he still there?"

"Yes, indeed he is. He has permanently relocated to Jerusalem. My husband and I were married shortly before he left, and at that time, he had not decided to make the move permanent. At that point, Mark and I felt this house would be perfect for us. Although he offered us the house when we were married, we stayed with my parents for a while. Mark is a physician now and currently at Cambridge, and it has proven a good choice.

"When my father-in-law lost Elise, he was depressed for months, and we were all worried about him. With Mark and Sam in medical school, and Lexi in nursing school, he was alone most of the time, and it was starting to take a toll on him. He lost his usual lust for life and seemed to grow old before his time.

"He originally accepted the offer to join a group of medical personnel traveling to Palestine to take part in assessing a research program at the Hadassah Hospital on Mount Scopus. It brought him back to life and gave him the boost that he needed,

"His decision to move there permanently was somewhat of a surprise to all of us. My sister-in-law Lexi, fresh out of nursing school, went with him and opted to remain there too. She is currently deeply involved in the Hadassah Hospital School of Nursing, and is contemplating going to medical school.

"She has built a nice life for herself there." Standing and walking over to the mantel, she picked up the photo of Lexi. Handing it to Marcus she said, "We recently received this photo of Lexi and her newborn daughter Zoe.

"Did you know Elise or Lexi? How do you know my father-in-law?"

"I did have the pleasure of meeting Elise a long time ago. I also had the pleasure of meeting Lexi a couple of years ago. I never met your father-in-law; I was inquiring about him for a friend."

"If you like, I am more than happy to give you contact information for him."

"I would appreciate that." In the back of his mind, he had already noted the information that Lexi could be reached at Hadassah Hospital School of Nursing. He would keep her father's information if the need arose to contact him.

He rose to leave. "Thank you Rosalie for the tea; I enjoyed our little chat. Good Luck to you and Mark, and I wish you much happiness and the best of everything. Now that the War In Europe is over, we Brits have a lot of cleaning up to do to get back to normal."

The earlier elation that Marcus felt learning that Jake was coming home was gone. He drove home devastated at Jake's latest loss and disappointed in himself that he had not kept in touch with Lexi. The photo of her and her newborn daughter Zoe did not add up. It was simply not possible she could be Jake's. It had been a year and a half since they had seen one another.

There was no way for Marcus to know that the photo had been taken almost a year earlier, and that the ring so visible on her left ring finger was the one that Jake had given her.

When he arrived home, instead of an upbeat happy man, Elena greeted a depressed sad man who once again had to deliver bad news to a young man who had already endured more than his share of loss and disappointment in his short life. Marcus had grown to love Jake as a son knowing their relationship was one that many fathers and sons never realize.

He was determined that nothing would mar Jake's long-awaited homecoming. He didn't know exactly how or when for that matter, he would tell him, but he would find a way, he had to find a way to soften the blow that he knew it would be.

Jake spent a week in the hospital, where test after test proved he was in good health and good shape. He attributed all the credit to the Walsh family who took care of him, and their uncanny good fortune to stay in the good graces of the German Commandant, allowing them to avoid the starvation and deprivation endured by the majority of Islanders.

Jake reported back to Coltishall to a resounding welcome. *Jitterbug Jake* was home—they knew it; they never lost faith. The first item on his list was to take to the air—he yearned to feel the euphoria of flying a Spit once again. It had been over a year since he had last flown; the night he and his plane had gone down in the Channel.

On a beautiful sunny afternoon, he was told a Spitfire awaited him. He was not the least bit nervous. This was not at all like the first time, but he quickly recalled he hadn't been nervous then either.

He taxied the plane to the holding point on the runway; he did his run up and instruments check. On getting the green light, he released the brakes and glided the stick back gradually, opening the throttle to takeoff power. A few seconds later, he felt the plane fly itself off.

Sitting in the snug cockpit with that beautiful wing in his field of vision, Jake was home. With speed building up, he retracted the undercarriage, closed the canopy and climbed to a safe height over the base. After flying for over an hour, he reluctantly headed back. He flew every chance he got over the next few days. For Jake, flying was his elixir.

In June, he was granted a ten-day leave, and he caught the train to London.

This time, instead of simply showing up at De Beers, he rang up Marcus and told him his plans prior to leaving the base. He turned down his gracious invitation to stay with him and Elena, and opted to check in to the Savoy. He had a lot on his mind—first and foremost was getting in touch with Lexi.

To Marcus, the time had come. He had thought of little else since Jake's return than how he would deliver the news that Lexi was married, had a daughter, and no longer lived in England. He discussed it at great length with Elena. Neither could contemplate what this would do to Jake; he had been through so much and managed to rise above it all. Could he possibly do that once again?

CHAPTER SEVENTEEN

J ake arrived at Charing Cross Railway Station and decided to walk to
the hotel. It was a clear day, a little on the warm side, but it felt good to
be back in London. The destruction left by the German air raids was a
reminder that although the War in Europe was over, it would be a long time
before everything was rebuilt and looked as it once had.

After checking in and leaving his bags in the room, he set off for the East
End. He stopped at the Brady Street Cemetery first, left a pebble on each
headstone, and bowing his head recited the Kaddish.

His next stop was to see Rabbi Levin. He found him sitting on a bench
in the small garden behind the Great Central Synagogue, deep in thought.
Not wanting to startle him, Jake called out as he approached. He turned, and
immediately a big smile spread across his face. "Jacob Lyons, my boy, how
good it is to see you. How are you?"

Jake noticed how frail he had become. "I'm fine Rabbi, and you?"

"I can't complain. I have aches and pains that generally come with age,
but they are worse in the winter. When the weather is warm, they subside."

The years of war had taken a toll on this gentle old man. He had lost
many of his parishioners; in some cases, entire families were wiped out during
the air raids. Just that very morning, he had learned that two of his former
students were not returning from the War—Ivan Portman was one of them.

He spent most of the afternoon visiting with Rabbi Levin. So many people
were gone; others moved away and joined family outside the London area.
The East End had sustained a fair amount of damage that in all probability
would not be rebuilt. Where once a vibrant community thrived, stores stood
idle and vacant.

The streets were empty of children playing and busy adults rushing to and fro.

It saddened him to see the East End's Jewish Quarter that his parents had wholeheartedly embraced when they arrived in London, and that had wholeheartedly embraced them in return, in such a depressed state of disrepair. They lived the best twenty years of their lives in the East End—free of oppression and free to realize the dreams they brought with them from Russia.

They bid one another goodbye, and Jake had the feeling that he would not see him again.

He had asked Marcus to set aside a day when they could discuss business matters, and they planned to meet at his office first thing in the morning. He was due to be discharged in the near future, and wanted to get his affairs in order so that he and Lexi could get married and get on with their lives. He had kept his promise to return to her, and now he had the rest of his life to fulfill his promise to love and take care of her. He had to find a place to live, and he needed a job.

He spent the evening alone at the Savoy, having an early dinner in the Grill Room. Returning to his room, he unpacked, made a list of items to discuss with Marcus, and then went to bed—lost in thoughts of Lexi.

Jake arose early the next morning, showered, and dressed. After a quick breakfast at the hotel, he left for his meeting.

As Marcus greeted him, Jake sensed a hesitation on his part to get down to business. He offered him coffee, tea, a scone, and asked if he had eaten breakfast.

When Jake replied, that he was all set, Marcus had no choice but to began the hardest conversation he had ever had. He did not wait for him to ask.

"I know I disappointed you by not having Lexi with us to meet you when you docked in Portsmouth. I am sorry I let you down, and I apologize."

When Jake started to object, he motioned him to let him continue.

"After both of us lost contact with you, I spoke to her on several occasions while she was still at Birmingham. She told me she had written to you, but had not received an answer. The last time we spoke, she told me she was graduating in April, her brother Mark was getting married in May, and that although her father had returned to England for her graduation and Mark's wedding, he was returning to Jerusalem in June. Not wanting to leave her alone in London, he urged her to accompany him.

"By the time I learned that you were officially missing, she had set sail with her father. She did not leave me any information of how to get in touch with her.

"When I was told in strictest confidence that you were on Guernsey Island, and that the information could not be shared for security reasons, I was so relieved to learn you were safe, and I certainly would have confided in her, but all attempts to contact her were a dead end.

"When I first learned you were missing, I went to the Portman house several times, and called the number you had given me, but neither the phone nor the door was answered.

"When I received the call that you were coming home, I made one last attempt. I drove to the house on my way home, and much to my surprise, the door was answered by Mark's wife Rosalie.

"I introduced myself and told her I was inquiring about someone who had once lived in the house. When she left the room to prepare some refreshment, I looked about at the photos on the mantel. There were several taken at the wedding, and I noticed a photo of Lexi holding a newborn baby girl.

"When Rosalie returned, and we continued our conversation, she assumed that I was seeking information about Manny Portman. At first, I was taken aback, but then I realized that my age obviously caused her to reach the decision that I was interested in locating her father-in-law, not her sister-in-law.

"She told me that months later, Manny decided to relocate permanently to Jerusalem, and that Lexi was remaining there, as well. She and Mark are now living in the house. She lifted the photo of Lexi from the mantel and told me that the child was her newborn daughter Zoe. I could see in the photo that she wore a wedding ring."

Jake sat frozen in his chair. He felt as if he had been punched in the gut. He was utterly speechless, and he was having a hard time processing all that Marcus had said.

Marcus grew alarmed. He had no idea what he expected Jake to say— what could he say? Once again, the rug had been pulled out from under him.

He rose and came around his desk and stood in front of Jake putting his arm on his shoulder. "I've agonized over telling you since I learned the news from Rosalie, and try as I may, I saw no other way. I do have contact information for both Lexi and her father. You don't have to use it now, but the time may come when you will want to get in touch with her."

Jake stood and thanked Marcus for being honest with him. "I have a list of things that I want to go over with you, but I can't do it today. Maybe if you have time later in the week, I can meet with you then."

"Of course, I always have time for you. Just ring me up when you're ready. And please come for dinner; Elena so wants to see you and pamper you a bit. She won't take *no* for an answer."

They shook hands and hugged. "I need a couple of days to get my bearings. Rest assured, I have no intention of turning down one of Elena's delicious home-cooked meals. I'm due to be discharged soon, although I'm not sure of the exact date. I plan to take care of as many pressing issues as possible while I'm on leave so that when I am discharged, I will have a place to live. I also have to give some thought as to what I want to do with the rest of my life, and that includes getting a job."

—————※∭※—————

Jake left Marcus' office and walked back to the hotel stopping along the way to pick up two bottles of whiskey. He had never had anything stronger than beer or ale or ultra sweet Jewish wine. He generally never finished a single glass or bottle at any one sitting when out with friends; it was only mid-morning, and he had only eaten a light breakfast. Nonetheless, he returned to his room at the Savoy, leaving word at the desk that he did not want to be disturbed.

He stripped down to his skivvies, consumed three-quarters of one of the two fifths he had purchased, and passed out. His head was on the verge of exploding. Getting drunk and passing out was the only way he could stop the overpowering questions and thoughts running rampant in his mind.

Hours later, he awoke disoriented, his head throbbing. He stumbled to the loo, glanced at the horrible image that stared back at him in the mirror, and returned to bed sleeping until morning.

The following day was an entire blur. He was sick as a dog with a hangover that consumed his entire body. He spent most of the day emptying his stomach of its contents over and over until there was nothing left. By evening, he began to feel a little better. He took a hot shower, put on his robe and called for room service. He hadn't eaten in over twenty-four hours.

The hot broth was just what he needed. As he continued to sober up, Marcus' words of the day before came rushing back. How could this have happened? Lexi married to someone else—that was impossible. Just as she had known he would never leave without contacting her all those years ago, he felt that way now. She just wouldn't pick up and move out of the country and not leave word for him or how she could be reached. He recalled Marcus telling him that she had written to him, but he didn't know when. He had never received the letters; and they were not among his things waiting for him when he came home.

Lexi was married with a daughter and no longer living in England—how could this have been part of God's plan for him? When he survived the air raid that took his family, his faith had been unwavering throughout that He had a plan for him and that He would watch over him. Now, once again, he was alone—back to square one, as they say. He had no idea what he was going to do. He had seven days of leave left before returning to Coltishall. He had business to attend to, and he would use the time he had left on leave to set them in motion.

He rang up Marcus at his office. "Good morning Jake, I'm so glad you called. I was worried about you. How are you doing? I hope you're planning to stop by and meet with me."

"I'm doing okay. I needed some time to think things out. I'm calling to see if you have time to meet with me today, or if not, perhaps tomorrow."

"Today is fine; come over straight away. I have the entire day free, and I'm hoping you will tell me that you're available to come home with me for dinner tonight. I can ring up Elena as soon as we hang up."

"Sounds like a plan. I'll walk over, I should be there within half an hour."

His stomach was still a little queasy, but he felt much better and thinking much clearer. He decided to take care of the more pressing issues concerning his immediate future. He needed Marcus' help and hopefully all would be settled by the time he had to return to base.

Marcus welcomed him, and this time, Jake accepted his offer of hot tea. He had heard that coffee was actually better for a hangover, but preferred tea for his unsettled stomach.

Marcus suggested they be seated at the conference table. He brought the box of papers that Jake had entrusted to him and placed it before him. He urged him to open the box and handed him a list that he had made of the contents.

"I made this list the very day you left the box with me. You will note, there are additions with coinciding dates of their receipt. As I told you when you returned from the States, I set up a bank account in your name with the proceeds of your parents' funds and all that was left to you by Max and Reba Lerner.

"Since that time, I sold Max's shop as you instructed me to do and deposited the proceeds into your account. The contents of the shop are stored in the basement of the house in Middlesex, along with your jeweler's tools and also your father's and Max's. There is a considerable amount of diamonds, gold, silver, and various jewelry items that represented Max's business. The contents of the Lerner flat are there also; I think you should go through them to see if there is anything you wish to keep.

"In addition, there was a small safe at the shop that was hidden behind the workbench; the contents yielded both cash and additional diamonds—the cash was deposited in your account and the diamonds are packed away at the house along with the others.

'In the past, you never showed an interest in the contents of this box; you entrusted me with everything, and I did my best to keep track of all your assets by updating the list and monitoring it constantly."

Marcus reached in the box and retrieved a bankbook. Sliding it across the table to Jake, he urged: "Open it and tell me what you think."

Jake opened the bankbook and was shocked to see that excluding the house in Middlesex, its contents, and all that was stored there, he was worth a small fortune—he was actually quite wealthy—it was more money than he ever imagined.

"Marcus, am I reading this correctly? I had no idea, and you are right; I never really had an interest in learning what I inherited. There was really no need to know while I was off fighting the Germans." Briefly, he recalled the note he had given Marcus leaving everything to Lexi if he did not return from the War. Neither made mention of it; he had removed it.

"The other day, you apologized to me. I want to make it quite clear, and I will only speak of this once—here and now. Marcus Hirsch you have never done anything that requires you to apologize to me.

"I don't recall if I told you that I am due to be discharged within the next couple of months, but I am; I do not have an exact date. I plan to sell the house in Middlesex—I can't bring myself to live there even after all this time. I had no idea my financial situation was so solid, so I assumed that I would sell the house and look for a new place simultaneously.

"I would like to purchase a country cottage with acreage. I can set up a workshop in the basement—perhaps a replica of Max's shop where my father and I worked side by side. I don't want you to worry that I plan to live in the past; I do not. I adored my parents, and I was extremely close with my father. It's been a long time since I cut and polished a diamond, and just as I got to fly a Spitfire again when I returned to Coltishall, I want to cut diamonds again.

"I would like to get in touch with someone who can search for a house for me prior to my discharge. After I am settled in and have gone through the items I plan to keep from the house in Middlesex, I will put it on the market."

As he had been years before, Marcus was in awe of Jake's acumen.

"I have a friend who sold real estate before the War. I haven't been in touch with her in years, but I will ring her up and see if she's available. If not, maybe she can suggest someone."

"I can never thank you enough. I don't know what I would have done without all your help. I really had no one else to turn to; thank goodness you and Elena were and continue to be my guardian angels. I'd like to leave the box and all my papers with you until I'm discharged, if that's okay.

"Now that we're finished with business, what time is dinner?"

"Dinner is at six o'clock but please come as early as you like. I will be home no later than four. There is one thing I haven't mentioned—your father's Ford V-8 car—I have it stored in a friend's garage. I still remember when he bought that car."

For the first time, Jake smiled. "He loved that Ford V-8, and I did too. My parents arranged for me to learn to drive it for my sixteenth birthday. My friends were so jealous. Again, I thank you. I definitely want to keep that car, at least for now."

Although, they spent several hours together, the name Lexi Portman was not mentioned. And there were no more apologies.

Walking back to the hotel, Jake stopped to pick up wine for dinner and a big bouquet of flowers for Elena. He had never before purchased wine or flowers for anyone. He loved Marcus and Elena—they were family—his family.

Elena opened the door to Jake bearing gifts. "My goodness, what is all this? Come in, come in, and give the flowers and wine to Marcus so I can get a big hug and a kiss." She held onto him tightly. "You don't know how happy we are to have you safely home. I made all your favorites so I hope you're hungry."

Jake thought about the previous two days and hoped his stomach had returned to normal.

He refused their offer of wine, but enjoyed the appetizers and dinner immensely. They didn't press him to talk about Guernsey, but he did so on his own.

After dinner, they retired to the sitting room. The War was over, so he could tell them about the night they flew escort to France and how his Spit went down into the English Channel ahead of him.

"Guernsey Island is only 70 miles from the UK, but it was under German Occupation. I spent eleven months on the Walsh Dairy Farm not as a prisoner but not free to leave either. Bill Walsh found me unconscious, and his twin sisters Lulu and Lila cared for me and nursed me back to health. If the Germans had found me, things might not have worked out so well.

"Lulu fell under the good graces of the German Commandant, and the remote location of their farm kept us safe. Their farm produced dairy products for market, but they grew vegetable crops for their own consumption. By the end of the occupation, the farm was approaching rock bottom. Even with the help of the Red Cross, the Islanders were starving and in desperate need of supplies.

"It was Bill who contacted other clandestine operators on his shortwave radio to relay that I was safe on the Island.

"Speaking about my time on Guernsey makes me realize what I owe the Walsh family. As I said, by war's end, their farm was down to one cow and little else. Marcus, I would like to send a draft of 500 pounds to restock the Guernsey Cows and allow them to put in new crops. They even had to slaughter their pet sheep for food to sustain us through last winter. In fact, Lulu and Lila prepared a fine mutton stew to celebrate my 21st Birthday."

Though Jake started out on a serious note, the Commandant's infatuation with Lulu, and their efforts to teach him how to milk a cow, and grow vegetables had them all laughing and realizing that even in the face of adversity, one can find good. It felt good to laugh; it felt better to see Jake laughing.

It was growing late. "I think it's time for me to head back to the hotel. Elena, the meal was terrific, as I knew it would be, and honestly I expected no less. You have been so gracious; I know I can never repay all you have done and continue to do for me. I love you both with all my heart."

They walked him to the door. "I'll ring you up when I hear from my friend about finding a cottage for you. I hope to set it up so that you can meet with her while you're on leave."

Jake took the Underground back to the Savoy. He had accomplished almost everything he set out to do; by the end of his leave, he hoped to take care of the rest.

After he was discharged and settled into his new home, he would make a decision about employment. Then, he would be better prepared to find out anything and everything he could learn about Lexi, her move to Jerusalem, her daughter—her husband.

Jake arose early and planned to take the Underground to the house in Middlesex. He wanted to get an idea of how much space he would need for his workshop and how big a cottage he should be looking to buy.

When the phone rang, it was Marcus. "Jake, I have good news. Although my friend Meg Wentworth no longer deals in real estate, she knows of a cottage that has stood vacant for most of the war years, and is available immediately. She has a car, and if you' re up for it, she can take you to see it today."

"That's great news: let's do it. If you're free, why don't you and Elena come with us?"

"We would love to. I am certain that if Elena has something planned, she will cancel and join us. I will ring Meg back, and let's say meet here at De Beers at eleven. Is that good for you?"

CHAPTER EIGHTEEN

In the heart of England is a rural idyll of peaceful rolling hills where traditions abound and life is unhurried. Historic villages contain stone cottages so perfect they're called *chocolate boxes*. Footpaths cross scenic fields and valleys leading to rivers, canals, woods, and civilized pubs. This is the Cotswolds, an area of limestone hills in the English countryside west of London, between Bath and Stratford-upon-Avon.

Holiday cottages in England need little introduction. A cottage break has long been considered the quintessential English holiday, and there is no better way to explore the history and heritage the country has to offer.

A majority of cottages were owned by the wealthy before the War, and were primarily built or purchased as holiday cottages with the possibility of a good place to retire. Jake was not seeking a *cottage* for holiday use; he wanted a smaller house with acreage outside of London but easily accessible by train into the City.

They met as arranged at eleven; introductions aside, the four of them embarked on their adventure. As Meg drove, she gave them an overview and a little history of the area and the cottage they were going to view.

"Jake, when Marcus told me what you were looking for, the Wentworth Cottage came to mind at once—Wentworth as in my name—it has been in our family since the turn of the century. My father purchased the cottage as a holiday destination, but looked to ultimately retire there. After my Mum passed away, he didn't seem to have much interest in the place.

"The cottage has stood empty and unused throughout the War. My father died almost three years ago, and I've kept up the maintenance as best I could.

My brother has no interest in keeping it nor do I, so I decided to place it on the market after the War ended.

"When I got the call from Marcus, I was thrilled. If it turns out to be what you are looking for, it will be a good deal for both of us. My father spared no expense when he purchased it, and even added a few things like the garage when he bought his first car. I have many fond memories of family gatherings there, including the Christmas my husband and I became engaged."

The drive took not quite two hours, and the conversation helped pass the time. Suddenly, Meg announced, "We're here—welcome to Wentworth Cottage.

There before them stood a charming turn of the century, natural stone terraced cottage set in an idyllic and peaceful location on the edge of the village overlooking the surrounding countryside.

Meg unlocked the door. They entered the cottage and found—a delightful, spacious yet cozy, single story home with high ceilings, skylights, and solid wood floors. The beautifully furnished home looked comfortable and welcoming, and one could see that each piece had been selected with special care for its special place.

The entrance hall with a staircase to the loft led into the large open sitting/dining area which—Meg called the *great room*—with its massive Victorian style fireplace; the large kitchen was equipped with a cooking island and yet large enough to hold a round wooden table and six chairs. There was an oversized front master bedroom, three further bedrooms in the rear, and two water closets.

The landing and deeply pitched roof lent themselves well to the excellent location of the loft.

At the front of the cottage, the small garden had been somewhat neglected but could be brought back to life with a little tender care. Leading out from the great room to the upper patio there were steps leading to another patio below, and beyond that was an area of lawn with shrubs and a larger garden that led to a small carriage house on the far side of the property.

Jake was overwhelmed, as were Marcus and Elena. "Meg I can't believe you want to sell this magnificent home. This is many times over what I am looking for or actually need, but there is no way I'm going to turn this cottage down. It is beautiful in every way and best of all, I can see myself fitting in here quite nicely. What about the furniture? Do you plan to take all of it, some of it, sell it?"

Meg laughed. "I know how you feel. I always loved this place, but it's time for me to move on, and like I said earlier, it's enough for me to know I'm selling to someone who will cherish and enjoy it as much as my family did. I have no use for any of the furniture remaining. I long ago removed the many personal photos and trinkets that were special to us. I'm selling the house including the furnishings.

"I'm quite certain it will be a while before a lot of things will be available once again, and we're still at war in the Pacific."

"You're absolutely right. I love everything about Wentworth Cottage; there is no need nor do I wish to look further. So give me a price, and we can seal the deal."

Twenty minutes later after a handshake, a hug, and a kiss, Meg excused herself and came back with a large picnic basket. Placing it on the table in the dining room area, she began placing cheese, crackers, fruit, and two bottles of wine on the table. She removed four glasses from the cupboard and four plates.

This time, Jake took the wine and for the next hour, they ate and drank and walked about the cottage, inside and out. "You must have been pretty sure that I was going to love Wentworth Cottage as much as I do, sure enough to pack a picnic basket anyway."

Meg laughed. "I confess, I was pretty sure you were going to love it. But I love picnics and never miss a chance to have one. I just thought that since no one has lived here for awhile, we would have this one indoors."

Jake learned that not only was the cottage perfect, but so was the location. A short walk from the cottage to the local train depot would take him to London's Underground Paddington Station—allowing him to travel to London by train from the Cotswolds in a little over an hour and a half.

Everyone pitched in; packing everything up and washing the glasses and plates only took a few minutes. Soon they were on their way back to London.

Meg dropped them off at De Beers. Jake was too exited to call it a day.

"You've come through for me once more. I'm over the moon about the cottage, and it's too early to call it a day; have dinner with me. Please, let me take my two most favorite people in the whole world out for dinner and a little celebrating."

Marcus and Elena couldn't resist. They too were excited, and Marcus still felt terrible about the situation with Lexi. They chose a small, out of the way pub near Hatton Garden where it was less crowded on weekdays, and the food was good.

Jake had a hard time falling asleep and when he finally did, he thought only of Lexi—he pictured her in every single room in the cottage, in the garden, and making love to her in the big beautiful master bedroom. But that wouldn't happen. She was thousands of miles across the world with a baby daughter and a husband.

He returned to Coltishall and soon learned his discharge date—11 August 1945. They asked him to remain in the RAF as an instructor, but he declined. He had done his part; he was anxious to get home and get on with whatever the future held for him.

6 August 1945, President Harry S. Truman orders the first Atomic Bomb to be dropped on Hiroshima from a B-29 flown by Col. Paul Tibbets.

9 August 1945, the second Atomic Bomb is dropped on Nagasaki from a B-29 flown by Maj. Charles Sweeney—Emperor Hirohito and Japanese Prime Minister Suzuki request immediate peace with the Allies.

11 August 1945, Jake is honorably discharged and returns home to London.

14 August 1945, the Japanese accept an unconditional surrender; Gen. Douglas MacArthur is appointed to head the occupation forces in Japan.

World War II is in the history books.

PART TWO

CHAPTER NINETEEN

South Africa located on the southern tip of the African continent is bordered by the Atlantic Ocean on the west, and by the Indian Ocean on the south and east.

Cape Town, South Africa's first city was founded by the Dutch to provide fresh produce and meats to the members of the Dutch East India Company, who were traveling between Europe and the Orient.

In the early nineteenth century, the Colony switched hands and became part of the British Empire. The Union of South Africa became an independent nation within Britain's Commonwealth of Nations, and Cape Town was chosen as its parliamentary capital.

Religious freedom, granted by the Dutch and guaranteed by the British, attracted Jewish immigrants from Britain, Germany, and Holland—among the first British settlers to come to Cape Town were 20 Jews. They formed a Jewish congregation and met for services in private homes; eight years later, the first Synagogue, Tikvat Israel (Hope of Israel) was founded.

Over the next five decades, British Jewish immigrants established additional synagogues, plied the trades they brought with them, and developed philanthropic institutions evolving Cape Town into a thriving community.

Discovery of diamonds in the Cape Colony radically modified not only the world's supply of diamonds but also the conception of them; and it changed South Africa from an agricultural society to a modern metropolis.

The story of diamonds in South Africa begins in December 1866 when 15-year old Erasmus Jacobs and his sister found a transparent rock on his father's farm, on the south bank of the Orange River. They showed the rock to a neighboring farmer who found the rock intriguing and offered to buy it from them. The Jacobs family, believing it was of no value, simply gave it to him.

When confirmed that it was in fact a diamond—a diamond weighing 21.25 carats—it was aptly named the *Eureka*--the single most important diamond find in the history of South Africa. This single discovery triggered a *diamond rush* that attracted people from all over the world seeking to get rich mining diamonds.

The first discoveries were alluvial; by 1869, however, substantially richer lodes were found far from any stream or river—first in yellow earth and then deep below in hard rock.

By the 1880s, South Africa's mines produced 95% of the world's diamonds and became home to great wealth and fierce rivalries; most notably that between Cecil John Rhodes and Barney Barnato, English immigrants who consolidated the findings of early prospectors into ever larger and larger holdings and mining companies thus forming the Premier Transvaal Diamond Company.

Franz Schiller was a boy of sixteen when he left Hamburg, Germany and hopped a freighter bound for South Africa in 1882. The Schiller family was dirt poor. His Lutheran father spent most of his time drinking with his friends in the town's plentiful beer halls, and the remainder of his time sleeping it off. He had five younger siblings, and a Jewish mother who supported the family by doing laundry and mending for the wealthier families in town.

Since the young age of seven, Franz worked to bring in whatever he could to help the family. Frustrated that he was going nowhere and tired of his father's beatings that had become more frequent of late, he confided in his mutti that he was leaving. She was heartbroken, but gave him what little money she had knowing that when her husband found out, he would surely beat her as well.

Almost fifteen years had passed since the discovery of diamonds, when Franz arrived in Cape Town. No longer were hopeful prospectors arriving on a daily basis seeking to strike it rich. What he found was a thriving community comprised of an assortment of business establishments. With little cash in hand, his priority was to find a job and a place to live.

As he was leaving the dock area to head into town, he noticed an older gentleman struggling to carry a rather large parcel. Approaching him he said, "Sir, may I help you with that? How far are you going?"

The old man looked up gratefully. "Yes, thank you. It seems as if I do need some help. This package is quite heavy, heavier than I thought. I'm headed into town. Where are you going?"

"That's a good question. I just arrived on that freighter, and I too am headed into town—looking for a job and a place to stay. Maybe you can give me a few suggestions."

"That I will."

Franz left the man long enough to go back to the freighter and get some rope. He tied it securely around the parcel creating a handle making it easier to carry.

The man introduced himself as Simon Abel. Although Franz was carrying both the man's parcel and his own bag, he had to maintain a slower pace to allow Simon to keep up with him. By the time they arrived at The General Store, they had both learned quite a bit about one another; and Franz had a job and was told he could stay in the back of the store for a few days until he found a more permanent place.

Franz was a big help to Simon. In return, Simon had given him a lifeline. He taught him all there was to know about the business. Franz built a cart so that on future trips down to the dock to pick up goods, they could load up and easily pull it back to town with little effort.

Simon grew quite fond of Franz, and as his dependence on him became more and more evident with each passing day, he feared losing him. One evening, on the anniversary of his arrival in Cape Town, Simon invited him to have dinner with him at a restaurant that had recently opened.

Seated at a small table in the corner, Simon explained. "We are celebrating the one-year anniversary of having found one another. Have you forgotten that it was exactly one year ago today that you helped me get my package to the store?"

Actually he had. Simon paid him well; well enough to take a room at a small boardinghouse where he could get his meals and meet other people his own age. On weekends, Franz met up with the friends he made, and they often attended events at the many synagogues that had formed to accommodate the immigrants that continued to arrive and settle in Cape Town.

He made it a point to stay away from the many pubs that dotted the town. When his friends urged him to join them, he refused and simply returned to the boardinghouse. He had left home because of his father's drinking, and didn't want to fall into the same trap.

"I can't say I forgot. It just didn't come to mind." For a moment, Franz wondered if he was letting him go.

Simon continued. "I can honestly say that it was my *lucky day* when you offered to help me; and it has never stopped being just that. I hope you know that the business is doing much better since you came to work for me. I must, however, face the reality that I'm getting on in years; I'll be ninety on my next birthday; and I have no family left.

"I was born on a farm on the Orange River that my parents owned. Once diamonds were discovered in the area, farming went down hill. When my parents died, I boarded up the farmhouse, and moved to Cape Town, purchased the property, and built The General Store. Been here ever since.

"Don't know what you aspired to when you came here a year ago, but I'm quite certain it wasn't to be a clerk in a shop like mine. The one thing the past year has taught me is that if we hadn't met that day, I would in all probability have closed the store months ago.

"Don't know how much longer I'm going to be around, but if you stay and continue to work with me, when I pass on, The General Store will be yours. At that time, you can continue to run the business or sell it and move on.

"If you accept my offer, there are a few requests that go with it. I would like to be buried on my family farm alongside my parents and my brother who died when he was a boy. The farmhouse has been boarded up since I came to Cape Town, and I'm thinking it should be torn down. Been meaning to do that for years."

Franz was totally surprised by Simon's offer. He had grown fond of him too. No one had every treated him with the respect and kindness that Simon had, certainly not his abusive drunken father.

"I don't know what to say. Of course, I will stay. Where else would I go? I had no aspirations other than to get away from a bad situation at home and save up enough money to help my mother and siblings in Germany. I wasn't heading anywhere in particular when I signed on to the freighter that brought me here to Cape Town where I met you."

Simon clapped his hands. "Then it's settled. I will have the papers drawn up to make everything legal. I want to take you to the farm and show you around so that my final wishes may be carried out."

Six months later, Simon Abel passed away in his sleep. Franz closed the store leaving a sign on the door: *Closed due to a death in the family.* He rented a wagon and set out for the farm with Simon's casket and tools to dig his grave. He made a mental note when he visited the farm with Simon to clear the area where the graves were and to surround it with a small fence to deter animals and vandals; he brought supplies to built the fence too.

He agreed with Simon's suggestion that tearing down the farmhouse and leveling the ground would be the best thing to do.

Bringing enough provisions with him for three days, he hoped he could get everything done in that time. He planned to camp outdoors weather permitting; if it rained, he would seek shelter inside the farmhouse.

The first day, everything went as planned. He dug the grave and buried Simon. He cleared what little debris there was and erected a small fence enlarging the area to include a beautiful, low growing tree nearby. As he stood back and surveyed his work, he realized he had no marker for the grave, but that would be remedied on a future visit.

He was tired but pleased that he was carrying out Simon's final wishes.

He set up a campsite down by the Orange River and made himself something to eat. As he lay on the ground staring up at the multitude of stars in the dark night sky, he couldn't believe all that had happened to him since leaving home. The first thing he was going to do when he got back to Cape Town was to contact his mutti, let her know where he was, and tell her that he wanted her to come live with him.

He lay there for a long time, but sleep eluded him. He had a couple of big days ahead. Foremost on his mind was what if tearing down the farmhouse alone turned out to be a bigger job than he anticipated. Perhaps he should have given it more thought.

He decided to take a walk along the river's edge. He hoped gazing upon the water would be calming and clear his mind to help him find sleep. As he neared the shore he could see the stars twinkling in the sand. Not as many as in the sky, but shining brightly nonetheless in the darkness of night.

Suddenly, he reached down and touched a twinkling star—it was a pebble in the sand. He reached for more, finding fifty in all—pebbles, stones, and rocks. Unsure exactly what they were, he searched for more and then suddenly they seemed to disappear.

Gathering what he had found and wrapping them in his shirt, he returned to the campsite. He had put out the small fire before laying down to sleep, so he opted to wait until morning to look at his findings in daylight.

As sleep continued to elude him, he lay patiently waiting for the sun to come up so that he could inspect the pebbles, stones, and rocks he had collected—could they possibly be diamonds? He knew nothing about diamonds. Simon made no mention that diamonds had ever been found on their farm, only in the area of the Orange River.

They had sparkled in the dark night; in daylight, he found they sparkled even more. A change in plans was necessary; he decided to return to Cape Town immediately. He packed up his tools, supplies, and camping gear and put them in the back of the wagon. He hitched the horse to the wagon and headed home.

The day after he returned, he took three of the small pebbles and made his way to the Assayer's Office. When he arrived, the place was empty except for the mustached man behind the window who inquired, "What can I do for you?"

Feeling a little nervous although he had rehearsed what he was going to say, Franz did not speak soon enough. Again, the man asked, "Is there something I can help you with?"

"Yes sir, there is. I have three small pebbles a friend left me when he died, and I would like to know if they are diamonds, as another friend of mine suggested they might be."

He handed them to the man through the window. The man disappeared into the back, returning a while later with a smile on his face. "My boy your friend was right—these three pebbles are definitely diamonds."

Franz grew quiet and thoughtful. "Can I sell them?"

"Of course, you can. I can give you a value and put you in touch with someone who is interested. We don't have folks buying up diamonds like we used to, but there are people who continue to buy and collect them.

"Thank you. I'm going to think on it. I'm the new proprietor of The General Store, and I might need the money for additional supplies.

"I'll get back to you when I've made my decision."

That very night, he wrote a letter to his mutti telling her he was in South Africa running a general store and urging her to come live with him. Adding that his siblings were also welcome, he requested her to reply as soon as possible at which time he would book passage for them.

One month later, he received word that his beloved mutti had died in childbirth along with the baby—another girl.

No mention was made of his father or his siblings. In fact, it was unclear to him who had responded to his letter. Again, he was heartbroken. One of the main reasons he left Germany was to help his dear mutti, and now she was gone.

—⁂—

For the next twenty years, Franz ran the store. It was his only means of support, and he was doing quite well. The General Store had originally opened for business to equip prospectors heading off in search of diamonds. That no longer the case, Franz opted to amend his inventory by adding a variety of items in hopes of attracting not only locals but visitors as well.

Selling the three small diamonds for cash, he laid out his vision for the store. He rearranged his stock and eliminated the storage area in the back where he built a living area that suited his needs. As his business continued to grow, he purchased a wagon to replace the small cart he had built to carry supplies from the dock.

The wagon was also his way of traveling to the farm where he continued to return and collect diamonds on the shore. At times they were plentiful; other times they were almost non-existent. Each time he returned home, he placed what he had collected in a crate he built, which he hid beneath the floor of his living quarters in the small cellar.

His visits were short in duration, and at times, long between. It meant closing the store, and he did not want to draw attention to that fact. He also planned his visits sporadically so as not to establish a pattern that would be noticed. Although he felt quite secure with the placement of his cache, it was the first thing he checked when he returned. The farmhouse remained boarded up; he preferred to camp along the river. On each visit he tended the graves of Simon and his family and made certain that the fence was intact.

In 1903, Franz departed Cape Town for the farm. His last visit was exactly one year prior when he came on the anniversary of Simon's passing. Now he was again going for the same reason. It had been over a year since he had found not a single pebble or stone but he continued to return to check on things honoring his friend's wishes.

As he approached, he saw a work crew of several men putting in stakes and roping off the area around the farmhouse. He stopped the wagon when he could go no further. A man came up to him inquiring both who he was and what he was doing there.

When Franz inquired the same of him, he replied. "I represent the Transvaal Government."

Starting in the late 1880s and into the nineteenth century, legal instruments through legislation such as resolutions, acts, proclamations, and ordinances played a key role in legitimizing systematic land dispossession and segregating South Africa.

In 1903, the Crown Land Disposal Ordinance was passed in the Transvaal, replacing the Occupation Act of 1886. Crown land was defined as all un-alienated land, and all land that was property of the government regardless of how that land was acquired.

Franz had no claim to the farm. His only concern was the gravesite and what would happen to it. He made his explanations to the official who in turn assured him that the site would remain untouched for the foreseeable future.

Franz's ties to the farm ended that day. He never returned. Over a period of twenty years, he had single handedly collected thousands upon thousands of uncut diamonds along the shore of the Orange River at the edge of Simon's farm, selling only the three original pebbles years before.

———〰———

When Franz left Germany and arrived in Cape Town, he was a boy merely sixteen years of age. His good fortune of having met up with Simon Abel was a blessing—or was it? When Simon died, it was too late for him to help his mutti.

After finding the stones and learning they were truly diamonds, he became obsessed. Each time he returned to the farm and added to his cache, he felt like a thief stealing what didn't belong to him—though he had no idea who could stake claim to them. He had long ago given up the friends he made when he arrived in Cape Town, and he knew no one else to ask.

As his cache grew, he became paranoid that someone was watching him, fearing that at any time, he could be confronted. The crate he built to hold the diamonds remained in the space under the flooring of his living area hidden by a rug and furniture on top. He very rarely looked at the diamonds anymore.

Twenty-one years later at the age of thirty-seven, he basically had no life, no wife, no family, no friends, and had no conception whatsoever of what his assets were worth. He couldn't sell the diamonds—they would ask where and how he acquired them. He had no need to sell them—what would he do with the proceeds?

With his ties to the farm severed, he no longer had a reason to leave town. At times when he felt melancholy, he wondered how different his life might have been if his mutti and siblings had come to South Africa. He would have had a family. He also wondered what had become of them—his father, his four sisters, and the youngest, his brother Michael.

He never wondered how different his life might have been if he had not found the diamonds. Yet finding the diamonds had the biggest impact; it affected his every thought, his every move.

Aside from customers in the store, he saw no one. One day, the thought occurred to him to begin attending services at the synagogue in an effort to become acquainted with others in the community—the community that he had been a part of for almost twenty-five years, and yet knew so few and so few knew him.

Although his father was not Jewish, and no religion was observed in their home, his mutti had seen to it that he took Hebrew lessons and became a Bar Mitzvah. His father had not attended, but his grandparents came and celebrated his day with his mother and siblings.

CHAPTER TWENTY

In 1871, the British entrepreneur Cecil Rhodes bought a claim to the De Beers mine, and using it as a financial base, eventually bought up most of the diamond mines in South Africa. He incorporated his holdings into De Beers Consolidated Mines, Ltd., in an effort to keep prices high and demand steady, allowing him to take control of the world's diamond distribution. By the time Rhodes died in 1902, De Beers controlled 90% of the world's rough-diamond production and distribution, but it was Sir Ernest Oppenheimer who made De Beers an Empire.

Oppenheimer was a German-born industrialist, financier, and one of the most successful leaders in the diamond mining industry in South Africa. At the age of sixteen, he became a junior clerk with one of the largest diamond brokers in London, and by 1902, was relocated to South Africa as their representative.

With backing from J. P. Morgan, he formed the Anglo-American Corporation of South Africa, Ltd., and moved aggressively into the diamond industry by gaining control of the South West Africa mines. By 1927, he became Chairman of the Board of De Beers Consolidated Mines, essentially having bought his way onto their board over a period of years.

Under Oppenheimer's leadership, De Beers and its Central Selling Organization established exclusive contracts with suppliers and buyers, making it impossible to deal with diamonds outside of De Beers.

Around the world, *De Beers* became the preeminent name in *diamonds*— d*iamonds* and *De Beers* became synonymous.

In 1925, Benjamin Lyons arrived in Cape Town, South Africa. He carried one bag that held all that he possessed in the world, his diamond cutting tools, and enough cash to last him for three months, if he was frugal. He had the promise of a job and the name of the person to contact, given to him by a friend he had grown up with in Russia. If the job did in fact materialize, he would make his plans permanent.

After leaving the ship, he headed into town. His first stop was at the first store he came upon—The General Store. When he entered, Franz noticed immediately that he seemed new to the area. "Good afternoon, may I help you?"

"I'm sure you can. I just arrived in town, and I am looking for an address on Adderley Street—Zeller Jewelers. Are you familiar with the store?"

"Why yes, I am. It's one of the best and quite well known. I know the owners, Paul and Phil Zeller. Are you planning to stay in Cape Town or are you just here on business?"

"You might say a little bit of both; I'd like to stay if everything works out. I arrived this morning from Russia, and I'm looking to settle here and build a new life for myself. By the way, my name is Ben Lyons. I'm a diamond cutter, and I'm hoping to get a job working for the Zeller brothers."

"Franz Schiller here; I'm pleased to me you. I've been in South Africa for over forty years, and although I have seen many changes come to pass, our stories remain the same—we all come seeking a better way of life. Where are you staying?"

"Actually, I haven't gotten that far; I came here directly from the dock. Maybe you can suggest a place close by. Of course for now, I'm only interested in something temporary.

"Welcome to Cape Town Ben Lyons. I will write down directions—it's only a short walk; and I will include directions to the Hotel Metropole, which is in the same general area. I hope you will come back and let me know how you make out with the Zeller brothers, and with the hotel, as well. If there is anything further I can do for you or help you with, please do not hesitate to stop by."

They shook hands and Ben thanked Franz. With directions in hand, he made his way to Adderley Street. As he observed the variety of shops along the way, he found himself liking what he saw and feeling good about coming to South Africa. He hoped the position he was seeking would become his.

Paul and Phil Zeller were born in London, England, and spent their early childhood working in and around their father's jewelry business starting at the bottom, sweeping floors and emptying trash. By the time they reached adulthood, their father had taught them the art of watchmaking, and perfected their skills as jewelers working with gold and diamonds.

The brothers saw their father as *old school* quick to criticize and short on compliments. He made it abundantly clear that it was *his* business and *he* wanted it run *his* way. They yearned to spread their wings and show what they could do on their own.

In 1905, the brothers decided to embark on a new beginning and saw South Africa as the *land of promise.* They left behind family and friends, and with what little they had, journeyed to Cape Town. They began with a modest jewelry establishment—Zeller Jewelers—on Adderley Street, and stocked with only a small amount of watches and rings opened their doors for business.

They came to realize that their success was derived not only from their skill but also from the personal and individualized service provided by an owner-run business. They continued to build upon that success by satisfying the ongoing special requests of their clientele who began coming from far and wide as word spread.

Soon they had their own jewelry workshop where they could fix and alter a myriad of items for their customers; and they began designing unique pieces to fulfill the many growing requests they received from wealthier clients.

Their product inventory grew immeasurably, and in no time, they were offering a wider range of jewelry, diamonds, and watches. Despite WWI, their business continued to prosper, and they decided that it would be both beneficial and profitable to set up a gem-cutting workshop right in Cape Town, eliminating the need to deal with Antwerp.

Although De Beers controlled the diamond industry for larger buyers, sources of uncut diamonds were plentiful on a smaller scale. With this thought in mind, they purchased and renovated a small warehouse building turning it into a brightly lit and fully supplied workshop solely to cut and polish diamonds and other gemstones.

When Ben Lyons arrived, they had but one cutter—an elderly gentleman, a fellow congregant from their synagogue; he was retired and required a bit of coaxing to come work for them. Upon learning of their search for diamond cutters, his friend who also knew the Zeller brothers from the synagogue offered to write to Ben in Russia and see if he was interested.

At the time, he was not. When his parents died within a few months of one another, and he and his brother Sydney both decided that the time had finally come when they too were contemplating leaving Russia, he reconsidered. He could not, however, convince his brother to come with him. Sydney remained determined to relocate in the United States. He travelled by way of Cuba where he was unfortunately detained and forced to wait for the moratorium on entry quotas to be lifted.

Cape Town's Long Street was the *pulse of the town,* its pavements throbbing with the constant movements of travelers, locals, shoppers, diners, and those that found a relaxing walk on the street energizing. Running up the hill from the corner of Coen Strytler Avenue near the docks up to Multensigel Road, from where it becomes Kloof Street, it lies between Loop and Adderley Streets in the center of town.

Ben reached Adderley Street, walked to the middle of the block and entered Zeller Jewelers. His was impressed. It was immaculate, well lit, and inviting. The jewelry was displayed in various cases about the store, and towards the back was a jeweler's bench.

The gentleman approaching him extended his hand. Good day, I'm Paul Zeller; welcome to Zeller Jewelers."

Ben took his hand. "Good day to you, as well. I'm Ben Lyons. I believe my friend Leon Abrams spoke to you about me. I'm a diamond cutter, and I heard you are looking for someone with my abilities."

With a big smile on his face, Paul continued shaking Ben's hand. He seemed quite happy to learn that he was not a customer, but someone who possessed a skill Zeller's needed and had been actively seeking for well over a year.

"My goodness, what a surprise. My brother and I were not expecting you so soon, but this is wonderful, just wonderful. Phil is not here, but let me try to reach him."

Ben put his bag down off to the side. As he waited for Paul to return, he looked about the store. He saw several unique pieces that he took to be Zeller designs. His eyes came to rest on a case that held engagement rings. He was surprised to find diamonds cut and polished in so many different shapes he was unaware of, and was intrigued by their placement in the mountings.

Paul returned. "Phil will be here in a few minutes. Have you found a place to stay?"

"No, I haven't. I came here straightaway from the dock. The Hotel Metropole was recommended to me; in fact, I passed it on the way here, and thought it rather nice. I'll stop by when I leave here."

"Excellent. There are others, but I would say that it's the best. The Metropole has been in Cape Town for thirty years and only seems to get better as time passes. If for any reason there are no rooms available, the Carnival Court is another longtime hotel that's good; it too is on Long Street a little further down."

When Phil finally arrived at the store, they made plans for the evening. "Ben, I would like to suggest that you get your room squared away, and you might want to freshen up. Please have dinner with us, where we can discuss our offer in a more relaxed atmosphere.

"How about meeting back here at 6:00 p.m. when the shop closes? We will have dinner at my house. My wife Lena is an excellent cook, who loves having company, I might add, especially since our girls are away at school in England. Paul and his wife Rene live nearby and will join us."

Ben felt truly welcomed by the Zeller brothers. They were complete strangers, yet he felt he had known them for a lifetime. "You are too gracious, and I can't thank you enough. I will be back by the time you close, and I look forward to a delightful evening."

Hotel Metropole opened in 1895 in Cape Town, South Africa and quickly became one of the City's Landmarks. Five stories high, it was a tower at the corner of Long and Castle streets, rising over 90 feet above street level. Its very imposing and grand appearance was designed in the old German Renaissance style that featured red pointed brickwork and artificial stone facings, an upper story veranda, quaint dormer windows, pediments, and a cupola on the Mansard roof.

Ben entered the hotel and approached the desk. After paying for and securing the room for a week, he was given the key and apprised of various eating establishments in the area—they were numerous.

His room was located on the third floor on the front side of the building, and had a balcony overlooking Long Street. He unpacked, checked the time, and lay down for a brief rest before bathing and heading back to the store by 6:00 p.m.

Ben arrived at the store to find Paul and Phil waiting for him. They set off for Brooklyn where both brothers lived. It was a short drive of 7 kilometers. While Paul drove, Phil pointed out various retail and eating establishments in the immediate area of the store to give Ben an idea of the neighborhood.

As they neared their destination in the Good Hope Model Village in Brooklyn, Ben saw a synagogue and several newly built cottages where the Zeller brothers lived on the same street.

In his small village in Russia, there were only one or two room dwellings with dirt floors, meager furnishings at best, and certainly no table set as fine as the one before him—even on the Sabbath. The china and crystal sparkled on the beautiful cloth that covered the table. And the aroma coming from the kitchen was heavenly.

Introductions aside, they sat down to a fine meal and an evening like no other Ben had ever experienced.

After the meal, the men retired to the sitting room to discuss business.

Paul began by asking Ben about himself. "I grew up in Minsk, Russia—life was very hard. My brothers and I watched our family and friends abused and killed by the pogroms and other catastrophes over and over again. My father's family goes back generations in the gem cutting business; my grandfather taught my father, and they both taught my brothers and me. We also learned to be jewelers working with gold and silver.

My brother Harry left Minsk a year ago and with his wife settled in London. When our parents passed away several months after their departure, my brother Sydney and I also decided to leave Russia. He sailed for America while I sailed here to South Africa."

He removed a small bag from his pocket. "I have brought a few samples of my work; not only stones that I have cut, but rings that I have crafted as well. I am also quite accurate at rating stones. In addition, I have come up with a device that allows me to measure the size of a stone more precisely."

Paul took the samples from Ben. He began by telling him the history of Zeller Jewelers. "Now, twenty years later, we have added gem cutting and polishing to our endeavors. We have dealt with cutters in Antwerp, and we have tried dealing with others in India. Quality has never been an issue; it's been all about time.

"We purchased an old warehouse, refurbished and subdivided it into three separate spaces; we leased two of them. The third space, we fashioned into a workshop, fully equipped with the latest tools, benches, lighting, and the myriad of items needed to produce a finished product—cut and polished diamonds for our customers—right here in Cape Town.

"Everything went according to plan, that is almost everything. The one thing we didn't anticipate was the difficulty finding cutters willing to relocate and come to work for us. We searched first in South Africa and then started contacting people out of the country; no one seemed anxious to join us.

"We convinced Saul Davis from our synagogue to come out of retirement to help us out. He agreed but stated emphatically that he was only willing to do so on a temporary basis.

"Phil and I are not looking to make the cutting center into any type of massive production entity; we envision three to four cutters at most. But one never knows. If time proves the facility can do more, then we will deal with it when that day comes.

"We came up with the idea of the center exclusively for Zeller's; cutting and polishing the rough stones that we purchase from various sources—all in South Africa. If we build a team of cutters that allows us to offer these services to others, we are open to that; but to offering our services only—we do not want to purchase rough stones for anyone but Zeller's. They would have to supply the stones to be finished.

"We realize that once the workshop is manned and running at full capacity, our options are limitless—we can provide these services to other jewelers in Cape Town, as well as all of South Africa and beyond.

"Tell me Ben, does this sound like something you might be interested in?"

Without hesitating, he replied. "It actually sounds better than I anticipated. The part I like best is the growth potential. To me it says, *the harder you work, the more successful you'll be.* In Russia, there was no growth, no potential, and no future."

Phil rose, excused himself, and left the room. When he returned, he turned to Ben. "Please come to the dining room where you can enjoy a second cup of coffee and dessert with Lena and Rene. Not only are they going to feed you, but perhaps bore you a bit with family pictures and the like. Phil and I need a few minutes."

Paul and Phil smiled as they heard laughter coming from the other room. At last Paul asked Ben to join them again.

"We discussed your compensation at great length. Coming up with a fair offer proved to be more difficult than we expected. Should we pay you by the piece? Should we pay you for your time? Should we just offer you a flat salary?

"After learning that you have so much more to offer, it was necessary for us to go back and look at hiring you in a different manner.

"As we tried to come up with an offer that would be beneficial to both you and Zeller's, we took into consideration the fact that you came here to relocate, and we realize this makes your needs greater at the onset.

"So Ben Lyons, we reached the decision to offer you a percentage in Zeller's Annex—the official name of the diamond cutting center. We are hereby offering you a salary and a 25% interest in the net profits of the Annex. We own the property outright so there will be no rent involved. Net profits will be figured and payable at the end of each calendar year.

"Zeller Jewelers will be the first Annex client and will pay the same rate for services as any future clients. Of course, we will look to you for guidance at setting prices based on what is involved in each particular case.

"To begin with, we will sit down with you to come up with fair compensation—enough to cover your living expenses, etc. We anticipate increasing your salary as business increases.

"There is no title for the position, at least there wasn't before this evening. Learning that you have abundantly more to offer than we were seeking has required us to take a different approach. We are still searching for additional cutters. When they come on board, yours will be the lead position. At that time, your title will become *Manager*.

"To be fair to all of us, if you accept our offer, we are proposing a probation period of ninety days where either party can change their mind. In the meantime, we will help you secure a place to live, introduce you to our community, and show you that a life in Cape Town can be good."

Ben sat silently. The Zeller brothers had given him a lot to think about. He came to South Africa for a job; they were offering him a life—a life far beyond his wildest imagination.

CHAPTER TWENTY-ONE

When ninety days had come and gone, neither the Zeller brothers nor Ben chose to cancel their agreement. Ben found an apartment on Long Street that was ideally located. As promised, he returned to The General Store and struck up a friendship with Franz Schiller. They attended services at the synagogue and learned about each other's pasts, and their reasons for leaving home. As Franz had stated that very first day at their very first meeting, "We all come seeking a better way of life."

Ben fell in love with the Annex. It was a far cry from the makeshift area his grandfather and father taught him and his brothers the art of diamond cutting and polishing. The newness, the cleanliness, the brightness—he actually loved getting up each morning, stopping at the corner café for a quick breakfast, and briskly walking to the Annex two blocks up from the harbor.

He quickly proved to the Zeller brothers that they had made a good choice in hiring him. Originally, the brothers felt offering him a percentage of the business would be incentive, but they quickly learned that Ben's incentive was inherent. He would never deliver less than his very best.

Six months after Ben's arrival, the Annex hired two brothers from Johannesburg, and Saul Davis returned to retirement. Ben, Jonah, and Nathan were a good team. They worked well together, and as each day passed, the Annex came into it's own. Their reputation grew, and the Annex began acquiring additional clients.

For the most part, Jonah and Nathan Kahn were loners. They were good workers, never late, eager to please, and willing to learn. They even managed to teach Ben a thing or two about the new *brilliant cut* they had first seen in

Johannesburg. Once they felt their jobs at the Annex were secure, they moved their families to Cape Town.

Ben assigned their work and helped them if needed. Nothing makes time pass faster than being occupied. With the additional clients, the Annex was consistently busy, and the months turned quickly into years.

Although several attempts were made to introduce Ben to widows at the synagogue, no one caught his eye. His business life was phenomenal; he had even purchased a small cottage of his own, yet he yearned for family.

One evening, as Ben sat relaxing with Franz after they had met for dinner, he commented. "We've been inundated with orders; trying to keep up gets harder by the day. I've been thinking of speaking with Paul and Phil about hiring one or two more men. If we don't, we will have to stop accepting new orders at the rate we have been."

"What about your brother Sidney? He's still in Cuba, is he not? Is he still hoping to get to America?"

Suddenly, Ben was all smiles. "Why Franz that's an excellent thought. I had given up on asking him to join me here; he turned me down many times. Now that years have passed, and he remains waiting to get to America—you might say, so close and yet so far—he might be more open to coming to Cape Town. I'll send him a wire in the morning."

Three months later, Ben met Sidney at the dock. The Annex now had a staff of four cutters. Business was good; business was about to get even better.

Extensive new diamond discoveries were made in South Africa in 1926 and 1927, first in Lichtenburg and then in Alexander Bay. By 1929, Oppenheimer secured controlling interest in both; however, the markets were flooded by these massive discoveries, and De Beers suffered considerably just as he took the helm at the onset of the Great Depression. Stagnant sales in the early 1930s—poor to nonexistent—resulted in mining coming to a complete halt in 1932.

For the next decade, Oppenheimer instituted important structural changes to De Beers and the diamond sales pipeline as he moved forward with his vision—a single organization that would be an exclusive marketing channel for world rough diamond production through a single central selling entity—the Diamond Corporation, Ltd., which was founded in 1930.

With rumors of war rampant; Nazism on the rise and spreading; and the world heading towards chaos, De Beers continued to increase its stockpile in London; the mines remained closed; and with each new discovery of diamonds, moved quickly to gain control of these new finds and shut them down.

For De Beers, it was *business as usual* with one goal in mind—*control*.

The looming war was about to add a new dimension to the diamond industry causing Oppenheim to shift focus to industrial diamonds.

The 1930s brought many changes to the diamond industry and to diamonds in South Africa, mostly due to the events leading up to and the eventual outbreak of World War II. Cape Town continued to prosper and grow; immigrants continued to arrive, but not as much to seek their fortunes in diamonds and gold as to escape the rise of Nazi tyranny all across Europe.

As Jews fled Nazi Germany during the mid-1930s, large numbers relocated to Cape Town. These new immigrants were mainly shopkeepers seeking to open their own establishments and carry on their trades from whence they came.

A number of groups sympathetic to Nazism emerged in South Africa. Perhaps the best known was the South African Nazi Party or more aptly known as the *Gryshemde* (Grey Shirts in Africa) because their paramilitary *Sturmabteilung*-like uniforms.

Its platform was the basic Nazi anti-Semitic rhetoric that extreme rightwing groups favored. The Grey Shirts were active in organizing large and sometimes violent street protests that for the most part were staged for show.

Headquartered in Cape Town, they opened a branch office in Pretoria and published a newsletter called *The Bulletin* where they attempted to justify the actions of the national socialists both in Germany and South Africa. Although the government closely monitored any and all of the Grey Shirts' activities, they were largely left alone.

The General Store had been open for business since diamonds were discovered in Kimberley. Simon Abel opened the store when his parents died, leaving their farm on the Orange River that had ceased being a working farm years prior.

Realizing Cape Town was the port of entry for a majority of the prospectors who came seeking their fortune in diamonds and gold, he equipped the store with the myriad of items including provisions that they needed to embark on their quests.

His store's location so close to the harbor was generally their first stop; and they came with cash in hand eager for advice and equipment. This worked out quite well for Simon, and he prospered.

Once De Beers gained control of the mines and closed them down, it became an ongoing problem for Franz to stay ahead of the game and continually shift his inventory to items he thought would appeal to his customers. The store's location had proven excellent for a general store, but others saw it as a prime location for other types of businesses.

Through the years, he had received offers from time to time to purchase the property for these other types of establishments, but he wasn't interested. If he gave up the store, what would he do? How would he spend his time? In addition, in the back of his mind loomed the diamonds hidden beneath the floor of his living quarters.

He had become good friends with Ben Lyons when he arrived in Cape Town, and since Sidney's arrival, considered him a good friend too. He decided to seek their advice about The General Store and what he could possibly do to increase business. On several occasions, the thought crossed his mind to seek advice from the brothers about the diamonds, but he wasn't quite ready for that decision, as yet.

Asking Ben and Sidney to meet him at his store one evening after closing, was the first step, and he awaited them.

They entered the store, and Ben called out, "Hello, are you here Franz?"

Coming into the store from the back, he greeted them warmly. "I asked you here tonight my good friends for a little advice, a little business advice. I'm hoping you can help me make a few changes to The General Store."

He gave them a brief overview of how and why Simon Abel opened it over sixty years before. "Now, all these years later, times have changed and continue to change and business has fallen off. I do not want to sell; nor do I want to go out of business. I really don't know what I want to do. What I do know is that the store is in an excellent location, and I'm trying to come up with a new entity to put in its place."

Sidney looked at Ben. "What did I tell you when I first arrived in town? If you remember, I said this would make a fantastic *smoke shop* featuring the best in *Cuban Cigars*. There is no such shop around here—this would be the first."

Ben nodded. "You did say exactly that, and I thought you were just missing your Cuba experience."

When Sidney arrived in Cuba, the only job he could find was working in a cigar factory. At first, he wasn't too happy, but after learning all aspects of the business from the owner himself, began to enjoy it immensely. Except for the fact that he had the distinct feeling that the owner was looking at him as a possible husband for his not too attractive daughter, he remained in the position his entire stay. The factory not only produced the best and most popular cigars in all of Cuba, but also several varieties of cigarettes.

Franz was quiet as he listened to his friend's suggestion. Sidney walked about showing Franz that he could make the store smaller and enlarge his living quarters, indicating where he envisioned cases and shelving could be installed. "You can put several chairs out front of the store where customers could enjoy a cigar and visit."

At first, Franz wasn't too keen on the idea, but as Sidney laid out a plan, he too began to envision—The Smoker's Shop.

"How involved would it be to turn this place around? I'd have to get rid of most of my merchandise. Of course, I have a lot of materials that can be used to transition the space, and if I do most of the work myself, the job should prove less costly.

"I know a couple of the vendors that sell their wares at the street markets, and they would probably be interested in some of the inventory. How long would you estimate making contact with suppliers and getting delivery of what I would need?"

"I think you can probably do it in two months, three at most. The biggest part would be here redoing the shop. As far as orders go, if you wire cash for payment until you set up an account, your merchandise would be shipped immediately. I might add that the factory I worked at is only one of many all over the Island. You would be wise to do business with several. I can recommend contacts and even place the initial orders for you."

Franz went to work on his new venture the very next day. He went to the street market in search of Jamilia who sold among other things, ornate wooden boxes that her son Afram carved by hand. The first time Franz saw them, he was amazed at the detailed carvings that featured tribal symbols and African animals. At the time Afram was a small boy.

He found her at her usual spot, and she greeted him warmly. Years earlier when her husband was killed, Franz helped her find work so she could support herself and her son. Afram was now ten years old, tall, and devoted to his mother. She taught him to read and write English, and instilled in him the importance of learning often telling him *if you learn something new each and every day imagine what you can learn in a lifetime!*

Although Franz had sought Jamilia out to offer her his inventory to sell, he left with far more. He hired Afram to help him build the cases and shelves for his new shop, and he commissioned him to supply hand-carved cigar boxes and humidors for his new customers.

Sidney helped place the initial orders for cigars, and cigarettes. They also ordered an array of pipes and tobacco and ashtrays. Once Franz had disposed of all of his inventory and the shop stood totally empty, Afram came to work to help make The Smoker's Shop a reality.

At last, they stood in the street in front of the store looking up at the big new sign that read *THE SMOKER'S SHOP*—then looking down at the chairs that sat on either side of the front door. The inside was clean and new and smelled of fresh paint. Several of Afram's hand-carved boxes sat on the shelves; two small humidors sat on the floor. A beautiful handcrafted rug of many colors covered the floor. All that was missing were their shipments from Cuba—due to arrive any day. The cases sat ready to receive the merchandise.

Even the living quarters in back of the store looked shiny and new. It too had a fresh coat of paint, and Franz purchased a larger rug to cover the expanded room. Everything was in place.

When the shipments arrived, Afram helped Franz display the cigars, and cigarettes in the cases. They built a special case with hooks to hold the pipes, and the loose tobacco was placed in bins to keep it fresh. The next day they would open for business and Franz told Afram he was expecting him to bring his mother to the *Grand Opening*.

After Afram left for home, Franz had one more thing to do. He summoned Ben and Sidney to the store where they lit up three of the best and most expensive cigars, and seated themselves out front on the chairs. If the numerous inquiries of passersby were any indication of how the shop would fare, success was inevitable.

The town welcomed the new shop, and Franz felt more alive than he had in years. Business was brisk with both locals and visitors. Once again he had come through for Jamilia and her son, but he felt they too had come through for him. The hand-carved boxes proved to be a popular item keeping Afram busier than ever.

———⟋⟋⟍———

Ben and Sidney kept in touch with Harry sporadically at best. They were each busy in their own world as the years passed into history. Rumors of war were just as rampant in South Africa as in London, especially with the continued influx of immigrants to Cape Town.

December 1936, the brothers received a letter from Harry telling them of Jacob's impending Bar Mitzvah the middle of January next. It had been almost seventeen years since they had seen one another. They decided to surprise Harry and Ada, meet their nephew and nieces for the first time, and celebrate Jacob's becoming a man.

When Ben told the Zellers of their plans, they urged them to stop by their father's jewelry store in London and introduce themselves. They planned to be in the London area for one week. They knew that Harry was working for De Beers, and although their primary reason for going was to see what little family they had left, they intended to see as much as possible on this visit; after all who knew when they would get the chance again.

As brothers growing up, they were close, but fate had cruelly separated them. They felt fortunate they were all doing well and living much better lives than what they had in Russia, but family was family. Ben and Sidney had never married so carrying on the Lyons name fell to Harry.

Franz and the Zeller brothers saw them off at the dock as they set sail for London, England. They carried with them a hand-carved box holding one dozen cigars—to celebrate Jacob's Bar Mitzvah. On the lid of the box was a beautifully and intricately carved head of a *Lion*.

Harry's surprise at looking up and seeing Ben and Sidney at the Great Central Synagogue attending Jacob's Bar Mitzvah was the ultimate blessing.

The brothers spent the week together—a week like no other in their entire lives.

Harry and Ada ushered them all around London, and introduced them to Max and Reba Lerner. They stopped by Zeller's and spent time with Paul and Phil's father; they went to Hatton Garden—London's diamond hub--and Harry took them to De Beers, where Marcus Hirsch welcomed them.

They spent time with their nephew and nieces. When they left Minsk,

Ada was barely eighteen, skinny, and somewhat awkward. She had blossomed into a beautiful woman whose contentment with life showed. Ben and Sidney envied their brother, his beautiful family, and their life in the Jewish community.

In the back of his mind, Ben had thought about asking Harry to join them in Cape Town so they could once again be together. After seeing what Harry had built for his family and how happy they all were sadly convinced him otherwise, and he abandoned his plan.

The week flew by quickly and although it seemed they had just arrived, it was time for the brothers to leave and return to Cape Town. It was a solemn goodbye at the dock. It took seventeen years to bring them together; they all hoped that their next meeting would be sooner rather than later.

As year after year of the 1930s peeled away, and the inevitability of war became reality, when and where would the quirks of fate that govern life and death unite them once again?

CHAPTER TWENTY-TWO

Ben and Sidney returned to Cape Town and their small circle of friends came to meet them at the dock. The Zeller brothers and their wives, Franz, Jamilia, and Afram were all happy to see them. As they made their way up the hill to The Smoker's Shop, Franz invited everyone in. He closed and locked the door, and asked Jamilia to help him bring in an assortment of sandwiches, cheese and crackers, fruit, and bottles of wine to celebrate their safe return.

Although Ben and Sidney were exhausted, they were overwhelmed at their friends' gesture of kindness. They had all become family.

They learned Franz's shop was doing good; Jonah and Norman had been working overtime to keep up with demand; and Franz surprised everyone by announcing he had a lead on a new client for the Annex—to be discussed in the coming days.

In turn, Ben and Sidney told them about their experience in London. They spoke of Harry, Ada, Jacob and the twins, and what a fine family their brother had; they described their visit to Hatton Garden and De Beers where Harry worked; and they told them about their visit to their father's store. Ben reached into his pocket and removed an envelope handing it to Paul. "Your father asked me to give this to you."

It was late when everyone reluctantly decided it was time to go home. Although it was only a short walk, the Zellers offered Ben and Sidney a ride home. Jamilia and Afram stayed to help Franz put everything away.

As much as they enjoyed London, it was good to be home. It was even better to want to be home

Franz was true to his promise of a new client for the Annex. Allowing Ben and Sidney time to settle back in after returning from their trip to London, he decided after two weeks had passed to arrange a business meeting.

For the most part, during the week, everyone was busy working; it was on weekends that they generally met at Sabbath Services. On occasion, Franz and the brothers had dinner together, met to discuss or seek advice on a specific topic, or just for a little company.

Franz realized how important Ben and Sidney's friendship had become to him in the weeks they spent travelling to, during, and from London home. He and Ben had become friends when each needed a friend; Sidney had been key in turning his life around by coming up with the idea of his new shop. If he couldn't trust the Lyons brothers, whom could he trust?

He chose Sunday for the meeting suggesting they meet for an early dinner, after which he planned to invite them back to his living quarters. The store closed, and Sunday normally a quiet day on the streets, led him to believe he could at long last relieve the burden of guilt that he carried most of his life.

They dined at one of their favorite restaurants next door to the Metropole Hotel. They were all in a good mood. The brothers were pleased with their decision to visit Harry and his family, and they actually were quite taken with London. For a brief moment, Franz felt sad that he had no one—even 6,000 miles across the ocean, but as the moment passed, it only confirmed that he was doing the right thing.

They arrived at the store and made their way to the back. He offered them cigars; they accepted; and as they sat back relaxed, Franz took center stage.

From Hamburg, Germany, to Cape Town, South Africa, to the Orange River, he kept his friends spellbound for almost an hour. Speaking from the heart, he left no reason to doubt him. When he reached the end of his story, he stood and left the room, coming back with a bottle of wine and three glasses.

"I collected thousands of rough diamonds—exactly how many I can't tell you. I never counted them. I came home after each visit and simply added them to my cache. I had no idea what I was going to do with them, yet I continued to return to the farm, continued to collect the stones, and continued to deny I had a right to them."

He challenged Ben and Sidney. "I realize this is a lot to comprehend in one sitting; does anything come to mind? Do you have any suggestions?"

Ben and Sidney were stunned. For what seemed a long time, no one spoke as they collected their thoughts.

At last Ben asked, "Where are the diamonds?"

Franz smiled for the first time. "I keep them in a crate hidden beneath the floor upon which we are sitting."

The brothers looked at one another amazed. "Are they secured under lock and key? Weren't you ever worried that you would be robbed?"

"No to both of your questions. I never told anyone about the diamonds; I basically had no life; I became a loner. No one ever came to the store except for customers, and honestly I guess I didn't look smart enough to be concealing anything, let alone thousands of rough diamonds. They saw me as a young man trying to make a living, and they all knew I was a hard worker who had helped Simon immensely.

"When I took over the store, I was welcomed by the Town, managing to increase business in the early years although I was not yet twenty years of age, and had never run a business. In the ensuing years, I helped a lot of people in the community in any way I could whenever the need arose.

Once I no longer had ties to Simon's farmhouse, I started attending services at the synagogue to meet people. I welcomed your friendship Ben, and Sidney's when he moved here. We've been good friends and spent some good times together, have we not?

"While you were away, I did a lot of thinking about the diamonds, certainly more than I've thought about them in all the years since I first found them. I still don't know what to do with them. I did, however, make the decision to become a client of the Annex that is if you will accept me. I would like to have the rough diamonds cut, polished, and appraised. I will pay you for the services, of course. The time has come for me to know what I have."

Sidney turned to Ben and asked, "What do you think? Can we help our friend?"

"We can, and we most certainly will. On the other hand, we must not act hastily; we must think the situation through thoroughly leaving no loopholes. I cannot justify picking up a new client of this magnitude without discussing it with the Zellers, but I think it best that Franz remain anonymous by setting up an account bearing an anonymous name and paying for our services with bank drafts.

"We start by counting and sorting the diamonds which will have to be done right here. This limits our time to evenings and weekends when the store is closed. Although I don't feel you have kept them secure all these years, I cannot deny that they have in fact apparently been quite safe after all. Moving them elsewhere is not an option; there is no way and nowhere safer to move them.

"Once we know how many stones we are dealing with, we will get a better idea of how to proceed to cutting and polishing. They will have to be given to the Annex in batches based on availability of the cutters and workload. My suggestion is to begin with smaller stones, and appraise each batch as it is finished.

"I have no knowledge whatsoever of any legal ramifications where you would have to show how you acquired the rough diamonds. I just don't know. In all the years I've worked at the Annex, we have never had an instance where a client was questioned about the stones they sent us."

Ben looked at Franz. "Can we see the diamonds? See what we are dealing with?"

Franz stood and pushed the table in front of the sofa aside. He rolled the rug back and lifted the door, revealing a stairway leading down below to the small storage area that Simon had included when he built the original store. He beckoned them to follow.

On a bench against the wall sat a large covered wooden crate—it had a latch but was unlocked. Slowly, Franz released the latch and opened the lid. Filled to capacity the crate's contents sparkled in the dimly lit space. It had been years since Franz had viewed them; and there he stood as much in awe as Ben and Sidney.

"Diamonds have been in my life since I was born yet I have never seen this many stones—certainly not at one time. This will be a huge undertaking to say the least, but you are a good man and our good friend, and there isn't anything within my power I wouldn't do for you. I am sure Sidney agrees with me."

Without removing his eyes from the diamonds, Sidney nodded.

"I welcome you as a client of the Annex. We have a lot of work ahead of us, but proceeding cautiously and diligently is paramount. I will not speak to the Zellers until we are ready to accept the first batch of stones."

They shook hands on the deal. Ben promised to formulate a plan with Franz to begin sorting and counting the diamonds.

———✺———

Perhaps he never felt the diamonds belonged to him because he had gathered them to help his mutti—the diamonds belonged to her.

After his friends left, Franz fell into a troubled sleep. He dreamt of his mutti reaching out for help—he hadn't been able to help her—he was too late.

He chided himself how different his life might have been if he had been able to bring her to Cape Town—finding the diamonds would have had meaning, would have changed their world.

He never learned what had become of his father, his four sisters, and his brother who was an infant when he left. With the rise of Nazism in Germany and fleeing refuges' reports of their treatment of Jews, he thought about his Jewish grandparents; in all probability they were no longer alive.

CHAPTER TWENTY-THREE

They met as often as they could, on weekdays after The Smoker's Shop closed and on weekends. Ben suggested that Franz build three crates—small to hold the larger stones, medium to hold the medium stones, and large to hold the smaller stones. They went to work sorting them by placing them in the crates according to size. They were surprised to find that there was an equal amount of smaller and medium stones, but also a fair amount of larger rock-size diamonds.

By the time they finished sorting and counting, they made plans to move forward. Franz chose *Shiloh* as his client name—meaning *the one to whom it belongs*—in Hebrew. He advised the Zeller brothers of their new client, seeing no need to offer the number of diamonds involved or the client's true identity. Their decision to submit them in batches made the information unnecessary.

Ben regulated the number of rough stones submitted by Shiloh based on the workload of the Annex. When times were slower, he accepted more; when they were swamped with other orders, he accepted less, but always accepting some regardless of how few.

Franz assigned the task of building a chest to hold the finished diamonds to Afram. He wrote *Shiloh* in Hebrew on a piece of paper and asked him to carve the letters of the name on the lid. As Ben and Sidney delivered each batch, he deposited them in the chest that sat in his sitting area in full view— placing them there only after the brothers left. A shallow tray sat atop the stones hiding them from view when one lifted the lid on the chest.

Month after month after month, the finished pile increased while the rough diamonds in the storage area decreased. As each batch was delivered to Franz, he presented the Annex with a bank draft from his account. Through the years, he had amassed a small fortune. He lived frugally, had very few expenses, and The General Store had done quite well up to the time he turned it into The Smoker's Shop, which in turn was passing all expectations.

9 November 1938—*Kristallnacht—the night of broken glass* was a night of horror. The Nazis torched synagogues, vandalized Jewish homes, schools, and businesses and killed 100 Jews. It was the start of Nazi Germany's march across Europe, invading and occupying country after county.

On 1 September 1939, the Nazis invaded Poland; Great Britain under a Mutual Assistance Treaty were committed to defend the Poles. When Germany did not respond to the ultimatum issued by Neville Chamberlain for immediate withdrawal of German troops, Great Britain declared War on Germany.

Now that Britain had entered the War, the strategic importance of industrial diamonds became acutely clear to the Allies, and to the United States.

Diamonds were needed to stamp out the millions of precision parts necessary for mass production of airplane engines, torpedoes, tanks, artillery, and other weapons of war.

However, diamonds and only diamonds could be used to draw the fine wire needed for radar and the electronics of war; diamonds and only diamonds could provide the jeweled bearings necessary for the stabilizers, gyroscopes, and guidance systems for submarines and planes; diamonds and only diamonds could provide the abrasives necessary for rapidly converting civilian industries into a war machine.

Without a continuing supply of diamonds, a war machine would slow to a halt. Yet, De Beers who controlled the world supply of diamonds, kept the mines closed, and continued to stockpile any additional diamond acquisitions under the leadership of Sir Ernest Oppenheimer—a British subject.

In preparation of war, Hitler had been stockpiling diamonds since 1936. Once hostilities broke out, he continued to import diamonds from South

American producers over which De Beers had no control, namely Brazil and Venezuela.

When Britain declared war against Germany, although the United States remained neutral, they pledged their support to Britain. As Hitler's armies swept across Europe in a Blitzkrieg and threatened to invade England, it became clear a very real possibility existed that the world's diamond stockpile could fall into Hitler's hands. The loss of De Beers' stockpile would render the UK impossible to continue fighting a war.

At that time, the United States had less than a year's supply of industrial diamonds. When economic planners estimated that America needed at least 6.5 million carats of industrial diamonds to convert its factories to war production, President Roosevelt ordered the War Production Board to purchase the diamonds necessary from De Beers.

Oppenheimer resisted. He personally opposed the sale of diamonds to the United States; it ran counter to all De Beers stood for and all he had accomplished. Its entire system of monopolizing diamonds depended on its controlling the available stockpile. If they honored the purchase, and the war suddenly ended, they would have no control over the release of the remaining diamonds, undercutting the entire world order that he had so vigorously constructed.

Eventually an agreement was reached where the diamonds would be supplied on a continual, as needed basis.

Poland's defeat by Germany was followed by the *Phony War;* over the winter of 1939-1940, neither Germany nor Britain and the Allies launched a major attack. In the spring of 1940, Germany invaded France, Belgium, Holland, Norway, and Denmark. These offenses became known as— *Blitzkrieg* meaning *lightening war*—due to the speed of the attacks.

During the Battle of Britain, which lasted from June to September 1940, Germany's Luftwaffe failed miserably in their attempt to dominate the British Royal Air Force. The Battle, was Hitler's first defeat, and rendered him unable to move forward with his planned invasion of Britain, but not without leaving a wide path of destruction—the devastating air raids on London.

In November 1940, the Zeller brothers received a wire from London from their father notifying them that Zeller's—a London landmark established by their grandfather, carried on by their father, and where the brothers had learned all they knew about the business—had been destroyed by a Luftwaffe air raid.

Zeller's, on track to celebrate 75 years of business in the spring of 1941, was a total loss. When Ben and Sidney returned to Cape Town, they brought with them a letter from the brothers' father. He wrote of health problems both he and their mother were facing, and he urged them to consider leaving South Africa, return to London, and takeover the Landmark store.

For over three years, Paul and Phil had agonized over their father's request. The brothers did not wish to leave what they had built, the success they enjoyed, or the lifestyle they had grown accustomed to. As upstanding members of the Town's business and Jewish communities, they viewed their thirty-five years in Cape Town as an investment that had truly paid off. They considered South Africa their home and their future, not England.

They had never given their father an outright denial or acceptance of his proposal. They were planning to travel to London to celebrate Zeller's 75th Anniversary; at that time they would have a heart-to-heart talk with their father and explain that their best interests were vested in South Africa.

The following week, they received a wire from Phil's eldest daughter. Their father had suffered a massive heart attack. She urged them to drop everything and come immediately.

After making arrangements for the store, and the Annex in their absence, they set sail for London. By the time their ship docked in England, their father had died.

World War II escalated dramatically when Germany formed the Axis Alliance with Italy and Japan in June 1941.

The South African government acted swiftly and issued a proclamation. For the next four years, the Union of South Africa was officially at war with Imperial Japan.

Although the South African economy was not immediately affected, the foundation was laid for a war economy and for massive war production.

The government saw Japan's entry into the War as a very real threat to South Africa with emphasis on the vulnerability of her coasts and harbors. The Country's coastal defenses were planned to meet simple hit-and-run raids, but with the Japanese forces overrunning one area after the other in the East, they feared a full-scale invasion.

Although the Japanese war machine was formidable in December 1941, it was the Japanese Navy that posed the greatest threat to the Allies. It was of the highest urgency that South Africa ready herself for a possible Japanese incursion into the Indian Ocean.

Ben and Sidney were beside themselves with worry. They had not heard from Harry since the air raids had begun. They had written twice, but had received no response as yet. In January 1941, they decided to send a wire to Harry at De Beers; it was a good decision. Several days later, they received a wire back, stating that despite the unending air raids on London, they were all safe. Harry added that they had purchased a house outside the city limits and were due to move within weeks, putting them at a distance from the attacks on the City and its harbors.

The Zeller brothers remained in London; their mother was not fairing well. Phil and Lena's daughters both living in England, urged their parents, aunt, and uncle to take whatever time was needed to make arrangements for their mother's care and to settle their father's estate. With the War escalating, they pointed out the possibility existed that the time might soon come when they would be unable to return to England at will.

Ben had no idea how Zeller Jewelers was doing; the employees the brothers had placed in charge seemed to be taking care of business as usual; and it was not his responsibility. The Annex, however, had seen a decrease in new orders, and in the brothers' absence, no work was being processed for the store.

Ben utilized this down time to continue to satisfy what had become the Annex's No. 1 client—*Shiloh*. At long last, the end seemed in sight. He estimated that if all went well, by mid-April, if not sooner, Franz's cache of rough diamonds would be cut and polished. All that remained was for Franz to catalogue the appraisals and summarize the number of diamonds and their weight to determine what they were worth.

As Ben had calculated, the first week in April, he notified Franz that he and Sidney would bring the final batch by his shop after the Annex closed for the day.

When the brothers arrived at The Smoker's Shop, Franz beckoned them in and locked the door behind them. He took the diamonds and asked that they wait for him. He entered his living area, and hastily placed the diamonds inside the chest. He picked up the bank draft, and grabbing a jacket came back into the shop.

He handed Ben the final payment on his *Shiloh* account, shook hands with both brothers, and said, "You have my undying gratitude. I can never thank you enough for what you have done for me, nor could I ever repay you. To start, however, please join me for a celebratory dinner."

"We were happy to help you in any way we could. As far as repaying us, you paid for our services, and no further payment is required; the Annex profited and kept us busy. And don't be so sure there won't be an occasion to call on you for a helping hand. That's what friends are for, are they not?"

The three of them left the shop for the short walk up to Long Street to the restaurant, but not before Franz grabbed three cigars for an after dinner smoke.

Their friendship had endured for years without a single disagreement. They began as friends, but they had become family.

Exactly one week after their celebratory dinner, Ben and Sidney received a wire from Marcus Hirsch. Their minds unwilling to comprehend what their eyes saw, as they read and reread the words on the paper Ben's trembling hand held.

PLEASE ACCEPT CONDOLENCES—STOP—SORRY TO ADVISE, BROTHER HARRY AND ENTIRE FAMILY EXCEPT FOR NEPHEW JACOB KILLED IN AIR RAID ON FRIDAY NIGHT LAST—STOP—JACOB LEFT TO JOIN RAF—STOP—WILL SEND INFO AS AVAILABLE—STOP

MARCUS HIRSCH
DE BEERS, LONDON, ENGLAND

Franz urged Ben and Sidney to go to the synagogue and seek out the Rabbi for comfort and spiritual advice. Sidney was willing; Ben adamantly refused. As he vowed never to set foot inside a synagogue again, Sidney continued to accompany Franz to the Sabbath Services relentlessly seeking advice to help Ben.

In the following months, they received three additional wires from Marcus Hirsch. The first notified them that a Memorial Service had been held one week after the tragedy, and that Jacob after being sworn in had reported for basic training in England.

The second notified them that Jacob was en route to the United States for flight training to become a Royal Air Force pilot.

The third notified the brothers that the remains had been recovered and Harry and his family were buried in the Brady Street Cemetery per Jacob's instructions.

To Ben, although each wire was encouraging, there was a deep sadness that engulfed him. At times, Sidney saw signs that gave him hope his brother was returning to his usual self; but all too often that hope was dashed when he caught him staring into space for long periods of time. He worried about him constantly. Neither he nor Franz could get through to him, and he remained adamant against speaking with the Rabbi.

When the Zeller brothers finally returned, hardly any aspect of Cape Town life remained unaffected by the War in some way. The rationing of petrol restricted the movement of people; commodities such as motor vehicles, building materials, rubber, wood, paper, and agricultural implements were declared *controlled goods.*

A shortage developed in food, such as meat, wheat, corn, and sugar, and wholesale and retail price indexes rose, causing the government to implement price controls.

There was greater austerity in the country, as people began feeling the pinch of shortages and the accompanying rising costs. The realization that *war has its price* settled on the residents of Cape Town.

All business establishments were affected. With profits down and prices up, people had less to spend on unnecessary items. The Annex still had several active accounts, but was barely turning a profit.

Paul met with Ben to discuss letting Jonah and Nathan go; there was barely enough work for two cutters. Ben wouldn't hear of it; they had families; where could they go? He convinced him to keep the brothers saying he and Sidney would take a reduction in pay until things improved. Paul was grateful.

Ben, Sidney, and Franz continued to have dinner and enjoy a good cigar together albeit less frequently since rationing became a way of life. At times, they had dinner at the brothers' cottage by pooling their rations.

In April 1942, Franz was greeted by his *old friend* Ben opening the door bidding him, "Come in, come in. Dinner is almost ready, but first we will have a drink together."

Franz had no idea what had occurred to bring the old Ben back, and he didn't much care. It had been one year since learning the devastating news of the tragedy in London. As the days and months passed, Ben remained withdrawn at best, and it had been a long time since a smile lit up his face— until tonight.

There was no wine this night. Three glasses and a bottle of Vodka 100%

Proof sat on the table. Next to the bottle laid the wire from Marcus Hirsch that had arrived that afternoon.

JACOB SAFELY BACK IN ENGLAND—STOP—FULL-FLEDGED RAF PILOT—STOP—WILL NOTIFY WHEN POSTED—STOP—MAZEL TOV—STOP

MARCUS HIRSCH
DE BEERS, LONDON, ENGLAND

CHAPTER TWENTY-FOUR

From the beginning of the War, South African Air and Naval Forces played an important role in watching over the trade routes along the Country's shores. In addition, far away from enemy air force bases, South African air space was ideally suited for training purposes.

As early as 1940, the South African government announced the British had accepted their offer of facilities for training airmen—a scheme that resulted in far reaching consequences for both the Royal Air Force and the South African Air Force. The Joint Air Training Scheme turned out to be one of the Country's great success stories of the War. Even after the War had ended in Europe, it continued to provide a steady stream of pilots in the struggle against Japan.

By the end of 1943, the war at sea and the threat of Japanese invasion of South Africa began to abate.

For the most part, Cape Town residents felt fortunate that the War had not come to their doorstep. Enduring rationing and shortages seemed inconsequential compared to other countries around the world.

On the eve of the War, ninety percent of Antwerp's diamond businesses were in Jewish hands. It was at that time the most important center for diamond trade, totaling eighty percent of the world's production and commercial activity. Only the distribution of raw diamonds was beyond Antwerp's control; that control rested in the hands of the London Syndicate—The Diamond Trading Company—an affiliate of the South African conglomerate De Beers.

In 1934, a partnership established the first financial institution to focus solely and entirely on the needs of the diamond industry, and opened its registered office in the very heart of Antwerp's diamond district—*Comptoir Diamantaire Anverois*. In 1937, Belgium passed reform legislation that allowed the entity to become a Bank.

Throughout the ensuing years leading up to the War, and as Jewish immigrants fleeing persecution in Germany and Eastern Europe poured into the country, the vast majority settled in the diamond districts of Antwerp and Brussels.

The diamond industry in Antwerp so disproportionately Jewish in membership was of great concern to the Bank. Adopting a proactive stance, in 1940 before the German invasion of Belgium, the managing director and his staff moved their clients' diamond stock, consisting of loan collateral and goods in custody, and shipped them via France to England and ultimately into the United States. When the German occupation forces arrived, they found the safes, deposit boxes, and accounts empty.

Although Germany's goal was to eliminate the Jews, before they did so, they would have to tolerate them until they could exploit the Jewish diamond dealers in order to supply the German war machine with vitally needed raw materials. In short order, they rendered Antwerp's diamond industry non-existent.

As part of the *Final Solution*, from 1942 forward, the persecution of Belgian Jews escalated, but they were not alone. Important politicians who had opposed the Nazis before the War, Prime Minister Paul-Emile Janson, and thousands of Catholic workers accused of plotting a large-scale strike became victims, as well.

News from the War and reports of the Allies' victory after victory was a welcome start to the New Year—1944. With the debilitation of Antwerp's diamond industry, the Annex acquired several new accounts and coupled with Zeller Jewelers increasing their demand, business picked up.

It was good to be busy again, and to add to their elation Ben and Sidney were surprised and overwhelmed with emotion to receive a wire from Jacob.

HOPE ALL IS WELL—STOP—ALL IS WELL HERE—
STOP—WILL VISIT WHEN WAR IS OVER—STOP

JACOB LYONS
LONDON, ENGLAND

To Ben the wire was so heartfelt that he folded the paper and carried it on his person wherever he went. It gave him hope that the War would soon end, and even if just on a visit, they would spend time with Jacob again.

The Smoker's Shop was holding its own, just as most of the town did the same. Business was down somewhat, but it was more difficult and took longer to receive shipments from Cuba, so it all seemed to work out.

The brothers and Franz continued to get together for dinner. On occasion, Ben and Sidney would drop by the shop for a good cigar, and they would sit on the chairs discussing all they looked forward to after the War.

By April, business at the Annex had increased substantially, and whereas in the past, being busy made the time pass faster urging one to move forward, Ben noticed that for several days now, Sidney appeared withdrawn.

"What's wrong my brother? Is something bothering you? Have I upset you in any way?"

"No, nothing you've done. I'm not feeling too well. Just tired I guess; we have been pretty busy of late."

"Do you think you should see a doctor? I'll go with you."

"I thought about it, but I really think I am just tired. Tomorrow is Friday; if I don't feel better over the weekend, I'll go on Monday."

The next day, as they left the Annex and walked home, Sidney decided to give it one more try. "Ben, I'm meeting Franz at the synagogue for services; why don't you join us? It's been three years since we lost Harry and his family, and Jacob seems to be doing well. I'm sure you're counting the days until he comes to visit us."

Ben's hand reached in his pocket covering the folded wire from Jacob. "You're right. They say *Time heals all wounds*. I guess some wounds just take a longer time to heal."

When they arrived at the synagogue, Franz was surprised to see Ben but decided not to say anything. He was truly glad to see him attend services, so he simply hugged his friend. They walked in and took seats.

Following the services, Ben was quite touched by the many congregants who welcomed him back, thinking perhaps he had stayed away too long or perhaps he reacted badly and shouldn't have stayed away at all.

As they walked down the steps to the street, Sidney collapsed. Almost immediately Dr. Berg was at his side. The ambulance arriving minutes later transported him to Groote Schuur Hospital.

The large government-funded teaching Hospital was founded in 1938, as the chief academic hospital of the University of Cape Town's Medical School providing care and instruction in all the major branches of medicine.

Sydney suffered a massive heart attack. For one week, Ben did not leave his side refusing to go home while Franz pleaded his case to hospital officials. At last, they relented and allowed him to stay—realizing that he wasn't leaving anyway. He brought Ben a change of clothes and visited each day to make certain he was eating.

Sidney remained unchanged. They stabilized him, assessed the damage, and waited for him to regain consciousness. Exactly one week to the day, hooked up to a myriad of tubes and machines, Sidney awoke. He was groggy and disoriented, but opened his eyes to see Ben hovering over him.

Suddenly surrounded by doctors and nurses, he answered questions, moved his limbs when asked, and lay there as they notated their charts.

Although the heart attack was extensive, he was not paralyzed, and they were pleased with his progress thus far. However, they warned of the long road to recovery ahead of him, and cautioned against speeding up the process. One thing for certain, Ben would see to it that when Sidney was released from the hospital, he would be moved to and remain in a healthcare facility until he fully recovered.

Ben returned to work at the Annex; he visited Sidney every day; he attended Sabbath Services with Franz every weekend praying for his full recovery.

Although the Annex continued to enjoy an increase in business, Jonah, Nathan, and Ben managed to keep up without Sidney by working extra hours when needed.

News from the War continued to be hopeful and many were predicting an end to the fighting in Europe mere months away. Although they had not heard from Jacob again, they realized that being at war had its limits, and they were grateful that Marcus Hirsch had kept them apprised all along.

Ben decided against sending a wire when Sidney suffered his heart attack. At first, the thought never crossed his mind. As he improved, Ben not knowing how long it would take or when the news would reach Jacob, thought it best to leave things as they were.

Sidney came home the middle of May. He couldn't return to work just yet, but he could do just about anything else. He walked all over the town and was surprised to see many things for the first time although he had lived in Cape Town for almost fifteen years. He stopped and talked with many of the merchants up and down the streets that converged in the center of town.

Ben hired Jamilia to cook for them; Sidney was on a restricted diet. Franz stopped by every day, and Afram too found time to visit bringing him a carved wooden Elephant with its trunk pointed up. On these visits, he got to know the boy who was quickly becoming a young man. He spoke to him at length about his woodcarvings and how they, in many ways, equated to cutting diamonds.

"How did you learn to carve? Did you just pick it up yourself? Did someone teach you?"

"My father began teaching me when I was a little boy, but then he died. After he died, I was so sad, my mother encouraged me to try perfecting it on my own, telling me that it would make me feel closer to him. She was right, and it helped me deal with losing him.

"In fact, carving came quite easily to me. I found I could pick up a piece of wood and in minutes create an animal as seen in the many books my mother bought for me. It was she who taught me what each animal symbolizes in

African culture. When I started making the boxes, I carved notches around the base weaving them into different designs. I guess you could say the notches resemble the cuttings on a diamond.

"This Elephant signifies strength, royalty, dignity, patience, wisdom, longevity, and happiness—all of which my mother and I wish for you. Its trunk pointing upward is a symbol of good luck."

Sidney was amazed. "Your story is similar to mine. When I was a small boy, my grandfather and father taught my brothers and me the art of cutting stones. When I've made a full recovery, I'm going to find the time to show you how we take a rough diamond and turn it into a beautiful and shiny gemstone."

Afram flashing a broad grin on his face said, "Thank you sir; I'd like that."

Jamilia and Afram left for home. Dinner sat waiting for Ben to arrive; Franz was joining them.

Ben left the Annex and met Franz at the shop for the walk home. They entered the cottage and found Sidney slumped over in his chair. Cold to Ben's touch, he had died peacefully shortly after Jamilia and Afram had left.

After years of agonizing over the loss of Harry and his family, Ben was finally in a good place. All indications that the War would soon be over buoyed his hopes and dreams for a future with his nephew. Whether Jacob came to Cape Town or he and Sidney moved to London, it made no difference. His dream was that they should and would be together.

Sidney's passing brought an abrupt end to that dream, and he began formulating a new plan.

Franz stood by his good friend and mourned Sidney as his own. He was amazed and yet concerned that Ben was calmly making arrangements and appeared so certain with each step he took.

He arranged for a memorial service at the synagogue. Against the Rabbi's advice and tradition, he had Sidney cremated. He intended to keep his ashes until the War ended, when he would bury them in London alongside Harry. At that time, he too would leave Cape Town and relocate to London to be with the only family he had left.

After his week of mourning, Ben sent a wire to Jacob via Marcus Hirsch at De Beers in London.

SIDNEY SUDDENLY PASSED AWAY WEDNESDAY
LAST—STOP—RECOVERING FROM HEART
ATTACK SUFFERED IN APRIL—STOP

BENJAMIN LYONS
CAPE TOWN, SOUTH AFRICA

The wires crossed in the sending. As Marcus Hirsch received the wire
from Ben, Ben received the following wire from Marcus:

JACOB LISTED OFFICIALLY AS MISSING—STOP—
NO PLANE WRECKAGE FOUND—STOP—WILL
ADVISE FURTHER INFO AS AVAILABLE—STOP

MARCUS HIRSCH
DE BEERS, LONDON, ENGLAND

6 June—D-Day, the Allied troops land along the Normandy coast and
begin the liberation of France. The news is broadcast all over the world.

Once again, Ben grew withdrawn and depressed, as once again Franz
grew weary. He didn't know how to help his friend. He made it a point to
have dinner with him every day. Jamilia continued to prepare meals for them
when she was asked to do so, and she and Afram helped in any way they could.

August brought news in the form of another wire from Marcus Hirsch.

JACOB ALIVE AND SAFE—STOP—NO FURTHER
INFO AVAILABLE—STOP—CONDOLENCES ON
THE LOSS OF SIDNEY—STOP

MARCUS HIRSCH
DE BEERS, LONDON, ENGLAND

Although Marcus had been told in strictest confidence about Jacob's
survival and whereabouts, he could not let one more day go by without

notifying Ben Lyons. He knew he had no other family left and could only imagine what he was going through.

The wire brought Ben back to life. He resumed making plans for the future. He had been in Cape Town for almost twenty years; his arrangement with the Zeller brothers had proven quite profitable. Having saved most of his earnings by living frugally, Ben was financially well off.

He would say nothing to the Zeller brothers until the War had finally ended, Jake returned to London, and he had a date for his departure. He would not allow anyone to change his mind. In the meantime, he wrestled with the thought of telling Franz his plans. He knew he had no family, and now with Sidney gone, he was his only friend and confidant just as Franz was his. Although he was nearing eighty years of age, he was in good health and showed no signs of slowing down.

After receiving the last wire, Ben's attitude became more positive, and he and Franz returned to dining at their favorite local spots. News of the War was good, and they often spoke of how nice it would be to return to a normal way of life; the way it was before the War. Ben continued to evade the issue and never summoned enough courage to reveal his plans to join Jacob in London.

CHAPTER TWENTY-FIVE

The North African Campaign of WWII took place in North Africa from 1940 to 1943, fought between the Allies and Axis powers, and dominated by the British Commonwealth and exiles from German occupied Europe. When the United States entered the War in December 1941, it offered direct military assistance to the Campaign.

Fighting in North Africa started with the Italian declaration of war in June 1940, included battles fought in the Libyan and Egyptian deserts, and ended when the Allies encircled Axis forces in northern Tunisia and forced their surrender in May 1943.

Rudy Schiller was sick of war. He joined the Hitler Youth Program when he was twelve years old to spite his father but soon regretted it, realizing he had simply traded one disciplinarian for another. Germany's rigid military regulations were not at all to his liking. Once he had joined, however, he saw no way out. At eighteen, he was inducted into the German Army.

When he learned his unit was being shipped to North Africa, his outlook brightened. He paid a visit to his father to bid him goodbye, planning to spend the afternoon with him. His real reason for coming home was to retrieve a letter found among his grandmother's things when she died. The letter was from his uncle, his father's older brother, who lived in South Africa. In the letter, he urged his mutti to bring his siblings and join him for a better life in Cape Town, further stating he ran a general store, and offered to send passage.

At the age of two, his father went to live with his grandparents. When his grandmother died, he was eight years old; he spent the next ten years in

Saint Martin's Orphanage for Boys. At eighteen, he left the orphanage to return to Hamburg. Pleased that Sister Margaret came to bid him farewell, he made no notice of the letter she slipped into his bag as she hugged him and wished him well.

Not knowing what to make of the letter and having no interest when he discovered it, his father chose not to pursue it. He never learned what happened to his four sisters who were also sent to orphanages.

The hour was growing late, when at last his father went down to the cellar. He quickly retrieved the letter from the box where his father kept it.

When his father returned, he was gone.

Rudy Schiller had no idea where Africa was located. He had no idea of the distance between the northern tip of North Africa to the southern tip of South Africa. He also had no idea how he was going to get from North Africa to South Africa while he was in the German Army and not free to travel at will. Yet, none of these facts deterred him.

For three years he fought in battle after battle managing to stay alive and unhurt. In May 1943, after their final defeat, the Axis troops were ordered to retreat to Italy. There was no way Rudy was leaving Africa without attempting to locate his uncle.

The night before they were due to move out, Rudy fled the Camp and began his journey to Cape Town. For the next eight months he traveled 5,000 miles from country through country, Algeria to Cape Town on the southern tip of South Africa. With no cash to speak of, he stopped in the larger cities where he found work easily staying until he had enough funds to continue his travels.

January 1945, Rudy Schiller finally reached his goal—Cape Town, South Africa. Although he did not arrive by ship, he wandered down to the dock seeking information about the local general store.

He stopped three people, asking them for the location and directions to a general store. Each of their answers was one in the same. "Town hasn't had a general store for years. Hasn't been a need for one in years."

Rudy stood speechless. It had all been for naught. He silently cursed his father for not having pursued the letter years before.

What was he to do now? He couldn't return home; there was nothing waiting there for him except possible arrest and imprisonment for having deserted. The War was still being fought, and the Axis had suffered numerous defeats in recent months. He determined he had but one option—find work until he could hop a freighter or book passage somewhere, anywhere but Germany.

He was successful in finding jobs along the dock during the day, spending his nights at the YMCA and eating as inexpensively as possible. After he had been in Cape Town a few weeks, he noticed as he approached the harbor that a large freighter had docked just that morning.

A large man stood in the middle of the road calling out to anyone looking for work. Rudy approached him. "Sir, what type of work are you offering?"

"Have to get the smaller shipments over to the office where they get picked up by the local merchants. There are quire a few packages, and it's a good day's work. If I can't find anyone else, it might turn into an additional day.

"Gus over at pickup has a cart you can use. Are you interested?"

"Sure am. Let's get started." He hoped this would be the final job that earned him enough for passage out of Cape Town.

Rudy was the only person interested, and although he put in a long, hard day, the man asked him to return the following day.

The next morning anxious to get down to the dock, he arrived early ready to finish transferring packages from the ship to the office, collect his pay, and see about booking passage. When he entered the office to pick up the cart, he overheard a young black man asking if any shipments had arrived for Franz Schiller at The Smoker's Shop.

Hearing the name Franz Schiller startled him to the point that he froze. The office clerk had to repeat three times, "If you're here for the cart, it's sitting where you left it."

Regaining his bearings, he thanked the clerk and left.

The day could not end soon enough for Rudy. He worked without taking a break and by noon he had finished. Pleased with his earnings, he thanked the man who had hired him, and left to return the cart.

Striking up a conversation with the clerk, he learned that The Smoker's

Shop had once been The General Store, both owned and operated by one Franz Schiller.

Armed with his newly acquired information, Rudy forgot all about looking into his options to book passage to leave Cape Town. Instead, he headed up the street to the YMCA where he had left his things. With letter in hand he planned to head back to The Smoker's Shop and introduce himself to his uncle.

When he entered the shop, Franz was finishing up a sale. After shaking hands with the man and bidding him to enjoy the cigars he had just purchased, the man left. Turning to Rudy, he said, "Good afternoon young man. What can I help you with?"

"I'm not here to purchase anything. I'm not a customer. I came here specifically to find you."

Franz had no idea what he meant by his statements. He didn't know the man, in fact, he was certain he had never seen him before. "Are you here to sell me something? Do you have goods that I could sell in my shop? What do you want with me?"

Rudy looked at Franz and saw an old man, certainly older than his father. His eyes scanned the shop; he was not the least bit impressed. Selling cigars, pipes, and cigarettes—how could that make a person rich?

"My name is Rudy Schiller; I'm your nephew, your brother's son. I have a letter you wrote your mutti inviting her to come live with you."

Franz was stunned. After all these years, out of the blue, his nephew was standing before him.

"I wrote that letter sixty years ago. The only response I got was a brief note telling me my mutti had died in childbirth, and I don't even know who sent it to me.

"Is your father still alive? Are my sisters still alive? I never heard from anyone. Why exactly are you here now?"

Rudy grew irritated. He had anticipated being welcomed with open arms. "My father is still alive, but in poor health. The last time I saw him was four years ago when I left Germany. He doesn't have any sisters that I know of; he grew up in an orphanage.

"Did your father send you to find me? Did he give you the letter?"

Rudy laughed. "No, my father didn't send me, and he definitely didn't give me the letter. When I learned I was coming to Africa, I took it and came to find you on my own.

"With the War still raging, Germany is not the best place to be these days. I've been fighting for our Fuhrer in North Africa, and when we were ordered back to Italy, I deserted. So you see, I can't go back to Hamburg; nothing awaits me there but prison or death.

"I'm here to accept the invitation you extended to my grandmother. The way I see it, you can teach me all about your business, and when you pass on, it will become mine. After all, I'm family."

Franz stood quietly mulling over in his mind all his brash nephew had said. He didn't like him, that much he knew. Rudy had shown him no respect, and he felt Franz was obligated to give him an inheritance his own father obviously was not providing.

"I don't know what you expected to find here. You know nothing about me; nothing about the life I've led, the hardships I've faced. And I faced them alone, without family. I wrote the letter to my mutti to help her; to give her a better life than my drunk of a father gave her. The only thing he ever gave her was child after child, year after year, to care for and parent alone until he killed her.

"Your father, my brother, was an infant when I left Hamburg. I never really knew him, and he never knew me, which is why he probably never tried to locate me. My urging my mutti to come to Cape Town for a better life has nothing to do with you. I sent that letter to her long before you were born.

"I don't even know if you are really my nephew; I only have your word. I owe you nothing; there is nothing here for you. Look around. Does it appear that I am living an opulent life? I live in the back of my store where I have always lived except for a short stay at a boarding house when I first came here.

"'I've worked long and hard my whole life even as a young child before I left Germany. I suggest you make your own way in life; if and when you do, you'll grow to appreciate it.

"You do know that you had a Jewish grandmother, do you not? How on earth did you ever end up a German soldier fighting for the Nazis? What did your father have to say to that?

"Now, please leave. We have nothing further to discuss."

Rudy Schiller was furious. His face turned beet red, as he cursed and left the store, slamming the door behind him.

After he left, Franz was so visibly shaken, he closed the store and made his way up the street to the Annex. He had no one else to turn to but Ben.

Trailing a good distance behind him, Rudy followed Franz and saw him knock on the door of the Annex that was opened by a man who appeared to know him. He entered and the door closed behind him. He wasn't exactly sure what type of business the building housed. There were no windows—just skylights on the roof. It was obviously under lock and key, since Franz had knocked on the door to gain entrance. The sign above the door that read *The Annex* revealed nothing.

He patiently waited for over an hour. At last, the door opened. Franz and the same man who had opened the door walked up the hill to The Smoker's Shop where he entered his store as the man continued walking toward the center of town.

Franz went in the back to freshen up before heading out to meet Ben for dinner. Rudy seized the opportunity to sneak into the store and hide behind the side counter. A while later when Franz left to meet Ben, Rudy had the store to himself.

He entered the back living quarters—two rooms and a water closet. In the larger open room, a sitting area consisting of a sofa, two chairs and side tables atop a large colorful rug. Behind the sofa, against the wall, stood a table that held an ornately carved chest. A dining table sat in the corner kitchen area. The smaller room was a bedroom with a bed, chest, and closet.

His uncle had been truthful. If he had means, he surely wouldn't be living behind the store with such meager furnishings. The chest on the table seemed out of place; it was by far the nicest piece in the room. He browsed through the store, again finding nothing that seemed of any value. He didn't smoke, and had no interest in the cigars. He noticed that several boxes on the shelves were smaller versions of the larger chest behind the sofa. Opening one, he found it empty.

In his mind, Rudy formed a new plan. Perhaps he had overplayed his hand. He would humble himself and apologize for what he said earlier, and implore his uncle to lend him enough money to book passage to a destination far from Germany and the War. Added to the money he had earned at the dock, he could leave Cape Town behind him and set sail for a new beginning. He would promise to repay him as soon as he could. If he didn't, there would be nothing Franz could do about it.

He crouched behind the counter waiting for Franz to return.

When Franz arrived at the Annex earlier, Ben could see that he was visibly upset. Actually, he had never been to the Annex before. It was not open to the public, and only a handful of people had ever been allowed inside. The building was highly secured—the walls were concrete, no windows, and large safes held the varying quantities of diamonds and gemstones on hand at any time. The door equipped with a peephole was never opened to persons unknown.

Franz was speaking so fast and making no sense whatsoever. Ben heard the word *nephew* and for a brief moment thought of Jacob. As Franz calmed down and related the story of Rudy Schiller's visit, Ben put his arm around his friend.

"Franz my dear friend, why are you so upset. I think you handled him beautifully. He spoke his mind and came across as brash and disrespectful. You, in turn, spoke your mind and sent him packing. So what's the problem?

"I think you are more disappointed than upset. You have wondered for years what happened to your brother and sisters, now you know. They were separated and sent off to orphanages. Obviously, your nephew has not had a very good start in life, but that blame belongs to the brother you never knew.

"The disappointment is your nephew. What a foolish naïve young man. If he had merely sought you out to get to know you and ask your advice, you would have opened your arms and welcomed him. By demanding what he thought was due him, he alienated you instead. Am I not correct in my assessment?"

How wise his friend Ben Lyons was. Always there for him; always knew what to say and when to say it, while fighting demons of his own as he faced tragedy after tragedy.

They left the Annex together; Franz went to the shop and Ben went home. They planned to meet for dinner.

After dinner, at Franz' request, they went to Ben's cottage. On a sheet of paper Franz wrote an informal Will. He knew he wouldn't live forever, and the altercation with his nephew made him realize that he should leave his life's earnings to a person or persons of his choosing. He had no idea what would happen to his assets if there was no one who could claim them.

> *I, Franz Schiller, being of sound mind and body declare this paper as my Last Will and Testament.*
>
> *The Smoker's Shop and all its contents are to be sold, as well as the furniture in my living quarters. All proceeds are to be deposited in my bank account held at the First National Bank of South Africa.*
>
> *I leave the entire sum of said account to Jamilia and Afram Botu—the sole condition being that Afram attend a University, and get an accredited education ultimately earning a degree.*
>
> *Signed, sealed, witnessed, and dated the 22ⁿᵈ day of the month of February in the year nineteen hundred forty-five.*
>
> It was signed by Franz and witnessed by Ben.

"I have given great thought to paying for Afram's education for some time. He is a fine young man and quite intelligent. Jamilia has taught him far more than his attendance at the limited number of missionary schools that are available could have. I think the time has come for him to attend a university of higher education where he can become a leader for his people.

"Although I have penned my intentions in this Will, I will speak to both of them within a week and see what we can set up. I will also go to the bank tomorrow and get a draft for Rudy. I can certainly help him on a smaller scale."

Ben smiled. "I knew you would soften a bit where your nephew is concerned. Do you know where he is staying?"

"No, I don't, but I can ask around the dock. If he's planning to leave town, that's where he will be."

"Franz, I've been meaning to ask you if you have any small crates around the shop. I'd like to pack up Sidney's tools and a few of his things and ship them to Jacob when he gets home."

"I have several in the cellar, just tell me what size you're looking for."

Franz penned a duplicate copy of the Will. He left one with Ben, folded and placed the other in his pocket. He would go to the bank first thing tomorrow morning.

"Good night Ben. Thank you for hearing me out. I'll catch up with you tomorrow.

No mention whatsoever was made of the diamonds. Ben had no idea where he kept them.

Franz left Ben's cottage and walked home. He let himself into the shop and went immediately to the back. He rolled back the rug, lifted the door, and as his foot hit the first step, Rudy appeared before him.

A look of sheer fright crossed his face as he fell backwards down the stairs, his head hitting the cold cellar floor with a thud. Rudy quickly lowered himself to the cellar, and ignoring Franz's cry for help began rummaging around only to find the space empty except for the three crates that had once held the rough diamonds.

Filled with rage yet again, he ascended the stairs, and ransacked the store leaving Afram's boxes, broken ashtrays, and strewn cigars in his wake. Finding the cash drawer, he took what little money there was and threw the drawer to the ground.

Fleeing the store, he tore up the street to his room at the YMCA. He would leave early and return to the dock. He would find a way to sneak aboard the freighter and hide out until it left port."

Afram found Franz the next morning. He was unconscious, but alive; the cold floor having saved his life. The Police and the ambulance arrived almost simultaneously, questioning Afram at length.

When Ben arrived, Afram was free to go, but he chose to stay. He never knew that there was a cellar beneath the living quarters. He began picking up the boxes, discarding the broken ashtrays, and in no time the shop was back in order. In the living quarters, he closed the door to the cellar, and replaced the rug.

The Police viewed it as a robbery, and with the cash missing, in essence it was. Ben told the Police about Rudy Schiller and the confrontation they had the day before. He suggested they check at the dock to see if they could locate him. Ben had no description—a young man in his early twenties was all he knew.

As Ben made his way to Groote Schuur Hospital, a thought occurred to him. After the ambulance left with Franz, he went down to the cellar, finding only the three empty crates that once held the sorted rough diamonds. He surmised that Franz must have gone to retrieve the crate he had asked him for when he was confronted.

Where were the diamonds? Could Rudy Schiller have stolen them?

CHAPTER TWENTY-SIX

F ranz was a tough old bird. He regained consciousness almost immediately. He confirmed to the Police and to Ben that Rudy Schiller had been the culprit, waiting in the store for his return. They correctly assumed that he had snuck into the shop while Franz was getting ready to meet Ben for dinner, and that he had confronted him when he had gone down to the cellar for the crate.

Ben found him sitting up in bed with a big bandage wrapped around his head. "I would have given him a bit more than what he managed to grab out of the cash drawer." He joked. "What I don't understand is why he came back. He must really think I'm hiding something big." He winked at Ben.

The young intern came in to check on Franz and extended his hand. "Christiaan Barnard here Mr. Schiller, how are you feeling?"

"I feel pretty good, but then they tell me I had a good night's sleep."

"That's what we like to hear, a positive attitude. We're going to keep you for a few days to thoroughly check you out and monitor your concussion. We'll probably send you home with the head bandage, but you'll have to return to have the stitches removed. You have a pretty wide cut on the back of your head."

"Thank you for taking such good care of me. Christiaan Barnard this is my dear, dear friend Ben Lyons."

Christiaan Barnard completed his internship and residency at Groot Schuur Hospital where in 1967 he became an international superstar virtually overnight when he performed the first successful human to human heart transplant.

After what happened, Franz was more determined than ever to get his Will and affairs in order and talk to Afram about attending a university.

Jamilia and Afram offered to run the store while Franz recuperated, but he refused and the sign *Closed Until Further Notice* remained on the door.

The Police searched the dock area for days, but Rudy Schiller was nowhere to be found. He had successfully hidden in the hold of the freighter and wasn't discovered until they were well out to sea.

When he was released from Groote Schuur, Ben insisted Franz stay with him until he was well enough to return to the store. Jamilia offered to care for him during the day while Ben was at work, citing Afram would stay with him when she had a class to teach. His first day at the cottage, he told them he intended to help with Afram's education both financially and finding a school for him to attend.

They were so moved by his offer, they thanked him in unison. Afram's education had long been a priority for Jamilia, and she viewed the opportunity for her son to further his education a true blessing. The arrangement proved a good one allowing Franz and Afram to discuss schools while Jamilia continued teaching the children.

He did not mention the Will and what would occur when he passed on; or that everything had been taken care of at the bank. He was planning to stick around for a while.

For the three weeks that Franz stayed with Ben, the four of them had dinner together each evening. Afterwards, Jamilia and Afram went home only to return in the morning after stopping by the market to pick up supplies for dinner. They spent their days researching the closest and most accredited university accepting black students.

When he returned to the hospital to have the stitches removed, he was in a good mood. The doctors were pleased with his progress, but urged him to take it easy and not rush back to the shop. After Jamilia and Afram left each evening, Franz would bring Ben up-to-date about the schools they were researching.

"You know Ben, although my nephew's coming here wasn't exactly a happy occasion for me, it did spur me on to do some good with my life's savings while I'm still here to see it. I do have regrets that I let life pass me by. I should have found someone to share my life, have a family, and dream with. My mutti always said dreams were an important part of the future; it took me a long time to realize that.

"You and only you have been there for me, and I thank you from the bottom of my heart."

Ben grew quiet, fighting back tears. Franz was to him exactly what he was to Franz.

"I agree wholeheartedly. In Russia, marriages were arranged. After Harry left for England, all Sidney and I dreamt of was leaving and starting a new life, just as he had. Although in good conscience, we could not and would not leave our elderly and ailing parents. By the time they passed on, we had turned down offers from the *matchmaker* in our *shtetl (town)* so many times she eventually stopped asking. We felt it would be easier to leave and strike out on our own without the responsibilities of a wife and possibly children.

"Like you, a wife and family have passed me by. Losing Harry, his family, and Sidney have left me all alone except for my nephew Jacob. After the War, I plan to get to know him; he's the only family I have left."

Ben purposely stopped short of telling him his plans to leave Cape Town and join Jacob in London. Once again, he just couldn't tell him he was leaving.

Early May, Franz left Ben's cottage and returned to the shop. He felt good, but had been experiencing headaches of late. Dismissing them as temporary, he mentioned them to no one—not his doctors, not to Ben.

He reopened The Smoker's Shop to a rousing welcome from his customers and fellow merchants. At Shabbat Services on Friday night, he received a warm welcome back.

The first few days home were fine. If he grew tired, he closed the shop early. One evening, he fell asleep while sitting on the sofa. He awoke in a cold sweat calling out, "Who's there? Is someone there?"

From that day on, he began having dreams of his nephew appearing in the shop. At other times, he envisioned him standing over him with a fist full of diamonds as he lay in his bed. Having recently resumed enjoying dinner out with Ben, he was on his way back home one evening when he spotted Rudy heading up the street ahead of him. His thoughts void of all logic caused him to hasten his pace towards home. Entering the shop and locking the door behind him, he went directly to the back. He rushed to open the chest and found the tray on top empty.

It was as he thought—Rudy Schiller had found and stolen the diamonds.

The pain that spread across his chest was excruciating. As he gasped for breath, there was no one there to hear him or help him. They found him dead on the floor of a massive heart attack—a look of horror on his face.

There were no explanations for his death. His doctors were in agreement that medically he had fully recuperated and was in all probability more fit than he had been before the incident with his nephew. Having never experienced heart problems, the massive heart attack that killed him coupled with the distortion of his facial features remained puzzling to his doctors and friends alike.

Ben Lyons dealt with his latest loss in robotic mode. He made all the arrangements for his friend's burial in the cemetery adjacent to the synagogue. He worked with the bank's representative to offer the shop for sale and moved towards finalizing Franz's final wishes.

One afternoon, he and Afram arranged to meet at the shop to determine the sale and disposition of its contents. Ben purchased all of his favorite cigars for himself. They entered the back of the store and decided that the furniture was of little value and would best be simply disposed of. Ben approached the chest and lowered the lid. Seeing *Shiloh* carved on the top in Hebrew, he lifted the lid, and removed the empty tray on top. The carved chest held Franz's cache—the diamonds cut and polished by the Annex that he had found over fifty years earlier.

Ben was amazed. All this time he often wondered what his friend had done with the finished stones, the stones he never quite came to terms with finding, and never quite accepted the fact that they rightfully belonged to him.

When one finds something, it is often because it has been hidden, but

Ben discovered the diamonds in the carved chest that sat unlocked in full view for as long as he could remember.

At first he wondered why his friend had never confided in him, and then he realized that perhaps if he had confided his plans to leave Cape Town, maybe, just maybe at that point, he would have told him where he kept them.

The Chapel of the Great Synagogue overflowed to standing room only. Some were fellow congregants, some were customers, while others were friends of friends and never knew him personally. They had all come to pay homage to a long-standing member of their Cape Town community. He was laid to rest in the cemetery adjacent to the synagogue he had attended for years. The Rabbi said it best: *Franz Schiller was a Mensch*—a decent human being.

Two weeks after Franz's passing, Ben received another wire from Marcus.

JACOB TO RETURN TO ENGLAND FRIDAY NEXT— STOP—HE IS SAFE AND WELL—STOP—WILL ADVISE FURTHER WHEN HE ARRIVES—STOP

MARCUS HIRSCH
DE BEERS, LONDON, ENGLAND

The wire was the best news Ben could receive. Once again, he moved forward with his plans, but first he had to settle Franz's affairs. The store stood emptied of its contents, as did the back living quarters. Everything had been sold or disposed of. Ben enlisted Afram's help to move the chest of diamonds along with the table it rested upon to his cottage making no mention of its contents.

In mid-June, Ben asked Jamilia and Afram to meet him at his cottage. The time had come for him to disclose the contents of Franz's Will, and to advise them that he planned to leave Cape Town in the near future.

Jamilia accepted but insisted on preparing dinner for the three of them.

The evening began on a light note. The previous months had taken a toll on all of them—crisis after crisis, loss upon loss. With the War over in Europe, and Japan's defeat imminent, it was time to look to the future.

After dinner, they cleared the table. Jamilia placed a pot of coffee and cups before them. When they were once again seated, Ben produced a single sheet of paper.

"I don't think I have to tell you what Franz meant to me; he was my best friend, and I loved him like a brother. I valued his advice I sought along with the advice he so freely gave when I needed it most. He was the first person I spoke with when I arrived in Cape Town seeking directions to Zeller Jewelers. From that brief exchange of words grew a lifetime friendship.

"First and foremost, he was a good man, an honest man who remained true to his beliefs. If you were lucky enough to fall under his good graces, it meant in his eyes, you were a good, honest, and decent human being.

"Afram, I applaud Franz's decision to further your education. He saw in you the potential to someday be a great man. He praised you Jamilia for raising your son alone and teaching him things that aren't learned from books. You showed him life as it exists, not as a fairy tale, while urging him to nurture his hopes and dreams believing if you can dream, you can achieve. I intend to continue to work with you both to find a university to attend.

"I have a paper before me which is the Last Will and Testament of one Franz Schiller. Jamilia and Afram, you are the sole heirs to his assets, all proceeds of which reside in one account in the First National Bank of South Africa. Proceeds from the shop will be deposited once it has been sold. We will make an appointment with the bank manager, and I will go with you to transfer the account to both of you.

"The one stipulation in the Will that you attend a university and further your education rests with you alone. Afram, I have no doubt whatsoever that you will honor his wishes, and I reiterate I will do all I can to help you."

Jamilia and Afram sat quietly without speaking a word. They had accepted Franz's offer to send Afram to school with profound thanks and humility. Now to be the recipients of his entire worldly goods was simply too much for them to comprehend. Neither spoke a word.

"I can see that you had no idea whatsoever that Franz had named you as his heirs. In his defense, when he drew up the Will, I don't think he had any idea that he would die so soon. I think he looked forward to seeing Afram graduate and begin his life's journey. He saw firsthand the sacrifices you made when your husband was killed, leaving you with a small child to care for on your own. In some way, I think he wished there had been someone to help his mother when she was in need."

Jamilia was crying. "I'm at a total loss for words. Franz was good to us from the very beginning, often telling me to come to him first if we needed anything or he could do anything for us. Through the years, he became an important presence in our lives, someone who watched over us time after time, and Afram and I both looked up to him, blessing the day he came into our lives. We too grew to love him as our own.

"For now, our lives will not change. I accept your help to find a school and get Afram enrolled. My place is big enough for me especially if Afram leaves Cape Town. If you would be so good as to make the appointment with the bank so we may accompany you to transfer the account, I would appreciate it.

Jamilia stood; Ben motioned her to be seated.

"There is one other matter we must discuss. I am about to tell you of the Franz Schiller you did not know." Ben began in 1882, the year Franz arrived in Cape Town—from Simon Abel to The General Store to the farmhouse to finding the diamonds.

"He felt as if he had stolen the diamonds, and never accepted the fact that they were indeed his. Having collected them over a period of twenty years, and finding them on property whose owners had passed on weighed heavily on his mind. For most of his life, the rough diamonds remained in a crate hidden in the cellar where Afram found him. He rarely even thought of his cache; it was never a part of his life, and with the exception of three small pebble-sized stones that he sold in the very beginning, his cache remained in tact.

"After he opened The Smoker's Shop, he summoned Sidney and me for advice. At that time he related the story I just related to you. He decided to get the rough stones cut, polished, and appraised to determine their worth.

I have no idea why or how he came to that decision after years of denying their existence. The Annex took him on as a client, and it took several years to complete the job. I never learned what he did with the finished stones or where he kept them.

"Franz was laid to rest, and we observed a week's mourning. Days later, I met Afram at the shop to begin clearing out the contents. Noticing that the chest's lid was open, I went over and closed it. It was then that I saw *Shiloh* carved in Hebrew on the top. *Shiloh* was the client name Franz set up with the Annex."

Ben stood. "Please come with me." He walked over and stood before the chest, Jamilia and Afram on either side of him. He opened the lid and removed the top tray revealing the diamonds.

If Jamilia and Afram were awestruck at learning the contents of the Will, nothing could adequately describe their demeanor with the sight they found before them.

Ben replaced the tray and lowered the lid on the chest. Once they were again seated at the table, Ben cleared his throat. "This is my dilemma. Nowhere did Franz make mention or provisions for the diamonds. Since he left his assets to the two of you, I feel they should be yours. There is no one else who could possibly lay claim to them."

Jamilia disagreed. "Perhaps he meant them to be yours. You were his true friend, his brother. He entrusted you with his lifelong secret and to cut, polish, and appraise them."

Afram who had not said one word the entire evening spoke. "I guess it's obvious we are overwhelmed. I know I am. If my mother agrees, I think we need to proceed slowly; we need time to process all of this. Franz asked me to make the chest shortly after he opened The Smoker's Shop. He handed me a piece of paper with markings unfamiliar to me asking if I could carve them on the top. I did not know they were Hebrew letters or that they spelled a name.

"He gave me the dimensions for the chest, and requested five trays. In addition, he asked that carvings resembling facets on a diamond surround the base. I practiced on small pieces of wood until I got the carvings just right before finishing. Franz was so pleased with the chest that he insisted I take more for my work than we had agreed to. I didn't want to accept any payment; he had done so much for my mother and me, I was happy to be able to do something for him.

"I also made the table it rests on. I never knew why he wanted the chest, or what he planned to put in it, if anything. In the years since, I've seen the chest sitting in full view in his apartment. He didn't ask me to provide a way for it to be locked. I thought perhaps he just wanted a larger container for cigars."

"I agree with my son; we are beyond overwhelmed. Two black Africans—a woman and a young man—with a cache of diamonds—what on earth would we do with them? What on earth could we do with them? They would be a larger liability to us than they were to Franz. His generosity in naming us his heirs goes far beyond our needs, and for now, I'm afraid that's all we can handle."

Ben agreed. "You are right. For now, the diamonds shall remain here. When things settle down, and Afram is off to school, we will work together on what we can do with the chest and its contents."

In agreement, they bid one another goodnight.

The meeting at the bank went smoothly. Franz's assets were transferred to a Trust Account for Jamilia and Afram Botu. For two years, each would receive a generous monthly stipend to live on. In addition, expenses for Afram's education would be paid directly from the account that had been set up prior to his death solely for that purpose. At the end of two years, the Trust provisions would be revoked and all remaining proceeds transferred to an account for Jamilia and Afram Botu.

As they rose to leave, the manager handed Ben an envelope and a small box that was sealed. "Mr. Schiller left these for you."

To Jamilia and Afram he said, "If there is anything further I can assist you with, please feel free to call on me. I would like to set up a schedule with you Jamilia to visit the bank once a month allowing me to go over management of the account with you. I feel this will be helpful to you when the funds pass to you permanently. Of course, when the shop is sold, I will notify you."

Leaving the bank, Ben headed to the Annex; Jamilia and Afram headed home. Walking in the same general direction, they started off in silence.

As they passed the open market with its array of fresh vegetables and fruits, and vendors offering freshly caught fish, Jamilia stopped. "Ben, I thank you from the bottom of my heart for taking care of Franz's final wishes for Afram and me. I'm quite pleased and truly relieved that the bank will be handling our assets for the next two years. At the end of that time, I feel I will be much better prepared to take over the account, and manage Afram's school needs.

"Tonight, I'm going to prepare a celebration feast for the three of us—celebrating Franz Schiller—celebrating Ben Lyons our dearest friend—celebrating Afram heading off to university—celebrating life itself."

Ben smiled. It was a fine day, a new beginning. The bank's arrangement for Jamilia and Afram was a good one—he felt a weight had been lifted from his shoulders. Now he could finally come clean and relay his plans to leave Cape Town to join Jacob in London without guilt. Tonight would be the perfect time.

"Jamilia, what a wonderful idea. Please, prepare what you wish, never has one of your meals disappointed, even when we were dining on Sidney's restricted diet. Of course, we will have dinner at my cottage; I look forward to a pleasant evening with my two very best friends, friends that Franz introduced to my life. I'll supply the wine and the cigars."

They parted laughing. Jamilia gathered vegetables and fruit and moved on to the stands selling fish. She was going to prepare a feast that she had watched her mother prepare many times, but had never attempted herself. She knew precisely where she kept her notes for the savory fish sauce. Moving on, she purchased two loaves of bread. At last, arms filled with their purchases they headed for home.

———✺———

Ben arrived at the cottage to the heavenly aroma of Jamilia's feast that she had promised. The table was set; a small vase of flowers stood in the middle.

Noticing that Jamilia and Afram had *dressed* for this special occasion, he excused himself. After freshening up and a change of clothes, he returned.

When they were seated at the table, Jamilia handed Ben the wine; he poured three glasses. Raising his, he said, "To Franz Schiller—may he rest in peace. To us—*L'Chaim (To Life)*! Jamilia and Afram echoed his words and the evening began.

A light Fish consommé with collard greens started their meal.

As Ben and Afram sat in amazement, Jamilia brought in platter after platter and set before them a true South African Feast—Baked Fish with Lemon Tahini Sauce, Sukuma Wiki (Pan Seared Greens with onions, tomatoes, and garlic, and Pilau rice.

Although his mother generally cooked native meals for the two of them, Afram had never seen her prepare any of the dishes she set before them, and he had certainly never tasted anything like them. Since there were no restaurants in predominantly white Cape Town offering authentic South African cuisine, Ben had not experienced the ethnic recipes that Jamilia deemed her *Feast*.

Ben and Afram were both delighted. They savored every bite, and complimented her every dish. Though the amount of food seemed overwhelming when the platters were first placed on the table, not a morsel was left.

For dessert, Jamilia had prepared a Spiced Ricotta Peach Tart and coffee. Ben could no longer contain himself. "You have outdone yourself my dear friend. I have never had a meal as fine as this. You could not have honored Franz better."

He pushed back his chair and stood. "Now, who wants a cigar? I have the finest cigars—from The Smoker's Shop, of course."

When Jamilia and Afram left for home, Ben opened the small box that the bank manager had given him. The box contained a small cloth pouch. He loosened the top and spilled the contents onto the table before him—five large rough diamonds. He removed the folded note from the bottom of the box.

Dear Ben,

These five rough diamonds are for you. We spoke many times of our friendship and what it meant to each of us, and for that, I am glad we did. Too many times, we do not speak our minds before realizing it has grown too late to do so.

Shiloh in Hebrew means—the one to whom it belongs; these now belong to you. Cut and polish them to their full potential just as you did our friendship.

May God be with you and watch over you Ben Lyons. May your new life in London with Jacob bring you happiness and contentment—no one deserves that more than you.

I love you my Brother.
Franz

Ben collected his thoughts. Try as he may, he could not recall ever telling Franz that he planned to join Jacob in London after the War. He had guarded that secret fervently not wanting his friend to feel that he was deserting him. He was certain that he had never revealed his plans to anyone. How could Franz have known?

When Sidney passed away, Ben was in a terrible place. Vodka became his drink of choice, and on several occasions Franz saw that his friend got home and into bed safely. On one such evening, Ben did indeed reveal his dream to once again be with the only family he had left.

Days later, Franz placed the five largest rough diamonds that he had pulled from his cache in a pouch, penned his note, and placed them in a small box. He planned to give them to Ben as a parting gift—what could be more symbolic of his friend's life in South Africa than diamonds?

CHAPTER TWENTY-SEVEN

Once again, Ben had not revealed his plans to leave Cape Town, but after opening the box and reading Franz's note, he was glad he hadn't. The evening he read the contents of Franz's Will, followed by the revelation of his diamond cache resulted in more than enough for Jamilia and Afram to handle at that point. In addition, he was committed to seeing Afram enrolled in school. In reality, his plans were just that—his plans.

The celebration dinner was what the three friends needed; a night free of worry and all that had befallen them—both good and bad—in recent months. First and foremost, Ben awaited word from Jacob that he was discharged and what his plans were for the immediate future. Then and only then, he would reveal his wish to relocate to England.

By the end of July 1945, the Imperial Japanese Navy was rendered incapable of conducting major operations and an Allied invasion of Japan was imminent. Together with the United Kingdom, and China, the United States called for an immediate and unconditional surrender—the alternative being *prompt and utter destruction.*

While publicly stating their intent to fight on to the bitter end, Japan's leaders were privately making entreaties to the Soviet Union to mediate peace on terms more favorable to the Japanese. Meanwhile, the Soviets were preparing to attack Japanese forces in Manchuria and Korea to further their own cause.

On 6 August 1945, the United States detonated an atomic bomb over the Japanese city of Hiroshima. President Harry S. Truman called again for

Japan's surrender, warning—*expect a rain of ruin from the air, the like of which has never been seen on this earth.*

On 9 August 1945, the United States dropped a second atomic bomb, this time on the Japanese city of Nagasaki.

Imperial Japan announced its surrender on 15 August 1945. Formally signed on 2 September 1945 brought the hostilities of World War II to an end.

The ideological framework for Bantu education had its origins in a manifesto crafted in1939 by Afrikaner nationalists. Based on the racist view that the education of blacks was the responsibility of whites, the document called for Christian National Education and advocated separate schools for each of South Africa's population groups—whites, Africans, Indians, and Coloureds.

Segregated education disadvantaged all groups, but was particularly devastating for black Africans. The white government made it clear that Bantu education was designed to teach African learners to be *hewers of wood* and *drawers of water* for a white-run economy and society, regardless of an individual's abilities and aspirations.

Education for blacks was left largely to Christian missions, whose resources, even when augmented by minimal government grants, enabled them to enroll only a small proportion of the black population. Missionaries did, however, run numerous schools, including some excellent high schools that took pupils through to the university level.

Missionaries were the dominant influence at the South African Native College at Fort Hare founded in 1916. It was the key institution of higher education for black Africans, offering a Western-style academic education to students from across sub-Saharan Africa, and created a black African elite who were frustrated by the fact that whites did not treat them as equals.

South African Native College alumni were part of many subsequent independence movements and governments of newly independent African countries.

Originally, Fort Hare was a British fort. Missionary activity led to the creation of a school for missionaries from which the college ultimately resulted at the beginning of the 20th century. In accordance with its Christian principles, fees were low and heavily subsidized, and scholarships were available for indigent students.

Several leading opponents of the African apartheid regime attended the College; among them Desmond Tutu, Oliver Tambo, and Nelson Mandela who later wrote in his biography—*For young black South Africans like myself, it was Oxford and Cambridge, Harvard and Yale, all rolled into one.*

The South African Native College at Fort Hare was located in Alice, Eastern Cape, South Africa. It was 925 km from Cape Town.

Ben made an appointment to meet with a fellow congregant at his synagogue who was a Professor at the University of Cape Town. Explaining his endeavor at finding a closer school for Afram, he asked if he could offer any suggestions or help.

Professor Abraham Morton relocated his family to South Africa from Austria in the mid 1930s. As a Professor at the University of Austria, he witnessed firsthand the initial edicts issued by Nazi Germany limiting education rights for Jews that included the rights of Jews to teach. He understood and sympathized with young black Africans who wanted a higher education.

"I am more than happy to help you, but you must understand that any help I'm able to offer you will be extremely limited.

"I've met the young man you speak for, and I also know his mother. She has taught English to many immigrant children and their parents who came here to escape the War in Europe.

"In South Africa, matriculation is a term commonly used to refer to the final year and the qualification received on graduating from high school, but basically it refers to the minimum university entrance requirements.

"Unfortunately as a black student, Afram cannot enroll in the University. I would like to speak with a few faculty members and see what I can do. I'm going to suggest that Afram be given the entrance exam to test his level of knowledge. From there, I will see if there is any way he can complete his courses on his own through textbooks, testing, and being allowed to attend lectures. Of course, any faculty support I can muster will be crucial."

"I don't know how to thank you. He is a special young man, and actually it was Franz Schiller who sought to help him. I'm just following up. I want to do this as much for Franz as he wanted to do this for Afram."

Abe Morton was true to his word and got back to Ben less than a week later. He arranged for Afram to take the entrance exams at the school in private. On the day they were scheduled to take place, Abe drove to the University with Afram seated beside him. Although the drive was short, the conversation between them allowed Abe to get to know him better and learn what he envisioned for his future.

Abe had arranged for him to take the exam in his office. When they arrived at the school, everything was set up and awaited him. Abe left him and told him he would return at noon.

Afram had never taken such an exam before. There were three parts and each had separate instructions. He began Part 1 slowly but quickly picked up the pace; moving on to Part 2, he found himself answering question after question with ease; math was actually his best subject. Part 3 tested him on English and ended with his writing a short essay on what he expected from and how he expected to use his education.

He looked at the clock on the wall; it was just 11:00 a.m. Abe was not due to return until noon. He went over the exam again and remained satisfied with his responses. Along the wall opposite Abe's desk was a bookcase filled with books.

He walked over and scanned the titles. One book in particular caught his attention—*An African American in South Africa: The Travel Notes of Ralph J. Bunche, 28 September 1937-1 January 1938.*

He removed the book from the shelf; on the cover was a picture of the author; on the back was a brief description of the book's contents—*Provides unique insights on a segregated society.* He opened the book and began reading; he was halfway into the story by the time Abe returned.

When Abe entered his office, Afram stood. "I finished my exam early, and as I was looking at the books you have, this one caught my eye. I picked it up, and I began reading. I hope you don't mind."

Abe glanced at the book he was holding and smiled. "I don't mind at all. In fact, if there are any others you would like to read, please feel free to borrow them. I assume you would like to take the book with you so that you can finish reading it."

"Yes, I would. Thank you."

"Well, how do you think you did on the exam? You said you completed it early and that's a good sign. I am working with two and possibly three other professors to grade you, and we will then present you with a course of study that we can offer you here with an eye on the future to actually get you enrolled in a University where you can earn a degree.

"Meanwhile, I'd like you to take another book with you today; a book I think you will not only enjoy reading but will serve as an inspiration for your goals. This biography of Ralph Bunche shows that although he is only in his early 40s, his accomplishments are many.

"I need a few minutes to check my messages, and then we can leave for home. My colleagues and I will get back to you in a few days."

"Thank you. I want you to know how much I appreciate all that you are doing for me. My mother has seen to it that I have had books to read since I was a little boy, instilling in me that reading is learning."

Abe dropped Afram at home, promising to get in touch with him as soon as his exam results and their recommendations were in place.

While waiting to hear from Abe, Afram finished the book, enjoying it enough to suggest his mother read it. The biography of Ralph Johnson Bunche was a game changer; he began equating himself with certain aspects of his story. Although they were worlds apart—Bunche was born in Detroit, Michigan in the United States; he lost both his parents during his early adolescence. As a result, he and his younger sister relocated to Los Angeles and were taken in by his maternal grandmother who became a major advocate for the education of her grandson.

The vast difference between the two was where they lived. The United States had many colleges and universities that accepted students of all backgrounds; South Africa's higher education was primarily offered to whites though whites represented only twenty percent of the population.

Abe Morton had been correct in stating that the book could serve as an inspiration. From that day forward, Afram set his goal—to attend Howard University in Washington, D.C., United States of America—7,900 miles across the sea. He didn't know how he would get there; he had no idea how long it would take to get there; but in his heart and head were his mother's words—*If you can dream it, you can achieve it; it's up to you to make it happen.*

To the surprise of no one, Afram aced his exam. When all arrangements had been made, Abe presented his recommendations to Afram, Jamilia, and Ben.

The essay he had written, and the results of the exam prompted more than one field of endeavor he could pursue.

Although he would be working at home, he would have access to the University's library for research, and he would be allowed to attend lectures pertinent to his course of study. He would be graded on the same standard as enrolled students.

Abe had consulted with the South African Native College about accepting Afram as a student. He outlined a plan that would allow him to take courses under the auspices of the University of Cape Town that would satisfy the first two years' requirements towards earning a degree in Political Science. At that time, Afram would physically attend the College in Alice. He cited the fact that it would be a hardship at present to leave his mother alone.

Before beginning his classes, Abe arranged for Afram, Jamilia, and Ben to join him on a visit to the school in Alice to meet the administrators and faculty he had spoken with.

The year was coming to an end. So much had happened. The War was over and around the world those who survived were left with picking up the pieces of their lives. Most simply wanted to get back to normal, but who really knew what normal was anymore. It would take a long time to heal emotionally, and so many bore scars that could never be erased.

On 2 September 1945, the Japanese envoys signed the instrument of Surrender on board the battleship USS Missouri. Although South African naval vessels were sent to the Far East, no Japanese military personnel set foot on African soil, and no South African military personnel was captured by the Japanese, consequently sparing them from the horrors of Japanese prisoner of war camps.

In relation to the role played by the Union in the overall Allied war effort during World War II, the Country's direct contribution towards the struggle against Japan was not very extensive. It did, however, play an important role in keeping the Allies supplied in the East, and this role continued until the cessation of hostilities.

Though, the war against Japan did not affect local politics or social matters in South Africa to any great extent, it did contribute to the economic growth experienced during the war years.

However, South Africa after the War was presented with a mixture of concerns—concerns that would not be resolved for decades to come.

CHAPTER TWENTY-EIGHT

As 1945 became 1946, Ben's year began on a high note. He was quite pleased with the way things worked out for Afram and school. The three friends met for dinner often with the premise that he was checking to make certain that all was going well. In reality, he was lonely. For the first time in his life, he was truly alone. Sidney and Franz were gone. At work, there wasn't much time to socialize especially when they were busy. Jamilia taught English to the immigrant children and Afram had his studies.

In mid-January, Ben received a long awaited letter from Jacob.

> *Dear Uncle Benjamin,*
>
> *I was saddened to learn of Uncle Sidney's passing. Although I only met both of you once on the occasion of my Bar Mitzvah, that visit proved to be a blessing allowing my father, you, and Sidney to be together one last time.*
>
> *I apologize for not writing sooner, but when I left to join the RAF, I left many loose ends that caught up with me when I returned.*
>
> *Marcus Hirsch tells me he has kept you apprised of my wellbeing, and I can never thank him enough for all he has done and continues to do for me.*
>
> *The past few months since I was discharged have been busy to say the least. I had to find a place to live, sell the house in Middlesex (I just couldn't see myself living there without my family), and decide what to do with myself for the rest of my life.*

I am considering accepting a job with De Beers, but haven't decided as yet. I'm planning to take my time and look into a few other options I am considering.

As promised, I do still plan to visit you in Cape Town; for now, however, I cannot in good conscience leave England so soon after returning. There are too many loose ends remaining, and I simply must attend to them as only I can.

You and I are the last two surviving Lyons, and I don't want to lose touch with you. I look forward to long and in-depth conversations with you about what my father was like as a boy and how the three of you became so adept at producing a true thing of beauty—a cut and polished diamond.

Stay well, and please write. I will do the same.

Your loving Nephew,
Jacob

Ben was overcome with emotion as he folded the letter and slipped it back into its envelope. How could he have expected Jacob to leave everything and come to Cape Town so soon after returning home? Reading between the lines, it was evident he was still trying to come to terms with losing his entire family.

He sent a short note letting Jacob know that he had received his letter. He wished him well and told him that he looked forward to his visit, but advised him to take the time needed to prepare for the future.

By War's end, Zeller Jewelers had been established in Cape Town for over forty years. From their meager beginning of a small amount of watches and rings, they had emerged as the premier jewelry shop in all of Cape Town. Their selection of jewelry, no matter the item, was unrivalled. The Annex in operation for just over twenty years had only added to their success.

De Beers continued to dominate every facet of the diamond industry for larger buyers. However, the many sources of uncut diamonds on a smaller scale that were once so plentiful were all but gone. There were now many gem cutters in the Cape Town area who had fled Antwerp and other European countries setting up small shops that gradually managed to siphon off some of the Annex clients.

The diamond cutting industry in Antwerp that was mainly run by Jews was virtually wiped out by Hitler's persecution of the Jewish population in the German occupied territories during WWII. The industry never recovered from this huge blow and diamond-cutting centers began emerging elsewhere.

For the most part, Ben ran the day-to-day business of the Annex; his contact with the Zeller brothers was and had been for many years limited to once a month unless there were problems or questions to resolve. At the end of each month, they met for an overview of accounts, business, and profits. The brothers were quite pleased with Ben; he was quite pleased with them. They had afforded him the opportunity to do what he did best and loved the most, and he had learned a great deal in the process.

For their meeting the end of March, Paul suggested that they meet over lunch and dispense with going over the accounts. Ben was a bit surprised at his suggestion, but doing things differently every once in a while was good, was it not?

It was a clear sunny day and Ben enjoyed the walk to the restaurant. When he arrived, Paul and Phil awaited him. They ordered lunch, had drinks while they waited, and by the time coffee was brought to their table, Ben was convinced that this had been precisely what he thought—something different every once in a while.

Phil cleared his throat. "Ben, we suggested this venue for our meeting because we didn't want to be overheard by anyone at the Annex. Paul and I have been doing a little soul searching and looking forward to the future.

"We have been here in Cape Town for over forty years and have been successful beyond our wildest imagination. We owe a good deal of that success to you and your management of the Annex.

"Times have changed dramatically, and although the War played a part, one cannot deny the fact that *times change* with or without war. We were fortunate that we set out to blaze a new trail when individuals could do just that by following their dreams. We see the future of the jewelry trade trending towards bigger and bigger entities.

"We are now in our seventies, and time seems to be catching up with us. We have no one to take over Zeller's when we are gone. My daughters both live in England, and Paul and Rene have no children. Of late, we have been trying to decide if keeping the store and continuing on is the right course for us to take.

"Lena, of course, would prefer to move back to England to be with our daughters and their families, and I have to admit, I agree with her. Before we make any decisions—decisions that affect you and the people that work at the Annex, as well, we felt it necessary to discuss the situation with you.

"None of this is going to happen overnight. It will probably take months and possibly a couple of years or more. Our initial thoughts are to seek a buyer for the store. If you feel you would like to take over the Annex, we have no doubt that we could reach an agreement beneficial to both of us. If, however, you are not interested, we could seek a buyer or simply close it down. But, that too is months away. For now, it will be business as usual. Ben, Paul and I have long blessed the day you came into the shop seeking employment. As we have told you numerous times, it was a good fit for both of us."

At first, Ben could not believe his ears. He had gone over and over many scenarios in his mind of how he would tell Paul and Phil Zeller he was leaving Cape Town. He owed them everything. They had provided him and Sidney with a good life, and he could easily equate with their desire to be with family. That's what life was all about—*family*. The War had proven that over and over again.

"I have to be honest and say *you beat me to the punch*. Since losing my brother Harry and his family, Sidney, and my dear friend Franz, I have yearned for the day my nephew Jacob, my sole living relative, would return from the War, planning to join him in England. He has returned safe and sound, and I received a letter from him earlier this year.

""He is trying to tie up the many loose ends left after his family was killed and he joined the RAF. He is planning a visit to Cape Town as soon as he is settled, and I plan to leave and return to England with him.

"Like your situation, I don't see this happening overnight, but I do feel that it will fit into your timeline for leaving quite well. I am also more than happy to help you with finding a buyer for the Annex and offering you any and all input that will be useful to you."

To say the Zeller brothers were relieved would be an understatement. They dreaded leaving Ben knowing he had no one in Cape Town. Over another cup of coffee and much lighter banter, they left the restaurant.

Ben felt good. He had seen to it that Afram was taking classes; and now the burden of telling the brothers he was leaving had lifted yet another weight from his shoulders.

When things are good, and when one awakens each day with a purpose, an eye towards the future, and better days to come, time has a way of passing quickly.

Afram completed his first round of courses. Jamilia was enjoying her English teaching duties with the immigrant children and acquired half a dozen adult students that she taught in the evening.

They allowed nothing to interfere with their dinners that averaged three to four evenings a week. Jamilia with her busy schedule managed a *feast* every now and then at the request of her two biggest fans.

Ben finally shared with them the fact that he was planning to join Jacob in England. If anything, they were relieved. They worried about their good friend who had lost so much.

The days turned to weeks; the weeks turned to months; 1946 became history. With the arrival of 1947, the Zeller brothers began aggressively seeking buyers for their shop and the Annex. Business continued as usual.

Ben developed a cough that although persistent, he chose to ignore. When questioned by Jamilia, he said it was simply a cold that was taking longer than normal to get over. After two weeks, he began noticing that he was not only losing weight, but often found himself short of breath. Not even the unbearable night sweats that left him too drained to go to work convinced him to seek medical help. When he began coughing up blood, he grew scared, scared enough to realize that something was seriously wrong, and at last, he made an appointment with the doctor.

The diagnosis was Pulmonary Tuberculosis in his right lung. The recommendation was Sanatorium confinement for six to nine months, and the prediction that in a year or so, he should be completely cured. The main thing being that for the first two to three months, he needed nothing but complete rest and fresh air. Then a further X-ray would indicate his progression and he would come out of quarantine.

Tuberculosis, including pulmonary TB, and lung disease was a common and serious condition occurring in Cape Town. Ben experienced all of the early symptoms, but although he chose to ignore them, it had been less than a month since the coughing had begun, and time was of the essence in seeking treatment.

Without the scientific understanding needed to develop effective therapeutics to fight tuberculosis in its many forms, doctors, patients, families, and charlatans looking to make a profit tried a wide range of treatments to offer any hope of relief and a cure.

One of the most universal and pervasive approaches for people with the most common pulmonary form of the disease was that of rest and fresh air for patients. This ultimately led to the creation and proliferation of sanatoriums offering the long-term treatment needed.

The rationale for sanatoria was that a regimen of rest and good nutrition offered the best chance that the sufferer's immune system would *wall off* pockets of pulmonary TB infection.

The Stoneham Sanatorium on the outskirts of Cape Town was a small but exclusive privately owned and run facility. The building consisted of eighteen individual patient rooms, and boasted of a beautiful courtyard and sun balconies where patients could relax and enjoy the outdoors. Once they were well enough to no longer require continual bed rest, they were allowed other privileges, as well.

March and April passed quickly. Ben followed the rules: Absolute and utter rest of mind and body; consume nourishing food; and have plenty of fresh air. His own set of rules included: No self-pity allowed; remain cheerful at all times; prepare for the future no matter what.

May brought news that he was doing much better and could go up and down stairs, begin short walks—a few yards more each day, and he could get up for tea and dinner. By month's end he was dressing himself and could walk without feeling shaky, although at times it left him breathless if he bent down.

June brought news that if all continued to go well, Ben could go home in three months. But the best news was he could have visitors.

When Jamilia and Afram came to visit in early July, Ben was overcome. He had not seen his friends for months. He missed them more than words could express. They had a wonderful visit and although visiting hours were from 1:00-3:00 p.m., they allowed them to stay as long as Ben did not grow tired.

He was pleased to learn that Afram was doing so well with his studies; that Jamilia was also doing well with her teaching, and she assured him that she was taking care of the cottage checking it out frequently. She also told him that she had spoken to the Zeller brothers, and they would be dropping by to see him in the next few days.

Paul and Phil did stop by days later and gave him an update on finding buyers for the store and the Annex. Two prospects looked promising.

Once he was feeling better, he decided there were important issues he needed to attend to sooner rather than later.

He drew up a Will of sorts leaving all his worldly goods to Jacob. He requested that he be cremated and that both his and Sidney's remains be shipped to England to be buried alongside their brother Harry. All of his personal papers and items along with Sidney's were to be shipped to Jacob, as well.

The cottage that he had purchased from the synagogue sat on property that under South African law could not be owned by a black African. Nevertheless, he was leaving the cottage to Jamilia to reside in as long as she wished, the deed to be held in Trust by the bank. When sold, the proceeds would go to her at that time.

Afram was tasked with the job of building a crate that would hold everything and ship it to Jacob in England. Any and all furniture could be kept or sold as they chose, and his clothing could be donated to the needy.

When he had completed the Will and instructions, he grew tired. There was one thing left for him to do, but he would take care of that tomorrow. He had not heard from Jacob in over a year. He was actually grateful that he had not received a letter once he fell ill, and purposely did not write to him not wanting him to think it was necessary to come to South Africa immediately. Until recently, he could not have visited him at the Sanatorium, thus he preferred to be back home when he came.

While sitting quietly in his room after returning from dinner that evening, Ben coughed and hemorrhaged. He continued to cough up blood three to four times a day—sometimes light, sometimes heavy. By Saturday evening, he couldn't move or speak above a whisper. As quickly as the hemorrhaging had begun, it stopped.

The damage to his morale was irreversible. If nothing else, it showed how frail he had become. How could he consider making the long voyage to England? He would never survive it. His intentions had never been to be a burden to Jacob.

The doctors assured him that despite his setback, he was doing quite well. They urged him not to give up, and it worked. He continued to have visitors, and Jamilia brought him books to read.

Abe Morton came to visit and offered firsthand assurance that Afram was doing splendidly and would probably be enrolled in the South African Native College the following year. He conveyed to him that each Friday at Shabbat Services, the entire congregation's *Amen* followed the Rabbi's prayer for his full and rapid recovery.

Although, he felt lonely and alone before he fell ill, his many visitors showed otherwise. There were people who cared for and about him, and he was touched.

Following Ben's setback, Jamilia approached Abe Morton and suggested that he speak with the Rabbi asking him to write to Jacob telling him of his uncle's illness; that he was on the mend; and that he would be returning home in a few months. There was no immediate need for him to come to South

Africa, but knowing that his uncle had not wanted to concern him with his problems, he was merely giving him a *heads up*.

Ben had decided against writing to Jacob. While he was recuperating, he felt it bought him time. Hopefully, he would make a full recovery before his visit to Cape Town. In the meantime, he focused on himself, growing stronger each day.

In November, Paul and Phil came to visit with news that a buyer had been found for Zeller Jewelers. It was a growing jewelry chain from the United States. If all went well, they would leave Cape Town in the spring. There had not been too much interest in the Annex until just last week when Jonah and Nathan along with three other gem cutters were looking to strike a deal. The brothers were more than willing to work with them.

Spring sounded good to Ben. If all went as the doctors predicted, he could be well by then. At that point, he would not wait for Jacob to come to Cape Town; he would tell him that he was coming to England.

In December, the doctors told Ben that they planned to release him in January. He couldn't return to work; he had to continue to take it slow and easy until he got his strength back. This was no problem; he would tell Paul and Phil that he was retiring and request that they pack up his tools. Jamilia agreed to cook and care for him and even stay at the cottage until he felt better.

He finally got around to writing to Jacob, but his intent was not to mail the letter. If all went well, he would send word that he was coming to England. If anything happened to him, the letter would tell Jacob of his dream to be reunited with him, and about his battle with the illness that had prevented his dream from becoming a reality.

1948 began with hope and renewal. The sale and transfer of Zeller Jewelers would become final on March 30th. The Annex transfer would also become final in March, earlier in the month. The brothers' cottages were both sold with the option to remain until they sailed for England in early April. The two additional stores adjacent to the Annex were sold to the existing tenants.

January 18th was the day that Ben was due to come home. Jamilia brought flowers for the cottage and supplies to prepare meals for Ben. She picked up new books for him to read, and Afram was setting aside his studies to have dinner and spend the evening with him.

Without warning, Ben awoke from a coughing fit and found himself covered with blood. For the next week, it was touch and go, and each time they thought they had lost him, he rallied. On January 25th, Ben lost his battle dying peacefully in his sleep. When the nurse arrived bringing his breakfast, she saw that he had passed.

Jamilia was teaching the children in the basement of the synagogue when the Rabbi's aide came down to tell her that the Sanatorium had called with the news. She was so upset, the young man urged her to leave promising that he would occupy her students until it was time for their parents to pick them up.

Afterwards, she could not recall how she reached Afram; how they got to the Sanatorium; or how she had the presence of mind to stop by Ben's cottage to pick up the envelope he had given her—the envelope that contained his Will and more importantly instructions for his cremation and the shipment of his personal effects to Jacob.

Once they reached Stoneham, she was composed and handled everything efficiently. As they were leaving, a nurse handed the books that she had brought for him to read and an envelope with the name Jacob Lyons written on the front.

Jamilia asked Abe Morton to arrange for a memorial service for Ben at the synagogue that he had attended since coming to Cape Town. It was the same synagogue where Sidney and Franz had been eulogized by the townspeople of their community.

They were all gone now, the three of them—Franz, Sidney, and Ben. Their hearts were heavy and ached with the pain of losing someone exceptional and good—*a real mensch (a person of integrity and honor)* as the Rabbi had said about Franz.

A week after Ben died, Jamilia and Afram went to the cottage to gather the items to be shipped to Ben's nephew. They placed everything on the table to get an idea of how large a crate Afram would have to construct. As they gazed about the room to see if there was anything they missed, they both spoke at once, as their eyes rested on one particular object. "What are we supposed to do with the chest of diamonds?"

They did not hurry their decision. Instead they put great thought into it. In the end, Jamilia concluded that Franz had never wanted to claim ownership of the diamonds, and therefore never felt they were his to give to someone else. *Shiloh—the one to whom it belongs* had been left to them to determine.

At Ben's request, Afram had made a small box and carved a Star of David on top to hold Sidney's ashes. He now did the same for him. The crate he built was long and narrow and resembled the size and shape of a casket. It was sturdy and well built to withstand the voyage to England.

It was large enough to hold the two boxes containing the remains of Ben and Sidney, a small box containing their personal items and mementos, another box containing their diamond cutting tools, and positioned dead center to equally distribute the weight was the carved chest that held Franz's diamond cache.

Afram made arrangements with a local funeral home to deliver the crate to the dock for shipment on the first available freighter to England. Before nailing the lid shut, Ben's letter to Jacob was placed on top. There was nothing identifying the sender of the crate other than the funeral home that they hoped would indicate that the contents were indeed a casket, thereby making shipment of the diamonds secure.

Jamilia took Ben's Will to the bank where she gave it to the manager. The Will was signed and witnessed, but someone who did not know Ben or Jamilia might not have thought it legal enough to accept. She gave him the address for Jacob Lyons and requested that he send a wire notifying him of his uncle's demise.

She further suggested that he advise him of Ben's burial wishes for his and Sidney's remains that were being shipped to him in England, along with various personal items. In addition, since Ben's account at this very bank was now Jacob's, she inquired when the bank would be notifying him to arrange the transfer of funds.

The bank manager smiled broadly. "Jamilia, I'm proud of you. The two years will be up soon, and I can honestly say that you have learned so much in the time I have worked with you in handling your inheritance from Franz Schiller. You are a quick learner, and I have no doubt that you will manage wisely. I understand that Afram is doing great with his studies, and I wish you nothing but the very best.

"I will send the wire immediately and include all of your recommendations."

After 1943, when Albert Schatz, then a graduate student at Rutgers University, discovered *streptomycin* an antibiotic and the first cure for tuberculosis, sanatoria began to close their doors. By the 1950s, Tuberculosis was no longer a major public health threat, controlled by antibiotics rather than extended rest and fresh air.

PART THREE

CHAPTER TWENTY-NINE

L exi was beside herself. It had been two months since she had any contact with Jake. She had posted two letters to the address he had given her and had not received a response. Her calls to Marcus Hirsch were equally as frustrating. His last contact with Jake had been about the same time as hers. To add to her dilemma, she was pregnant.

Graduation from nursing school was a month away, and the following month her brother was getting married. Her father had set sail from Jerusalem and would be arriving in London in two weeks. She hadn't yet decided how she would handle the situation, but felt that with her Pops back home, she could stay with him until the baby was born. She was due to give birth in late September.

Hopefully, by then she would hear from Jake, and they could make plans for their future together when he returned home. Unfortunately that was not to be.

Her graduation in April was a happy event. Her family lauded her accomplishments, amid her two older brothers teasing her endlessly. The Portman family had not been together for some time, and it brought back fond memories of when they were younger.

As May arrived, and Mark and Rosalie's wedding grew closer, she became more apprehensive with each passing day. She had not yet begun to *show,* but as her waistline disappeared her clothes became tight and uncomfortable.

One evening following dinner, her father motioned for her to sit beside him on the sofa. "I've been back in England for over a month, and you haven't said a word about what your plans are. Have you applied for any nursing positions? Have you thought about where you would like to work? It's not like you to be without a plan; you've always had a plan for what you wanted to do."

Lexi was caught off guard by her father's questions. He was right; she always had a plan. "I have several things I'm looking into. I just wanted to get through graduation and Mark's wedding, and then I'll decide."

She was totally unprepared for what came next.

"As I promised, I have returned to England. I would never miss two such important occasions in my children's lives. I only wish your Mum was here.

"That said, I have decided to return to Jerusalem to continue working with the Hadassah Medical Organization. I have learned so much about the organization's involvement throughout Palestine and what they have done not only for the Jews but for the Arabs too. The work is so satisfying and aspiring; they are growing famous for never giving up on a patient before they absolutely must. I agree with that wholeheartedly.

"Hadassah's first project in Palestine was directly connected with the welfare of women and children. Being a Pediatrician, I will always have a special place in my heart for helping children, for helping all children. I might add that their nursing school is unprecedented, and I can see you being a part of it. Why don't you consider coming with me? This tour is for six months. If we're lucky, the War will end by then, and you can return to England. Think on it.

Lexi sat quietly collecting her thoughts and digesting what her father had said. "Are you planning to move to Palestine permanently? You only mentioned my returning. Are you selling this house?"

"Whoa, not so fast. That might be what I decide somewhere down the road, maybe when the War is over. For now, I'm not thinking that far ahead. There is a ship sailing in early June under the guise of a hospital ship. It will not only carry medical personnel, but much needed supplies. The ship is coming from America to Liverpool and then sailing on to Haifa. There will be numerous doctors and nurses from the States when it arrives to pick up those who have signed on from all over England. I'm not certain what the final number will be."

"Pops, I'm truly happy for you. I know you miss Mum, and the work you are doing at the Hadassah Hospital agrees with you. You look happy and content.

"If you are not giving up the house, am I to assume that I can continue to live here? Since the War is ongoing, I'm not anticipating any difficulty in finding a position at a hospital nearby."

"Of course, you can stay here. This is your home."

Lexi figured she had approximately five weeks to make contact with Jake. She rang up Marcus successfully, but unfortunately he had no news for her. There had been no word.

The wedding came and went. She tried reaching Marcus again on several occasions, but when she was told he wasn't available, in lieu of leaving a message opted to say she would try again.

Two weeks prior to her father's sailing date, she was forced to make her decision—the most important decision of her life to date. Although it was hers to make, it would affect not only her, but Jake and their unborn child, as well. She had to get this one right; there was no room for error.

War weary London was depressing at best; Palestine was a total unknown; she only had her father's view of what her life would be like living in Jerusalem.

For days, she had gone over and over which path to take. First and foremost she thought long and hard about telling her father she was pregnant. What if he refused to leave her on her own to have the baby? He had finally found a life for himself after losing her Mum; could she risk ruining that for him? Mark had just gotten married, and she certainly didn't want to be a burden to him and Rosalie. Her brother Sam was in medical school, and she would be living in the house alone. What would happen when she went into labor? There would be no one to help her.

Marcus never entered her thoughts except to see if he had heard from Jake. He and Elena would have welcomed her with open arms and taken care of her and the baby until Jake returned home. She had only briefly met Marcus once and had never met Elena. The thought simply never crossed her mind.

She could wait no longer. As Manny sat reading the paper, she approached him. "We have to talk. I need some Pops advice."

Manny sat listening without interruption as Lexi returned to 11 April 1941 when Jake's family perished in *The Good Friday Raid*. She lowered her voice as she told him about the letter her Mum withheld from her until her last days and then begged her forgiveness. Her voice became more upbeat as she told of running into Jake when she returned home on holiday break from school.

"When Jake and I found ourselves attending the same party, we couldn't believe it. We fell into one another's arms and didn't let go for the remainder of the weekend. We were so young when we met, but we both knew from that very first moment there would never be anyone else for either of us but each other. We had both grown up during our separation; grown up too fast perhaps, but War has a tendency to affect every aspect of our lives. It certainly has ours.

"I returned to school, and Jake returned to his base. He rang me up at school the end of January and told me that he probably wouldn't be able to keep in touch on a regular basis, but he would write or call any time he could. That's the last time I heard from him.

"I have written a couple of times, but received no response. He introduced me to the gentleman who delivered his letter and gave him my contact information to forward any news. The gentleman's name is Marcus Hirsch; his father worked with Jake's father at De Beers. Having lost his entire family, Mr. Hirsch is listed as his contact.

"I have checked in with him from time to time, and he too has heard nothing. As he pointed out to me the last time we spoke, sometimes no news is good news so I try to keep my thoughts positive.

"I haven't said anything to you about any of this because you weren't here, and I knew you would be returning for my graduation and Mark's wedding. When you revealed your plans to return to Palestine, I was taken aback; I wasn't expecting that at all. Please understand, I am not asking you to change your plans in any way. I'm just trying to make some plans of my own, and I'm having a difficult time.

"Before the weekend was over, Jake asked me to marry him, and I accepted." She pulled the chain out for her father to see. "Jake gave me this ring before he left. If there had been time, we would have found a Rabbi to marry us, even though I would have been risking expulsion from nursing school."

Manny pulled her into his arms and held her close. "I am so sorry I have not been here for you. I see now that it was selfish of me to leave not only you but your brothers too, traveling thousands of miles away thinking only of myself. I know how close you were to Mum, and so soon after you lost her was not the time for me to exit your life too.

"I've always been aware of how much you and Jake care for one another; Mum and I discussed it often. You reminded us of ourselves. She never confided in me about the letter; never mentioned Mr. Hirsch's visit. I think she knew that I would have disagreed with her decision and insisted she give it to you.

"Why don't you consider coming with me? As I told you, the nursing school has an excellent reputation and you can take some specialized courses while you use your nursing skills in so many needed ways. The Hadassah Medical Organization is always looking for good people. When this damn War is finally over, we can return to England, and I'll throw you and Jake the biggest and best wedding you ever imagined."

Manny realized that Lexi was crying. "Pops, I'm pregnant. Our baby is due in September."

The next day Manny rose early and set out to make the necessary arrangements for Lexi to accompany him. At first contact with the organization that was sponsoring the trip, he was told that all slots had been filled, and unless someone cancelled, Lexi would be unable to join them.

He left the building disappointed and questioned being so naïve as to offer Lexi something that was not within his power to deliver. At that moment, he turned around and returned to the office he had just left. The same receptionist greeted him. "Did you forget something Dr. Portman?"

"No, but I need to speak with Joe Bergman again. I'll be brief."

She showed him into the office. "Is there something else I can help you with Dr. Portman?"

"No, I have just returned to tell you that I won't be able to go on this tour. I can't and won't leave my daughter alone in London. My wife passed away last year while she was in school, and I left shortly thereafter for Jerusalem. I returned to England for her graduation, and learning that she had not yet secured a position, I wrongfully assumed that she could come on board. She is a registered nurse, and knowing that medical personnel are always needed, I felt it would be good experience for her while she would be helping others, which is all she ever wanted to do since she was a little girl."

Joe Bergman was well aware of his efforts on behalf of the children's program; he did not want to lose Dr. Manny Portman. So close to sailing, there was little chance he could be replaced. "Perhaps I responded too hastily; I should have at least offered to look into the matter. I am offering that now, and although I cannot promise the outcome you wish, I would suggest that you get your daughter's passport and papers in order just in case."

"Thank you. I appreciate anything you can do." They shook hands and this time, Manny left more upbeat and hopeful.

He did not mention his conversations with Joe Bergman or that there was a possibility that neither of them would be sailing in two weeks. Instead, he sat down with Lexi and filled out the necessary papers. The next day, they would apply for her passport stressing urgency for immediate issue.

A young nurse who had been one of the first to sign on was having second thoughts. She had spoken with Joe Bergman twice about dropping out, but each time had reconsidered and remained ready to go. When he rang her up to notify her of the orientation meeting she was required to attend, she began crying and told him once again, she decided to drop out.

Manny and Lexi attended the orientation. On the way to the meeting, they picked up Lexi's Passport and Visa. They were set to go.

In mid-1942, Hospital Ships simply did not exist in the United States.

There was an Army-Navy dispute over how many Hospital Ships should be obtained and which service should build and operate them. As a result of these problems, the Joint Chiefs of Staff decided to procure only three Army Hospital Ships.

The debate continued, and precious time was lost as refitting and commissioning went slow, taking months to receive authorization to partially convert a single ship. The first US Army Hospital Ship only reached British waters a short time before the Normandy Invasion.

Continuing deliberations, additional requirements, lack of decisions, took their toll, and not much happened. In the spring of 1943, the Surgeon General requested ships for evacuation purposes not to be used as floating hospitals. This resulted in a decision to convert smaller troopships as hospital ships, and to register them under the Geneva Convention, in order to assure safe passage.

In May 1944, the USAHS Recovery bearing the Geneva hospital ship symbol—a large Red Cross—left Brooklyn, New York, for Southampton, England. The ship carried medical supplies and equipment and medical personnel en route to Palestine, stopping in England to pick up additional doctors and nurses who had signed on for a six-month tour. The ship was due to dock in Haifa in two weeks. From there, a convoy of busses and trucks would transport all personnel and supplies to Jerusalem.

The ship was equipped with comfortable sleeping quarters; food though basic was plentiful. The doctors socialized by spending time discussing medical issues; the nurses were mostly younger and discussed a myriad of things including boyfriends, life in the States as compared to England, and what they looked forward to when the War was over. None of the nurses were married.

For the most part, Lexi enjoyed the crossing. The nurses were friendly and meshed together well, expressing where they hoped they would be assigned.

The USAHS Recovery sailed into Haifa on a beautiful sunny day. Everyone was on deck as the small crowd that had gathered welcomed their arrival. They spent the remainder of the day unwinding. A buffet dinner was set up for two hours allowing individuals to eat when they wished. They stayed the night in Haifa.

Overnight the supplies had been loaded onto trucks. After breakfast, the busses awaited all personnel and luggage. At 10:00 a.m., the convoy started out for the 151 km journey to Jerusalem.

The nurses from America were much more outgoing than the British nurses. They were singing and talking most of the trip, but it felt good to be around them. Lexi was quiet and spent much of her time thinking about Jake. Where was he? Was he safe? Why couldn't he write to her? All questions that remained unanswered.

CHAPTER THIRTY

The origin of the earliest known civilizations is traced back to the Middle East where the land of Palestine was comprised of a human habitation existing even before Biblical times. Its land area refers to the region that lies between the interior of Syria and the southern Mediterranean coastal plains. In the Old Testament, the land is not called Palestine but Canaan.

The land of Palestine populated by religiously diverse Jews, Christians, Muslims, and Druze people for the most part lived peacefully between Biblical times and the modern era. However, with the Zionist movement of the 20th century, a large number of Jews immigrated to Palestine from many parts of Europe increasing the Jewish population drastically, leading to endless conflicts between Arabs and Jews.

The Palestine Mandate was instituted by the League of Nations entrusting Great Britain with the Mandate to administer non-self-governing territories under a temporary trust that would see to the wellbeing and advancement of its population.

The British Mandate authorities granted the Jewish and Arab communities the right to run their internal affairs. In August 1929, the Jewish Agency was established with a council, an executive committee, and an administrative committee. Each of these bodies consisted of an equal number of Zionist and non-Zionist Jews.

The Zionists settling Palestine brought one great asset—organizational acumen. This allowed the movement despite deep ideological differences to achieve a centralized Jewish economic infrastructure in Palestine while promoting religious, educational, cultural, and medical services.

The Jewish community wanted to help their fellow Jews who were being murdered by the Nazis all over Europe, but strict immigration quotas prevented them from fleeing to Mandatory Palestine, resulting in the Jewish Agency organizing and pursuing illegal immigration from 1939 to 1942.

This proved to be a very dangerous operation. Many of the ships sank or were caught, and compared with the number of attempts, few ships actually arrived successfully to Mandatory Palestine. Despite the danger and failures, tens of thousands of Jews were saved by illegal immigration. Those who arrived during this time were part of the Aliyah Bet.

During World War II, Palestinian Jews volunteered in large numbers resulting in 30,000 serving in the British Army, mainly in North Africa. Others were sent to Europe as emissaries to organize local resistance and rescue operations. While 5,000 others in the Jewish Brigade were dispatched to participate in the Italian campaign in late 1944, and later took part in the 1945 spring offensive in Italy against the German forces.

When the caravan of buses and trucks arrived in Jerusalem, the excitement on the bus carrying the nurses was infectious. None of the young women had been to Palestine before, and they all seemed to be talking at once.

It had been a long trip, but it was worth it. Lexi's last minute decision to join Manny had not allowed time for him to talk about what to expect; he spoke mainly about the medical center. She was quite impressed. As she stepped off the bus, she felt a flutter in her belly. Placing a hand over her stomach, she smiled to herself, confident that she had made the right decision.

They were shown to their temporary housing where they would stay until they were assigned to their posts. The doctors knew where they would be going as most had been on previous tours serving in their specialty. The nurses would be allowed to choose their first option followed by monthly rotations so that they could gain experience serving on different units.

However, for the first night, everyone dined together, and what a night it was. The food was unbelievable, and the nurses being a little less serious with their singing and dancing managed to loosen up the doctors' moods. By the time everyone returned to their rooms, they were exhausted.

Lexi fell asleep with her hands resting on her abdomen. She felt her baby move; their was no denying, she was carrying their child who would be born in Eretz Israel (the land of Israel)—a *Sabra*.

The Hadassah Medical Center is a medical organization established in 1934. The cornerstone for the Hadassah Hospital on Mount Scopus was laid that same year, and after five years of construction, the complex opened its doors in 1939 offering schools of medicine, dentistry, nursing, and pharmacology all affiliated with the Hebrew University of Jerusalem.

Its declared mission: *to extend a hand to all, without regard for race, religion, or ethnic origin.*

Lexi was assigned to the Pediatric Ward of the hospital. Her Nursing Supervisor was Bella Kahn. At their very first meeting on her very first day as she showed her around the ward, she asked, "When is your baby due?"

Lexi could not believe it. "I'm due the end of September."

"Well then, maybe we can keep you here in Pediatrics until you have the baby. At that time, if you wish to move to another unit, we can certainly see to that. In the meantime, I will introduce you to Dr. Henry Kahn who happens to be my husband, and who will take very good care of you and deliver your baby."

Everyone at the hospital was so nice. They were efficient in every way, and although she had come to serve, they seemed to be serving and helping her. She told Bella about Jake, and that her father was Dr. Manny Portman. Bella had met him briefly, but never worked with him. She thoroughly understood that he could not leave her in London.

Her father was based in Hebron 29 km away at the Medical Organization's infirmary—*the Beit Hadassah Clinic.* Although he spent a good deal of time in Hebron, he often visited their widespread system of clinics in Jewish centers and hospitals in the principle towns throughout Palestine. Therefore, they didn't see one another every day.

At the end of June, he arranged to spend the weekend with her. He wanted to introduce her to the city of Jerusalem and its surroundings, take her to dinner at the King David Hotel, and simply show her why he fell in love with Palestine hoping she would share his enthusiasm for the program.

He also wanted to make sure she was feeling good, and that she was seeing a doctor. Working at the hospital was the perfect place for her to be. She was never alone, ate regularly and well, and the nurses' quarters were on the hospital grounds.

"How do you like this place? Is it not inspiring? They do such wonderful things here, and help so many people. They've managed to thrive under the Palestine Mandate, and one can only imagine what they will accomplish when the State of Israel becomes a reality."

It was fun being with Pops. As a child, the two of them often went off for an afternoon together. It all seemed so long ago. She wondered what kind of father Jake would be. If they had a girl, would he take off with her for an afternoon of adventure as she and Pops had on so many occasions? Of course, he would, but he would insist she go along too. If they had a boy, he would undoubtedly teach him the art of diamond cutting.

As the weekend was coming to an end, Manny sat holding her hands. "I received a letter from my brother telling me that Ivan has shipped out to the Pacific. He also wrote that before he left, he learned that Jake was listed as *Missing*. There were no further details. It was reported in the papers as they do from time to time once the families have been notified.

"I know it's useless of me to tell you not to worry. You'll worry anyway. I thought about not telling you, but I didn't think that was right either. You have to believe in your heart that he is okay. When he returns, just think how happy he will be to find out that he's a father."

After their beautiful weekend, the news about Jake was upsetting. Although she tried her best to contact him and had not succeeded, she never feared or had a gut feeling that he was in danger, hurt, or worse. He promised to come back to her, and she never for one minute believed that he wouldn't keep that promise.

She was glad her father told her what Ivan had learned. There had been enough secrets between her and her parents. She wondered if Marcus had tried to contact her at the house in Middlesex. There was no one living there, but he could perhaps have left a note or posted a letter. Mark was checking the house for mail, but there had been no word.

In hindsight, she realized that she should have told Marcus that she was leaving for Jerusalem with her father. Although she blamed the oversight on her last minute decision and their hasty departure, there was nothing stopping her from posting a letter and apprising him now that she was settled. She made no move to do so.

She enjoyed working with the children at the hospital. When she was in school, none of the patients were children; most were military. Bella kept an eye on her to make sure she didn't overdo.

Lexi felt good. Being pregnant agreed with her. She was more beautiful than ever with the glow of pregnancy. How she wished Jake was here as she guided his hands to feel their baby move. But most of all, she yearned to feel his protective arms around her keeping them safe.

In July, a few of the nurses went on a day trip to Tel Aviv. It was the last month the doctor would allow her to travel. It was a perfect beach day and the girls brought bathing suits so they could go swimming.

Lexi had never seen water as blue at the Mediterranean. It reminded her instantly of Jake's deep blue eyes. As her friends frolicked in the water, she was content to sit on her blanket and watch.

They ate dinner at a small local restaurant recommended by one of the doctors. They had no idea what they were eating; the owners just kept bringing dish after dish. Finally they could eat and drink no more. They thanked the couple for their hospitality, and left to catch the bus back to Jerusalem.

They were quiet on the trip back. Lexi slept on and off dreaming of Jake, unaware that 2,000 miles across the sea on Guernsey Island, Jake struggled to recall who he was and put a face to the name *Lexi* that Lulu Walsh said he called out for in his sleep.

In mid-September, Manny came to Jerusalem to stay with Lexi until the baby was born. 25 September 1944, Lexi gave birth to a girl weighing exactly eight pounds; she had her mother's red hair and her father's deep blue eyes, ten perfect fingers, ten perfect toes, and a button nose. Manny called her a

Lexi *clone* and accepted many a *Mazel Tov on* becoming a *Zeyda* (grandfather). Lexi named their beautiful daughter *Zoe Elise Lyons*.

She returned to work at the hospital in mid-October. Bella told her she could bring Zoe with her, and they would put a crib in one of the small offices. This would allow Lexi to nurse her, and look in on her throughout the day. The tour was due to end in December. By then, Zoe would be three months old.

The arrangement worked to everyone's benefit. Lexi could continue working; she did not have to find someone to care for Zoe while she was at the hospital; and she could spend every possible moment with her daughter. She couldn't have planned or hoped for a better outcome.

Once a month, they called London at an arranged time to talk with her brothers. Each time, Manny asked if there was any mail for either of them. There was nothing other than the bills for the house that Mark was taking care of.

As the end of the year approached, Manny decided the time had come to make a few decisions.

Lexi had been thinking about what she should do, as well. The War was still ongoing although the Allies had proven victorious of late. Many felt the War would be over in months. She knew deep in her heart that her father wanted to remain in Palestine. He loved what he was doing, and she did not want her responsibilities to spill over into his life.

If she returned home alone, she would have to find someone to care for Zoe while she worked and hospital hours could be sporadic at times. If she worked days, she would be home nights when Zoe was sleeping. If she worked nights, she would have to sleep during the day so she could go to work at night.

She had approached Bella asking if there were classes she could suggest in specialized pediatric care, and if she could continue working at the hospital part time. As she and her father sat down to discuss the approaching end of the tour, she had a plan.

"I know you would like to stay and continue your work. What I need to know is are you planning to make the move permanent? As for Zoe and me,

I would like to some day go back to London. Until the War is over, I feel that I'm in a better place here, especially while Zoe is a baby.

"I've spoken with Bella, and there are classes I would like to take, and she has agreed that I can continue to work part time at the hospital. I would, however, have to get my own apartment and find someone to care for Zoe.

"When the War is over, and I learn of Jake's fate, I will deal with it. I have no other choice, but I have not given up hope nor will I until I learn the truth.

"I have a plan Pops. What do you think?"

Manny hugged her and held her close. "I love you, and I'm very proud of you; that's what I think. I am leaning toward staying here permanently, but not just yet. As I promised, I will throw you and Jake the grandest wedding ever when he comes home.

"I have to see about getting our Visas extended. If I do decide to make my move permanent, I will look for a permanent position, as well. It would be nice to live close to you and Zoe. Perhaps we can find a small house that would give us more room and prove a better choice if I do decide to stay on. It would allow me to see my daughter and granddaughter each and every day; I could help with Zoe while you study.

"You should make signing up for your classes a priority. When we find a place to live, we can look into getting someone to care for Zoe."

Although Lexi was confused and uncertain of the choices she made in London, she had given great thought to her plans to remain in Palestine. For now, it seemed both practical and logical to remain where they were.

Lexi loved being a mother. She loved cuddling Zoe and singing to her and telling her about how she and Jake had met and fallen in love. The child didn't have a clue what she was talking about, but as her deep blue eyes looked into Lexi's she seemed to be absorbing each and every word.

She was a happy child content to entertain herself looking at the big Teddy Bear Manny bought her or chewing on her teething ring, or rattle. Each month, Lexi took her to the photographer, and he took a picture of the two of them. She wanted the pictures to be in color so that Zoe's red hair and deep blue eyes were prominent. Her intent was to capture as much as she possibly could of the time Jake missed seeing her grow. She also bought a camera.

—~m~—

On 2 November 1917, Britain's Lord Balfour announced that His Majesty's Government views with favor the establishment of a national home in Palestine for the Jewish people. One year later, World War I came to an end. Euphoric over the Balfour Declaration and certain that England was on their side, the Jews of Palestine presented the British with a gift of land on Mount Scopus for a cemetery. The site on a mountain top 834 meters above sea level with vast military and historical significance was the perfect location.

In 1925, Mount Scopus became the site of the world's first Hebrew University. It was joined soon afterwards by Hadassah Hospital, without question the most modern and well-equipped medical facility in the entire Middle East. But there was a serious drawback to the location; the single road to both the hospital and the university was surrounded by hostile Arab neighborhoods.

It didn't take the Arabs long to realize how easy it would be to blockade the road. They ambushed many Jews naïve enough to try passing through, despite the fact that the British, who still controlled Palestine, had promised the Jews safe passage to Mount Scopus. Realizing that the Hadassah Hospital benefited many Arabs, as well as the Jews, the attacks abated.

In the six months since Lexi arrived in Palestine, there had been isolated incidents of Arab attacks but none involved the immediate area surrounding the hospital and the university.

Manny found a small house near Mount Scopus and thought the location aptly suited their needs. Lexi would be attending the university and working at the hospital which were both in walking distance or a short ride by bus. He was also seeking a position at the hospital for himself.

At the end of the year, a farewell party was thrown for the doctors and nurses leaving to return to England and the States. Everyone was saddened to say to goodbye to all the wonderful people they worked with and especially to Lexi, Zoe, and Manny who were remaining.

For Lexi, the New Year brought thoughts of happier times, and sadness that she and Zoe were without Jake by their side. She could not fathom that it was just one year ago that she and Jake had found one another only to lose contact with one another again one brief month later.

Moving into their new home and enrolling in the university helped get her mind back into perspective. Once she had the schedule for her classes, she would speak with Bella about her hours at the hospital and begin searching in earnest for someone to care for Zoe.

By the time her classes started, all was going according to plan. Bella recommended a friend to care for Zoe. Eva Goodman was a retired nurse whose husband had passed away five years ago, and whose only son was killed in an Arab attack. Being alone, she welcomed taking care of a small child and offered to prepare dinner to give her something to do.

Eva Goodman was an excellent cook, and it became the norm for her to join them for dinner each night before leaving for home. She and her husband had moved from Poland to Jerusalem when their son was a little boy. Lexi loved hearing the stories she told about what the Country was like when they arrived and how far it had come. On weekends, they played it by ear, often inviting Eva to join them when they went on what Lexi called *an adventure*.

Manny was successful in landing a temporary position at the Hadassah Hospital. They were in the process of expanding the Pediatric Department to include a research lab devoted to eliminating childhood diseases. The current head of the department was due to take over the responsibilities of setting up and running the new lab. At that time, the position would become permanent, and Manny would become the new head of the Pediatric Department.

The months flew by. Being busy was the key. It didn't allow much time to dwell on the past or to worry about the future. Zoe brought much joy into their lives. With each new accomplishment—*rolling over, sitting up, crawling, her first tooth, and first words*—Lexi thanked God for her each and every day.

In March when the new lab opened, Manny accepted the permanent position as Head of Pediatrics. On their call to London at month's end, he excitedly told his sons adding that Lexi was taking courses at the university and working at the hospital. Her plans for the present were to remain with him. He urged Mark and Rosalie to reconsider moving into the house. There was no mail or messages for either of them. Before ending the call, Lexi promised she would send long awaited pictures of Zoe.

Zoe was a virtual chatterbox. Mama, bye-bye, Pops were her favorites. She was standing, and when she thought no one was watching, dared taking a step or two. On nice days, Eva would put her in her stroller and take her for walks around the campus of the university. She was often stopped with exclamations of—*What a beautiful little girl you are!* Zoe always acknowledged her admirers with a big smile.

April brought continued good news about the War, but May brought the news everyone had long awaited—on 9 May1945, the Axis surrendered and the War in Europe was over.

Businesses closed; schools were dismissed; there was dancing in the streets. The Nazis had finally been defeated but not before millions died in gas chambers, starved in concentration camps, and bled on the fields of battle. One could not find a single human being in the Palestine Jewish community that the War did not affect. Entire families had been lost, lifetimes of achievement had been erased, scholars, writers, doctors—the heritage of a people, all gone.

For those who survived, Palestine was their future. The British Mandate had promised a Jewish State, and the time had come to collect on that promise.

Lexi would look back on that time as a *waiting game*. She didn't expect to hear from Jake immediately, but four months later when the War ended in the Pacific, she became apprehensive that no news was forthcoming, good or bad.

In September, Zoe was one year old. Eva baked a cake, and they sang

Happy Birthday and urged her to blow out the lone pink candle. When they called London, they learned Rosalie was expecting, but there was no mail, no calls, no mention of a visitor inquiring about Manny; Rosalie had completely forgotten about Marcus's visit months earlier. Actually, when she gave him the contact information he was seeking for his friend, she never gave thought to mention it to Manny.

CHAPTER THIRTY-ONE

After leaving the base, Jake caught the train to the Cotswolds. He arrived at the cottage to find that Marcus and Elena had fully stocked the kitchen with food basics, along with towels and sheets and many other necessary items that Elena insisted needed a woman's touch. There was a vase of flowers and a bottle of wine on the dining table with a note: *Welcome home Jake. We Love you.* It was signed Marcus and Elena.

Marcus had taken care of everything on the list that Jake had left with him—a thorough house cleaning, touchup painting inside and out, utilities and phone hookup, and moving the Ford V-8 from storage to the garage. The landscaper cleaned up the areas that had been neglected and planted flowers both front and back. Lastly, the outdoor furniture had been removed from the shed, washed down, and placed on the upper and lower patios.

It was good to be home; it felt right; he and the cottage were a perfect fit. He would have preferred to share it with Lexi, but that wasn't the case; he was on his own. In the next few weeks, he would hire a moving service to move the items that he decided to keep from the house in Middlesex to the cottage.

The first priority was setting up his workshop in the cellar. It had been years, since he cut and polished a diamond, and he was anxious to get back to it. But first, he had to catalogue the diamonds both polished and rough, as well as, the gold and other items of jewelry that were part of the inventory in Max's shop.

And last but certainly not least he would have a safe installed where he could keep everything secure.

He rang up Marcus and Elena to tell them he had arrived home. He thanked them for all they had done, and invited them to join him for dinner at the cottage the following evening—instructing them to bring absolutely nothing but themselves.

Jake rose early the next morning and made breakfast. He checked out the supplies that Elena had brought and found he had several choices. He opted for a cheese omelet before realizing that it brought back memories of Lexi. As he ate, he mulled over in his mind what he needed to pick up in the Village for dinner.

He checked the cupboards for dinnerware and flatware and found a couple of tablecloths with matching napkins in the drawer below.

He washed the pan, dish, and utensils he used for his breakfast, and placed them back where he found them.

He decided to walk to the Village to scope it out and see what restaurants and shops carrying groceries were available. There were several—a café, two pubs, a cozy restaurant that advertised authentic homemade meals, a small grocery, and seasonal stalls selling fresh produce.

The restaurant was closed, but as he peered through the glass door, a woman inside opened the door and asked if she could help him. Inviting him in, they chatted for twenty minutes. He introduced himself and told her he was the new owner of the Wentworth Cottage; that he had invited two very special people to dinner; that his cooking expertise was limited to omelets; and asked if she could offer any suggestions.

Mandy Hastings laughed aloud. "My suggestion would be to take them out; it would be easier. I sense, however, that you want to entertain them in your new home, am I right?"

Jake felt relieved. "Yes, you are spot on right. Am I that obvious?"

"No, not at all. There are men that feel at home in the kitchen; men that want to learn to feel at home in the kitchen; and men who wouldn't be caught dead in the kitchen, except to eat, of course. I think you're the second kind.

"Let's put our heads together, figure out what the main course should be, and I will prepare a meal for you to take home and simply put in the oven, giving you all the particulars to cook it to perfection. Add a starch, vegetables, and if you think you can handle preparing a salad, you can pick up fresh produce at the stalls up the street. For dessert and bread, you'll find that the Café has an excellent selection."

Jake could not believe his good fortune. "Thank you from the bottom of my heart. My guests are the two most important people in my life, and I want this evening to be the best."

Mandy offered to prepare the meal in her own pans and deliver it to the cottage later that afternoon, telling Jake he could return them along with any utensils the next day.

He walked up the street to the produce stalls and selected an array of greens, peppers, radishes, cucumbers, and tomatoes. He picked up vinegar and oil for salad dressing, and then made his way to the Café where he bought a hearth-baked bread, and a small pear flan for dessert.

Among the supplies Elena had brought were coffee and an assortment of tea. He hurried back with his purchases excited that he was entertaining in his new home. It was quite fitting that his first guests would be Marcus and Elena.

It was too early to prepare the salad so he put everything in the refrigerator including the flan. He found a large bowl and salad servers and set them on the counter. Next, he selected the ecru tablecloth and covered the table. Removing plates, cups, glasses, and utensils, he began placing them at each seat.

As he stepped back to view his first attempt at setting a table, he recalled the many special dinners his mother had prepared and how the dishes and glasses had sparkled under the lights of the chandelier like diamonds. Instead of making him sad, he found himself smiling and wondering. What would Ada Lyons think of his table? She would approve; of that he was certain.

Finding himself with time to spare, he went to the cellar and sketched a layout of where to place his workbench, install the safe, and add storage bins.

In the morning he planned to go to the house in Middlesex. His clothes were there, and he could bring the smaller personal items such as photographs to the cottage. The writing desk that stood in the upstairs hallway that had been his mother's, and a few of the wall paintings that they brought with them would be moved later. He planned to offer the new furniture that had come with the house to the new buyers as part of the package.

Everything in the cellar would be relocated to the cottage when the workshop had been completed. He planned to meet with a contractor to get an estimate and timeline when the work could begin.

Once everything had been moved, he would put the house in Middlesex up for sale.

Mandy was true to her word and arrived at the cottage at 4:00 p.m. The larger pan held the Roast seasoned and marinating ready to be placed in the oven. Two smaller pans held the potatoes and vegetables also ready for the oven.

She removed the salad makings from the refrigerator and showed Jake how to tear the lettuce instead of cutting the greens with a knife. With a small paring knife, she showed him how to cut the cucumbers, the radishes, and the tomatoes on an angle. Covering the bowl with a towel, she placed it back in the refrigerator.

For the salad dressing, she produced a small cruet that held vinegar on one side and oil on the other that when poured came out in one stream.

She checked out the table and told Jake he had done a fine job. The wine was chilling in the refrigerator to accompany the petite vegetable pies Mandy's restaurant was noted for.

The kettle sat on the stove with water; an assortment of tea, cups, saucers, dessert plates, and utensils sat out on the sideboard.

He hugged her spontaneously and stepped back embarrassed. "Thank you Mandy. I think my friends are going to know I sure didn't do all of this myself. The next time, I plan to bring them to dine at your restaurant. I'll see you in the morning to drop off the pans.

"You don't know how much this means to me, but more than your helping me pull off dinner tonight, I have a new friend and what I hope is the beginning of a long and mutual friendship. I think I'm going to enjoy living here."

"You are so welcome Jake. We don't get too many new people around here, and the War has brought too many changes. We need some new, young blood in the community, and I am pleased that I could help you with your first guests."

Mandy left; Jake checked everything out one last time. He showered and changed clothes walking into the great room as Marcus and Elena drove up.

Jake had turned the tables on his friends. He knew they were intent on making his homecoming special; he knew that Marcus felt terrible about losing contact with Lexi, but he faulted no one. Tonight was all about Jake giving thanks to the most important people in his life just as he had told Mandy.

He reiterated to himself he could never repay them. He had no idea what he would have done or who he would have turned to if Marcus had not come looking for him. They had taken care of all the particulars, including worrying about him, but most of all loving him, and for that he would be eternally grateful.

Marcus opened and poured the wine while Jake brought in the tray of petite pies and placed them on the table in front of the sofa. He returned to the kitchen and put the roast, potatoes and vegetables in the oven noting the time.

As they sat sipping wine, they complimented Jake on the pies. "You have to give me this recipe." Elena teased. "These are delicious."

Jake smiled. "I can always whip you up a batch if you like. It's a family recipe, and I have never shared it before."

Jake started the conversation by telling them his plans to move the contents of the cellar at the house in Middlesex to the cottage. He showed them the sketch he had made sectioning off a room for the workshop adding that he hoped to have the work done and the items moved as quickly as possible, if the contractor he had yet to hire cooperated.

As they savored their wine and petite pies, Elena could no longer contain herself. "Jake, I don't know what we've having for dinner, but the aroma coming from your kitchen is heavenly. I might need to get those recipes too."

Jake accepted the compliment and stood. "The meal will taste just as heavenly if its not overcooked, so I better check on things."

The roast had a few more minutes, so he called out. "Grab a seat and if one of you would be good enough to dish out the salad, I'll bring in the main course."

Mandy had promised a fabulous dinner and that it was. The compliments were often and many, and finally Jake couldn't take anymore. "I know you guys don't believe I made this meal, but the truth is I did do part of it. I made the salad—with help; I put all the food in the oven to cook although I didn't prepare it; I purchased the bread; and I might as well confess that I bought the dessert too. But you have to admit it was better than my taking you out to dinner, was it not?

"The best part is everything is local so you are tasting the best of the Cotswolds, and it's because of you putting me in touch with Meg Wentworth that I found this wonderful cottage—my new home."

They laughed all evening. Jake admitted that he brazenly invited them to dinner before he checked out the Village and what it had to offer. "I don't know what we would be eating if I hadn't found Mandy Hastings; and I promise you we will dine at her restaurant very soon.

"I can, however, make a pretty good omelet; so beware if I invite you to breakfast."

Jake accepted their offer to help clean up. They all pitched in and did the dishes, putting everything back in its place. When they were finished, Jake asked them to take a seat in the Great Room. He had something to tell them; something he should have told them a long time ago.

He began the story of Lexi and Jake; how they met when they were twelve; how they fell for each other that very first time. He told them about the letter; how he didn't feel he had the right to ask her to wait for him; how her mother had withheld his letter until days before she died; how they met by chance at the Savoy New Year's Eve 1943; how he asked her to marry him and she accepted.

"I thought that when I brought her to De Beers to meet you, she would stay in touch with me through you. I don't know what happened; I don't understand why she decided to leave London and move to Palestine with her father without at least telling you or leaving word for me through you.

"At any rate, I've been doing a lot of thinking. My first instinct was to find out everything I could about the man she married and has a child with, but it's not my place. Just as my choices were mine to make, so are hers. My father used to tell me that we control our destiny by the choices we make, but not our fate. Our fates are sealed. When I lost everyone, I realized once again that my father was a very wise man.

"I'm not over Lexi by a long shot. I love her more than ever, and in my heart, I do believe we were meant for each other. I can't imagine that the time will ever come when I no longer love her. I have to accept the fact that we were not fated to be together; I have no other choice.

"My focus right now is to get my life back on track. I told you my plans for moving my things and selling the house in Middlesex. I want to return to cutting and polishing diamonds; I feel close to my father whenever I remember how he nurtured me when I was still a young boy. He was my Hero, and I adored him.

"I was sorry to learn that my Uncle Sidney passed away while I was on Guernsey Island, and I must write to my Uncle Benjamin. Maybe I can schedule a visit to South Africa when I get some of my priorities out of the way. He's alone now too. We're the last two surviving Lyons.

"I love flying, and one of the first things I did when I got back to the base was take a Spitfire for a spin. Aviation is the way of the future, and I plan to get a private general aviation license as soon as I can, maybe buy a small plane.

"Somewhere along the line, I'm going to need a job, so I have to decide what I want to do with the rest of my life.

"That's everything I wanted to tell the two most important people in my life. I love you both, and I intend to see a lot of you. I will always have time to spend with you."

Everyone was crying and hugging and sniffling. Elena stood. "If you don't mind, I'm going to put some water on for tea—just one cup, and then we will head home. I don't want to overstay our visit and chance not be asked back again."

"You may rest assured, that will never happen. My door is and always will be open to the both of you."

The next two months were hectic to say the least, but Jake accomplished what he set out to do. He found a local contractor that was available immediately, but it took two weeks to gather the supplies that were needed causing them to get off to a slow start. It took another two weeks for the contractor and his helper to finish the job, but when all was said and done, he was quite satisfied.

After having the safe installed, he hired a moving service to pick up the boxes he had packed, the small writing desk, and contents of the cellar at the house in Middlesex.

Before he could tackle setting up his workshop, and unpacking, he took the train to London. His first stop was the Brady Street Cemetery where he visited the graves of his family and recited the Kaddish. As he walked back to exit to the street, he came upon a recently dug grave. There was no headstone as yet, but as he glanced down to the temporary card that sat atop the freshly dug earth, he saw the name *Moshe Levin*—Rabbi Levin. Reciting the Kaddish again, he decided to stop by the Great Central Synagogue to see what he could learn.

The last time Jake had seen the Rabbi was months ago when he was granted leave after returning from Guernsey Island. The toll of losing so many friends and congregants during the War had taken a toll on this gentle soul who Jake fondly remembered as a good and decent human being although he had initially viewed him as a harsh and mean Hebrew teacher. He learned the Rabbi had passed away just before he returned home.

He made his way to the Underground and took the train to Middlesex. When he arrived at the house, the realtor awaited him. They went through, room by room, and Jake told her that the furniture was included in the sale, and that no one had ever lived in the house, so it could be presented as *new*.

She liked what she saw. Most of her recent listings were older homes in disrepair after having been neglected during the long years of war. "I have several people in mind that are seeking everything this home offers. One couple in particular that were recently married upon his return from service will be my first choice. So if we can agree on a price, I will get to work. I don't think a gem like this will be on the market long."

"I'm not looking to make a killing on the sale nor am I looking to give it away. I'm hoping we can simply determine a fair price for the buyers and me. I prefer your handling everything through my bank; they will represent me for the closing. There is no mortgage to pay off; I own the home outright. Of course, if any questions or problems should arise, please do not hesitate to contact me."

They shook hands; the realtor left. Jake went through the house one last time. There wasn't as much a feeling of sadness at never having lived in the house, as there was a feeling of those he lost. He could now add Lexi and Rabbi Levin to that list. He had come full circle; there was no one left. It was almost as if the first seventeen years of his life never existed. Throughout the War, he yearned to return to a normal life, the life he knew growing up. He knew now that simply wasn't possible.

His next stop was De Beers; he rang Marcus up and planned to meet him for lunch. As he walked from the station, there was nothing *new to* be seen. The bombed out areas of London remained, indicating it would be a long road back.

They had lunch at Phil's Pub. Jake filled him in about all that was going on at the cottage, and that he had put the house in Middlesex up for sale. He also told him about his visit to the cemetery, and learning that Rabbi Levin had died.

Marcus was happy to see that Jake was moving on. "It's sounds like your *To Do List* is getting shorter; you've accomplished a lot since you've been home.

Have you thought about a job, or what you would like to do?"

"Well, for the immediate next few months, I've got to set up my workshop, inventory what I have from Max's shop, and get back into a little cutting and polishing for personal reasons.

"I know things have changed in the diamond industry. To be honest, I don't see myself cutting diamonds for the rest of my life anymore. Even my father was no longer cutting when he went to work for De Beers.

"Are you asking for a reason?"

Marcus leaned back in his chair; Jake knew him pretty well. "Of course, I am. You are right; the diamond industry has changed. Some changes came about because of the War, but others came about and are ongoing by design. De Beers is about to launch a massive advertising campaign in the United States next year.

"Although what I'm offering is months down the road, I hope you're interested; and if you are, I will work with you and acquaint you with the areas that I think you can help us with. Are you in?"

"Yes, yes I am. Months into next year will allow me to finish up a lot of loose ends, and by the time the campaign gets going, I'll be free to offer you my undivided attention."

They made plans to have dinner over the weekend.

The workshop setup was as he had envisioned. Cataloguing the diamonds, gold, and jewelry took less time than he thought, and when the day arrived for him to return to diamond cutting, he was ready. At first, it was hard for him to get started; memories kept getting in the way. But then the only memory that remained was his father's voice gently guiding him through the process.

The realtor had been right; the house in Middlesex sold to the newly married couple she had mentioned. The sale was complete, and they planned to move in by Christmas. Per his request, the realtor had taken care of everything. If he had chosen to learn the buyers' names—*Thomas and Elizabeth Butler*—would he have connected them in anyway to *Tommy and Betsy*? Probably not, but perhaps he would have.

The end of the year was approaching fast. One evening, Jake decided to go into the Village and have dinner at Mandy's restaurant. It had been some time since he had seen her.

A light snow had fallen days earlier, and the Village enhanced by the holiday decorations was bright and festive. Jake could hardly believe he had been home almost five months. He entered the restaurant and Mandy came over to welcome him.

"Hi stranger. Where have you been?"

Since August, he had eaten at the restaurant a couple times a week. "I apologize to both you and my stomach. I've been preoccupied of late and I don't think I've eaten a complete meal since I was last here."

"We'll take care of that straight away."

She brought him chicken and dumplings; it was the *Special of the Day*. With his dessert and coffee, she included a cup of coffee for herself, and sat down to chat.

Suddenly the door opened and a young woman with a small boy came in.

The boy ran over to Mandy and she lifted him onto her lap. "Auntie Mandy, Mum bought me a book about St. Nicholas."

"Well aren't you a lucky lad; lucky to have a Mum who loves you so much."

The boy jumped down. "Jake, I'd like you to meet my sister-in-law Wendy and my nephew Jason. They're staying with me for a bit."

They left as quickly as they had come. "See you at home."

Mandy's husband John was the eldest of eight children. He suffered a fatal heart attack a few years after they opened the restaurant; and having nowhere else to go, she decided to stay on. She managed to keep the place profitable during the War by availing herself of locally grown produce and reinventing her favorite recipes.

Wendy married John's youngest brother, and *very* soon after, Jason was born. When Britain declared War on Germany, he enlisted in the Royal Navy serving in the Pacific; he was killed when a Japanese torpedo sunk his ship.

Wendy had no family she could count on for help, finding herself alone with a six-year old son to provide for she could think of no one else to turn to except Mandy. Without warning, she had shown up on her doorstep a week earlier.

"I don't know what to do with them. Of course, I want to help them, but the restaurant is not doing well enough to support two more people. She knows nothing about food or cooking and working here is out of the question. And I have to admit, I like my *alone* time and *personal* space. John and I didn't have any kids, and Jason is a good boy, but at my age, I'm just not up to it.

"I was kind of looking forward to business picking up with the War being over and people coming back to their cottages, including bringing new people to the area like you."

Jake asked for another cup of coffee. She brought the pot, and poured them each a cup. "Mandy, when I came into the restaurant looking for your help, I told you then, and I feel even stronger now that what I found above and beyond your help was a friend. Friends help each other. Now it's my turn to help you.

"I'm looking for a housekeeper. There's not a whole lot to do, just general housework, laundry, changing linens, and the like. I may be travelling in the future, and she can keep an eye on the place for me when I'm out of town.

"Do you think that's something she might be interested in? Do you think she could handle the job? I'm the only person living there so her tasks will be minimal and not at all time consuming."

"Why Jake, I had no idea you would be the person to rescue me from my dilemma. I'll ask her when I get home, and if she agrees, I'll bring her around in the morning."

"I've had another thought. She and Jason can live in the carriage house on the far side of my property. That way, they won't be infringing on your space; Jason can go to school in the Village; and if Wendy can take care of the cottage with time to spare, she will be free to work for one of the local shops for extra income.

"I intend to pay her for my housekeeping, but I see no need for her to pay rent on the small house as it isn't being used."

This time, Mandy hugged Jake, and she wasn't the least bit embarrassed.

They all pitched in, and by Christmas, Wendy and Jason were living in the carriage house. Mandy provided them with a small tree and all the trimmings. Christmas Day, Jake brought presents for everyone; Mandy brought dinner; Wendy and Jason had the best holiday in a long time.

Marcus and Elena were spending the holidays with their daughter and her family and were not due to return until after the first of the year. They invited Jake to join them; he declined.

Jake opted to spend New Year's Eve 1945 alone. He knew how fortunate he was, and he felt truly blessed. Compared to others returning from the War, it appeared he had everything. But how could it be said that one had everything when one did not have the one thing one wanted most?

CHAPTER THIRTY-TWO

B y the end of the War the economy of the United Kingdom was exhausted. More than a quarter of its national wealth had been spent, and its war debt was described, by some in the American administration, as a *millstone round the neck of the British economy.*

London was in desperate need of rebuilding on a large scale. All across the City, years of Luftwaffe air raids had left an endless trail of destruction. Architects and planners were quick to see and seize the opportunity for not only rebuilding, but for remodeling. Meanwhile, the population reorganized and rejuvenated itself.

Parks, farmland, and recreation grounds subject to outdated and strict building and development regulations had to be dealt with in order to move forward. High-rise housing and the construction of eight satellite towns were touted as the solution to London's growing population, replacing housing lost during the War and London's slums.

In addition, hundreds of airfields were built across Britain before and after the outbreak of war to accommodate the last generation of heavy bombers. These bases were hurriedly constructed amid the quiet British Countryside, as the new aircraft required extensive runways, hangars, and support buildings. For the vast majority, 1945 saw wartime airfields returned to the farmers and landowners they were purchased from. Others that did not remain in operation were abandoned.

Those with foresight saw General Aviation as the future. A majority of RAF pilots went from high school to flying, and had never considered a career to return to. Some chose to remain in service as flight instructors, while others opted to become a part of the public's growing interest in flying.

In April, Jake learned of the opening of *Eagle Aerodrome* on the former site of RAF Northleach near the Cotswold town of the same name in Gloucestershire. It was one of the first private airfields to open after the War. The abandoned airfield purchased by two recently discharged RAF pilots began with two reconditioned planes—a Beechcraft Model 17 Staggerwing and a Piper J-3 Cub—both built during the War. The new aerodrome offered flying lessons, and the planes were available to rent by licensed pilots at an hourly rate.

Determined to get a private flying license, Jake set out for the airfield to see what he could learn. He yearned to fly again, and if he could rent a plane from time to time and take off into the wind blue yonder, what could be better than that? The airfield's proximity to the cottage was simply another plus.

The aerodrome was owned by cousins Tim and Joe Hanks, both RAF ace pilots, and employed two mechanics and an additional flight instructor. Since the base had recently closed, it was in pretty good shape and did not require any major renovations. A fresh coat of paint on the hangars and buildings topped off with the large brightly painted *Eagle Aerodrome* sign was an impressive sight to see as one approached the airfield.

Jake found a home. He signed up for lessons to get acquainted with flying the two planes and applied for his private license.

De Beers Consolidated Mines, Ltd. took control of the world diamond trade by closing the mines, stockpiling diamonds, and selling them strategically in order to control both distribution and price.

A worldwide decline of diamond prices in the 1930's led the Oppenheimer family to figure out a way to not only control both supply and demand but to stabilize the market. They determined In order to accomplish this feat, they would need the help of an ad agency.

As early as 1938 when they began their search for an ad agency, the global economy was suffering and Europe was under the threat of war. Their challenge was to figure out which country had the most potential to support a growing diamond market, and then hire an ad agency to implement a marketing campaign in that country.

Because of Europe's preoccupation with the oncoming war, the United States was chosen—even though the total number of diamonds sold in the States had declined by 50% since the end of World War I.

Sir Oppenheimer's son Henry travelled to New York to meet with advertising ad agency N.W. Ayer based on their idea to conduct extensive research on social attitudes about diamonds, and then strategically change those attitudes to appeal to a wider audience.

The game plan was to create a situation where almost every person pledging marriage felt compelled to acquire a diamond engagement ring! Although the concept of an engagement ring had existed since medieval times, it had never been widely adopted. In addition, before World War II, only 10% of engagement rings contained diamonds.

Ayer used traditional marketing tools such as newspapers, magazines, and radio; they created entertaining and educational content supporting their product but not explicitly about it. There was no direct sale to be made; there was no brand name to be impressed on the public's mind; there was simply an idea—the eternal emotional value surrounding the diamond. They sold their story about people who gave diamonds or were given diamonds, and how happy and loved diamonds made them feel.

Between 1938 and 1941, a 55% increase in America's diamond sales was reported; the increase was attributed solely to De Beers' ad campaign.

Now that the War was over, De Beers was stepping up their campaign; they had a large new market—returning soldiers, sailors, and marines eager to become engaged and marry the girls who had faithfully awaited their return.

Marcus rang up Jake and asked if he could come to London for a meeting.

The De Beers ad campaign was about to make history, and Marcus wanted Jake to be a part of it.

By the spring of 1946, the RMS Queen Elizabeth, having fulfilled her wartime role, was refitted and furnished as an ocean liner and entered Cunard White Star's two-ship weekly crossings to New York.

In June, Marcus, Elena, and Jake set sail aboard the Queen Elizabeth departing Southampton for New York. They would be gone approximately six weeks including crossing time. Marcus took the opportunity to combine business with pleasure by including Elena so they could celebrate their 40th Anniversary in the States the end of June. They had never been to America.

Jake had spent an entire year in the States learning to fly. He had never been to New York, although he had been on a train that passed through New York, on its way south; his time was spent in Georgia and Alabama. He too was about to celebrate an anniversary—one year since his return to England from Guernsey Island.

The crossing was exciting. People were once again beginning to venture beyond home shores and America was the #1 destination for most. Marcus and Elena had not left England since before the War, and this trip brought back fond memories of their trips to Paris, Florence, and Milan; it had been too long. Marcus looked forward to taking care of business for De Beers, but while at sea, he was determined to relax and enjoy being on holiday.

One morning following breakfast, Elena excused herself. "You are on your own for the remainder of the morning. I'm off for a bit of *personal pampering* at the Beauty Salon."

Marcus decided to take the opportunity to fill Jake in on what to expect at their meetings in New York. After a brisk walk around the deck, they found two empty deck chairs set apart from the long row offering privacy.

"When we met in my office to discuss this trip, I placed my emphasis solely on the ad campaign and the Company's plans to upgrade and extend it. There are, however, other sides to the story, a personal side and a side that includes you.

"I will begin by explaining my thoughts that include you. As an employee of De Beers, my position is that of consultant and advisor on behalf of the Company but in no way do I have the final say. I see my position as another view for the future of De Beers and diamonds; a view that is all about the next generation and the next and the next. Our young men and women are our future—you are our future.

"I realize that your experience in the world of diamonds is limited, however, the many times I have watched you exhibit integrity, resilience, ingenuity, loyalty, and just plain common sense in dire situations puts you in a class of your own. All of these attributes are quite valuable in the business world. I might add, when De Beers hired me, I had not been tested by any of these attributes.

"You will learn when we get to New York that there are many opportunities available to learn anything and everything you ever wanted to know about diamonds that goes far beyond the talent that you possess to cut and polish a rough stone into a magnificent thing of beauty. Your father often told me that he learned so much from De Beers, and it was true; but we learned a good deal from him.

"Cutting and polishing will ultimately evolve into a quicker process, a more precise process as new innovative ideas are introduced. That is inevitable. I see your inherent ability and talent going far beyond sitting at a bench transforming rough stones.

"The position I am offering you is actually mine. Now we come to the personal side of the story. Elena and I have been talking about my retiring, not immediately but definitely in the near future. This position will require a good deal of travelling to and from the States, and other countries, as they get onboard.

"At this point in my life, I'm looking forward to a quieter and slower pace, not the exciting and hectic one that the Company is aiming for, and I have no doubt will accomplish.

"I think you know me well enough to know my offer is not without merit. Your qualifications especially for someone so young are impressive, and as I've told you there are many opportunities available to expand and learn.

"After we return from New York, we can discuss your feelings and if you wish to proceed. I expect nothing less than your own truthful decision; a decision based on your desires and needs, not mine."

Jake sat quietly and gathered his thoughts. "Marcus, I don't think I ever told you, but one of the reasons my father accepted the position you offered him was his gut feeling that you were a good and honorable man, and he trusted you.

"As I have repeatedly told you, you are my Guardian Angel, and I am deeply honored by and grateful for your offer. It not only sounds exciting, but working with you would be a dream come true. My gut is telling me that this trip could be just the beginning of a whole new life for me. On that basis, you have my word that before making my decision, I will take everything into consideration.

"I never gave thought to getting a university degree; growing up, it was never discussed. From the time I was a young boy, I only wished to emulate my Papa, my Hero. Just after my sisters were born, Rabbi Levin met with my father to tell him that I had been skipping too many Hebrew classes, and that although years away, my becoming a Bar Mitzvah was in jeopardy.

"After dinner that night, my father asked me to join him for a walk. When we stopped walking, he waving his hand around and said, *Jacob, this is Hatton Garden, better known as London's Jewelry Quarter and the center of England's diamond trade.* He went on to tell me that was where he aspired to open a Jewelry Emporium of his own.

"By the time we returned home, we had reached a deal. School would be out in a week. I gave up going to camp for the summer in exchange for my Papa's teaching me to cut and polish rough stones. Before that time, I had only observed my father at work. In the fall, I would resume my Hebrew lessons and make him and Mama proud.

"I will never forget that very first day. With the lunch my mother prepared for us in hand, we set off for Max Lerner's shop. In the back of the store at the workbench were my very own tools that he bought for me—a Scaif, measuring devices, and rough diamonds ready for cutting.

"I learned that the actual process of how diamonds are cut and polished consists of five steps—planning, cleaving, bruting, polishing, and inspecting. He instilled in me that planning although time consuming is the most important step as it determines the final value of the finished product.

"I was equally as enthusiastic as I learned each new step, but the Scaif fascinated me to no end. He showed me how to infuse the polishing wheel with a mixture of olive oil and diamond dust making it possible to polish all the facets of the diamond symmetrically at angles that reflected the light best. When he deemed the very first diamond I cut on my own *excellent*, I was hooked.

"My Papa did indeed end up in Hatton Garden not exactly as he had envisioned, but his dream did come true, and he owed it all to you. The War changed everything for me, but it also changed the world. We spoke of a return to normal, but what was normal before the War is no longer so today.

"I left school two months before graduating to join the RAF. Scholastically I was an A student, but I never gave thought to extending my education. I only saw the world of diamonds in my future. I was asked to stay on as a flight instructor in the RAF, but declined; that never interested me even though I love flying, and I strongly believe that general aviation will play a big part in the future of the world.

"So Marcus, this was a good talk. It's probably the first real heart-to-heart talk we've had, and the most important for me. New York here we come. Do you think they're ready for us?"

Marcus couldn't help thinking to himself New York has no idea who's about to come to town. "Well if they're not, they only have two days left to get ready."

The Queen Elizabeth arrived in New York on Tuesday, 11 June 1946. She docked on the north side of Cunard's Pier 90 in the North River, Manhattan. A car had been sent to pick them up and take them to the Waldorf Astoria the stately hotel on Park Avenue.

The New York City that emerged from WWII was a dramatically different place than the one that had entered it four years earlier. The change was in large part due to the War itself, which had finally lifted the City out of the Depression and ushered in an era of unparalleled prosperity.

The explosion in commercial activity brought on by the War reignited the City's economic engine propelling it to a level of economic power and dominance like nothing before or since.

By the late 1940s, New York City became the world's largest manufacturing center, the Nation's largest wholesaling center, the world's biggest port, and the world's financial capital. Above all, it was home to the immense corporations that now dominated life in the United States, and increasingly, around the world. One hundred thirty-five of the Nation's 500 largest industrial companies called it their *Headquarters City*.

Along with the economic boom came exciting cultural growth, and after four years of darkness, Broadway's dazzling lights shone brightly once more.

By the end of 1946, the United Nations selected New York as the location for its permanent headquarters; work would soon begin on a 16-acre site along the East River, where a magnificent new complex would rise over the coming years.

Jake was mesmerized by the view of the City from the car taking them to the hotel. The shops, the office buildings, the people hurrying about the streets, the restaurants were all so vibrant. The London of his youth mirrored New York City while postwar London was forced to endure the long slow process of rebuilding.

By 1946, the Waldorf Astoria was well on its way to becoming one of the most prestigious and best known hotels in the world. In 1929 to make way for the construction of the Empire State Building, its original site was demolished, and a new building at 301 Park Avenue between 49th and 50th Streets was erected.

From its inception, the hotel gained international renown for its lavish dinner parties and galas, and was often at the center of political and business conferences involving the rich and famous.

Their meetings for the most part were scheduled to take place at the Waldorf Astoria hence it was the obvious place for them to stay. As they were shown to their suites, Jake remained in awe of everything around him, unable to shake the bombed out images of London from his mind.

Their first evening, they dined at Voisin on Park Avenue and walked the City's streets until they were exhausted. The Broadway lights, Times Square, the retail shops brought back memories of Piccadilly Circus to Jake. They couldn't resist stopping in at Horn and Harder's Automat for coffee and pie before returning to the hotel. Inserting a coin into the slot to get a piece of pie was a totally new and delightful experience for the three of them; it was fun.

Most days, Elena was on her own to shop, do a little sightseeing, visit the many art museums, or sample the eclectic tastes of the City. She made notes of the places she thought Marcus and Jake should visit, and she made reservations each night for dinner at a new and different restaurant.

For the first week, Marcus and Jake were tied up in meetings pertaining to the ad campaign; the second week, they spent exploring. Marcus had three specific organizations in mind that he wanted to introduce to Jake.

In 1906, Jewelers of America was founded by jewelers for jewelers, with the goal of advancing the professionalism and ethics of the jewelry industry while representing every facet of the jewelry supply chain. Members' benefits included not only buyer discounts, but also education programs that covered relevant business topics such as profit strategies, selling techniques, jewelry marketing, product knowledge, legal issues, and more.

The Gemological Institute of America was founded in 1931 to protect all buyers and sellers of gemstones by setting and maintaining the standards used to evaluate gemstone quality. The Institute's ultimate goal was to develop an International Diamond Grading System and the Four C's (cut, clarity, color, and carat weight) as a standard to compare and evaluate the quality of diamonds.

The Diamond Council of America was founded in 1944 as a forum to educate jewelry sales professionals. DCA was a nationally accredited school that offered jewelers the opportunity to earn professional certifications in diamonds and colored gemstones through distance education that ultimately became known as correspondence courses.

Each evening at dinner, they discussed their *visit of the day*, and each day brought new revelations. They took in Broadway, and Jake fell in love with the theatre—in particular, musicals. They saw *Annie Get Your Gun* at the Shubert and *Showboat* at the Ziegfeld. For days after seeing each show, he found himself humming or singing the tunes endlessly.

"Elena, I can't begin to tell you what I have learned in the past few days. It is overwhelming at times, and yet at others it is so invigorating and inspiring. It shows me that today's world of diamonds is all about the future far different than my father's that was all about the past.

"Once again Marcus, I have you to thank. I gave you my word to think carefully about making my decision to accept your offer, and though you are not expecting an answer until we return to London, I'm going to break my word here and now. I'm in; I'm onboard, however you wish to phrase it. Before we leave New York, I'm hoping to set up a series of future meetings and courses that I can take.

"Next week belongs to the two of you. Celebrate your Anniversary and explore New York to your hearts' content. I will be busy taking care of things, but I plan to do some sightseeing on my own. I have but one request; allow me the honor of taking you to the Rainbow Room for dinner to celebrate your Anniversary.

"As my Papa said to me so long ago, *do we have a deal?*"

The next week went by in a whirl. Striking up a conversation with Al Cohen after their meeting at Jewelers of America, he asked for suggestions of must see New York attractions. Al took a liking to the clean-cut young Brit who he learned was an ace RAF pilot. When he said he would be on his own, Al offered to check with his receptionist Molly to see if she would like to show him around the City.

Jake rose early each day scheduling meetings for his mornings only. Afternoons, Al allowed Molly time off to show Jake around.

They had such a good time that he invited her to join him for dinner each evening. The last night before he was due to sail for England, Al managed to secure reservations for them at the Stork Club and picked up the tab.

As they walked to the station for Molly to catch the subway to Brooklyn, they talked about the evening and how much fun it had been. "I don't remember when I had so much fun Jake. I hope you're taking back the best of New York."

"That I am, and I have you and Al to thank for a good portion of that. I hope all Americans realize how fortunate they are that the War didn't land on the doorstep of their homeland. England was not so lucky. But that aside, as the saying goes *I love New York*, and London will be back."

Suddenly, Molly turned and kissed him full on the lips. He pulled her close and kissed her back then quickly released her. "I'm sorry; I can't."

Embarrassed she said, "No, I'm the one who should apologize. It was presumptuous of me at best and totally out of character for me. I took advantage of you after you've treated me like a lady and showed me nothing but kindness and respect. You're one in a million Jake Lyons; I hope the one who has your heart knows and appreciates what she has coming home to her."

Jake was speechless; he made no attempt to correct her. "No apology necessary; I had a wonderful time, and I would do it all over again. I enjoyed every minute I spent with you. We did have fun, and we laughed a lot. Laughing is good for the soul."

They reached her station; Jake hugged her and thanked her again.

Walking back to the hotel, he thought of the Empire State Building—the tallest building in the world, the museums, Rockefeller Plaza, Central Park, the restaurants—"21" Club, the Brown Derby, El Morocco, Voisin, the Stork Club, the Rainbow Room, Tavern-on-the-Green, Horn and Harder's Automat, and Diamonds. He was excited just thinking about what lay ahead.

For a few brief moments, he had allowed himself to be lost in the kiss until he realized that as Molly was kissing him, he was kissing Lexi. Proving once more neither he nor his heart was close to letting her go.

They sailed for London the next day. It had been quite a crossing. Marcus and Elena had celebrated their 40th Anniversary; Marcus and Jake had taken care of business for De Beers; and they had taken New York by storm.

Eager to begin and up for the task, Jake was about to embark on the adventure of a lifetime.

Throughout the 1930s, Pan American Airways (Pan Am) and Trans World Airlines (TWA) were in competition to establish the first commercial transatlantic flights.

Howard Hughes the owner of TWA arranged a meeting with executives from Lockheed Aircraft Corporation to outline his vision of what he called the *airline of the future.* Expressing his concerns that Lockheed's L-044 Excalibur under development at the time did not meet his requirements.

When the meeting ended, Lockheed agreed that in lieu of modifications, it would start from scratch using some original characteristics of the Excalibur. The new design was given the designation of L-049 Excalibur A. Hughes dissatisfied when called in to look at a scale mockup called for additional modifications. Ultimately, the name Excalibur was dropped, as the new aircraft had nothing in common with the original design. The name *Constellation* was picked up as a nickname until the intervention of the military.

When the United States entered WWII, the Constellation was selected for wartime production placing Lockheed's production lines under military control for the duration of the War.

As WWII drew to a close, large quantities of military surplus became available on the civilian market along with the cancellation of those remaining in production. With the Constellation's design at risk, Lockheed purchased the remaining transports in production and reconverted them to civilian airliners putting them up for sale. This placed the development of the L-049 months ahead of the competing Boeing 377, Douglas DC-6, and Republic RC-2 Rainbow which were all still on the drawing board.

It was from the exigencies of WWII that the crossing of the Atlantic by plane grew to become an even more practical and commonplace possibility; a possibility whose future was now.

The first production L-049 flew on 12 July 1945 and was delivered to TWA on 14 November 1945. Pan Am received its first L-049 on 5 January 1946. TWA and Pan Am both began offering flights to and from the United States and England five days a week.

From their return in late July from the States until November, Jake made two additional trips to New York. His first return trip was in September to meet with the Diamond Council of America about the courses he had completed. He flew on TWA from Heathrow to La Guardia; the trip took 15 hours and 15 minutes.

On his second trip in November, he and Marcus were scheduled to attend a meeting with the Ayer Agency. Marcus was not too keen on flying and Jake had his work cut out for him. They were due to leave in less than a month and time was growing short.

He arrived for dinner and rang the bell. Marcus opened the door. "Come in Jake. It's good to see you."

"Thank you. It's good to see you too. Since we returned from the States, the time has just flown by; it seemed the year had just begun and now it's almost at its end."

Over dessert, Jake decided to give it one more try. "Marcus, I have admitted on many occasions that you have never steered me wrong. Now, I'm asking you, have I ever steered you wrong?"

Marcus could see what was coming. "No Jake you haven't, at least not that I recall. But I also can't recall your ever steering me right or wrong. But, I will make this easy for you. I've considered your argument, and you are absolutely right about one thing. It simply does not make sense to travel for two or three times the length of our stay. I've already arranged for our flights."

"Good for you. I can't wait to see your reaction."

Though nervous at first, Marcus actually enjoyed his first flight. He marveled that you could barely feel the plane moving; that you were served meals and drinks mid-air; that in little more than half a day you were across the ocean and once again on land.

Upon their return, Jake received a letter from Lulu Walsh. Hoping it was not bad news; he hastily tore open the envelope.

Dear Jake,

We hope this letter finds you well and enjoying your return to civilian life. We three are getting along just fine. We find ourselves talking and wondering about you often.

Please accept our long overdue Thank You for the draft you sent to help get the farm up and running full speed. Though totally unnecessary, it was a big help, and we are once again solvent because of you.

Under the worst of circumstances, we met a young man that has come to mean so much to us—we miss you Jake. Hope you miss us too.

Watching over my shoulder, Lila is prodding me to get on with it, and so I shall.

We are inviting you to come to Guernsey Island for the holidays; that is if you don't have other plans. Although you were here for one long year, you didn't get to see much more than our farm.

Please come and let us introduce you to our beautiful Island. This is the perfect time to pay a visit.

Love and kisses from all (including Bill), Lulu.

Jake was pleased with the progress he had made since being discharged from the RAF. He was satisfied with his choices. He loved his cottage, his home; the house in Middlesex had sold immediately; his workshop was to his liking allowing him to spend time with *diamonds* when he felt the need; he had received his private pilot's license and spent as much time flying as he could; and he had an actual job other than the military—Consultant for De Beers.

It was the right time to accept their invitation to visit Guernsey Island. The holidays brought back too many memories; it would be nice to be away from London, away from the memories that haunted him and with whom better than the people who kept him safe.

The Guernsey Airport is located in the Forest, three miles west southwest of St. Peter Port, the Island's capital. The Airport was officially opened on 5 May 1939, but the development of regular air services was not commenced until October 1946.

Jake inquired about renting a plane and flying to the Island himself, but if the weather was bad, it could delay his plans. Instead, he opted to use a regular scheduled passenger service leaving from Southampton using a super marine Sea Eagle flying boat that settled on the waves off St. Peter Port.

Lulu had been right. Exciting things come to Guernsey during Christmas season. Festive events are planned throughout December with holiday markets, late night shopping in St. Peter Port, and the main man himself— Father Christmas no less turning on the Christmas lights. Throughout the Island families open their homes offering refreshments with all proceeds going to charity.

Lulu, Lila, and Bill were all there to greet him. They thought he looked splendid and told him so. He had gained weight; his deep blue eyes no longer hollow; his smile warmer than ever. He spent two weeks on Guernsey. They partook of each and every event; they went late night shopping and Jake bought them gifts—sweaters, scarves, and gloves. They took him all over and introduced him to what he believe amounted to the entire population of the Island though they assured him they had missed a few.

The farm looked good. The sheep that had supplied his 21st Birthday dinner had been replaced. They added two additional Guernsey cows and the farm once again produced and sold dairy products. It was winter, but Lulu's spring garden had yielded enough vegetables to get them through until next spring. They were proud of what they had accomplished, but didn't hesitate to thank Jake over and over for his help without which it would have taken much longer. When they tried to return the money he had sent, he wouldn't hear of it. He made it clear; the matter was closed.

On New Year's Eve, they invited him to attend church to pray for a blessed year to come. At first he declined, but reconsidered when he equated it to the Jewish New Year when Jews pray to be inscribed in the Book of Life for another year. He hadn't been in a synagogue in years, since before he lost his family. The only part of his Jewish faith and his Hebrew lessons that he observed was reciting the Kaddish. It had been a good year for him, and it seemed fitting to enter a house of God and pray for a good year for others.

It was a new experience for him to observe that everyone sat together, men, women, and children, unlike the orthodox synagogues in the East End where women sat off to the side and at times behind a curtain. He liked that families sat together; that everyone was equal in the eyes of God.

The two weeks on Guernsey were wonderful. He was grateful for the invitation, and that it had come at a time when he could accept it. He knew that 1947 was shaping up to be a very busy year, and that he would be travelling back and forth to the States. There was no doubt that flying would make his life a whole lot easier.

They traveled to St. Peter Port on January 2nd for his return trip to England.

He promised that he would fly himself the next time. Bill jokingly told him to make sure he landed at the airport.

Marcus and Elena had returned a day earlier; they decided to surprise him by meeting him in Southampton. They drove him home, and Jake suggested they have dinner at Mandy's. Jake told them all about Guernsey and what a beautiful Island he had been on for an entire year and yet saw so little of it until this trip.

It was good to be home.

CHAPTER THIRTY-THREE

Francis Gerety spent her career at the Philadelphia advertising agency N.W. Ayer, where she dedicated herself to one client—*De Beers*. Starting in 1943 and for the next three decades, she wrote all of the Company's ads, including the iconic phrase *A Diamond Is Forever*.

When she first suggested the phrase at a routine meeting in 1947, her male colleagues in the copy department argued that it had no meaning; that the word *forever* wasn't even grammatically correct. Gerety didn't think the line was one of her best either, but by refusing to let it get lost in the shuffle it too became *forever*.

The audacity of the statement *A Diamond Is Forever* placed its emphasis on sentiment and eternity focusing on permanence and timelessness. The more they told their story, the more the public came to see it as fact.

By associating itself with eternal romance, the diamond solitaire was established as the standard token of betrothal and in the process proclaimed the diamond by far the precious gemstone of choice.

The success of the De Beers ad campaign would become known as one of the most successful of all time; and *A Diamond Is Forever* would become known as the best advertising slogan of the twentieth century.

Once again, the best-laid plans can go awry.

Marcus and Jake were due to fly to New York in late January for meetings; they only planned to be in the City for three days before returning to London.

Although serious snowfall events happen rarely, when they come, the UK normally isn't prepared. From 22 January to 17 March, snow fell somewhere in England every single day. The snow accumulated quickly, causing major problems compounded by temperatures that rarely rose more than a degree or two above zero.

London was at a standstill. The armed services were brought in to drop supplies to people in danger, trapped in their homes due to blocked roads and railways, as villages throughout England became cut off and isolated.

Early March was also bad, with gales and heavy snow. Meanwhile in the southwest much milder air pushed northeast bringing a thaw and heavy rain. Flooding was widespread as the frozen ground prevented melting water from being absorbed. Eventually the floods subsided, but the devastation remained and only added to the frustration of post war efforts to rebuild.

Unaffected, the Underground became a lifeline to those areas in and around London. From time to time, Jake went to the City and met with Marcus at De Beers, later having dinner with him and Elena who joined them. He continued with the courses offered by Jewelers of America; he kept in touch by phone when the lines weren't down; and he pored over the many articles and magazines he had picked up in New York covering the diamond industry.

He also spent a great deal of time at the cottage. Wendy was grateful that he was around to check on her and Jason. For days at a time, there was no school, and Jake welcomed the company when Wendy came to do her housekeeping and brought Jason along. When the weather allowed, they ventured into the village for food supplies and dropped in to see Mandy.

Evenings found Jake in front of the fireplace with thoughts of Lexi. Try as he may, he could not bring himself to accept the fact that she was living thousands of miles away with a husband other than himself and a child that was not his. Where had he gone wrong? If they had not met in London and her actions were based on his letter, it made sense; after all he did tell her he felt he had no right to ask her to wait for him. But meet they did; and he proposed and she accepted, so it made no sense to him whatsoever.

His life since being discharged from the RAF was more than he ever dreamed. The cottage couldn't suit his needs better than if he had built it from the ground up. He was flying again, and he was travelling by plane to

New York regularly. The world his father had introduced him to, *the world of diamonds*, was his world now, and he was anxious to put all that his Papa had taught him to good use. He loved New York, and all it had to offer; it was vibrant, alive, and spoke of the future. A future he only yearned to share with Lexi.

Though there were no upcoming meetings with De Beers, Jake was planning to return to New York in late March. He planned on making a few personal contacts that would aid him going forward. Al Cohen at Jewelers of America offered his help. Two days prior to his flight, he received a call from Al requesting a postponement due to a recently declared medical emergency.

In mid-March 1947, New York City faced a smallpox outbreak that lasted for one month. The outbreak marked two milestones for the Country. First, it became the largest mass vaccination effort ever conducted for smallpox, and second, it marked the last outbreak of smallpox in America. The rapid response was credited with limiting the outbreak to 12 people, ten of whom recovered, while two died.

In April, after months of delays, Jake boarded a Pan Am flight to New York. On the plane, to his surprise was Joe Hanks. They arranged to switch seats so they could sit together.

"You're the last person I expected to see on this plane.

Joe laughed. "Well, I could say the same. Where are you off to?"

"We know each other through the aerodrome, so I know what you do; but I have another life, and it's diamonds. I'm a consultant for a large diamond distributor. I've been trying to get to New York for months, but the weather and other issues have put me off until now. I only plan to be there for less than a week.

"Why are you headed to New York?"

"I too have business in New York; I'm meeting with two banks. Then I'm on to Kansas to meet with Beech Aircraft. They have a new plane that debuted last month, and we're looking to purchase one, possibly two for the aerodrome."

He reached into his briefcase and pulled out an advertisement that was due to appear in the May issues of several magazines. "Have a look Jake; this is the Beechcraft Model 35 Bonanza. Isn't she a beauty?"

Jake read and reread the specifications; the more he read the more excited he became. The full-page ad featured a picture of the Bonanza 35 and touted it as the first economical plane for business—fully equipped for travel anytime, anywhere, with two-way radio, landing lights, and heater.

The Beech Aircraft Corporation, confident in its manufacturing capacity after building more than 7,000 combat aircraft during WWII, positioned itself for the postwar era by designing a revolutionary single-engine aircraft with a V-tail configuration that trimmed weight without compromising control.

The Beechcraft Model 35 Bonanza was a four-passenger state-of-the-art aircraft built like the fighters developed during the War, featuring an easier to manage horizontally-opposed six cylinder engine, a rakishly streamlined shape, retractable nosewheel undercarriage, and was a relatively fast, low-wing, all metal monoplane at a time when most light aircraft were still made of wood and fabric.

By the time the company announced that full-scale production would begin in March 1947, it already had a backlog of 1,500 orders. It was a moment for the benefits of wartime experience to pay off; about 1,000 deliveries were due to be made by the end of the year.

For a price tag of $7,975, you could own your very own plane.

For the remainder of their flight to La Guardia, they spoke of aviation. Joe outlined his vision for the aerodrome. He told Jake that business was good, and that although they were holding their own and turning a fair profit, they felt that moving forward they had to offer the newest and the best to their customers, or they would be left behind. "The new planes will introduce our newest service—Charter Flights."

Jake agreed. "You're absolutely right about being left behind. I knew that general aviation would probably be one of the biggest advancements to come out of the War. It was well on its way, when war broke out. Take us for example.

"How fantastic is it that we can leave London and be in New York City fifteen hours later? Aviation will be the travel venue of choice sooner than any of us expected.

"Please let me know if you have any problems with the banks; I have a few contacts that may be able to help you."

They kept in touch, and had dinner together the night before Jake was due to return to London. At the restaurant, Joe told Jake that he was only able to secure a loan for one plane.

The next day instead of returning home, Jake accompanied Joe to the bank where he personally guaranteed the loan for the second plane. That afternoon, they boarded a train to Wichita, Kansas to meet with Beech Aircraft. Joe purchased two planes for Eagle Aerodrome; Jake purchased a plane for himself; the plane would be kept in a hanger at the aerodrome. They were promised delivery in the spring of 1948.

Two days later, they were on a train back to New York for their flight home.

The Bonanza 35 had a range of 1,024 miles. He couldn't fly the plane from England to the States, but he could fly it to many places in Europe—Paris, Rome, Venice, and more. If and when De Beers expanded its ad campaign, his plane could be a real advantage.

Before leaving for New York, Jake had gotten tickets for *Bless the* Bride opening at the Adelphi Theatre in London on April 26th. He invited Marcus and Elena to join him for dinner and the theatre in the City.

He had been back for a week, and although he had seen Marcus at a business meeting, they didn't have a chance to discuss his recent trip to the States. At dinner, Jake took the opportunity to fill them in.

"I met a friend on my flight to La Guardia; he and his cousin own Eagle Aerodrome in Northleach where I occasionally rent a plane and take it up for an hour or two. He was on his way to Kansas via New York to purchase two new planes for their new charter service that will begin when they take delivery.

"He showed me an advertisement coming out in several magazines in their May issues featuring a Beechcraft Model 35 Bonanza, and what a beauty she is. I'm afraid I flipped out when I saw the ad. Anyway, to make a long story short, I accompanied him to Wichita, Kansas.

"He purchased two planes for the aerodrome; and I purchased a plane for myself. It's a four passenger with a range of over a thousand miles and quite economical to fly and maintain. We won't have delivery until sometime next year in the spring."

They had dessert, and left the restaurant for the short walk to the theatre.

After the show, Jake caught the train back to the Cotswolds. Marcus and Elena picked up their car; on the drive home, Marcus commented.

"Did you notice that Jake did not mention the word *diamonds* a single time?"

"No, I guess I was caught up in his obvious excitement about the new plane. I'm sure you didn't miss that. Were you expecting to discuss business? You usually stay away from anything *De Beers* when we dine out even when we have no plans afterwards."

"It was a lovely evening, and we have Jake to thank for it. The show was marvelous. Don't you agree?"

"It wasn't a matter of expecting our conversation to lead to anything in particular; I guess I was just taken aback about his enthusiasm, and as you put it, his obvious excitement about a plane. I've never known him to show this kind of passion for anything—anything except his Love for Lexi Portman.

"Yes, I agree; it was a lovely evening, and the show was marvelous. I'm amazed he was able to get the tickets; the show has been sold out for months."

"Why Marcus, are you jealous? Are you upset that he is channeling his passion to flying instead of diamonds since he lost Lexi? I don't think you're being fair to him, and that's not like you."

"Elena, you know me better than I know myself; that's why I love you so much."

As the weather improved, he found himself at the aerodrome taking up a plane when one was available every chance he got. He became good friends with Joe who readily shared with him his vision of the future of Eagle Aerodrome, as well as the fact that his cousin didn't share the same vision.

After spending his morning flying, Jake returned home to find a letter from South Africa addressed to him. Noticing that the return address was not from his Uncle Benjamin, he hurriedly tore open the envelope and removed the letter.

Dear Jacob,

As Rabbi of the Great Synagogue your Uncle Benjamin attends, I am writing to you at the request of a concerned friend.

Ben was diagnosed with Tuberculosis earlier this year and has been confined to a Sanatorium for treatment. I am happy to inform you that I visited with him recently, and he is doing quite well. If he continues to improve as the doctors expect him to, he will be released in several weeks.

Friends close to him have informed me that he has not written to you because he didn't want to give you the impression that it was necessary to come at once to Cape Town to see him. I've been told you were recently discharged from the RAF.

I might add that I knew your Uncle Sidney too, and I am sorry for your loss. He was a fine and decent man.

I am certain as time passes, and the day for Ben to return home approaches, he will write to you. He has told us all that you are planning a visit when you get things settled in England. His upcoming release appears a better time for you to plan that visit.

Ben is lucky to have friends who care so much for him that they encouraged me to write to you. It will be our secret. I ask that you allow him to tell you about his illness when he is ready.

God Bless you, and may he keep you safe and well.

Rabbi Reuben Morris

Jake's first reaction was guilt. It had been over a year since he had written to his uncle. He had been so wrapped up in travelling back and forth to New York, getting his license and flying again, and now actually buying a plane.

In all fairness, he hadn't heard from his uncle either, and he didn't really know Benjamin. He was sorry to hear that he was not well, but happy to learn that he was on the mend. He made a mental note to make definite plans to take a trip to Cape Town as soon as he learned Benjamin was home.

The engagement of Princess Elizabeth to Philip Mountbatten, Duke of Edinburgh was officially announced on 9 July 1947. Though secretly engaged for over a year, they granted the King's request to delay the announcement until Elizabeth's 21st birthday the following April. She had fallen in love with Philip at the age of thirteen. As Jake heard their story repeatedly over the BBC, his thoughts were of Lexi.

Marcus needn't have worried. He followed through on everything he was asked to do for De Beers. In September, he traveled once again to New York to coordinate the ad campaign for the upcoming Holiday Season.

Upon learning he was in town, Al invited him to sit in on a meeting with Jewelers of America's planning committee. Seeking to expand the sponsorship of their upcoming New York Trade Show, they not only encouraged input from De Beers, but also assured Jake that any part the Company wished to play would be welcomed.

At a time when Trade Shows were becoming both *Grand and Central,* they were planning to hold their next show at Grand Central Palace on Lexington Avenue, between 46th and 47th Streets, in late January 1948. Invitations to exhibitors would be in the mail by month's end. The Show would be heavily advertised in their monthly publication *National Jeweler* and showcased as a *must* for exhibitors and retail jewelers alike. Side meetings, classes, and evening events were encouraged and a majority of the bigger names in the business were already onboard.

De Beers' commitment to promoting an extension of their ad campaign ultimately resulted in *A Diamond is Forever* appearing in every De Beers engagement ad from 1948 and lasting throughout the twentieth century.

As the big day grew closer, London was abuzz with excitement. The wedding of Elizabeth II and Prince Philip, Duke of Edinburgh took place on 20 November 1947 at Westminster Abbey in London.

The royal parties were brought by carriage processions. Eight bridesmaids and two pageboys attended Princess Elizabeth. Prince Phillip left Kensington Palace with his best man; Princess Elizabeth arrived at the Abbey with her father, King George, in the Irish State Coach as well wishers lined the streets waving and shouting to the happy couple.

The wedding ceremony was officiated by the Archbishop of Canterbury and the Archbishop of York. The ceremony was recorded and broadcast by BBC Radio to 200 million people around the world. Elizabeth and Philip proceeded to Buckingham Palace where a breakfast was held at the Ball Supper Room.

Upon their marriage, Elizabeth took the title of her husband and became Princess Elizabeth, Duchess of Edinburgh. They departed for their honeymoon at Broadlands in Hampshire, home of Philip's uncle, Earl Mountbatten.

The couple received over 2,500 wedding presents from around the world and 10,000 telegrams of congratulations.

In November, Jake received an Invitation to attend the Jewelers of America Holiday Party on December 20th. The venue for the event was the Rainbow Room atop Rockefeller Plaza. He was excited to learn that Marcus and Elena had also been invited and were looking forward to the party, as well. Knowing

Elena had never flown, he set out to convince her, just as he had successfully convinced Marcus, to fly to New York.

There was no need. Elena not only welcomed the party invitation but also looked forward to her first flight. She was eager to see for herself what this *flying* was all about and get a better understanding of how and why it had captured Jake's heart and soul.

They left London on December 17th for a week's stay in New York. This would allow them to attend the JA Party, see a Broadway Show or two, and have a mini holiday before returning home and spending time with their daughter and her family as they normally did.

The party was *The Party* of the year. The food, the music, the entertainment was all unlike anything Jake had ever seen or experienced. When he learned Molly had come to the party alone, he invited her to spend the evening with him; the two friends had a great time together.

They took in the *Radio City Christmas Spectacular* featuring the *Rockettes*, and spent an evening at the Cinema watching *Miracle on 34th Street*, which was originally released in the UK as *The Big Heart*. They dined at a different restaurant each night and allowed themselves to absorb the magic of the holiday-decorated winter wonderland of New York City, the likes of which hadn't been seen since before the War. To Marcus and Elena's delight, Jake invited Molly to join them.

As time drew close for them to fly back to London, Molly asked Jake to remain in the City and spend New Year's Eve in Times Square counting down the seconds to 1948. He accepted.

Marcus and Elena left for London on December 24th. The December 26th forecast for New York called for *occasional flurries*, but steady snow started falling in the wee hours of the night and was inches deep by the time most people were leaving for work. It continued falling hard all morning, making it impossible at times to see across the street. The snow clogged the switches to the Long Island Railroad, and many people never made it home. The lucky ones found hotel rooms, but others slept in railway stations. Theatres were kept open all night to provide shelter.

The Great Blizzard of 1947 was a record-breaking snowfall that began the day after Christmas without prediction and brought the northeastern United States to a standstill—25.8 inches of snow fell in less than 24 hours.

For Jake 1947 ended exactly as it had begun—in a *Blizzard*. He spent New Year's Eve alone in his room at the Waldorf Astoria. The City's streets piled high with snow were in no condition to accept revelers bringing in the New Year.

It wasn't until a full week later that he was able to get a flight back to London.

CHAPTER THIRTY-FOUR

1948—the New Year—what would it bring? A week had already gone by, a week of being snowbound in New York unable to get a flight home. He and Marcus were expecting to attend the Jewelry Trade Show at the Grand Central Palace in the City at the end of the month. Meanwhile, he awaited word of his Uncle Benjamin's release from the sanatorium so he could follow through with plans to travel to Cape Town.

After giving it much thought, he decided he would ask his uncle to consider moving to England. It would be good for both of them. He wasn't sure how old he was, but it would be unnecessary for him to work; he would take care of him, see that he had everything he wanted and needed.

Marcus and Jake were set to fly to New York for the Show on January 27th three days prior to the opening. The weather was cold but dry and they hoped there wouldn't be a repeat of last year.

There wasn't; their flight left on time. They enjoyed a smooth uneventful trip with Marcus telling him about the first trade show he had attended in Italy several years before the War.

"The Italian event was heavily concentrated on gold, especially 18K and featured original designs found only in Europe at that time. Although hundreds of manufacturers will be representing jewelry composed of an array of metals and gemstones, I anticipate that De Beers has gone all out to put diamonds front and center at the upcoming JA Show."

As they flew across the Atlantic, a wire addressed to Jacob Lyons was delivered to the cottage. Wendy was there when it arrived and signed for it.

She placed it on the dining table where she normally put all the mail that came when he was travelling.

———✺———

The JA Trade Show was a huge success all around, and they were pleased with De Beers' efforts. Jake's suggestion to produce a short film version of the campaign's magazine ads, and presenting it to retail members, proved a big hit.

They returned home Wednesday evening. When Jake arrived at the cottage, it had already turned dark. He let himself in, dropped his bag at the door, and turned on the lights. He was tired, but it had been a good trip, a good week.

Taking his bag into the bedroom, he decided to leave it until morning to unpack. He opted to take a shower instead, and then check in the kitchen for something to eat.

The hot water felt good, relieving the tension of the long flight home. Clad in pajamas and a robe, he felt refreshed as he headed to the kitchen. Passing the dining table, he stopped to check his mail. On top of the pile lay the wire.

PLEASE ACCEPT CONDOLENCES—STOP—SORRY TO INFORM YOU BENJAMIN LYONS PASSED AWAY SUNDAY MORNING LAST—STOP—FINAL WISHES REQUEST BURIAL OF HIS REMAINS AND THOSE OF HIS BROTHER SIDNEY IN LONDON ALONGSIDE BROTHER HARRY—STOP

REMAINS AND PERSONAL EFFECTS BEING SHIPPED DIRECT—STOP—PLEASE CONTACT ME AT YOUR EARLIEST TO ARRANGE TRANSFER OF FUNDS TO YOU—STOP

GORDON HEMMING, MANAGER
FIRST NATIONAL BANK OF SOUTH AFRICA
CAPE TOWN, SOUTH AFRICA

Once again he was engulfed in feelings of loss, sadness, and being alone. He was now truly alone, the last of the Lyons. The Rabbi's letter came to mind. If he hadn't received it, he would not have known Benjamin was sick. The wire made no mention of how or what caused his death. Emotionally, Jake was a mess. Why now? Everything in his life was going so well. Why then was he feeling guilty?

Sleep eluded him. He sat on the sofa throughout the night trying to make sense of his feelings, especially the guilt. As the sun came up, his thoughts became more transparent. He put a pot of coffee on to brew, looked through the remaining mail, and decided to get dressed.

Relying on his track record of making sound decisions, he was confident that his current choice would be equally so. As he awaited his uncles' remains and personal effects to arrive, he would make arrangements for their burials in the Brady Street Cemetery, and arrange for the new Rabbi at the Great Central Synagogue to perform the service. He chose not to contact the Bank just yet.

He rang up Marcus to tell him that he had received a wire notifying him that his Uncle Benjamin had died while they were in New York, offering no further information. Surprised by the absence of emotion and the tone in Jake's voice, Marcus sensed there was more, much more to the story than he had revealed.

While waiting for the shipment from Cape Town, he found himself thinking about family. Although he had been blessed in many ways, having a family was not one of them. His hopes of marrying Lexi and having a family of his own were no longer in the cards for him. Not only did he realize that his feelings for her had never waned, they seemed to be growing stronger. He found himself in a dilemma for which he had no solution.

Whenever the weather cooperated, he could be found at Eagle Aerodrome.

Flying became his salvation. High above the ground, in and out of the clouds, his thinking was crystal clear. He could hear his Papa's voice: *Choices control your destiny, but your fate is sealed.* He had once believed he and Lexi were inevitable only to discover that fate decreed otherwise.

Mid-February, Jake received word the shipment had arrived from South

Africa and requested arrangements be made for delivery. The next day, the truck pulled up at the cottage. The crate was much larger than he anticipated, and he was unsure where to put it. Opting for the garage, he asked the deliverymen to slide it alongside the car against the wall.

Retrieving tools from the cellar, he backed the car out and moved the crate away from the wall so it could be accessed from all sides. It was so solidly built and nailed shut that it took him almost an hour to pry open the lid. His eyes came to rest on the envelope that bore his name, *Jacob*.

Picking up the envelope, he opened it, and removed the folded piece of paper from inside.

Dear Jacob,

If you are reading this letter, than I have gone to join my Brothers.

For many months, I have been in a Sanatorium recovering from Tuberculosis, a terrible illness quite common in South Africa. It requires a long and slow recovery often riddled with setbacks, and I take it one day at a time. Unable to have visitors for the first six months of confinement, I decided to wait before writing to you.

I didn't want to concern you with my problems; waiting until I was home seemed a better choice. You wrote of many loose ends that you needed to tie up since your discharge, and I sensed it wasn't an easy task you faced.

When I came to Cape Town to make a new life for myself, I had no great expectations, but the Lord blessed me many times over, and I was happy. My happiness increased tenfold when Sidney left Cuba and joined me. We had a lot of good years working together, attending services at the synagogue, and we had good, good friends.

Recent years have not gone as well. When we learned what happened to Harry and family, we were devastated. The ache in our hearts was eased only by the fact that you survived. Learning you were missing we prayed for your safe return. As we waited for word that you were alive and well, Sidney suffered a heart attack and died. The wire I sent to Marcus Hirsch advising of his passing crossed with the wire he sent advising you were safe.

Sidney's passing was very hard for me to accept. Without the help of my dear friend Franz Schiller, I don't know what I would have done. We became friends the very first day I arrived in Cape Town.

When you returned to England and wrote of visiting, I began to think once more of family and possibly moving to be near my only living relative. When Franz suddenly died, once again I fell into a state of sadness. In the weeks following his death, I became more determined than ever to leave South Africa and relocate to England.

Diagnosed with Tuberculosis, I had no choice but to put my plans on hold and place my faith in the doctors who were caring for me; they tell me I am on the mend, but one never knows. Hence, I am writing to you just in case.

I cannot in good conscience leave this world without telling you how much I love you; I only wish we could have had a relationship, a chance to get to know each other. I often wonder if you are like your Papa, like Sidney, or even a little bit like me.

God Bless you Jacob. May He always watch over you, as your Papa, Sidney, and I will. Never forget that you are a Lyons.

Love, your Uncle Benjamin

He began removing the items. There were two small wooden boxes with a carved Star of David on top that contained his uncles' remains; each was identified by name. There was a box that contained jeweler's tools; there was another that contained watches, several rings, a hand-carved elephant, a cigar box similar to the one his uncles had brought his father when they came to London, a small cloth pouch, and an envelope containing assorted papers.

That left the crate emptied of everything except the chest resting in the center. At first glance, Jake could not identify the Hebrew lettering carved on the lid. Slowly, he opened the chest. The shallow tray on top was empty except for a card with the same Hebrew letters written on it. As he picked up the card, the tray shifted, and he removed it.

His fixed gaze stared and stared rendering him unable to believe what he was seeing—diamonds, more diamonds than he had ever seen at one time or in one place or in his entire life for that matter. Yet here they were in his garage, in his possession with no explanation whatsoever. The finished stones cut and polished to perfection were blinding to his eyes.

Jake's thoughts were rampant. They must be worth a fortune. Who could have shipped them in a nailed-shut crate under the pretense of delivering human remains for burial? The return address from a funeral home in Cape Town revealed nothing; could they possibly have been shipped to him in error? What would happen when they discovered their mistake? Could the diamonds possibly be spoils of a heist? A robbery of such a magnitude would have surely made news around the world, yet he recalled no such incident.

He suddenly realized, he had a violent headache. Not a single answer came to mind for any of his questions. Needing to think things through, he decided to put everything away.

He collected the smaller boxes and took them into the cottage. Returning to the garage, he replaced the tray and lowered the lid on the chest. Grabbing the handles on either end, he slowly lifted it out of the crate, surprised that it was not as heavy as he thought it would be. He carried it into the cottage and placed it on the dining table.

He broke down the crate piling the wood pieces against the wall, making a mental note to move it all to the cellar. He pulled the car back into place and lowered the door to the garage.

The next morning, he rose early and set about taking care of the items he removed from the crate. The tools were taken down to the cellar. He set the two boxes that held his uncles' remains on a table in the sitting room. He carried the chest into his bedroom and placed it deep in the closet putting blankets on top. The box containing the personal items, he placed on the dining table.

With a pot of coffee brewing, he made himself eggs for breakfast. When he finished eating, he sat down to go through the box.

His uncles most likely wore the two wristwatches; the gold pocket watch possibly belonged to his grandfather. The rings were all what Jake called *old country*. He assumed the gold wedding band and diamond lady's ring were his grandmother's. There were two men's dome rings in heavy gold settings with a sizable European cut diamond in each that he also assumed belonged to his uncles.

Picking up the elephant, he examined the intricate carving as he turned it over and over in his hands; every detail was so precise that he wondered if it had anything to do with the carvings on the chest. He made a note to compare them.

Loosening the cord on the cloth pouch, he emptied its contents onto the table—five sizeable uncut diamonds and a folded piece of paper. He began reading the note Franz had written to Benjamin. When he reached its end and saw the signature, he determined the reference his uncle's letter made to his friend Franz Schiller to be one in the same.

The last item in the box was an envelope crammed full of papers. The majority were fastened together and appeared to be diamond appraisals on sheet after sheet of *Annex* letterhead. Could this mean, the diamonds were not spoils of a heist and actually legitimate? Too many questions remained. Why were they sent to him and who sent them? Why had Benjamin made no mention of the diamonds? Who had cut and polished them?

The remaining papers consisted of every wire Marcus had sent the brothers, as well as Jake's letters and wires. He found himself more confused than ever.

He rang up Marcus to notify him that he needed a few days to take care of some personal matters. He told him that in accordance with Benjamin's final wishes, his and Sidney's remains were shipped to England for burial alongside his family in the Brady Street Cemetery. Having made prior arrangements, the service and burials were due to take place on Thursday. He promised to be in touch soon. When asked if he and Elena could do anything, Jake thanked him for the offer but stated it was a private matter for him, hoping he understood.

After his uncles had been laid to rest, Jake asked the Rabbi if he could have a few minutes of his time.

"It's been many years since my Hebrew lessons prepared me for my Bar Mitzvah. I can, of course, still read the prayer books, but I wonder if you could help me make sense of the Hebrew letters written on this card." He handed it to the Rabbi.

"These letters spell a name—*Shiloh*. The Hebrew meaning of the name is: *the one to whom it belongs*.

"Does the name *Shiloh* mean anything to you? Where did you get this card? Did someone give it to you?"

"I found the card among my uncle's things. I don't know if he wrote the name or someone wrote it and gave it to him. I was just curious as to what the letters meant; I had no idea they indicated a name."

"In translation, one cannot determine the significance of the name and it's meaning without knowing what to apply it to.

"*Shiloh* is also the name of a place; a place that appears 33 times in the Old Testament referring to an area of Israel. It's hard to tell what whoever wrote the name was referring to. I don't think I've been much help."

"No, quite the contrary Rabbi. I thank you for the service. I know that cremation is not normally accepted by Orthodox Jews, and I appreciate your consideration allowing me to honor my uncle's final request.

"If you don't mind, I'll stop by from time to time to chat with you when I come to the cemetery. My entire family is buried here; and I often visit when I have the need to be close to my father; he was my Hero."

"You're welcome Jacob. I look forward to seeing you again soon under better circumstances."

They shook hands and Jake caught the train back to the Cotswolds. He thought about stopping in to see Marcus but decided against it. Once again, his world had been turned upside down, but this was a world Marcus knew nothing about. For some reason, he chose not to confide in him.

Slow and steady was the way forward; he had a lot of sorting out to do.

On the way home from the train to the cottage, he stopped in the Village and headed toward Mandy's restaurant. As always, she was glad to see him.

"Hi Jake. What brings you here so early in the day? Are you planning to set up another dinner?"

He laughed. "No, nothing like that, at least not today. I'm going to be holed up for the next few days working at the cottage, and I thought it a good idea to pick up some food to see me through the weekend."

"I can certainly do that. Just tell me what you have in mind, and I'll put it all together and send it home with Wendy later today. Meanwhile, have a seat and let me fix you something before you leave. Do you prefer tea or coffee?"

"Thank you. Coffee will be fine; it energizes me."

Throughout the weekend, the chest sat on the dining table in front of Jake surrounded by the items he thought could be connected in some way to the diamonds—the cloth pouch, the carved elephant, the card, the appraisals.

He made a drawing of the items and tried to connect them. The pieces he had been given to the puzzle simply did not fit. Presented with what seemed an impossible task, he reached the conclusion that the answers could only be found in South Africa; only Cape Town could connect the pieces and complete the puzzle.

He removed the trays of diamonds from the chest, took them down to the cellar, and put them in the safe along with the cloth pouch and its contents.

Commercial flights direct from England to South Africa did not yet exist. After weeks of trying to piece together a flight from London to somewhere in Europe and ultimately to South Africa, he booked passage and sailed from Southampton to Cape Town.

Jake stood on the dock surveying his surroundings. He had been given directions to the hotel on Long Street and decided to walk the short distance allowing him to get a feel for the place his uncles had called *home*.

The path he took was exactly the same as that of Benjamin and Sidney before him. On the site where The General Store and The Smoker's Shop had once stood welcoming newcomers to the town was a clothing store. He continued on to the Metropole Hotel where he had booked a reservation purely by coincidence, having had no way of knowing the hotel had been Benjamin's first home in Cape Town.

He had no idea how long he would be staying as he searched for answers.

He began by meeting with Gordon Hemming at the First National Bank of South Africa, his sole contact. He produced a copy of Benjamin's Will, stating that the only item left unsettled was the transfer of funds.

"I presume that your uncles' remains and personal effects arrived safely in England and all was in order since I did not hear otherwise. If you will note, Ben left his cottage to a black African woman, Jamilia Botu, who was a good friend and great help to both your uncles during their illnesses. Under current laws, the cottage is located in an area where black Africans cannot own property. The bank holds the property in Trust for as long as she wishes to reside there; however, when it is sold, all proceeds will go to her."

Everything was in order and Jake realized that if not for the chest of diamonds, a trip to Cape Town would have been unnecessary. "You have carried out all of my uncle's final wishes, and I thank you. I didn't really know my uncles having met them only once as a boy when they visited London before their brother's family, my family, was killed in an air raid.

"Since I am the last surviving Lyons, I came to Cape Town in an effort to learn about the uncles I never knew solely for my peace of mind. In a letter Benjamin left me, he indicated that his good friend Franz Schiller had predeceased him not too long after Sidney died. Is there anyone else here that he was close to you can suggest I speak with?"

"Yes, of course there is."

Jake left with directions to the synagogue; a good place to start.

He met with the Rabbi and learned that Benjamin was a lot like his father. His trade was important to him, and he took great pride in his accomplishments. He was full of love and would do anything to help someone. His sole regret in life was that he never married and had a family. When Jake stood up to leave, the Rabbi beckoned him to follow.

They walked out of his office down a hallway and took the stairs to the classrooms below. He stopped before a door where Jake could see that a class was in session. "Please wait here. I'll be right back."

The Rabbi returned with the woman teaching the class. "Jake Lyons, let me introduce Jamilia Botu; she teaches English to Jewish immigrant children here at the synagogue. She was a good friend to both your uncles."

It was a surprise Jamilia never anticipated. Finding herself face-to-face with the nephew Ben Lyons hoped to join in England was unnerving, but she quickly regained her composure. "I'm am so pleased to meet you. Ben and Sidney spoke of you often throughout the years, especially when they returned from their trip to London."

"Likewise, I am pleased to meet you. I wonder if we could perhaps have a chat when you are not teaching. Would this evening be convenient?"

Jamilia hesitated. Was he seeking information about the diamonds? Was he looking to claim ownership of the cottage? No, not if he was Ben's nephew. He most likely just wanted to get to know his uncles, and she would like to get to know him too; after all it was she that had made the decision to bequeath the diamonds to him.

"Where are you staying?"

"I'm at the Metropole Hotel on Long Street. Why do you ask?"

"My classes end at 4:00 p.m. Meet me here, and we can have our chat."

"Thank you so much. I will be back at 4:00 p.m."

Jake stopped in to thank the Rabbi before he left. He decided to walk through the town and up and down the side streets. He found himself in front of Zeller Jewelers; a sign in the window noted *Under New Management*. There were many colorful shops selling books, clothing, giftware, and more.

He came to a small Café and stopped for a bite to eat—the very one that Benjamin had frequented for breakfast his early days in Cape Town.

Promptly at 4:00 p.m., he arrived at the synagogue. As he started down the stairs, she was coming up to meet him. "I'm sorry, I should have told you to wait for me in the lobby."

"No apology necessary. Are we meeting here?"

Jamilia smiled. Jake noted she was quite beautiful; he hadn't realized she was so young. "My first thought was to meet here, but they lock up by 5:00 p.m. and not knowing how long we would be, I thought you might like to come to my cottage; it's close by."

Jake thought of Benjamin's Will; could this be his uncle's cottage? "That will be fine, but I certainly don't want to inconvenience you."

"No inconvenience at all. It's home."

He stayed longer than he anticipated. Jamilia was pure delight. They made plans to meet again.

In the following days he learned more about his uncles than he could have imagined. Her story began with Franz Schiller coming to her aid after her husband's sudden demise that left her with a small son to care for. Franz befriending Ben when he came to work for Zeller Jewelers at the Annex, and Sidney's arrival in Cape Town to work alongside Ben were the good times.

The War years taking its toll when they learned their brother and his family were killed, worrying about their nephew, Sidney's sudden death, followed by Franz' passing, and Ben's illness contributed to the downward spiral. With Ben's ultimate death, the journey came to an abrupt and final end.

On days when she had no classes, she ushered him around the town and took him down to the Annex that was also under new management. They couldn't gain access, but he learned where his uncles had spent their days cutting and polishing the roughs into beautiful diamonds.

She told him how she had cared for Sidney while he recuperated from his heart attack, and how she had readied the cottage for Ben's homecoming that wasn't meant to be. She also cooked him a meal or two noting they were his uncles' favorites.

She bragged about her son Afram attending the South African Native College where he would soon be graduating with degrees in both Political Science and Economics, giving all the credit to Franz and Ben for helping him.

When it was time for him to leave, although he had learned all about the uncles he never knew, he had learned nothing about the diamonds. What he had gleaned from his conversations with Jamilia was that her friendship with Franz had led to her friendship with his uncles. His uncles were associated with diamonds, not Franz. Therefore, he simply saw no connection between Jamilia and the chest of diamonds, completely forgetting about the cloth pouch and its contents.

Jamilia was sad to see Jake leave. With Afram away at school, she was lonely, and although hesitant at first, she welcomed the days she spent with him. She was the only person who could relate what she told him about his uncles, and she was glad she had the opportunity to do so. She answered all his questions honestly; he had not mentioned the diamonds nor had she.

She liked Jake Lyons; he seemed a fine young man both genuine and sincere, and she wished him the very best. She told him there was no better way to honor those he had lost than to get married, have a family, and live a good life.

When Afram came home, she would tell him of Jake's visit, making a mental note to affirm her decision to send the cache of diamonds to him. She had no doubt whatsoever that Jake Lyons would see that the diamonds ended up with whom they belong.

CHAPTER THIRTY-FIVE

Zoe was the light of Lexi's life, her reason for living. Her studies were going well, and she loved working with the children at the hospital, but as month after month passed by with no word from or about Jake, she grew despondent. The news that Ivan had been killed in the final days of war in the Pacific only added to her already fragile state of mind. She cried for days unable to imagine that the cousin she had been closest to was gone. It was hard for her to believe, eleven years had passed since Ivan had introduced her to Jake at his party.

For many survivors of WWII, the Zionist dream of a Jewish homeland was their anchor of hope; a place to rebuild their lives and gain material security and safety. When Manny was invited by a fellow physician at the hospital to attend a Zionist meeting, he had no idea that the speaker's message would change the course of his life. Fighting for their cause soon overtook him. By March, only one year after accepting the position as Head of the Pediatric Department at the Hadassah Hospital on Mount Scopus, he stunned everyone by resigning.

Though he was not a survivor of the Holocaust, his sympathy for his fellow Jews who had suffered under the Nazis led him to become a member of the Irgun, a Zionist paramilitary organization. Viewed as a terrorist organization, its tactics appealed to a certain segment of the Jewish community that any action taken for the cause of the creation of a Jewish State was justified, including terrorism.

Lexi was horrified; she no longer recognized her father. The gentle compassionate yet strong man that for her entire life had been the backbone of their family no longer existed.

Her Pops had vanished into thin air.

To Lexi, Eva was a godsend; she spent more and more time with them as Manny spent less. In her father's absence, Eva often spent the night, not wanting to leave Lexi and Zoe alone.

The King David Hotel bombing was a terrorist attack carried out on Monday 22 July 1946 by the Irgun on the British Administrative Headquarters for Palestine, which was housed in the southern wing of the hotel—91 people of various nationalities were killed and 46 were injured.

Disguised as Arabs, the Irgun planted a bomb in the basement of the main building of the hotel. The huge explosion caused the collapse of the western half of the southern wing, and was the deadliest attack directed at the British during the Mandate era.

Lexi began having thoughts of leaving Palestine and returning to England. She had left a war-torn London only to find herself in the middle of another war, a war that was closer and deadlier, and she was now responsible for Zoe. Who could she turn to for help? Her brothers had no idea what was happening in Palestine; if they did, they had never voiced their concern.

Returning to England would take a great deal of planning. Leaving her father and Palestine would be no easy task, and she found the thought of traveling alone with Zoe on a ship for days daunting at best. She had only her brothers to rely on for help to get settled in London. Mark and Rosalie had welcomed a son in the spring, and Sam was in Residency. It seemed not a good time.

In September, Zoe turned two. Lexi and Eva did their best to make it a happy occasion, but Manny was nowhere to be found as Zoe held up two little fingers and proclaimed as she danced about the room, "I'm Zoe Elise Lyons and I'm two years old."

The year came to an end quietly, but 1947 started off with a series of Irgun attacks that grew deadlier with each passing month. In January, the bombing of British Headquarters resulted in four fatalities; in March 17 British officers were killed during a raid; April saw four British policemen killed in a bank robbery; and the ensuing months saw the number of fatalities steadily rise. Only days before Zoe's third birthday, 13 were killed and 53 wounded in an attack on a British police station.

Throughout the year, Lexi continued her efforts to arrange passage back to London for her and Zoe. She had finished the courses she planned to take, and when she wasn't working at the hospital, she was home with Zoe and Eva, who for all general purposes was living with them.

Following the vote in the UN General Assembly in favor of the 1947 United Nations Partition Plan on 29 November 1947, the Jerusalem Riots occurred. The Arab Higher Committee declared a three-day strike and public protest against the vote; the riots began on 2 December 1947.

Arabs marching to Zion Square were stopped by the British, causing them to turn instead towards the commercial center of the City at Mamilla and Jaffa Roads, burning buildings and shops. The violence continued for two days.

January 1948 began with good news, which Lexi welcomed with a sigh of relief. She had secured passage on a supply ship similar to the ship she had arrived on. The only drawback being the ship's arrival was not due in Haifa until March. It was scheduled to embark on its return trip three days later carrying not only Lexi and Zoe but also several additional passengers.

She felt bad about leaving Eva who assured her that she would be fine just knowing they were safe and back home; it was the right decision. The time for them to return to England was long overdue. For better than a year, the situation in Jerusalem had been explosive, and with the conflict centered on Mount Scopus, they found themselves living in the middle of it.

Lexi's attempts to get word to her father went unanswered until the end of February when he suddenly showed up at the house. At first glance, his disheveled appearance was frightening to Zoe and she began to cry. His visit did not go well.

"I've been trying to reach you for months. Have you gotten any of my messages? Where have you been? I've been so worried about you."

"I have received messages from you, it just wasn't possible for me to leave what I was doing and come running home. I'm here now, but I can't stay long."

Lexi was shocked; she had never heard her Pops speak to her this way.

"I've tried reaching you to tell you that Zoe and I are returning to England. I no longer feel that we are safe here, and my priority as a mother is to protect my child. I don't want her growing up in the hostile environment that has engulfed Jerusalem. I'm on edge constantly worrying about our wellbeing, and I can't take anymore. It's having an adverse effect on every aspect of our lives.

"When I speak with Mark and Sam, I don't know what to tell them when they ask for you. They haven't heard from you in months; and can't understand the lack of interest in your new grandson and what's going on in their lives. You've abandoned all of us."

Manny slumped in his chair. The weight of the world seemed to be on his shoulders. Lexi's words had cut to the truth. "I know I've let you down. I brought you here to protect you and Zoe, and then I deserted you. I'm sorry for that, so sorry. I know these are only words, but they are heartfelt.

"I'm happy that you are returning home; this was never home to you, and I never meant it to be. I believed that when the War was over, you would return to Jake. Since there has been no word, we have to assume that he is gone.

"I will stay with you until your ship sails. It will give us precious few days before we must say goodbye."

The end of March, Lexi and Zoe boarded the ship in Haifa. During the voyage, they kept to themselves with Lexi helping to pass the time by reading to Zoe and telling her about the new home they were sailing to in a place called *London*. She was taken aback when Zoe asked, "Is my Daddy in London? Is that where you lost him?"

"He's not in London now sweetheart. He used to live there just as I did. I guess you could say that is where I lost him because it's where I saw him last. When you get a little older I'll tell you more, and when I show you around the City, I'll take you to all the same places where we used to go."

The child accepted her answer. "Okay Mama; maybe we'll find him. Maybe we'll find Daddy in London."

Her father had insisted on giving her a sizeable sum, and together with the money she had earned and saved, it would allow her to take the time she needed to find a place to live and secure a job.

She had not notified her brothers she was coming; she didn't want to upset their lives or be a burden to them. She planned to stay at the Savoy until she found a flat; then she would contact her brothers. She also planned to pay Marcus Hirsch a visit; it was time she learned of Jake's fate. She had put off the inevitable far too long.

On the ride to the hotel, Zoe gazed out the window in awe at the new sights. Her Mama had told her that their new home, London, would be very different from Jerusalem and so it was.

She held Zoe's hand as they walked into the Savoy. Suddenly, memories came flooding back; Zoe had been conceived in this very hotel; conceived in Love—Love that promised a million tomorrows. How young and naïve she had been.

As Lexi and Zoe were checking into the Savoy, Jake was on his way to the Cotswolds. His long overdue trip to Cape Town was now in the past. Jamilia had thoroughly charmed him, and he was thankful for every morsel of information she had fed him. Her prophetic words to marry, have a family, and live a good life remained foremost in his thoughts.

His journey failed to unlock the mystery of the diamonds, yet he viewed it as successful in other ways. At long last, he felt he knew his uncles; learning about family was always a good thing.

He couldn't predict how the many pieces would ultimately fall in place, but at least one clue had emerged. The appraisals were printed on Annex letterhead leading to the strong possibility that his uncles had cut and polished the stones. Nothing he learned indicated either Franz or Jamilia had any connection to them bringing him back to Benjamin and Sidney which would explain why they were sent to him.

He had done all he could for now. He had to return to work and get back on track moving his life forward.

He would ring up Marcus in the morning and tell him he was home and that he would see him soon. If weather permitted, he planned to drop by the aerodrome, take a plane up, and check with Joe to see if there was any word on the delivery of the new aircraft.

Once again, the diamonds were set aside.

Lexi planned to spend the first few days in London taking Zoe on a tour of the City. She wanted to show her all the places her parents had taken her as a child, and introduce her to new foods that weren't available in Palestine.

But first, they were going shopping: they both needed clothes. Zoe seemed to grow overnight and clothes that fit her just weeks ago were now too small. Their first stop was a children's boutique; after trying on almost every item in her size, they left with two large shopping bags. Shoes were next on their list; they purchased a pair of Mary Jane patent leather dress shoes and a practical pair of oxfords both to Zoe's delight.

They stopped into a café for a quick lunch before heading to Selfridge's Department Store where Lexi picked up several outfits and necessities for herself.

Loaded down with bags, Zoe talked and talked all the way back to the hotel.

"Mama, can I put on my new clothes and shoes when we get back to our room? I like my shiny shoes best. If I get up close, I can see my face in my shoes. Did you know that?"

Lexi felt better than she had in a long time. To her, this was what being a mother was all about. For the first time in Zoe's three and a half years, she had spent a delightful day with her daughter—shopping, having lunch, stopping for ice cream, having fun, feeling safe—all basics of motherhood. Best of all was seeing Zoe so happy, and that made her happy too.

The next day, clad in new outfits—Zoe had chosen her own—they set off to take in the sights of London. After breakfast, Lexi took Zoe to the Underground; they rode to the end of the line and returned to London where they took in a film at the cinema—*Easter Parade* an American musical featuring music by Irving Berlin had just opened. They lost themselves in the singing and dancing of Judy Garland and Fred Astaire. Zoe loved it all—it was her first film.

The next day, Lexi allowed Zoe to again pick out her outfit, but told her they were going on an adventure that required sturdy shoes. She wore blue overalls, a striped blue and white shirt with a matching jacket.

Zoe's curiosity was relentless. "Where are we going Mama? Why couldn't I wear my shiny shoes? Are we almost there?"

They boarded the Underground and headed to Regent's Park. The London Zoo opened in 1828 and is the world's oldest scientific zoo. It was renovated in 1927. Repair to the bomb damage from the War began in 1946 and lasted through most of 1947.

They didn't miss a thing—the Clock Tower, the Raven's Cage, the collection of buildings that housed animals, birds, and reptiles, and the East Tunnel that linked the North and South parts of the Zoo. They covered every inch of the park and it left them exhausted but exhilarated.

On the train back to the hotel, Zoe hugged Lexi. "Mama, I love you. Thank you; the Zoo was so much fun." She put her head on Lexi's shoulder and slept until they arrived at their station.

Energized after her short nap, she convinced Lexi to stop at the Tea Shoppe for a snack before returning to the hotel.

Jake was on his way back to De Beers when he saw her, the hair, her beautiful red hair. Walking beside her was a little girl, her clone. He slowed his pace and followed a distance behind them. His mind was racing; his heart was pounding. It was Lexi; he would know her anywhere.

He continued to watch as they entered the Tea Shoppe. Unsure of what to do, he stopped and stood in the doorway of a building. Deciding it would be easier to control his emotions in a public place, he opted to stop for a cup of tea. They sat at a small table with her back to the door, and she did not see him come in.

As he approached the table, Zoe looked up, her deep blue eyes staring into his own. At the sound of her name, she thought she was imagining his voice, Jake's voice, as she heard, "Lexi?"

She turned and realized this time she hadn't imagined it at all. It was Jake, her Jake. The cup slipped from her hand and clattered on the plate. "Mama, be careful. You almost broke it."

Neither spoke; they continued to stare at one another. They had both been disappointed so many times over the years they didn't trust themselves to believe.

"Mama, do you know the man? Man, do you know my Mama?"

They both laughed; Zoe had broken the spell. "Yes sweetheart, we know each other; we've known each other for a long time."

As Jake was about to ask her when she had returned to England, his eyes rested on the finger of her left hand where she wore the ring he had given her when he asked her to marry him. He turned to Zoe. "My name is Jake. What's your name?"

"My name is Zoe Elise Lyons and I'm three and a half years old. Mama took me to the Zoo. Have you ever been to the Zoo?"

Jake kissed her on the cheek. "Yes I have; isn't it fun?"

He turned to Lexi and without a word lifted her out of the chair, pulled her into his arms and kissed her. As Zoe tried to get between them, much to her delight, Jake lifted her onto his shoulders.

"Can we go someplace and talk?"

"We arrived back in England three days ago, and until I find a flat, we're staying at the Savoy."

They talked throughout the night as Zoe slept in Jake's arms. He couldn't take his eyes off of the beautiful little girl that their Love had created. She took to him immediately, and when Lexi gently told her Jake was her *Daddy*, that they had found him in London after all, she said, "I told you we would."

There was still a lot of ground to cover, but when morning came, Jake was determined. He was not leaving without them. They packed up their things and checked out of the Savoy and made their way to Charing Cross Station.

They took the train to the Cotswolds, and less than an hour later they were at the cottage. As Zoe ran in and out of the rooms talking a mile a minute, and Jake showed Lexi around, Jamilia's prophecy came to mind.

Zoe was the most excited little girl on the planet. "What are we going to do today? Are we going to live here? Is this our new home?"

"Let me tell you what I would like to do today, and you tell me if you agree. First, I think you should pick which bedroom you would like to be yours. Then we have a wedding to plan. There are some people that are very important to me that I would like you to meet and get to know; and you have uncles, an aunt, and a baby cousin in London that are your family. How does that sound?"

"I want the bedroom with the big window. Can I put my clothes in there? Can you help me Mama?"

Lexi smiled. "You go ahead; I'll be right there." To Jake she said, "I knew you would be the best Daddy to our little darling. She's so much like you; you'll see as time goes by that she's a real *Daddy's Girl*."

"What do you think of my suggestions? I will give notice with the register office, and talk with the new Rabbi at the Great Central Synagogue in the East End and ask him to marry us. We can plan a dinner afterwards here at the cottage; I have a good friend who can cater it. There are eight adults, Zoe and your nephew, and I think the cottage is the perfect venue. It's our home.

"You really should contact your brothers. Running into them on the street would be awkward to say the least. Marcus and Elena are my family, and I must tell them sooner rather than later. I was on my way back to the office when I met you yesterday, and I didn't even ring him up to tell him I wasn't coming back."

As Zoe called out for Lexi, she leaned over and kissed Jake. "Everything sounds good and right. Let's do it."

That night, Jake made love to Lexi as though it was their first time. As she lay sleeping in the safety of his arms, all adversity melted away. They had found their way back to one another once again, and that was all that mattered. They had Zoe; they were a family.

It took them less than a week to arrange everything.

Jake spoke to Marcus and asked if he could stop by their house the following evening. He would never forget the look on Marcus's face when he opened the door and saw Lexi and Zoe standing beside him. Elena's endless supply of cookies was not wasted on Zoe. When they left, she gave her a kiss and hugged her. Elena held her tight unwilling to let her go.

When Lexi rang up Mark, he was not in the least surprised. After Manny had seen them off in Haifa, he returned to Jerusalem a sad and beaten man. For the first time in a long time, he considered the error of his ways. It was perhaps too late for him, but not for Lexi and Zoe. He placed a call to London notifying Mark and Sam that they were returning home.

"Please don't be angry with your sister. It was a big decision for her to make, and she needs time to work it out for herself. Lexi will contact you when she's ready. I miss them as I miss all of you, and I miss your mother; she kept me grounded. It just took too long for me to realize it; I'm so sorry for the mistakes I made. The happiness and wellbeing of my children should have been my first priority, my only priority."

Manny left the Irgun and returned to work at the hospital. When he received the call from Lexi telling him they had been reunited with Jake, he was genuinely happy for them.

They were married in the Rabbi's study. Jake in a blue serge suit and striped tie stood beside Lexi, the Love of his life, wearing a blue silk dress that had been her Mum's. A very happy Zoe stood smiling in her blue party dress and shiny patent leather shoes.

As the Rabbi pronounced them *man and wife*, she added, *"and Zoe too."*

Jake kissed his beautiful wife, and scooped his beautiful daughter up in his arms kissing her too to the applause of their guests.

Mandy had taken care of everything at the cottage. She brought flowers, and a case of her finest wine. Tables throughout the great room held a bounty of hors d'oeuvres that included her petite vegetable pies, set out for all to enjoy.

The dining room table was formally set for a dinner of roasted Cornish hens and fresh local vegetables.

The tiered wedding cake was heart shaped, and adorned with red, pink, and white roses. Guests were given a choice of coffee or tea.

Jake insisted that Mandy shed her apron, and join them for dinner. Elena entertained them with the story of their first invitation to the cottage when he returned home. Zoe stood guard over her cousin Ethan like a mother hen.

As Jake looked about the room at *his family*, emotion engulfed him. He had forgotten how much the family dinners at their flat in the East End meant to him. How ironic that the only one he missed had saved his life.

One of the visions of the Zionist movement was the establishment of a Jewish university in the Land of Israel. The cornerstone for the university was laid in July 1918, and seven years later in April 1925, the Hebrew University campus on Mount Scopus opened.

By 1947, the University had become a large research and teaching institution. During the 1948 Arab-Israeli War, attacks were carried out against convoys moving between the Israeli-controlled section of Jerusalem and the University.

The leader of the Arab forces in Jerusalem threatened military action against the University and the Hadassah Hospital if the Jews continued to use them as bases for attacks.

On April 13, 1948, an armored convoy of Hadassah and Hebrew University doctors, nurses, and civilians set out attempting to bring medical supplies and personnel to the Hadassah Hospital on Mount Scopus.

The convoy was attacked on the way by an ambush of Arab terrorists and after being besieged and under fire for hours, all 77 members of the convoy were killed; among the dead was Dr. Emanuel Portman. Hadassah evacuated all its Mount Scopus medical facilities due to the difficulties of the Arab siege and set up a makeshift hospital near Ein Karem.

Nobody was ever prosecuted for this crime against humanity nor were British collaborators investigated; the planners of the massacre became heroes of the Arab Palestinians.

The Hadassah Hospital on Mount Scopus would not be restored for 30 years hence.

CHAPTER THIRTY-SIX

J ake took a leave of absence from De Beers determined to make up the years that he had missed with Lexi and Zoe. He was no longer the same Jake Lyons that grew up in the Jewish Quarter of the East End; that person ceased existing that awful night he lost his family. The War brought an abrupt end to the first seventeen years of life as he knew it, and impacted everything that occurred in his life from that time forward until he was discharged.

Losing fellow RAF pilots was the hardest to come to terms with; one had to accept God's choice as to who lived and who didn't. In retrospect, spending an isolated year on Guernsey Island was not so bad compared to what others had to endure though it had resulted in him losing touch with Lexi. He was no longer naïve; the world today was not the world of his youth, and he was well aware of that. He was merely twenty-four years old, and yet he had lived a lifetime.

Having been raised by parents who placed more emphasis on love and family, and less on strict religious observance, finding himself alone was devastating. Thankfully, Marcus and Elena Hirsch had stepped up immediately to fill that void becoming his surrogate family. He couldn't imagine what going through the hardest times in his life would have been like without them.

Now to his delight and good fortune, in addition to Marcus and Elena, he had a wife, a daughter, two brothers-in-law, a sister-in-law, and a nephew; he felt truly blessed.

He planned to spend the remainder of 1948 getting to know his daughter, and loving Lexi, which was all he ever dreamt of. He wanted to introduce them to the new Jake, to his new world. He would leave no stone unturned.

He began in the Cotswolds. He took them to the Village and introduced them to the shopkeepers he knew; they stopped in to see Mandy; they shopped for food and prepared meals together—the three of them. They were inseparable.

Wendy told Jake she would be leaving at the end of the school year. She had met a young chap, and they were planning to be married in June.

On a bright sunny day in May, he excitedly told them he had a surprise planned. When they arrived at Eagle Aerodrome, Lexi grew apprehensive. She was nervous about watching him fly. Their long separation had taken a toll, and the thought of losing him if anything went wrong was more than she could bear.

He introduced her to Joe, and asked if a plane was available. "Yes, as a matter of fact, both planes are available; you can have your choice.

"I'm glad you stopped by; I was going to contact you to give you a heads up that the new planes are due to arrive by the end of the month."

Jake let out a whoop. "That is great news, really great news. It's been a year since we placed the order."

"Let me know which plane you want. It's been my pleasure meeting you Lexi and you too Zoe." Joe walked away.

"Jake, why are you taking up a plane today? How often do you fly?"

"I didn't exactly come here to *take up a plane*, as you put it. I want you and Zoe to let me take both of you flying; I guarantee that once you try it, you'll be hooked. You'll experience a feeling like no other. I do some of my best thinking up there. When I missed you most, ironically flying was the only thing that brought me back to earth."

Lexi's hesitation gave Zoe an opening. "Daddy, I want to fly. Can we go, please, please?"

"Your Mama has to decide. I can't take you if she doesn't want you to go."

Zoe turned to Lexi, but before she could speak, Jake said, "I'm sorry; that wasn't fair. Let me start over.

"I would like to take my two best girls for their very first flight. It is a perfect day for flying, not a cloud in the sky, and once we are in the air and you can look down and all around, I'll even point out the cottage. It looks really small from up there. I can assure you our safety is very important to me, but my flying credentials are solid; I'm an ace pilot, I'll have you know."

Lexi melted. How could she have possibly thought that Jake would endanger them in any way?

He chose the bright yellow Staggerwing. Once they were seated, Jake taxied to the end of the runway and suddenly they were airborne. Zoe clapped her hands. "Daddy, you did it. Look Mama; look how high up we are."

As she sat frozen in her seat, Jake looked over at her with a big grin on his face. "Come on Lexi, that wasn't so bad. I got us up here, now you only have to worry about my getting us down. Why don't you relax and enjoy the ride for now?"

To Zoe who was seated behind them, he said, "How's it going Zoe? Do you want me to point out the cottage? I'll point out the Village too."

Lexi relaxed and began to laugh and laugh and laugh. He was right; flying was euphoric. One could see for miles the open countryside, the cottage, the Village, and places beyond. "I love you Jake Lyons; don't ever forget it."

God promised Abraham, Isaac, and Jacob concerning their descendants: *I will bless those who bless you, and I will curse the one who curses you.* The rise and fall of many great empires in history can be traced to how they blessed or mistreated the Israelites.

The survivors emerged from the Nazi Holocaust a different people. The Jews of Europe became the Israelis of Palestine, tough, disciplined, and courageous in the face of overwhelming odds. They fought against British immigration restrictions; they fought against a hostile Muslim population that was being flooded with new Muslim residents from all over the world.

When the British disarmed them and heavily armed the Muslims, they organized freedom fighting cell groups that gave the British more than they could handle causing their ultimate withdrawal.

The land of Palestine was proclaimed the Jewish homeland on 14 May 1948. They providentially named the new State *Israel*. Never before in history had such a thing happened. Scattered across the face of the earth for 2,000 years they returned to the same piece of real estate from which they were driven.

After World War II, the Empire on whose flag the sun had never set found itself progressively diminished. The UK emerged only a shadow of what it once was.

Manny Portman died one month shy of Israel's Declaration of Independence. Although his brief involvement in the Irgun overshadowed his relationship with his family and his years of accomplishments as a physician for the Hadassah Medical Organization, he managed to set things right before he died.

—⚏—

They returned to the aerodrome when weather permitted, Lexi as avid as Zoe. When Jake got the call that the planes had been delivered, they dropped everything and headed off excited and anxious to see the beautiful new plane Jake spoke nonstop about.

It was all white with a blue stripe along the body and on the tips of the V tail; the under wings were red. They climbed aboard the plane sitting back in the plush seats while Jake checked out the instruments. She was a beauty. As Zoe urged Jake to take off, he explained to her that he had to fly the plane himself before he could take them along.

They returned two weeks later, and boarded *Lady Lyons*, the name Jake had painted on the side. Throughout the summer they flew often mostly at the behest of his two best girls. In September, Jake arranged a surprise for Zoe's fourth birthday. He flew them to Guernsey Island for a few days.

They stayed at the Old Government House Hotel in St. Peter Port with its cobbled streets and picturesque seafront marina and historic gardens, not far from the airport. Lulu, Lila, and Bill Walsh welcomed them with open arms. They rented a car, and spent their days as typical tourists boasting they had *the best guides ever.*

Their tour began at Castle Cornet standing at the mouth of the harbor with its museums including the 201 Squadron RAF Museum. Next they visited Candie Gardens, once a part of a private estate offering spectacular views across the harbor, and a public flower garden home to the oldest known heated glasshouses in the British Isles. They stopped for lunch at a Café housed in a Victorian bandstand.

The Victorian Shop and Parlour, probably the earliest remaining complete building within the town's medieval boundaries, was Zoe's favorite. The National Trust of Guernsey had done a magnificent job restoring the exquisite 18th century house to the delight of the Islanders and the many tourists who came to visit.

Through its doors, they entered into a bygone age where sweets came from jars and were measured in pounds and ounces; where the popular old type cottage garden and vegetable seeds are still available; where all gifts, souvenirs, and confectionery are offered in rooms of working gaslights with their fragile mantles. A bygone age kept alive.

No trip was complete without visiting the Walsh Farm on the far side of the Island. Zoe loved everything about the farm; the sheep, the cows, and Bill lending her a hand at milking. Lulu baked Zoe a cake and recanted the story of celebrating her Daddy's 21st Birthday with mutton stew at a time when there was precious little to eat on the entire Island.

Zoe proclaimed, "This was my best Birthday ever!" as she hugged and kissed Lulu, Lila, and Bill goodbye. Jake and Lexi bid them goodbye promising to return soon.

If they thought Zoe would sleep on the short flight back to London, they were mistaken. She did, however, fall asleep in the car on the way to the cottage.

As the months ticked by and the end of 1948 grew closer, Jake had one more surprise for his girls. He booked a flight to New York where they would spend the last two weeks in December; it was the final part of his life he wished to introduce them to.

New York was a sight to behold decked out in its holiday finest. Jake took them to Jewelers of America and introduced them to Al Cohen; he stopped by De Beers and introduced them to the people he worked with. With that out of the way, they took the City by storm.

Their days consisted of Broadway shows, marveling at Radio City Music Hall's Rockettes, waiting on line at Lindy's for cheesecake, eating the biggest sandwiches they had ever seen at Stage Deli, and dining at the finest of restaurants the City had to offer. Riding in a horse-drawn carriage through Central Park, and trying their hand at ice skating at Rockefeller Plaza finally brought their visit to an end.

On 2 January 1949, they flew back to London. Jake promised them that when they came back again, he would take them south to the State of Georgia where he had learned to fly and introduce them to *southern hospitality.*

It was time to return to a normal routine. The months he had taken to show Lexi and Zoe the life they had signed on for was well spent. He was pleased that he had accomplished what he set out to do; his girls were overwhelmed.

He promised Marcus he would return to work in January, and he was true to his word. Marcus was glad to see him. "Jake my boy, welcome back. I've missed the three of you and so has Elena; we must get together soon."

"Thank you, Marcus. We've missed the both of you too. I've had the time of my life with my two best girls, and I'm ready to get back to the world of diamonds."

In March, Lexi learned they were expecting. They were over the moon; Zoe only wanted to know *for sure*—was she getting a brother or a sister. They learned in May that she was carrying twins, but were still unable to answer Zoe's question. The twins were due in late September around Zoe's birthday.

They decided to look for a larger house; one that would accommodate their growing family and located in a better school district for Zoe to begin in the fall when she turned five. The cottage would be their getaway place to go on holiday.

Their goal was to be settled in their new home by the time the twins arrived and the school semester began.

They purchased a six bedroom detached home in Pembridge Square, Notting Hill, London whose commanding corner position overlooking the garden square was a remarkable fusion of traditional and contemporary that had undergone extensive refurbishment prior to the War.

An imposing entrance hall on the ground floor led to extremely generous proportioned rooms. The formal dining room overlooked Pembridge Square. The second and third floors were dedicated to a master suite with two dressing rooms, a large en-suite bathroom with a walk in shower, a private seating area, and five additional front to back bedrooms and bathrooms with each bedroom having its own en-suite facilities. They fell in love with the house the minute they saw it.

Quiet residential tree-lined Pembridge Square is located in one of Notting Hill's most prestigious areas. It sits between the highly fashionable and ever popular Westbourne Grove and Notting Hill Gate, and offers all the wonderful amenities of excellent schools within easy walking distance, wide open green spaces of Kensington Gardens and Hyde Park, and transport links that provide easy access to the West End, City and Canary Wharfs, as well as the main thoroughfare leading west.

In addition to a new home, Jake purchased a Standard Vanguard car made by the Standard Motor Company in Coventry, England. It was the Company's first post-WWII car, and the first model to carry the new Standard Badge, which was a heavily stylized representation of the wings of a griffin.

They spent the summer months getting the house ready for their move to Notting Hill. As was common practice in selling estate homes, they acquired a good deal of the furnishings from the previous owners leaving only Zoe's bedroom and the nursery to be dealt with.

Jake contacted the contractor that he hired for the cottage and had him install a duplicate workshop using the same plans he had originally drawn up, including the installation of a larger safe and a state-of-the art security system throughout.

Jake moved everything from the workshop at the cottage with the exception of the cache of diamonds, which he left secure in the safe; the chest empty of its contents sat on the floor in the master bedroom.

He hadn't thought about the diamonds for well over a year; with the twins due and their impending move to the new house, he had no idea when he would have the time to get back to them.

The first week in September, Zoe started school at Ealing High School, an independent day school for girls, ages 4-18. The school's strong traditions and leadership earned it a reputation for academic excellence at both the Junior and Senior levels. Jake and Lexi viewed it a good choice for their daughter's natural desire to learn and overactive curiosity about everything.

The twins, both boys and both weighing in at exactly six pounds each, were born on Zoe's fifth birthday; they named them Harry and Adam in memory of Jake's parents. Nanny Paige arrived the day before they were due home.

Elena could not be deterred and arrived with bag in hand to stay as long as she was needed. Insisting that she should not abandon Marcus, they invited him to join her to stay at the house, as well.

Because the twins were born on Zoe's Birthday, they celebrated when Lexi and the boys came home from the hospital. They invited their family; Mark, Rosalie, and Ethan, and Sam and Ellen who had recently become engaged. Elena insisted on preparing the meal. When all were seated, Jake stood with glass in hand. "To my beloved Lexi, I thank you for Zoe, Harry, and Adam, for making my life complete, for loving me. In case you aren't aware, I love you with all my heart."

As everyone echoed, "Here, Here," he handed her a small ring box. As their guests looked on, she opened it to reveal an eternal wedding band of alternating marquis cut diamonds and blue sapphires. Jake had cut and polished each stone himself. September's birthstone, the blue sapphire, represented not only Zoe, Harry, and Adam's birth month but their first meeting at Ivan Portman's Bar Mitzvah in September 1936. The ring was magnificent.

As tears streamed down her face, she said, "I don't know why I'm crying; I couldn't be happier. In case you aren't aware, I love you with all my heart too." Jake removed her gold wedding band and slipped the ring on her finger. He kissed her and pronounced that he considered the day they met the anniversary of their love and life together.

"One more toast, and I promise we can eat. To each of you here tonight, I love you too, and I am proud to call you family. As we celebrate the birth of Harry and Adam, Lady Zoe's birthday, moving into our new home, and Sam and Ellen's engagement, I assure you this is only the first of many gatherings Lexi and I plan to host. To Marcus and Elena, no thank you is sufficient.

"Now, let's eat." Everyone began talking at once as the two helpers Elena had hired began serving the meal.

When it came time for dessert, a Birthday Cake with candles aglow was brought in and placed in front of Zoe. After cake and ice cream, came the gifts. Jake fondly recalled the many presents his parents had given him that made each and every birthday special; driving lessons were the best ever.

Jake and Lexi gave her one of the rings he had made for his sisters years before, a pretty new outfit from Sam and Ellen, and a baby doll and carriage from Rosalie, Mark, and Ethan. Marcus excused himself from the table. He returned with a beautiful Dollhouse fully furnished and set it on the floor. As Zoe stared speechless at the tiny furniture, Elena said, "We have a table for the house to sit on when you decide where you would like to keep it."

When Jake tucked Zoe into bed, she clung to him not willing to let him go just yet. "I love you Daddy; I'm so glad Mama and I found you in London. I knew we would."

The family Jake so longed for was his. As the decade of the 1940s ended, he had regained all that he had lost at its onset—and more, so much more.

CHAPTER THIRTY-SEVEN

T he 1950s commonly known as simply the *Fifties* was a decade that began on 1 January 1950 and ended on 31 December 1959. By its end, the world had largely recovered from World War II, and the Cold War matured from its modest beginning to a power competition between the United States and the Soviet Union.

Communism and Capitalism clashed with conflicts that included the Korean War, the beginning of the Space Race with the launch of Sputnik I by the Russians, and increased testing of nuclear weapons. Decolonization of former European Colonial Empires, and on a larger scale in Africa and Asia, first began in the early fifties.

King George VI died; his eldest daughter ascended to the British Throne as Queen Elizabeth II at the age of 25. Winston Churchill resigned and Anthony Eden became Britain's Prime Minister.

Joseph Stalin, the leader of the Soviet Union, died leading to the rise of Nikita Khrushchev who pursued a more liberal domestic and foreign policy, stressing peaceful competition with the West rather than overt hostility.

America became the most influential economic power in the world under the presidency of Dwight D. Eisenhower. During his Administration, Alaska and Hawaii become the 49th and 50th States; and his approval of the first U.S. space mission in 1955 ultimately led to the creation of NASA in 1958.

Television matured with larger screens; the first transistor computer was built at the University of Manchester; Bell Telephone Labs produced the first solar battery; and the first solar powered watch was invented.

On 5 December 1952, a *killer fog* first appeared over London; it lifted four days later with an estimated death toll of at least 12,000 people, 150,000 were hospitalized, and thousands of undocumented animals died. The Clean Air Act was passed in response four years later, but the actual causes of the incident would remain unknown for decades.

In the medical world, Jonas Salk invented an immunization vaccine for Polio; the first successful ultrasound test of heart activity was conducted; the first cervical cancer cells were cultured outside a human body; and Francis Crick and James Watson discovered the double-helix structure of DNA.

Halfway through the decade, classic pop was swept off the charts by Rock-and-Roll when Elvis Presley became the leading figure of the newly popular sound of music. The endless groups of singers and bands of the fifties paved the way for The Beatles and The Rolling Stones, British rock groups that shaped not only the music world but also an entire generation.

In America, Marilyn Monroe performing in *Gentlemen Prefer Blondes* proclaimed to all—*Diamonds are a Girl's Best Friend*.

On 15 November 1957, Sir Ernest Oppenheimer, Chairman of Anglo American Corporation and De Beers Consolidated Mines, died at Johannesburg, South Africa. He was 77 and had been in uncertain health for some months. His son Harry Oppenheimer succeeded him as Chairman.

By the end of the *Fifties,* Fidel Castro overthrew the regime of Fulgencio Batista in Cuba, establishing a communist government in the Country—a mere ninety miles from the coast of the United States.

Winston Churchill had warned that Britain could be bankrupt when WWII was over; and immediately after the conflict there emerged a very depressing atmosphere across the Country. There were problems with transport; factories ran out of fuel; people had no electricity to cook with; and rationing remained in force far too long after victory was declared.

De Beers continued its involvement in primarily promoting diamonds in America rather than in the UK, as London struggled to rebuild the bombed out areas throughout the City that included Hatton Garden.

Hatton Garden located in the Holborn District of the London Borough of Camden, had long been noted as London's Jewelry Quarter and center of the UK diamond trade representing the largest number of jewelry retailers in all of Britain.

The largest of these, De Beers, represented a family of companies that dominated the international diamond trade. Their headquarters were located in a complex of offices and warehouses just behind the main Hatton Garden shopping street.

This was the very same Hatton Garden where Harry had walked with Jake and told him he envisioned a *Lyons Jewelry Emporium* in their future.

The *Fifties* were considered a conservative decade in jewelry, as many designers and manufacturers looked back to styles of the late 1800s. Flowers were reintroduced and reinterpreted by important jewelry houses like Van Cleef & Arpels and Cartier, who were doing more elegant versions with diamonds and emeralds; flowers became a way of showing off big diamonds and other gems.

Women once again desired parures and suites of jewelry that included either—bracelet, necklace, brooch—or—bracelet, earrings, brooch, ring. After the War, people began to entertain again, and a whole new brand of jewelry came into play with the introduction of the diamond cocktail ring, which grew quite popular.

For Jake, the decade became a turning point. His personal life couldn't have been better; his family was doing well; everyone was happy. When the twins turned five, they were enrolled in school, and Lexi returned to nursing.

By the mid-fifties, he found himself growing bored with his job at De Beers. Consulting was not where his interests in the diamond industry were rooted. He realized for the first time that his father had given up his dream for a position that would allow him to better provide for his family when he went to work for De Beers. By accepting Marcus' offer, he had done the same thing.

In his mind, success was measured not only by earnings, but also by what you brought to the table that enabled you to make a difference whether that was by innate ability or ingenuity. He viewed his expertise as diamond cutting and polishing not advertising and marketing. It had all been exciting and fun in the beginning travelling to America and actually learning about the many sides of the jewelry industry. Of late, he felt he accomplished more when working in his workshop.

He spent a lot of time at Eagle Aerodrome not only flying but also visiting his friend. His friendship with Joe Hanks had grown to the point that he confided in Jake from time to time often seeking his advice. Recently, Jake had helped him secure a loan for the purchase of two planes to expand the new charter business he had undertaken.

A week earlier, Joe had approached him with a business offer that he had been mulling over and over in his mind. He weighed the pros and cons a million times; arriving at the same conclusion each and every time led the way to reaching his decision

Unfortunately, the day he realized that *diamonds* were no longer his first love he was faced with a dilemma. How could he tell Marcus without disappointing him, especially after all that he had done for him? He had become a father to him. It was on a par with disappointing his Papa; an action he would never have considered.

With dinner over and the children in bed for the night, Jake asked Lexi to sit beside him on the sofa; he was seeking her input and sound advice he had come to rely on.

"I've been offered a business proposition that I want to tell you about; what I would like to do about it; and since it affects all of us, I want you to tell me your thoughts.

"Last week, Joe Hanks told me that his cousin Tim who is a part owner in Eagle Aerodrome wants out of the partnership. Joe is not in a position to buy him out at this point in time having embarked on a major expansion of their charter service less than a year ago. He asked me if I would be interested in becoming his new partner. Although Tim only owns 30% of the business, if I were to buy him out, Joe is offering me a 50-50 partnership.

"I have so many great ideas for the aerodrome and especially for expanding the charter services even further. There are new achievements in aviation happening almost every day, and there is so much opportunity out there just waiting to be tapped into.

"I've been thinking long and hard about his offer before speaking with you because I want to explain to you why I'm considering it. There's no need on my part to tell you how I feel about flying, about the future of aeronautics, about my friendship with Joe; you know everything about me.

"When we met at the tender age of twelve, I was all about diamonds and following in my Papa's footsteps; it was a given, but it was a way of life that no longer exists. The War changed a lot of things. Marcus offered me a job when I was discharged; a job in a field that I once thought was my destiny. I can't deny that I loved every minute of travelling to America and learning what the industry was all about and what it had to offer.

"Somewhere along the line, I began to realize that the part of the diamond industry that my father passed onto me is no longer sustainable on an individual basis. The areas that I am now involved in are just not me; they don't represent my interests. I've become bored with the process, and disappointed that instead of selling diamonds, De Beers' advertising campaign is based solely on selling an idea. The ability to produce a beautifully cut and polished gem has nothing to do with it.

"I would like to accept Joe's offer; I think we are a good fit and would compliment one another. I intend to tell Marcus that I'm leaving De Beers, not because of the offer, but because I think it's time. I don't enjoy going to work anymore. When Marcus hired me, it was on the premise that I would take over his position when he retired; I feel that leaving would upset his plans, and I don't want to do that. So my Love, that's my quandary. What say you?"

Lexi had listened intently; she had felt for some time that Jake wasn't totally into his job. In fact, it was evident he was far happier working on diamonds in his workshop which he often used as a means of relaxation when he wasn't flying. At first, she attributed it to Zoe's interest in watching him work and ultimately asking him to teach her as his father had taught him. She soon realized, however, that many times Zoe wasn't around yet Jake continued to frequent his workshop.

"I haven't seen you this excited in a long time. When I think back on other times you showed this kind of enthusiasm, it was always about something that had to do with flying. I think you should follow your heart, as I know that

Marcus would want you to. He loves you Jake, and there is no way you could ever be a disappointment to him.

"You know what I think? I think he idolizes you as much as I do."

Jake laughed out loud. He pulled her into his arms and kissed her. "I've spent a whole week agonizing over this; I should have come to you immediately; I could have saved myself from so many disparaging thoughts.

"Do we have any ice cream? Suddenly I feel like ice cream in a big bowl with hot fudge and nuts on top that's so popular in the States."

Jake's revelations were not in the least a surprise to Marcus. He recalled the night he told him and Elena that he had purchased a plane with all the passion and excitement he had once shown when he spoke of diamonds. Although Elena had viewed his interest in flying as a distraction for having lost Lexi, he had felt otherwise; the ensuing years had proven him right.

However, Lexi was right too. He idolized Jake who could do no wrong in his eyes. In fact, the only way Jake could disappoint Marcus would be by not following his heart, by not being honest about his own feelings in an effort to spare his.

Two months later, the partnership of Joe Hanks and Jake Lyons was finalized. Eagle Aerodrome continued to operate as a UK Civil Aviation Authority accredited pilot school. They began undergoing a much-needed expansion to accommodate the charter services. Two new jet planes were purchased; new hangers were constructed, and longer runways for the new jets were installed. New hires were in the works; pilots, mechanics, and an office manager for the charter services were needed immediately.

While Jake dealt with the construction and expansion, Joe was kept busy interviewing the new employees they were seeking. As soon as word went out, two mechanics were quickly hired.

Holly Reynolds was the first to apply for the office manager's position, and by the end of her interview, Joe offered her the job. She was actually overqualified for the position, but as an accountant and a licensed pilot, he felt the opportunity each afforded the other could be a win-win situation for her and their Company as it grew and expanded.

Joe hired two ex-RAF servicemen as pilots; both were also qualified to be flight instructors if the need arose. One of the men he hired had recently left the RAF having stayed on as a flight instructor after the War. Following the interview, they chatted for almost an hour, and finding one particular part of his story intriguing, Joe insisted he and Jake meet. He set the meeting up for the following afternoon.

When Jake walked into Joe's office, he was totally unprepared for what awaited him. As the two men stared at each other, Joe said, "Jake, I'd like you to meet one of our new flight instructors Tommy Butler. Tommy, this is my partner Jake Lyons."

After the interview, after Joe had hired him, as they compared stories of their service during the War, Tommy casually mentioned that he had learned to fly in the States and related that he and two other young chaps had experienced a year of *southern hospitality* at its best; it peaked his interest knowing that Jake had also been sent to flight school in America.

He lost contact with both friends during the War, but had recently read a newspaper article about Andy Barbour, now a Barrister, announcing his run for Parliament. He had no word on the whereabouts of his other friend Jake Lyons.

At first, Joe was inclined to tell him that Jake was his partner; on second thought, he opted to surprise them both. He was impressed with Tommy Butler; he seemed genuine—what you saw was what you got—and he liked that.

"Is that really you Tommy? Hey man, you look great. How are you? Where have you been? What have you been up to? Wait a minute. Did Joe say you're coming to work with us?"

"Yes, it looks like I am. I had no idea you and Joe are partners."

They both turned and looked at Joe who stood grinning from ear to ear. "Don't look at me like that. I had already hired Tommy, and as we were talking he mentioned your name, and I just couldn't resist setting up this little meeting."

That evening after the children had gone to bed, Jake gave Lexi an update on the expansion of the aerodrome and the new people Joe hired. "I met with one of the pilots today. His name is Tommy Butler."

Lexi thought for a moment. "Why does that name sound familiar? Is that your friend that I met years ago at the Savoy?"

"Yes, it is. And he's married to your friend Betsy Bromwell that you went to nursing school with, and they have four kids and another on the way. They live in Middlesex, but they recently bought a bigger home and will be moving soon."

"I can't believe you waited until after dinner and after the children were in bed to tell me. How could you not say *something* to me the minute you walked in the door Jake Lyons? Do you have their number? I have to ring her up. My God, it's been ten years or more. How are they? I remember when we said our goodbyes. Tommy said he was *sweet* on her. They actually kept in touch and got married. How wonderful."

Jake playfully tried to pull her towards him to kiss her, but Lexi playfully pushed him away. "Not so fast. You're not off the hook yet. Can we get together? I'd love to see them."

"Of course, we can get together; in fact, I invited them to dinner Saturday night, and I told them to bring the kids. Tommy and I worked it out that we would tell you after the kids were in bed. I'm sure they're having this same conversation as we speak. Here's their number so you can ring up Betsy. Why don't you give it a try now?"

She took the piece of paper he held out to her but not before giving him a big kiss. "Thank you; thank you. I love you. You're forgiven for holding out on me." And she was off to make her call.

During the months of renovation, contracts had been negotiated and by the spring of 1955, Eagle Charter Services was off to a great start. The two jets they ordered were due to be delivered by mid-summer; and it seemed as if everyone wanted to learn to fly considering all the applications they had received for their next class.

The twins were growing up; they were good scholastic students. Living too far from the East End to send them to Hebrew School at the old synagogue led Jake and Lexi to hire a tutor to come to the house. Their teacher was a woman whose milder, gentler way of approaching their lessons than Rabbi Levin had been with Jake, resulted in Harry and Adam liking her immensely and actually looking forward to the days she came.

Zoe no longer a child had become a young lady. To everyone, she was a normal teenager with many friends who attended parties and dances for young people her age, and who liked nothing better than spending time with her Daddy in his workshop perfecting her ability to cut gems. To Jake who knew his daughter better than anyone, he saw in Zoe what his Papa had seen in him. *Passion*—the powerful emotion he had for diamonds, she had for flying.

For her fourteenth birthday after many discussions and considerations, pros and cons, Lexi agreed to Jake's suggestion of her gift. She could begin taking flying lessons. She couldn't solo until she was sixteen and couldn't get her license until she turned seventeen, but by that time, the upside would be the vast knowledge, experience, and flying hours she would have to her credit. Jake planned to teach her himself until the time came for her to solo.

As the decade of the fifties drew to an end, Eagle Aerodrome and Charter Services was totally solvent with no outstanding loans and turning a hefty profit. Jake and Joe had parlayed their friendship and partnership into a multi-million dollar enterprise. A new venture to kick off the New Year was in the works. Lexi had made the suggestion and Jake had followed through. Eagle MedAir, providing medical transport for doctors, patients, and supplies, was set to begin service in January.

In an empty hanger, decorated for the season, with tables of ample food and drink, and a small band providing music, employees and their families gathered to celebrate Eagle Aerodrome's success that each had contributed to.

Jake had invited their family to join them, including Marcus and Elena whose pride in Jake's accomplishments was written all over their faces. Mark and Sam, both physicians, welcomed the news of Eagle MedAir.

There were other things to celebrate too. Marcus had finally retired. He was seventy-five years old, and he and Elena had celebrated their 50th Wedding Anniversary a couple of years back. Spending time with family and traveling was their sole agenda for the coming years.

An already wonderful evening ended with a surprise Christmas Bonus for each and every employee. Jake and Joe predicted it was the first of many to come.

When it rains, most birds head for shelter; the Eagle is the only bird that, in order to avoid the rain, flies above the clouds.

High above the clouds, Eagle Aerodrome Services soared into the future. Happy 1960 to one and all!

CHAPTER THIRTY-EIGHT

T ime is not measured by the passing of years but by what one does, what one feels, and what one achieves. The bad news is time flies; the good news is you are the Pilot; to the Pilot—the sky is the limit; the sky is home.

Zoe knew the instrument panel backwards and forwards. Through the years, Jake had answered her endless questions straightforward disregarding the fact that that for most of those years she was a child. She absorbed and remembered everything he taught her, often seeking further explanation if something was not clear in her mind. They had flown together many times just the two of them, and in retrospect, each flight had been a lesson in itself. Therefore, it was without question that she knew a good deal about aviation the very first time she found herself at the controls in the cockpit.

At first, it seemed to her that it was going to be a long two years before she could solo, and an additional year before she could get her license, but once she was at the controls, these thoughts evaporated into thin air. She was flying, actually flying a plane; Zoe Elise Lyons was on her way to becoming a pilot, a pilot like her Daddy.

Jake's busy schedule at work, Zoe's school commitments, and the weather to contend with did not afford them a great deal of time, but they flew whenever they could.

He considered having one of their flight instructors take over to prepare her to fly solo, but she wouldn't hear of it. Secretly, Jake was pleased. She was a natural and by the time she was old enough to get her pilot's license, he had no doubt whatsoever that she would ace the exam.

An article in the London Times caught Jake's eye; Paul Zeller died. The lengthy article identified him as the son and grandson of the proprietors of Zeller Jewelers one of the oldest establishments in Hatton Garden. They had been in business for seventy-five years at their landmark corner location when the store was demolished in one of the Luftwaffe air raids during the Blitz on London.

Paul Zeller and his brother Phil left London at the turn of the century and struck out on their own settling in Cape Town, South Africa. For over forty years, Zeller Jewelers was a well-known fixture on Adderley Street in the heart of the business district.

Seizing the opportunity to increase their profits, they ventured into gem cutting and polishing by opening the Annex, which they operated as a separate entity hiring gem cutters fleeing Europe and the Nazis. Upon the death of their parents at the end of the War, they sold the store and the Annex and returned to London. The Hatton Garden location never reopened.

Jake tore the article out of the paper. The funeral had been held a week earlier, but the name of the funeral home was listed, as well as the synagogue where the services had taken place.

He decided to go to the synagogue first. Finding the main doors locked, he walked around to the side of the building and entered. A woman in the office called out to him. "May I help you?"

"Good Morning. My name is Jake Lyons, and I'm hoping you can help me get in touch with Phil Zeller." He pulled the article from his pocket. "My uncles worked for the Zeller brothers, and I would like to offer my condolences."

When the woman hesitated, Jake added, "I will be happy to leave you my name and number to have him contact me. If you are not at liberty to give out information to strangers, I thoroughly understand your position."

The woman said. "I know Phil and Lena personally. Please have a seat while I try to reach the Zellers, and I'll leave the decision up to them."

"Thank you. I appreciate that."

She returned and handed Jake a piece of paper with a phone number and address in the Hyde Park area. "Ring them up. They're expecting to hear from you."

He walked out to the street in search of a phone. He could have asked to use the phone in the synagogue, but the woman hadn't offered, and he didn't want to press his luck. At the corner, he stepped into the booth and dialed the number. Phil Zeller answered.

Minutes later, he pulled up to the house, walked to the door and lifted the knocker. Lena Zeller opened the door inviting him in.

Jake never made it to work. He spent the better part of the day learning about Benjamin's arrival in Cape Town and how it was actually his uncle who ran the Annex. "Hiring your uncle was a business decision Paul and I never regretted.

"We didn't know anything about diamond and gem cutting. In retrospect, it was presumptuous of us to open a business we knew nothing about. Ben was a godsend, and we prospered because of his expertise and vision. When Sydney came to Cape Town, we welcomed him too with open arms. Except for a short period of time towards the end of the War, the Annex was a huge success.

"We originally came up with the idea of the Annex as an extension of Zeller's. With our own cutting and polishing facility, we envisioned larger profits and the ability to deliver a finished product to our customers in a more timely fashion. Ben, however, saw it as a separate entity allowing us to pick up other accounts. At that point, the two businesses were separated, and Zeller Jewelers became an Annex account. Ben had full control of day-to-day operations, managing all our accounts, and hiring additional cutters.

"Although the War never really had an affect on Cape Town, when Sidney died, Ben hit a rough patch. His friend Franz Schiller never let up on him until he finally came back around and returned to the Ben we knew and loved.

"When Franz died, he told Paul and I he planned to leave Cape Town after the War and join you in London. Sadly it wasn't in the cards. Ben was a good man, an honorable man. He helped so many people, and he was well respected in the town. His memorial service at the synagogue was attended by an overflow of the many people whose lives he touched."

In all that Phil had told him, there was nothing that offered a clue to the diamonds. He learned, however, that Ben had been the main force behind the Annex in spite of the fact that the Zellers were the owners. The appraisals on Annex letterhead should have gone to the owners of the diamonds. Why did Ben have them?

"I cannot thank you enough for all that you have told me today. I never really knew my uncles having only met them once at my Bar Mitzvah when they came to London. When I arrived in Cape Town after Ben died, you and Paul had already left and there was almost no one for me to speak with about them. I met the Rabbi at his synagogue and Jamilia Botu who I learned had taken care of both my uncles when they were ill. You have shown me a different side of their lives.

"When Ben's personal effects were shipped to me in England, among his papers was a card with the name *Shiloh* written in Hebrew. Would you have any idea what that could mean?"

"We had an account at the Annex with the name *Shiloh* but I don't recall seeing the name written in Hebrew. I have no idea who the account belonged to or where they were located. Most accounts were businesses and were listed as such. I do recall, however, that *Shiloh* was by far our largest account at the Annex, and we did business with them for years. Ben handled all of that.

"The account was actually acquired during the time Paul and I were in London after my father passed away. When we returned, he had hired three additional men in order to keep up with demand. I don't recall exactly when the account was closed, but I am certain it was before Sidney died."

Jake rose to leave. "I'm sorry for your loss. I had no idea you and Paul were living in London or I would have tried to get in touch with you sooner. Thank you for seeing me and spending so much time with me. I really appreciate it."

He was deep in thought as he drove home. It had been years; the mystery of *to whom they belong* remained. Other than Phil Zeller, he knew of no one else who had known his uncles; no one who could shed any light on the diamonds. With no one left to answer his questions, how could he possibly see that the diamonds ended up *with whom they belong*?

Phil Zeller did, however, verify his original thought that Ben and Sidney had cut and polished, if not all, a good portion of the diamonds.

The United Kingdom's initial interest in space was primarily military as was the case with other post-war space faring nations. The British government having obtained much of their rocketry knowledge from captured German scientists, performed the earliest post-war tests on captured V-2 rockets in Operation Backfire. Beginning in 1962, the Ariel program developed six satellites, all of which were launched by NASA.

In November 1960, John Fitzgerald Kennedy was elected President of the United States. His proclamation: *From Dream to Reality in 10 Years* before a joint session of Congress on 25 May 1961, set the stage for an astounding time in America's emerging space program.

First, I believe that this nation should commit itself to achieving the goal before this decade is out of landing a man on the moon and returning him safely to the Earth.

The goal, fueled by competition with the Soviet Union was dubbed *The Space Race*. What was to ultimately become Kennedy Space Center grew from a testing ground for new rockets to a center successful at launching humans to the moon and back. Neil Armstrong's *one small step* on the lunar surface in 1969 achieved a goal that sounded like science fiction just a few years earlier.

At the dawn of the decade, the two-year old space agency was launching rockets along the east coast of Florida. Project Mercury already underway launched the first American, Alan Shepard, on a suborbital flight 5 May 1961—just a few weeks before President Kennedy's bold proclamation. On 20 February 1962, John Glenn lifted off from Launch Complex 14 aboard an Atlas rocket to become the first American to orbit Earth.

Zoe's interest in aviation skyrocketed. She read each and every article on space exploration she could get her hands on. She followed America's space program with great interest, and often discussed each new achievement by the American astronauts with Jake.

America and Zoe had a new set of heroes—the Mercury 7 Astronauts.

Zoe was not the only Lyons sibling who had a passion for flying; Adam had become just as avid. Harry enjoyed going on family holidays with Jake as their pilot, but he was more into sports, soccer in particular. He made the school team and led them to their first championship in recent years.

They did, however, share a love for the game of tennis, which grew into a friendly competition that would last throughout their lives. The twins had their father's blond hair and deep blue eyes, which were not in the least wasted on the young admirers they met at school dances; both were quite popular with the girls.

In September 1961, two days after her birthday, Zoe earned her wings. They celebrated with a big dinner at the house.

The following June, Zoe graduated at the top of her class. In August, Jake and Lexi accompanied her to the States where she became a student at the Massachusetts Institute of Technology in Cambridge. With a degree in Aerospace and Aeronautical Engineering the possibility of becoming an Astronaut was good.

From 1960 to 1962, twenty-five women reported to Lovelace Clinic, the aviation medicine hub that tested America's first astronauts for Mercury 7. All of the women were professional pilots, several of whom ranked among the most distinguished pilots of their time; they underwent the same stringent tests endured by the men and many outperformed the Mercury 7.

Those who passed the test were dubbed the First Lady Astronaut Trainees (FLATS)—the *Mercury 13*. Just days before reporting to the Naval Aviation Center in Pensacola, Florida, the women received telegrams canceling their training.

In July 1962, they testified before a special subcommittee of the House Committee on Science and Astronautics, but the panel decided that training female astronauts would hurt the space program. The FLATS never flew in space.

16 June 1963, Russian cosmonaut Valentina Tereshkova became the first woman in space. She spent more time in space than all of the astronauts of NASA's Mercury program combined.

It would take twenty years and almost to the day, 19 June 1983, for the second woman to fly in space. Sally K. Ride became America's first women astronaut, serving as a mission specialist on the Shuttle's seventh mission.

For the Lyons family, September was a month of celebration after celebration. It was Zoe's eighteenth birthday; Harry and Adam turned thirteen. Their Bar Mitzvah was held at the new London Conservative Synagogue that had recently opened, and they hosted a lavish party at night for the adults and young people combined. Zoe flew home on Friday returning to school on Sunday in time for classes on Monday.

When Adam turned fourteen, Jake gave him the same option he had given Zoe, his choice of instructors. He chose his father. Although he had flown with Zoe far more than he had with Adam, he was an excellent student. Like his sister before him, he knew the instrument panel, as well as the basics; he too having asked a million questions when they flew together.

Harry had no interest in learning to fly. He was, however, quite interested in becoming a physician. He was fascinated by the strides that were being made in transplants—the human heart in particular. He decided he wanted to become a Cardiologist.

For much of recorded history, doctors saw the human heart as the inscrutable, throbbing seat of the soul, an agent too delicate to meddle with. This way of thinking changed with World War II. Dr. Dwight Harken, a young Army surgeon managed to remove shrapnel and bullets from some 130 soldiers' chests without killing one.

Buoyed by such successes in the postwar years, rapid advances in heart treatments laid the groundwork for open-heart surgery; ultimately by the 1960s, surgeons were ready to tackle hearts too far gone for repair with transplants.

In 1964, a team of surgeons in Jackson, Mississippi, performed the first animal-to-human heart transplant on record—a chimpanzee's heart into a dying man's chest. It beat for an hour and a half but proved too small to keep him alive.

By 1967, at least four surgeons were poised to try. On December 3rd, Dr. Christiaan Bernard of South Africa got there first, sewing the heart of a young woman killed in a car accident into the chest of a middle-aged man. After four hours of surgery, a single jolt of electricity started it beating. The patient survived the operation, but the immunosuppressant drugs used to keep his body from rejecting the new organ weakened him. Eighteen days after the operation, he succumbed to pneumonia.

Dr. Christiaan Bernard, one in the same, who cared for Franz Schiller at Groote Schuur Hospital, Cape Town, South Africa, when he was an intern.

June 1967, the Lyons family flew to Boston for Zoe's graduation from Massachusetts Institute of Technology in Cambridge. Over lunch, she disclosed her plans were to come home to London for a month before returning to the States, having accepted a position with NASA in Houston, Texas. Although it had nothing to do with becoming an astronaut, she was over the moon.

Lexi was happy for Zoe and tried not to show her disappointment. She had so looked forward to having her closer to home and spending mother-daughter time together again. Jake did not see it that way. He was so proud of her and the fact that she had landed a job with NASA that distance was not a factor. After all, he could get on a plane, and in a few short hours be seated across from her at dinner; he planned to do just that. Three months later in September, Adam became the third licensed pilot in the Lyons family.

Under Jake's leadership, Eagle Aerodrome continued to grow and expand, while Joe ran the day-to-day business operations. Tommy Butler found his niche and was in charge of the flight school. Lexi, recruited to join a team researching and developing new inoculations for common childhood diseases, accepted and gave up her position as head of Pediatric Nursing at the hospital.

They could not believe that time was passing so quickly. It seemed as though they awoke one day and their children were suddenly grown. The twins graduated in June and September saw them off to Cambridge University, the second oldest University in the English-speaking world regarded as one of the world's top five institutions of higher learning.

Considered the top medical school in the UK, Harry had applied and was accepted as a pre-med student, following in the footsteps of his grandfather Manny Portman, and his uncles Mark and Sam who had also attended Cambridge.

Considered the top Aeronautical Engineering School in the UK, as well, Adam applied and was accepted. With Zoe in America, Jake and Lexi were secretly pleased that the boys were staying closer to home.

Where had all the years gone? By the end of the decade, they chided each other about being an old married couple, although they were not yet fifty. They were content with their life, and came to view their *empty nest* situation as a good thing. With the children no longer living at home, Jake and Lexi found themselves spending more and more time at the cottage in the Cotswolds. For the first time in their marriage, they found themselves alone, just the two of them.

News from Zoe was good; she loved her job at the Space Center, and she was seeing someone; someone she promised to bring to London on her next holiday so they could meet him. His name was David Handler.

With Lexi no longer tied to erratic hospital shifts, and Jake's time at

Eagle coinciding with hers, they eagerly took advantage of the freed up time they now had. They flew together whenever the weather allowed, laughed together, prepared dinner together, and acted more like newlyweds than a long married couple.

They made plans for the future; they decided the time had come to travel more. There was a lot of world out there they hadn't seen. Lexi wanted to take Jake to Israel; Jake wanted to take Lexi to South Africa. They had never visited Europe, and there were a whole lot of States in America they hadn't visited including the great State of Texas.

British Airways Concorde made just under 50,000 flights and flew more than two and a half million passengers supersonically. In November 1986, a Concorde flew around the world, covering 28,238 miles in 29 hours, 59 minutes.

Concorde used the most powerful pure jet engines flying commercially. The Aircraft's four engines took advantage of what is known as *reheat* technology, adding fuel to the final stage of the engine, which produced the extra power required for takeoff and the transition to supersonic flight.

Concorde's fastest transatlantic crossing was on 7 February 1996 when it completed the New York to London flight in 2 hours 52 minutes and 59 seconds.

A team of 250 British Airways' engineers worked tirelessly, together with the relevant authorities, to ensure safety on board and Concorde was subjected to 5,000 hours of testing before it was first certified for passenger flight, making it the most tested aircraft ever.

In April 1998 for their *Fiftieth Anniversary*, Zoe, Harry, and Adam booked Jake and Lexi on the Concorde from London's Heathrow Airport to New York's JFK where the entire Lyons Clan gathered to celebrate.

On 24 October 2003, British Airways withdrew Concorde, bringing to a close the world's only supersonic passenger service.

PART FOUR

CHAPTER THIRTY-NINE

His eyes came to rest on the most beautiful girl he had ever seen. Her flaming red hair came to her shoulders, framing her face and accenting her blue-gray eyes that seemed to be looking directly at him. He wanted to look away; he tried to look away; but he was mesmerized. It seemed like forever, as he stood caught in her gaze.

There were no symptoms until the cancer had reached an advanced stage and spread to other parts of her body. She first noticed that she was losing weight but attributed it to her recent lack of appetite and her busy schedule organizing plans for their annual family holiday.

From believing he was the last surviving Lyons to reuniting with Lexi and their daughter, the family had grown to twenty-six. The children and their spouses had blessed them with eight grandchildren and two great grandchildren.

Many years had passed since Jake declared the last week of December the annual gathering of the Lyons Clan for all to be together welcoming in the New Year, and it quickly became their family tradition. No matter where they were or what was going on in their lives, it was their mandate; no one dared to disappoint them by not showing up.

Jake and Lexi planned each get-together, and they seemed to get better every year as they celebrated all over the globe. The choice of New York City was a hit with everyone. Despite having returned from a week of non-stop festivities that included fabulous meals, high calorie desserts, and snacks galore, her clothes hung loosely on her thin frame; the scale confirmed her fears that she continued to lose weight.

Her annual physical was scheduled for month's end. She rang up the doctor's office and arranged for blood work prior to the visit as she normally did. Receiving a call from his office days later, she learned he had scheduled her for an MRI at the hospital.

When the day of her appointment arrived, Jake accompanied her. They planned to make a day of it by having lunch in the City. When Dr. Whitman asked to speak with them after the examination, they grew apprehensive. The news he delivered was not good.

She was diagnosed with Stage 4 Pancreatic Cancer. Having spread to the liver, it was inoperable. She could opt to have chemo treatments, but it would only buy her a few months at best, and her quality of life for whatever time she had would more likely deteriorate than improve.

Dr. Whitman leaned back in his chair. "Throughout my career as a physician as much as I cherish helping people, I detest delivering devastating news. I've known you both a long time, and I want you to know that my recommendations to you are the same I would give my family.

"I would pass on Chemo; the side effects are more often worse than the progression of the cancer. As a nurse, I don't know how much exposure you've had to cancer patients, but each case is different. I would estimate that you have three to six months with no treatment. Use that time for you, Jake, and your family with a clear mind for as long as you can.

"I would like you to come to the office in two weeks so we can monitor you; we'll make the visits closer when I feel it necessary."

They left Dr. Whitman's office hand in hand neither speaking.

When Jake headed towards where they had parked the car, Lexi stopped. "Where are we going for lunch? You're not trying to get out of wining and dining me, are you?"

Jake couldn't help smiling; Lexi was still Lexi. "Never! Your wish is my command; where to Lady Lyons?"

They had lunch at the Savoy. Somehow, they seemed to gravitate to the place that eternally united them. Afterwards, they walked around London, stopping at the Tea Shoppe where Jake had *found* her and Zoe, or as Zoe put it, she and Lexi had *found* Daddy. It was still there after all these years. A breeze had picked up and the air had grown chilly; they decided to head to the car and drive back to the cottage.

There were no tears; Lexi wouldn't hear of it. They agreed to take time for themselves doing all their favorite things and thinking things through. They clung to each other making love night after night. They laughed and joked as they recalled so many wonderful times, and thanked God for their family. They felt blessed.

While on holiday, they learned that Zoe and her husband David were moving to England. Their two sons, both married with children of their own were remaining in the States. Since they were due to arrive in early February to look for a place to live, it seemed a good time to tell the children. Telling them in person was important; they had recently been together before they learned she was sick, but Lexi preferred to speak to them face-to-face so they could see that she had come to terms with the devastating news.

At times, it was hard to believe that Lexi was dying. She had stopped losing weight, and although she had no appetite, she found herself eating at least some of the various offerings Jake placed in front of her. He plied her with proteins, vegetables, and best of all calorie-laden desserts in an effort to maintain her weight and possibly gain a little.

Two weeks had passed, and her appointment with Dr. Whitman went well. He confirmed that her weight was holding steady, her coloring was good, and her latest MRI showed very little progression of the cancer. He inquired if she was eating regularly; if she was experiencing pain; if she was sleeping well; if she was tired. She answered, "No. No. Yes. No."

They left the doctor's office, and suddenly Jake turned and picked her up in his arms and twirled her around. "I would say that was a good visit, a positive visit, a visit that needs to be celebrated. I have a surprise for you that I have to admit, I planned in advance simply because I Love You Lexi Portman Lyons; I've always loved you; I always will."

He had booked a suite at the Savoy for the night. Dinner reservations at the newly opened Polpetto; tickets at Charing Cross Theatre to see *A Tale of Two Cities Musical*, and a stop at the Tea Shoppe just for the two of them; it was perfect. They walked back to the hotel, Jake's arm pulling her close protecting her from the chill in the air. They were happy; they were content; they were Jake and Lexi.

Before retiring for the night, wrapped in his arms with a light blanket covering them, they sat on the sofa watching BBC news. Lexi reached for the remote and turned off the TV. "Jake, we should make some plans. Zoe and David will be here in a few days and aside from telling the children I'm sick, we haven't really discussed anything else.

"I think we should offer them the house in Pembridge Square. They're planning to stay there while house hunting anyway. In recent years, except for occasional gatherings, it has stood empty, empty of laughter, of family, of life; all the things we purchased the house for in the first place. Our home represented everything we stood for and believed in, and it all came down to family. With Zoe and David living there, the gatherings will continue long after we're gone, and I think Harry and Adam would like that too.

"In fact, I think it would be a good idea, to have dinner at the house when we tell the children. We can arrange to have help brought in to prepare and serve the meal, and afterwards, when we speak with them, we can tell them our plans.

"Although I seem to be holding my own, we both know that can change without warning. Once that happens, we will no longer be in control. I don't want whatever time I have left to be sad; I'm not sad. I've had an awesome life with you by my side. None of us lives forever, and being eighty-eight is an achievement many never attain.

Jake held her close; she was amazing his Lexi. Never thinking of herself, she only wanted to make things easier for their children when she told them. "You have thought of everything. I absolutely agree that Zoe and David should make the house their home. I also agree that dinner at the house would be much easier than having everyone come to the cottage. From there, we can go forward and take each day at a time; we can Skype the kids and grandkids wherever they are and keep in touch on a weekly basis."

"I feel better now that's settled, but I do have one further request—this one is for you. After I'm gone, I want you to take Zoe into your confidence and make a decision about the *diamonds*. We tried, but somehow we never connected the dots, never found all the pieces to the puzzle. I don't want to pass the onus on to the children.

"I don't believe there is anyone alive today that knows the truth about how they were acquired, where they came from, and who they rightfully belonged to. We tried our best, but we were never able to reach a conclusion. Perhaps Zoe will be able to decipher your notes and see our findings in a new light.

"Actually the diamonds are only part of my request. Part two consists of writing the Lyons story for the family. They should know their roots, and unless we tell them, there is no one who will be able to once we are both gone. The diamonds have made that quite clear. I'm sure Zoe will be more than willing to help you put it all together."

How does one accept the news their beloved Mother is dying? They were all stunned; she simply didn't look sick. Her mind was as sharp as ever, and she was definitely in control of her destiny; she accepted her fate with no regrets. She wouldn't change one minute of her life, except maybe leaving England when she was pregnant with Zoe and travelling to Palestine with her father. But, she truly believed that things happen for a reason, and it all worked out for the best.

Her proudest achievement was the family she and Jake had created.

For as long as she was able, life went on as usual. In April, she began experiencing pain in her back and abdomen, and she grew tired early in the day. There were no more outings, not even a walk to the Village. As her organs began failing, the pain increased, and she was confined to bed. Jake refused to move her to hospice; she remained at the cottage.

They had nurses round the clock to keep her comfortable and minister doses of morphine as needed. Jake sat at her bedside during the day, and when she was awake, they revisited happier times and laughed about Zoe's prediction of finding her Daddy in London; the first time he took her and Zoe flying; and the times, more than once, when he couldn't tell their newborn twins apart.

Each night, he got into bed beside her, and she slept in his arms. Her last night, as he approached the bed, he was surprised to find her awake. "I Love

You Jake Lyons; don't ever forget it." She died in her sleep, encircled in his arms in the love that had consumed them both for seventy-six years.

It was her wish to be buried in the garden at the cottage. From near and far, young and old, the Lyons family came.

For one month, Jake mourned his loss. The children respected his wishes and kept their distance for the most part. They couldn't resist checking on him, but he assured them, he was eating regularly and doing okay. Each day he said Kaddish at her grave. As the weather grew warmer, he found himself spending time in the garden making plans to fulfill Lexi's last request that he put the *diamond cache* to rest.

They were all gone: Marcus and Elena, Mark and Rosalie, Sam and Ellen, Joe Hanks, Tommy and Betsy Butler, Lulu, Lila, and Bill Walsh, Mandy Hastings.

The realization hit Jake hard.

He agreed with Lexi's reasoning that no one was still alive that could shed any light on the mystery of the diamonds.

CHAPTER FORTY

As a young man, Franz Schiller found the diamonds on the bank of the Orange River at the edge of the farmland owned by Simon Abel; the year was 1883 during the *diamond rush* that attracted people from all over the world seeking to get rich. Unwilling to draw attention to his find, he never filed a claim, and, therefore, he never truly felt they belonged to him.

Shiloh—the one to whom it belongs. *Shiloh* was his mutti's Hebrew name. When he learned she had died before he could offer her a new life, a better life in South Africa, the diamonds held little value for him, yet for twenty years he continued to collect them each time he visited the Abel Farm. When he decided to have his good friends Ben and Sidney Lyons cut and polish the rough stones, he set up an account with the Annex, and the name *Shiloh* came immediately to mind—he had left home in search of a better life for his mutti—they belonged to her.

When his month of mourning ended, Jake embarked on his mission—*Shiloh*. More than sixty years had passed since he opened the crate from South Africa revealing the intricately carved chest of diamonds. For the majority of those years, the diamonds remained secure in the safe at the cottage, low on his list of priorities. In fact, the rare occasions that brought them back into his thoughts were short-lived and unenlightening in his quest to find their owner.

He rang up Zoe and invited her and David to dinner at the cottage. Then, he was off to the Village to pick up groceries for dinner. He recalled his very first visit to the small town to get dinner for his first guests, Marcus and Elena. He was thankful that he had acquired a little more expertise in food preparation since then. He planned to make the entire meal from scratch including dessert, after which he would ask for Zoe's help to accomplish his mission. Lexi was right. He had put off the responsibility that had been given to him far too long.

Zoe marveled at the dinner her Daddy set before them. He had prepared a big salad, followed by roast chicken and vegetables, and whipped up a batch of brownies that he knew were Zoe's favorite. They finished the bottle of wine that he had placed on the table, and he opened another when they opted to have tea or coffee later. He hadn't realized how much he missed having her live close by.

"I am so impressed, aren't you David? The meal was excellent, but more important is seeing the Daddy I've known my whole life so ready to move forward as Mama would have wanted you to do and expected you to do. So tell us about the project you have in mind, and how we can help."

After great thought, Jake decided to approach his mission as a dual project. He wanted to document a biography of his life for their family, and in doing so lead up to the diamonds and the promise he had made Lexi. At that point, he would reveal the cache together with the notes he had gathered, and hopefully Zoe could help him unravel the mystery and/or determine what to do with it.

"Before your mother died, she suggested that I write a history of the Lyons family so that future generations could learn where their roots began. Our meeting was fate, but falling in love was our choice. I became who I am because of your mother; she was my every reason for living, every hope, every dream I ever had. Everyday we shared was the greatest day of my life. Nothing is more precious, more rare, or more beautiful than a love that is equally shared.

"My family perished in the Good Friday Air Raid, and my uncles lived and died in South Africa; I only met them once. On your mother's side, you got to know your aunts, uncles, and cousins and even though you probably don't remember him, your grandfather.

"I'd like to begin by starting at the beginning when my parents came to London from Russia and lead up to the present relating my story in person, but recording my every word so that any notes you may wish to make or questions you would like to jot down will be kept to a minimum. I'm asking for your help to actually put it all down on paper when I am finished.

"What do you think? Is it too big a job? Am I expecting too much? Please tell me exactly how you feel."

Zoe glanced at David. "Daddy, what a wonderful and beautiful thing to do. You and Mama never fail to amaze me. You always put family first and your devotion to all of us has not gone unnoticed or unappreciated. We knew we were loved and that's all that mattered; we were lucky to have you as parents.

"I would like nothing better than to hear your story from beginning to end, and learn about what I've missed while living in America. I think it would be a good idea to get out Mama's box of pictures; they tell a story in themselves.

"The first thing we will do is purchase and set up a computer here at the cottage. All you have to do is speak into it, and it will record whatever you say as though you were entering the information by hand. That will allow us to print it out when we edit it. The computer at the house is a little outdated to move. I'll take care of it tomorrow, but it will be a few days before we're up and running. Do you want to come with me? Why don't you? Pack a bag, and you can go back with us tonight."

David couldn't help thinking that their decision to move to England couldn't have been better timed. "Dad, in space talk I would say your mission *is a go*!

"If it would make things easier, I can return to the States, pack up our things, and make arrangements to have everything shipped here. In the meantime, the two of you can get started, and Zoe can stay here at the cottage. Well, what do you think? Do you agree?"

Zoe leaned over and kissed David. "Thank you. That sounds like a plan.

"Daddy, I agree, but one more thing. As part of the bargain, are you offering dinner every night, and if you are, can I expect it to be on a par with the one we just had?"

They laughed. Jake stood, "Shall I put some coffee on? There are more brownies, and I have ice cream in the freezer. You're well aware that your mother and I were ice cream junkies, and I have to warn you, you won't find vanilla, chocolate, or strawberry here. Our tastes grew more exotic when we sampled Baskin-Robbins' 31 flavors on a trip to the States. When they opened a store on Baker Street not far from Selfridge's, she was in heaven. In fact, earlier this year, they opened a store in Middlesex."

Days later David left for the States and Zoe packed a bag and returned to the Cotswolds. Throughout the years, she had often heard bits and pieces of her parents' life, but to hear it from her Daddy's own lips from beginning to end was something she eagerly looked forward to.

Knowing him as she did, she had the feeling he was holding something back; she fervently hoped he wasn't ill. Actually he looked wonderful for someone who was approaching ninety, and she believed the promise he had made her mother was a good thing. She was glad he had embraced it. Life goes on, and he was too.

Although they worked on the project every day, their schedule was not set in stone. They arose early, had breakfast, and sometimes began with Jake's story; other times, if the weather permitted, they went flying with Zoe at the controls.

It was these times that Zoe told Jake her story, and how wonderful it was to work on the space program. They spoke of the twentieth century and the milestones not only in aviation, but the Internet, automobiles, and unbelievable strides in the medical world. Harry was living proof with the numerous transplants he had successfully performed. Jake had no qualms about handing over the reins of Eagle Aerodrome to Adam; with him at the helm, the future looked mighty good.

As they flew high above the cottage and the Village below, Jake closed his eyes. Zoe, Harry, and Adam—we did okay Lexi; we did okay.

In June, England celebrated the Diamond Jubilee of Elizabeth II with a four-day bank holiday weekend that included a pageant of over 1,000 boats on the River Thames and a Pop Concert outside Buckingham Palace.

David returned from the States. Since they were living in the house at Pembridge Square and had no need for additional furniture, he had sold or given away the larger items. While awaiting the shipment to arrive, he spent time with Adam at the aerodrome and became acquainted with the many services they offered. He was particularly impressed with MedAir.

With David back in London, Zoe returned to the house. They altered their schedule to weekdays only, and she commuted to the cottage on a daily basis. On occasion, David accompanied Zoe, and if it was a good day for flying, the three of them took to the skies.

In August, the 2012 Summer Olympics were held in London. When all was said and done, Great Britain finished third in the medal table with 29 gold medals of the 65 medals in total.

In December, St. James' Palace announced that the Duchess of Cambridge was pregnant with their first child. She was hospitalized at the King Edward VII Hospital in London with acute morning sickness for a brief stay, and when she was released, everyone sighed with relief.

By the end of November, they had been working on the project for six months. They had reached the point where Lexi and Zoe had returned to England. Jake surprised her one morning by suggesting they take a break, not just for the day, but also for a few weeks. The end of the year was approaching, and he asked Zoe to help him plan their annual get together.

"I have to admit, although I made all the arrangements for everyone to get to our many destinations, your mother made all the other choices. I was thinking that we would have everyone come here to London. There's plenty of room at the house for your boys and their families, Harry and Adam and their families are local, and it's been awhile since we've all been together here except for the funeral. I think the kids might enjoy London, Piccadilly Circus, and we can check on theatre and cinema shows. It will be fun."

"Daddy, you don't have to plan anything; I don't think anyone expects a holiday this year. However, personally I would love it. David and I can check everything out and get back to you with what we find."

"Sounds good. When your mother and I thought the house at Pembridge Square would be the ideal place for you and David to live, she reasoned it would perpetuate family gatherings in our beautiful home; I agreed with her. It's a good choice to be *home* this year; New Year's Eve in London was our special time."

Jake, Zoe, and David were a good team; they planned the 2012 Lyons family holiday as a precursor of Jake's announcement of their project.

The first night of their holiday week, Zoe arranged dinner at the house. It would be overflowing, but it had been for some time. Being home would not only add ambiance to the evening, but would allow the younger children to play games or watch a film on television while Jake made his announcement to the adults.

After making sure everyone had a filled glass, Jake began. "Every holiday gathering has been *special* because it has brought us all together and not one Lyons family member has ever missed being a part of it. That fact alone made each and every holiday *extra special*. I love you all; God Bless you all."

As everyone clinked and raised their glasses, Jake continued. "Past years have been total holiday mode, a time to have fun together and to touch base and let one another know what's going on in our lives. We never discussed business. This year is no different. We will have a week to catch up while we partake of the festivities Zoe, David, and I hope you will enjoy.

"There is, however, something I would like to tell you, and there is no better time or way than with all of you here face-to-face. This year has been bittersweet for me; I lost the *Love of My Life, My Lexi*. She was your mother, grandmother, great grandmother and I know you feel her loss as much as I do.

"When I was a young boy, my Papa told me time and again, *our choices determine our destiny but our fate is sealed*. I can't tell you how many times I've recalled those words, and each time how profound they proved to be. My intention is not to cast sadness over our week together, it is instead to be thankful for having her in our lives. She was a part of all of us, and in all of us she lives on.

"I made her a promise, and that is what I am about to tell you."

Jake refilled his glass and sipped the wine. One could hear a pin drop, so quiet was the room as he told them it was simply all about family. "Zoe has agreed to help me put it all down on paper and perhaps by next year's holiday, we will have finished it."

Adam's broad smile said it all. "Dad, I am so proud of you and Mother. That's the best gift you could possibly pass on to all of us and any future Lyons, I might add. We all know bits and pieces, but I for one can't wait to read about your early days of flying.

"I knew you had something up your sleeve when Zoe moved into the cottage and the two of you showed up at the aerodrome every time the weather was good."

Harry nodded his head in agreement with Adam. "We were all wondering what was going on. You seemed to be in a good frame of mind, so we weren't worried about your wellbeing, but we definitely felt something was afoot.

"I, however, have a suggestion. Although I am selfishly as pleased as Adam that you are doing this for the family, I feel you should take it a step further and publish it for the public. You're quite renown not only in England, but also in America, in Israel, and in South Africa. You're a decorated Ace RAF Pilot, your philanthropy is unrivaled, and then there's that knighthood ceremony I recall when you became Sir Jacob Lyons."

Jake was taken aback. The children for the most part led private lives. Harry had never capitalized on his renown as a transplant surgeon; and Adam had never capitalized on the many humanitarian efforts of MedAir that were all done pro bono. So, never in a million years, did he think that they would want to share his story with the world. He and Lexi had always been about family.

Overcome with emotion, he spoke. "You amaze me and flatter me to no end. I had no idea you felt this way." Jokingly he said, "It appears you already know my story, and perhaps there is no need for me to tell it after all."

Everyone welcomed Jake's news. Zoe raised her glass in toast. "To Sir Jacob Lyons our very own *Diamond in the Rough*. Here's to equating each and every facet of your journey to the cutting of a stone and polishing it to perfection."

His family's excitement was overwhelming; Jake sat quietly. What just happened? His promise to Lexi was a personal thing, a family thing. What about the diamonds? He didn't know if he wanted that to go public. At this point, he didn't have a clue as to what he was going to do with them.

He repeated over and over again, "I didn't agree to anything. I don't want to make a big deal out of this. You're blowing this way out of proportion." But nobody was listening.

The week went all too quickly. All agreed that their 2012 holiday was one of the better ones, although there had never been a single complaint about any of their past gatherings. London proved the best choice; it was the family's home base. Regardless of how scattered they had been through the years with children attending school abroad or living abroad, home was home.

With their holiday at an end, Jake and Zoe returned to the project with gusto. She knew she had a lot of work ahead of her, but finding Harry and Adam as excited as she was about their father's story spurred her on. If they were to consider having the final manuscript published, perhaps she was not the one to edit or rewrite it. Maybe it wouldn't have to be rewritten. It would be much more authentic in her father's own words.

Her musings could wait. There would be time to polish the finished product. All she knew for certain was that it had to be perfect.

CHAPTER FORTY-ONE

J ake was unsure how to proceed. Before their holiday, they had left off at Lexi and Zoe's arrival in London. At that point in his life, the diamonds were already in his possession, and he had travelled to Cape Town and returned. Once Lexi and Zoe became his life, the diamonds were quickly forgotten. Many years would pass before Lexi would learn of them.

When Jake decided to leave De Beers, trading diamonds for aviation, the cache remained secure in the safe at the cottage. By that time, they were living in the house in Pembridge Square and visits to the Cotswolds were far and few between. The carved chest sat on the floor of the master bedroom where Jake had placed it emptied of its contents. To Lexi, it was part of the cottage's furnishings when she arrived, and she gave it no further thought.

As Jake continued relating his story, he purposely omitted mentioning the diamonds. Following their holiday and Harry's suggestion to publish, he revisited his thoughts and considered including them only in the family version and only when they determined who would receive them was resolved. There were other parts of his story that he also felt should be solely for the family because they represented his personal feelings. His growing up in the East End, his idolization of his Papa as he taught him about diamonds, his uncles Ben and Sidney—he thought too personal and inappropriate for a public version should it materialize.

When he declared, *The End*, Zoe was a little surprised. Where was the mystery? Had she missed something? What was it that he had wanted her to help him resolve? And there was that feeling again; was he holding something back?

For the next week, they began at the beginning and read through the pages stopping only when Zoe had a question or something was unclear. For the most part, they were satisfied with what they had accomplished.

"Daddy, why do I feel that something is not right? Is this really *The End*? Although we know a good deal of your story, and it is enlightening to learn your feelings firsthand, I sense that at times especially when you speak of your uncles, you seem disconnected, almost as if you don't consider them family. I know you didn't really know them having been quite young the only time you met them."

If Jake were certain of only one thing, that one thing would be that Zoe knew her Daddy. She had the same connection with him that he had with Lexi. She often knew what he was thinking, and sensed what he was feeling; he found it uncanny. After all, for decades she had lived thousands of miles across the sea. How could it even be possible that she knew him so well?

"From the very day we met up in London my darling Zoe, you have plied me with questions. To the best of my ability, I believe I answered each and every one convinced that if I hadn't, you would have continued asking. Now here we are almost seventy years later and nothing has changed. That and my love for you Zoe Lyons Handler will also never change.

"We've had a long week, and now the weekend is here. Time to go home and spend some time with David. I feel guilty taking up so much of your time since you moved back to London; he's been quite nice about it. How does he really feel about his daddy-in-law interfering in your life?"

"He would move heaven and earth for you and you know it. He feels guilty about having kept me in the States for so many years. It was actually his idea that we move to London, and I love him for it. It was the nicest, most unselfish act on his part especially since our boys and their families are still there."

The distance that had separated Jake and David was not reflected in their love and respect for one another, nor did it deter from the bond that developed between them on both a personal and professional basis.

"Give me the weekend to collect my thoughts. When you return on

Monday, bring David with you, and I will reveal the other part of my promise to your mother; the part that requires your help."

———❦———

When Zoe and David arrived on Monday, Jake awaited them. The table was set. He bade them be seated; he served them omelets, scones, and coffee as they chatted. Their banter was light and David commented on the bright sunshine streaming in the window on the otherwise cold winter's day. With breakfast done, they helped him clear the table.

Jake went to his bedroom and returned carrying the carved chest and sat it on the dining table. When they were seated once again, he began reading from the pages he had printed out. Beginning with his discharge to learning Lexi was living in Palestine to learning that Sidney had died while he was on Guernsey Island to starting a job with De Beers to returning from New York only to learn that Ben too had died before he had the chance to visit him in Cape Town as he had promised.

At that point he stopped reading and spoke from the heart. "Ben was my last surviving relative. I had promised to visit him, and it was my intention to bring him to London so that we could get to know one another; we were family. I thought I had lost your mother, and I didn't know I had a daughter. Your mother's last news about me was that I was missing in action; she came back to London to learn what happened to me so she could build a life for the two of you.

"Weeks after receiving the wire notifying me of my uncle's demise, I received a crate that held my uncles' remains with the request that they be buried with my family. The crate also contained their personal effects, their diamond cutting tools, assorted papers, and items that I knew nothing about. In the center of the crate was this beautifully carved chest. When I lifted the lid, it appeared empty, but after removing the shallow tray on top, I learned otherwise."

Jake stood, opened the chest, lifted the shallow tray and observed Zoe and David's reaction to the diamonds before them. They were speechless, of course, just as he had been. The only difference, he was alone. The questions began.

"Who sent them to you? Who did they belong to? Are they yours? What were you supposed to do with them?"

"I have no answers to your questions because they are the same ones that have remained unanswered since I received them. I travelled to Cape Town weeks later only to learn nothing about the diamonds. The crate had been shipped from the funeral home, but I wasn't successful in learning who actually packed the items for shipment.

"I did meet people who knew my uncles, people from the synagogue, the bank, and a black African woman who had cared for both Sidney and Ben when they were sick. I learned that my uncles were highly thought of in the community, and that they had been happy in South Africa. They were both diamond cutters and worked for the Zeller brothers who ran a fine jewelry emporium in Cape Town. When they opened the Annex, a gem cutting entity, Ben went to work for them and ultimately managed the day-to-day operations.

"I learned a man named Franz Schiller became a good friend to Ben and later to Sidney. He started out as the proprietor of the town's general store during the diamond rush, and later converted it to a smoke shop. As far as I could learn, Franz had nothing to do with diamonds or the jewelry business. He was simply Ben's first and lasting friend in Cape Town.

"By the time I arrived, not only were my uncles deceased, but Franz was gone as well. The bank manager I met knew them only through dealings with the bank, and to the Rabbi at their synagogue, they were among his congregants. The woman that had cared for my uncles taught English to the refugees at the synagogue, and I spent a couple of days speaking with her. She was the most informative, and I learned a good deal about my uncles from her. The diamonds never came up in any of our conversations, and I had no reason to believe that she would know anything about them.

"I returned to England with no answers and even more questions. Two days later, I met up with you and your mother at The Tea Shoppe. The rest is history. Once again, I had a family and that was of the utmost importance to me. The cache remained locked in the safe here at the cottage. Only once before did I remove them when I showed them to your mother; she's the only person I ever confided in. As close as I was to Marcus, I never even considered telling him although I can't explain why I felt that way.

"Throughout the years, I was always searching. At times I was drawn to articles about diamond heists particularly during the War. Nothing ever connected. When one of the Zellers passed away, I paid a condolence call to the surviving brother and learned about the Annex and that Ben had been the driving force behind its success. If I had known they were living back in London, I would have contacted them years earlier.

"I have some information, but very little. I'm hoping that when I show you what little I have, maybe we can research it on the computer. It's a long shot, but one never knows. You and David are more adept at that than I am.

"I have some items in the safe at the house that I want to share with you, as well. They were among the things that came in the crate. Your mother was adamant that I resolve the issue of the diamonds before I leave this world. She felt a new approach was needed.

"Perhaps I would have been more successful at finding answers to my questions had I pursued it when they first came into my possession. By now, it seems highly unlikely that anyone is still alive that knew my uncles and Franz Schiller that could shed any light on the matter. By process of elimination, instead of searching for the rightful owner, my mission is to find a worthy owner. In the long run, that might prove to be the easiest way.

"There's one more thing." He closed the lid of the chest and traced his fingers over the carved letters. "These Hebrew letters spell the name *Shiloh*. I found a card with these same letters written on it and showed it to the Rabbi in the East End. He translated them for me and told me the meaning of the name—*the one to whom it belongs.*

"Somewhere in the back of my mind, it seemed as though I had heard or read that before. Perhaps in my Hebrew lessons, but it never came to me. Years later, I learned from Phil Zeller that this same name was given to an account at the Annex. I'm fairly certain that my uncles cut and polished the diamonds."

Everyone sat quietly—thinking. Finally Zoe said but one word, "Wow!" David said, "I second that."

"Can you understand why I was slightly apprehensive when Harry wanted to go public with this story? I wasn't totally convinced I should include the diamonds in the family version."

"Why do you feel the diamonds were not meant for you? They must have some connection to one of your uncles or both since they were in Ben's possession when his things were shipped to you. I can't imagine someone just adding the chest to the crate, and I certainly can't imagine why anyone would want to give the diamonds away. They're magnificent."

"It's almost one o'clock. David, if you would be good enough to help me carry the chest down to the cellar, I'll put the diamonds back in the safe, and return the chest to my bedroom.

"As you pointed out earlier, it's a beautiful day; why don't we go flying for a while. I don't know about you, but the altitude always clears my head. I'll pack a bag and accompany you to London; we can leave from the aerodrome. Later today or tomorrow, we can go through the other items I was telling you about that came in the crate. It's also been on my mind to suggest we get a new computer setup for the house."

"I'm way ahead of you Daddy. David and I did just that months ago."

By the time they flew the plane back to the aerodrome, it was growing dark. The drive to London took longer because of heavy evening traffic, and Zoe whose thoughts weren't about to give it a rest took advantage of the situation.

"Do you think the items you're planning to share with us are connected to the diamonds in any way?"

"I recognized immediately the items that are totally personal. There are watches that I believe belonged to my uncles, as well as two men's dome rings. There are other rings that I can only assume belonged to my grandparents; the styles of the wedding rings, in particular, are definitely *old country*.

"Don't let your curiosity get the best of you my dear Zoe. We're almost there. Let's freshen up and grab a bite to eat at The Pub; they have the best fish and chips in town. When we get back to the house, I won't make you wait until tomorrow. I promise.

Jake retrieved the items from the safe in the cellar and placed them on the kitchen table. He pointed out the jewelry he had spoken of in the car, the intricately carved elephant, a cigar box similar to the one his uncles had brought for his father when they came to London, a covered medium-sized jewelry box, a small cloth pouch that appeared empty, and a large envelope containing an assortment of papers.

"Upon opening the crate, I found two small wooden boxes with Stars of David carved on top and each identified with my uncles' remains for burial. There was a box that contained jeweler's tools that are in the cellar. Zoe, as you watched me work and wanted to learn, I handed you tools from that box. Another box contained all of these items before you.

"The crate was rather large, large enough to contain a coffin, and it was shipped from a funeral home. When it was delivered, I had them put it in the garage. I backed out the car to allow me room to open and unpack it. The chest was the last item I removed. When I discovered it held a cache of diamonds, my first thought was how *unsecure* and *unobtrusive* the crate had been shipped. At first, I thought perhaps the diamonds were sent to me in error, but then as I began to rationalize, it occurred to me they had been intended for me and deliberately shipped in a way that would attract the least attention.

"Throughout, I have stuck to my original conclusion that to unravel the *mystery* of the diamonds, I had to identify the sender. Unfortunately, I have been unsuccessful in doing so. Time is like a river; the flow that has passed will never pass again. So I am changing course. I am no longer seeking *the one to whom it belongs*; I am seeking *the one to whom it shall belong.*"

Zoe began looking through the items on the table—the pieces of jewelry, the elephant carving, and the cigar box that she examined with curiosity. "Do you see any similarities in the animal carving on this box and the elephant or any comparison of the box's carvings to the chest?"

"I never compared the box to the chest. I do feel there is a similarity to the animal carved on the top of the box and the elephant; the detail in both is extensive. I've always felt the carvings on the chest paralleled the facets of a diamond and were done so intentionally, just as I have always felt that the chest was made to order to accommodate all of the diamonds with the trays separating the various sizes."

Before Zoe could move on to the covered jewelry box, Jake leaned forward and picked it up along with the empty cloth pouch. He removed the lid and placed the box before them. "Zoe, you called the cache magnificent; what do you think of these?"

The box lined in black velvet consisted of five sections; each section held a large diamond cut and polished to perfection. Beneath each stone was its name. The Alexandra was the largest—22 carats; Lady Lyons—18 carats; Princess Zoe—16 carats; Prince Harry and Prince Adam –just over 15 carats apiece.

Zoe and David stared at the beautiful stones sparkling under the light hanging above the table. "Daddy, these are awesome. It's obvious you named them; did your uncles cut them?"

"This pouch was among Ben's personal items. There was a note from his friend Franz Schiller gifting them to him. It seems as though Ben planned to move to England when I returned from the War and Franz gave them to him as a token of their friendship. They were uncut when I received them. It took many years and a lot of practice, for me to attempt to cut and polish such large and valuable stones. But cut and polish I did, and I named each finished stone in honor of my family—your mother, Harry, Adam, and you.

"Your mother loved them. She considered them too big to wear as a piece of jewelry—they were simply too ostentatious for her taste. She approved of my naming each stone, and was pleased that although I had left the world of diamonds behind many years before, I put all that my Papa taught me to good use.

"You said they were in the pouch with a note to Ben from Franz, and there was no note leaving them specifically to you. Why did you feel they were rightfully yours and the cache of diamonds was not? If you were Ben's sole heir, his entire estate would legally pass on to you, would it not?"

Jake collected his thoughts. "The note stated the five uncut stones were a gift to Ben from Franz. There was nothing that indicated who the cache belonged to. Timing was a big factor; I was so young. I had lived through losses that people two and three times my age had never endured, and when I returned from Guernsey and thought I had lost your mother too, I chose to move on. I accepted the job with De Beers that Marcus offered me."

Zoe picked up the envelope stuffed with papers. "Are any of these papers significant?"

"Ben saved all the wires sent by Marcus and my wires and letters too. I think he was desperately hanging on to the only family he had left. I truly regret for not having kept my promise to visit him in South Africa after I was discharged. Again, I was trying to get my life in order, and in doing so I lost him before I could make good on that promise.

"The majority of papers are appraisals on Annex letterhead and from what I can tell, they are for the diamonds that were in the chest. It would be more cumbersome to match up each diamond with its description on any given appraisal, than it would be to start over and have each stone appraised individually on a single sheet. The appraisals, however, do indicate that the stones were cut in batches."

Zoe pushed her chair back and stood. "Can I get anyone a drink? Should I put some coffee on or start the kettle for tea?"

"I think we've done a lot today. I'm hoping you'll take some time digesting all of this. Although I have had this on my plate for quite some time, it's new to you. I'm going to return everything to the safe. You both know the combination and you're free to go through any of the items and/or papers to help in your Internet search."

"You're right Daddy, as always. I know I've been relentless with my over-the-top questions. Actually, I think you have uncovered more insight than you realize, but the diamonds will take more time and effort than the history of the Lyons. I think your idea to treat the family version personally is a good one and the right one. Down the road if you should decide to go public, we can start with what we have, add to it, and edit it as you see fit.

"I've read and reread what you've done, and I think it's good, very good. By telling the story in your own words, your feelings come through genuinely, and I think the family will love it. Why don't we read through it one more time together, make any changes or additions, and see about getting it bound and printed. I suggest a note from you at the beginning would be the perfect touch. When we've finished, we can move on to the diamonds.

"In the meantime, while we are working at the cottage, David can get started on the Internet. He's quite good at it, and if there's something out there to find, I have no doubt he will find it."

With everything returned to the safe, they went to bed. Zoe was up most of the night; she couldn't sleep thinking about the diamonds. There were so many questions, and no answers. She hoped that she and David could help.

Sleep eluded Jake as well. His thoughts were of Lexi. He had put her first; a decision he never regretted. When he had revealed the diamonds to her, she couldn't imagine why he felt they did not belong to him. She viewed it as Zoe did.

They were considered a part of Ben's personal effects, and since he was Ben's sole heir, they were rightfully his.

Maybe, just maybe he couldn't find *the one to whom it belongs* because *the one to whom it belongs* had them.

—

On the first anniversary of Lexi's passing, Jake and the children gathered for a memorial service at the cottage. At dinner that evening, Jake handed each of them a copy of the Lyons story; he had taken Zoe's suggestion and included a note at the beginning. It was a heartfelt note intended solely for his children.

To Zoe, Harry and Adam,

The cornerstone of my life has been Love and Family
No two words proved more profound than when I lost everyone.

No matter how bad times are, they can always be worse;
Believe they can always be better.
Believe that family is God's ultimate Blessing.
Believe when love is given, it is returned tenfold.

Dare to dream the best; dare to soar above the rest!
Success in not an accident.

Learn, work hard, persevere and don't settle.
Love what you do and your happiness will be assured.

Of all the titles that we seek in life,
Father is the grandest of all!

Zoe was surprised he had addressed the note solely to her, Harry, and Adam; and she had no idea he had received the copies from the printer. Jake clinked his glass as he usually did to get their attention, and they grew quiet.

"Your mother encouraged me to document my story for our family, present and future, and I have done that. However, I decided that presenting the Lyons story to my children would allow you to add your stories and pass them on to your children, and so on into perpetuity. Much of what you will read you already know but there are parts that I never told anyone.

"In addition, there is an envelope in each copy that contains a letter from your mother. The contents are unknown to me; they were individually written to each of you, and although she offered to let me read them, I saw no reason to. I'm well aware of how much she loved you.

"You will note that I made no mention of how proud we both were, and I continue to be, of each and every member of the Lyons Family. I ask only that you remain true to yourselves, to your ideals, to your beliefs, never losing sight of the parts that love and family play in your lives."

When Jake finished speaking, they all stood, clapping and cheering. Zoe who thought she had the upper hand in bringing their project to completion was not surprised in the least that her Daddy never ceased to amaze. There were hugs, kisses, and teary eyes all around.

Harry and Adam were anxious to read what their father and sister had put together; Zoe was anxious to see if there were any more surprises.

"Dad, have you given any further thought to publishing your work?'"

Jake put his arm around Harry's shoulders. "I was going to mention that fact but decided against it. Tonight was all about the promise I made your mother. This version is what I call the *family version* meant for Lyons family members only. There are parts that are too personal for me to share with the world. When you're finished reading it, you will have a better understanding of how I feel.

"However, I am not adverse to editing and adding to this version in an effort to turn it into a manuscript that I would consider publishing. Zoe has agreed to continue working with me, and David has offered to help as well."

"I'm glad to hear that you're considering it. I think your story is amazing, and I'm sure there are a lot of people out there who will agree with me.

Although it's months away, I do want to give you a *heads up* for the end of the year. Our Matt will be a Bar Mitzvah in December and his parents are considering having the celebration in Israel. Do you think our annual holiday could be worked around their plans?"

"Absolutely. This is great news; I won't have to plan anything; and I'm certain Zoe will be relieved too. We'll talk soon; just keep me apprised of their plans, and I'll take care of all the travel arrangements."

He made all the arrangements in 1975 when he and Lexi visited Israel.

It was his first visit, and her first time back. They had returned one additional time when Zoe planned their annual end of the year holiday in Israel, but that had been years ago. He was ready to visit again, and celebrating his great grandson's Bar Mitzvah made it all the better.

To Lexi returning to Israel where she had lived for four years and given birth to Zoe was bittersweet. She had both good memories and sad memories of the time she spent there. The country she left in 1948 was not the same country she had come to visit.

In the almost three decades since declaring its independence, the State made great strides in creating a modern industrialized nation. Improvements and modernization were achieved in every sector from housing to agriculture to road systems to telecommunications to electrical networks. Israel had established a growing shipping fleet and a national airline (El-Al).

The land began to flourish and Israel became self-sufficient in almost every area of food production. Trees were planted on once barren land, and as industry grew and natural resources were developed, employment rose.

The educational system grew as well, and the government offered free schooling until the age of eighteen. Israel flourished culturally, as each immigrant group brought with them a unique set of customs and traditions.

The one problem that remained was *security*.

As a result of the 1948 War, Mount Scopus and the Hadassah Hospital were left as an Israeli exclave guarded by a small number of armed personnel, and all activities at the medical campus were abandoned. Alternative locations in West Jerusalem were selected for the evacuated medical staff to continue their activities. In 1961, a new medical complex was built in Ein Karem on the outskirts of Jerusalem.

During the Six-Day War in 1967, Israel conquered the entire area around Mount Scopus and the old medical campus was eventually reactivated after undergoing extensive renovations, reopening in 1975 coinciding with Jake and Lexi's visit.

She was relentless in showing Jake around Jerusalem where they had lived, where she took classes, and the newly renovated hospital where she worked and Zoe was born. They learned where her father was buried and visited his gravesite.

They spent two weeks In Jerusalem overwhelmed with emotions by a city that promised and delivered a religious and spiritual experience like no place else.

They had several stops scheduled along the way including an overnight stay at a Kibbutz, and a visit to the Dead Sea before continuing on to their final destination—Tel Aviv. They flew from Ben Gurion Airport home to Heathrow ending their month-long holiday.

Prior to leaving Jerusalem, Jake made arrangements to have the new Pediatric Wing of the hospital dedicated to *Dr. Emanuel Portman.*

Lexi was surprised but quite pleased; they hadn't parted under the best of circumstances, but she loved her Pops, and she loved Jake for honoring him.

While Zoe and Jake were busy at the cottage tying up loose ends before sending their work to the printer, David explored the Internet. He began his research in Cape Town. He made a list of all the names and places mentioned in the papers, and immediately, his search reverted back years before Ben had arrived from Russia.

He learned that Paul and Phil Zeller left London in 1905, opening a store in Cape Town; their father was the proprietor of Zeller Jewelers in London located in Hatton Garden. After 20 years, they were well established as a high-end jewelry emporium when they ventured into gem cutting by opening the Annex in 1925.

The article went on to describe the Annex and its success due in part to the Nazis' dismantling of the world's diamond-cutting center in Antwerp. Both the original store and the Annex were sold in 1948. He googled Zeller Jewelers in London and learned an air raid had completely demolished the store during the War. It was never rebuilt.

Most of what he learned from the article was not new information. He surmised that Ben had arrived from Russia shortly after the Annex opened. Jake's notes had accurately pieced together the history of Zeller Jewelers from what he learned on his first visit to Cape Town and from his meeting years later with Phil Zeller.

Next he tackled Franz Schiller. Several attempts were futile; the name was not found. He entered Cape Town General Store, and it was a hit. One Simon Abel opened The General Store in the late 1860s at the very beginning of the diamond rush. It was the town's sole general store and was one of its earliest business establishments. After his death in 1883, a young clerk who had worked for him took over the business.

It was converted to The Smoker's Shop in 1935. In later years, it became a clothing store.

David searched through Jake's notes. There it was; he found it. Franz Schiller must have been the clerk who worked for Simon Abel. He ran it as The General Store until he converted it to The Smoker's Shop some time before Ben and Sidney's visit to London when they brought a carved wooden box filled with cigars as a gift to their brother Harry.

Jake had noted that he vaguely remembered a lion carved on the top of the box. David went down to the cellar and retrieved the wooden box that had come in the crate. It too had a lion carved on its lid. Perhaps the lion carvings equated to the Lyons name.

Once again, nothing he learned was new or indicated any significance. Yet somehow a gut feeling began to kick in. Jake had dismissed Franz Schiller's involvement with the diamonds at the onset. He had predeceased Ben, and nothing indicated that he had ever been a prospector himself, although he was living in South Africa during the years of the diamond rush.

Perhaps there were prospectors who paid him with rough stones for the equipment they needed to work their claims. If this were the case, why would they have paid him with sizeable stones possibly worth a fortune as opposed to insignificant smaller pebbles? If not from prospectors, from where could Franz have acquired the five diamonds he had gifted to Ben?

David decided to take a break. He thought about Jake's statement that altitude had a way of clearing one's thoughts. Logging off the computer, he grabbed a jacket, and set out for the aerodrome.

He popped in to say *Hello* to Adam and was soon high above the clouds deep in thought. The one fault he found with his theory was the size of the cache. But try as he may, his gut feeling held steady—Franz Schiller was key to the diamonds.

He would have to continue to search for anything and everything he could learn about one Franz Schiller.

CHAPTER FORTY-TWO

Following the memorial service for Lexi, Jake suggested they take a brief respite. Zoe, after spending the better part of the past year at his side working on the project, wholeheartedly agreed. Stepping back would allow them time to collect their individual thoughts and then come together to determine the best way to proceed.

David, on the other hand, wanted to maintain his momentum. He felt he was on to something with regard to Franz Schiller. They were having a quiet dinner at home alone when Zoe asked, "I've been so busy wrapping up things with Daddy, I haven't asked how your Internet search is coming along. Have you uncovered anything we don't already know?"

"As a matter of fact, I have and I haven't."

"What on earth does that mean?"

He filled her in on what he had learned, acknowledging that there was really nothing new, but the facts revisited had led him to draw different conclusions. He further went on to say, "The diamonds came from South Africa; a fact that remains undisputed. This leads me to believe that the answers to all of our questions regarding them lie in Cape Town. Everyone involved worked and lived there.

"We know pretty much everything there is to know about the uncles, about the Zellers, about various other people that touched their lives, but the biggest *unknown* is *Franz Schiller*. I believe he is key to unlocking the mystery of the diamonds. Unfortunately, none of my searches unearthed one iota of information about him. It's almost as if he never existed."

"What do you propose we do? What can we do?"

Two days later, their plane left Heathrow Airport—destination Cape

Town, South Africa. So much for a respite, Jake thought, as he settled back in his seat for the long flight.

David had done his homework. He organized his notes and made a list of places to visit in search of the information they hoped to uncover. Although they spoke of his first trip to Cape Town after Ben's death, Jake hadn't disclosed much if anything about the time he had taken Lexi to South Africa on holiday.

Their 1976 trip to Cape Town was as enlightening to Jake as it was to Lexi. The Central Business District that had been the center of his uncles' lives had prospered and grown into a popular tourist attraction with little resemblance to the Town he had come to in search of learning about the diamonds.

His visit to the synagogue was equally surprising. In 1905 the fittings were dismantled and moved to the newly constructed Great Synagogue, leaving the historic Old Synagogue standing empty alongside the new building for years.

In 1941, the centenary year of the Great Synagogue, a society to establish a Jewish Museum and Archives was founded in Cape Town. Its object was to collect and preserve articles and documents, illustrating the history of the Jewish community in South Africa, but the project made little progress, and it was not until August 1958 that the museum was officially opened to the public.

They arrived early in the week and began their holiday on the Atlantic seaboard, regarded as one of the most scenic routes in South Africa and known as Cape Town's Riviera. From Clifton Beach to the beach at Camps Bay to the unspoiled beaches of Llandudno, they stopped at the many restaurants, cafes, and bars along the way acting as honeymooners.

Prior to moving on to Johannesburg, they toured the Central Business District with Jake pointing out the site of Zeller Jewelers (Wolf's Jewelers), the site of The General Store (a clothing store), and down towards the harbor, the Annex which was no longer there. On their way to attending Shabbat

Services at the Great Synagogue, Jake went in search of Ben's cottage. It too no longer existed.

When they entered the Great Synagogue, to their surprise, they found plagues for Ben and Sidney on the Memorial Wall in the lobby; in looking further, they found there was one for Franz Schiller too. They learned that a Jewish Museum had opened in the Old Synagogue since Jake's original visit, but unfortunately it was closed for the Sabbath. By the time it reopened on Monday, they had left Cape Town continuing on their holiday.

They rented a car at the airport and drove to the Victoria & Alfred Hotel located in the heart of the waterfront. Jake was hoping that they could enjoy a little R&R while they were there. At the check-in counter, there was a card advertising scenic flights over Cape Peninsula. As the clerk handed them their keycards, he suggested that they find the time to do so, exclaiming the experience was nothing short of *exhilarating*.

After a brief rest, a shower, and a change of clothing, they left for dinner and a night on the town. Although they knew they had not come for a holiday, Zoe and David were charmed with Cape Town, a vibrant and cosmopolitan place they never thought to visit but were rather pleased that they were actually doing so.

At the top of David's list was the Great Synagogue, and Government Hall where he wanted to check out property records hoping he could learn who might have received the proceeds from the sale of Franz Schiller's store. At breakfast, when Jake asked him where he planned to begin, and he mentioned the Synagogue, he told him about the Jewish Museum, and that he and Lexi had left without stopping in. David was excited; surely there had to be some information about one of the community's longest and most prominent members.

The new South African Jewish Museum was completed in August 2000, and quickly became one of the most state-of-the-art museums in the Country. The concept of the Israeli design required the existing Old

Synagogue be coupled in an entirely new building. The Old Synagogue would house a collection of original Judaica, and the new structure would house the museological zones of *Memory, Reality, and Dream*; together, these linked areas would comprise the new museum, celebrating the historical role of the Jewish community and its ongoing contribution to South Africa using the most modern techniques available.

Touch screens and interactive computers stand side-by-side with a peddler's cart, and documentary films and newsreel footage are shown alongside a 19th century Lithuanian village, as one explores the Jewish pioneers left behind and recognizes new ones that were discovered.

David's emotions were intense. From the moment he entered the new South African Jewish Museum, he was certain they would find what they were looking for; he felt it in his bones. They spent four hours at the Museum. They left buoyed beyond their greatest expectations.

There were dialogues of Ben, Sidney, and Franz Schiller. There were dialogues and a complete history of the Zeller brothers. All of which were comprised of interviews conducted in the early 1940s when the Society had first been founded to collect the history of the Jewish community in Cape Town. They were in their own voices and words; at the end of each dialogue, was the date and cause of their demise.

The information on Ben and Sidney was accurate and precise. All that Jake had learned and pieced together about his uncles mirrored what their dialogues stated. They had even mentioned their brother Harry and his family in England.

David adjusted the headphones and began listening.

My name is Franz Schiller. I was born in Hamburg, Germany, and left home at the age of sixteen to seek a better life, not only for myself but also for my mutti and my five younger siblings. I was determined to get them away from my abusive father. My mutti was Jewish, and she defied my Lutheran father by seeing that I took Hebrew lessons allowing me to become a Bar Mitzvah.

She further defied him by giving me what little money she had when I told her I was leaving Germany. I promised to send for her and my siblings as soon as I could.

Upon my arrival in Cape Town, I went to work for Simon Abel who was the proprietor of The General Store. He was up in years and needed help; I was new in town and needed a job; our meeting up was a blessing for both of us. He died a year later, and having no family, he left me his store.

After a time, I had saved enough money to send for my mutti and siblings. Following weeks of waiting for a reply, I learned my dear mutti had died giving birth to a seventh child. I never learned who sent me the letter; I never learned what became of my siblings; there was no mention made of my father.

My early years in Cape Town were somewhat lonely; I was obsessed with keeping The General Store up and running, although at seventeen years of age I knew very little about business. When I began attending services at the Great Synagogue, the Jewish community of Cape Town became my home, my family, and my friends. I converted The General Store to The Smoker's Shop in the mid-1930s; it became a popular gathering place from the onset.

I've always felt that my beloved mutti was watching over me and guiding me; and I attribute all my accomplishments to her having helped me when I left home. Her Hebrew name was Shiloh—the one to whom it belongs—the one to whom my good life in Cape Town belonged. My one regret was that I was unable to help her.

On March 22, 1945, Cape Town's Jewish community mourned the passing of Franz Schiller from a massive heart attack.

David removed the headphones. For several minutes he sat in the booth digesting Franz's dialogue. Although the picture was not yet complete, connecting the dots had begun. He went in search of Zoe and Jake urging them to listen to Franz tell his story in his own words.

They viewed documentaries that featured Ben and Sidney at the Annex; Zeller Jewelers as it had looked when the brothers first opened for business in 1905, and in the 1920s when they expanded the store. Another film showcased The General Store in its heyday when it was every prospector's destination, and when it was converted to The Smoker's Shop, a new entity for the town. There was also a film covering the changes that came to Long Street—new hotels, new restaurants, and numerous trendy shops featuring all that was the latest in fashion.

The next day they went to Government Hall in search of the Department of Land Records. All records for the year 1945 had long been archived. The clerk asked them to return in two hours, allowing her time to retrieve what they were seeking.

They stopped for lunch and ate quietly, each lost in their own thoughts.

"The Museum is amazing. For the first time, I feel as if I really know my uncles and what their life was like in Cape Town. They seem to have been as happy here as my parents were in London. I find it rather sad that neither married and had a family. I'm glad they had each other, had a good friend in Franz Schiller, and that they were there for one another."

"David, what are you hoping to learn at the Land Records office?"

"I'd like to find out who received the proceeds from the sale of Franz's shop.

I'm not certain that the information will answer any of our questions, but before we visited the Museum, the only information we had about him was that he was a good friend.

"As a shopkeeper, we naturally had no reason to connect him to the diamonds, but now that we've learned *Shiloh* was his mother's Hebrew name, the name carved on the chest, and the name of an Annex account, I'd say the diamonds appear to connect more to one Franz Schiller than to your uncles. I remain convinced, however, that Ben and Sidney did in fact cut and polish the stones at the Annex."

When they returned to the Land Records office, as promised, the clerk had pulled the information they sought. As David read that the sale of the store had been completed in August 1945, and that the proceeds were dispersed to the First National Bank of South Africa, Zoe observed his disappointment. "It was a great idea. It just didn't turn up anything."

They returned to the hotel and decided to relax for the rest of the afternoon.

That night over dinner, Jake opened up about the thoughts he and Lexi had over the years. "Your mother and I came to the conclusion that there exists one elusive unknown piece to the puzzle; without that piece, we will never learn who shipped the diamonds to me and thereby never learn who they belonged to or if in fact they do belong to me.

"We have concentrated solely on the only three people we know to be involved—Ben, Sidney, and Franz. But they were all deceased when I received the crate. With all indications pointing to Franz as the owner, perhaps he left them to Ben, and they were sent to me when I became his heir. In that case, they are mine, and I must determine what to do with them.

"When your mother and I planned our trip to South Africa that included stopping in Cape Town, we discussed making a sizeable donation in their memory to the Great Synagogue and erecting two memorial plaques for Ben and Sidney. However, we were genuinely surprised to learn that two plaques in their names already existed, as did one for Franz Schiller. At that point, we began to suspect the unknown piece to be an unknown person; a person who felt he or she was duty bound to honor the three of them.

"I love you both; and I can never thank you enough for helping me to try and put the diamonds to rest, once and for all. At times, I chided myself for not having resolved the matter years ago. I no longer feel that way. A decision I may have made years ago would not be the same decision I would make today. One tends to look at things differently as one gets older.

'David, just as you drew different conclusions from what Lexi and I had learned over time, I see things differently now that we have learned Franz Schiller was in all probability the owner of the cache.

"When we return home, I will tell you the conclusion I have reached and tell you what I plan to do with the diamonds; I am certain you will approve. At that time, I will add a chapter to the *family version* and bring Harry and Adam into the loop.

"Then, if my children feel that my story is worthy of publishing, I'm going to let the three of you write it." He winked at Zoe. "With my approval, of course."

She responded, "Of course Daddy; we wouldn't have it any other way."

"Starting now, I am declaring the three of us on holiday for as many days as you would like to stay. Tomorrow, the day belongs to your Daddy. We're going to rise and shine early, pick up bathing suits, and I'm going to introduce you to some of the most beautiful beaches in the world—famously known as Cape Town's Riviera.

"I'm also thinking we should take the hotel clerk's advice and take a scenic flight over Cape Peninsula, although I'm certain they won't let us fly the plane."

They returned to London 22 July 2013, as England welcomed the new Prince, third in line to the British Throne.

To register the birth of His Royal Highness Prince George Alexander Louis of Cambridge, Prince William, Duke of Cambridge gave his occupation as Prince of the United Kingdom rather than RAF helicopter pilot.

Once Jake made up his mind about the diamonds, there was no stopping his determination to fulfill the second part of his promise to Lexi. In his own words, he told his story from beginning to end, explaining in great detail exactly how he had determined—*the one to whom it belongs.* In the end, it all seemed so natural, so easy, and so right. He was confident that Lexi would approve.

The months flew by and as December approached, the entire Lyons family was involved in one aspect or another of their trip to Israel. At Jake's request, it was extended from their usual ten days to two weeks. First and foremost, they would be celebrating Mathew's Bar Mitzvah atop Mount Masada, followed by their annual welcoming in of the New Year. Behind the scenes, Zoe, Harry, and Adam were putting together yet another celebration, the occasion of Jake's 90th Birthday.

As they welcomed the arrival of 2014 in Tel Aviv, Zoe glanced around the room at her family. Of all her Daddy's accomplishments and successes, to her, the people in this room represented his very best. She raised her glass of champagne and looking upward said aloud, "Mama, I told you we would find Daddy in London, and we certainly did."

David came up behind her, pulling her into his arms. With a twinkle in his eye he asked, "Were you talking to someone?" Before she could answer he kissed her. "Happy New Year. I Love You Zoe Lyons Handler for always."

CHAPTER FORTY-THREE

J ake sat watching the falling snow out back of the cottage creating a winter wonderland as far as his eye could see. Each spring, though he and Lexi looked forward to the multitude of flowers adorning much of the grounds with their ability to brighten even the darkest mood, he tended to welcome the snow's calming effect, as well.

He had a fire going in the fireplace, and he had brewed a pot of coffee planning to spend the afternoon going over his notes in response to Zoe's recent inquiries. Although Harry and Adam had quickly relinquished their parts in writing his story, Zoe was eager to get started. He was due to meet up with her during the coming week, and he wanted to double-check his information.

Both were satisfied with the family version that was rightfully presented in Jake's own words; it was after all his story, and only he could tell it with the passion with which he lived it. When he suggested his children pen the public version, Zoe embraced it with a vengeance. In the back of her mind, she had a strong feeling that her brothers would opt out, and they did.

She started writing her novel *A Diamond in the Rough* soon after returning from Israel, using the family version as a basis. Thus far, she had written the first five chapters. Her intent was to write several chapters at a time, give them to her father to read and approve, and move on to the next series of chapters.

Winter became spring and spring turned to summer. While Zoe kept busy writing her novel, and David spent time helping Adam with the new computer system they had recently installed at the aerodrome, Jake decided to do some housecleaning at the cottage.

He started with the workshop in the cellar carefully packing up the cutting tools, making a mental note to bring the items that had been in the crate back to the cottage and pack them away, as well. Next he tackled the two boxes of items that he had brought from the house in Middlesex. There were pictures, books, odds and ends from his sisters' room, and to his surprise the wooden cigar box that Ben and Sidney had given his father; a lion was carved on the lid.

On a sheet of paper, he inventoried the items with a brief description, returned them to the boxes, and resealed them. He opened the safe, which had been emptied except for the trays of diamonds he had removed from the chest resting on the four lower shelves. Suddenly he noticed a piece of paper at the edge of the top shelf. He reached for it and recognized the note from Franz that had been in the cloth pouch with the five uncut stones. He stared in awe as his eyes fell on the second paragraph:

> *Shiloh in Hebrew means—the one to whom it belongs; these now belong to you. Cut and polish them to their full potential just as you did our friendship.*

How could he have forgotten so quickly after opening the crate and reading the note? It was only days later that he had asked the Rabbi to translate the letters on the card. Had he remembered, perhaps he would not have dismissed Franz's involvement from the onset.

On a warm August day, he decided to take a break and go flying; taking up his favorite Cessna for a spin. He was surprised to find David in the office when he arrived; they spoke for a while before he headed over to the hangar.

Since returning from Israel and celebrating his 90th Birthday, he found himself often thinking about growing old. Age never mattered to him in the past. He and Lexi had only experienced minor health issues until she was diagnosed with cancer, and his energy level of *full speed ahead* had never waned; that is until recently. He passed his latest physical, which allowed him to continue flying. He took no prescribed medications, and he wasn't despondent.

For the first time in his life, he was lonely. He and Lexi had existed almost as *one* for their many years together, and when she died, half of him died with her leaving a void. He missed her; he missed her terribly. For two years since her passing, he had been occupied with fulfilling the promise he made her. Now that he had done so, he found himself in a position he had not previously experienced.

The altitude that always cleared his thoughts only seemed to bring back memories—good memories, happy memories but memories represented the past. He needed to look to the future, needed to have a reason to get up every day; he needed something to do.

Without realizing it, he had been flying for over two hours. At first, he was disoriented, but quickly recognizing where he was, made a slight turn and headed back to the aerodrome. As he landed the plane, Adam and David stood awaiting him with arms folded and anxious looks. Breathing a sigh of relief in learning that he was okay, they decided to hold their tongues.

Subconsciously, he had already embarked on a plan.

Zoe and David's two sons lived with their families in Houston, Texas. Joel was two years older than Jonathon but they grew up closer than twins. They were both attorneys, both pilots, and both no longer practiced law. Twenty years ago, they purchased a private airport just outside of Houston and with Jake's help and advice launched Lyons Aviation, Inc.

Over that time, they built a program offering flight and ground training to an enrollment of 50 students at a time, most of whom study under the GI training bill. As a distributor for Cessna aircraft, Lyons Aviation was equipped to provide repair and service facilities, and on average 60 planes, rental and privately owned, operated from Lyons Airport at any given time.

Their latest venture, Lyons MedAir was set to launch in late December.

Jake received a call from Jonathon in September offering to host their annual family event of welcoming in the New Year in Houston. He did not tell him about the new venture; it was to be a surprise.

"Joel and I will take care of planning everything *Texas Style* offering our very own brand of *southern hospitality*. And Grandpa we want you to see all the latest things that are happening at Lyons Aviation.

"Are you in?"

Jonathon couldn't see the pleased smile that spread across Jake's face. "Of course, I'm in. You had me at your offer of *southern hospitality*."

Every member of the Lyons family from the youngest to the eldest was clad in western gear including cowboy boots welcoming the arrival of 2015 in Houston, as fireworks lit up the sky.

They returned from a warm Houston to a bitter cold and snowy London. Jake's housecleaning efforts had become an exercise in getting his house in order for when he was no longer here. He labeled each item and who each item belonged to.

He went through the box of pictures that Lexi kept and openly cried when he came across the pictures she had taken of Zoe as a baby in Palestine, the first three and a half years of her life. There were pictures of Harry and Adam as infants when it seemed only Lexi could tell them apart.

The camera she had purchased in Jerusalem came in handy, and she kept it close at hand; she refused a new more up-to-date version until one of the grandchildren dropped it breaking it to pieces. When Zoe gifted her with a smart phone, she said she had no need for it; but upon learning it was also a camera, she accepted it without question.

He put the box of pictures away. There was no need to label them. The family had gone through them at many family gatherings.

He spoke to Zoe every day; she rang him up to check on him to assure herself that he was okay. She continued working on the novel, but Jake told her it was no longer necessary for her to seek his approval. In his mind, she was the only person qualified and up to the job.

It wasn't until March that the weather began to improve. He took the train to London and surprised her. At Jake's request, they had dinner together at the Savoy. He spent the night leaving the next afternoon by train to the Cotswolds.

With April came the first signs of spring; Jake awoke each morning to birds singing and colorful daffodils, jonquils, and tulips sprouting up from the ground infusing new life as they pushed the dead of winter away.

He rose early, had breakfast, and after a second cup of coffee left for Eagle Aerodrome. It was the start of a beautiful day; he planned to get a little flying in and then he had a meeting in the Village. He had petitioned to have the Lyons Cottage designated as a historical site; he received word just yesterday that it had been approved.

This time, he called in advance and the Cessna awaited him. No matter how many times he took flight, that same euphoric feeling came over him as the plane lifted off the ground and began its climb.

His plan to request historic status for the cottage had come to pass. At first, when he presented his petition to the Village, he wasn't sure if they would grant his wish, but they had. Now he could share his plan with the family.

The children had long ago renamed it the *Lyons Cottage* and replaced the old Wentworth Cottage plaque as a gift to Jake and Lexi. When Lexi told him she wanted to be buried on the cottage grounds, he didn't hesitate to comply, but in hindsight learned the only way to assure that the cottage would never be sold was to preserve it historically and ultimately deeding it to the Village.

As the plane leveled off, Jake looked down below. It seemed a million times he had flown over the cottage, the Village, and the neighboring towns of the Cotswolds. He could see the Lyons Cottage perfectly; and he was flying low enough to see the flowers that grew more vibrant with color each day as the weather warmed.

He could pinpoint exactly when the thought came to him to convert the Lyons Cottage into a historic site. He had been in the midst of housecleaning and packing items away, when the thought occurred to him that the items should be shared just as his story was going to be shared. He envisioned a site that would exhibit his life and work in diamonds and aeronautics, and exhibit

Lexi's life and work in the field of Nursing and research, including the time she spent in Palestine.

He landed the plane, stopped in as always to see Adam, and returned to the cottage to shower and change before heading into the Village for his meeting.

He felt invigorated having been so occupied the past few weeks.

He invited the children to the cottage for drinks and appetizers and made a late dinner reservation in the Village. He began by asking Zoe, "How is the book coming along? Do you have a guestimate as to when it will be finished?"

"It's coming along just fine; as you know I've been editing each chapter as I write it so that when I'm finished, there will be very few changes to be made. I'm hoping that I will be wrapping it up by the end of the year at the latest."

"Good. Now fill your glasses and come sit down, and I will tell you what I've been up to."

He showed them the paper that granted historical site status to Lyons Cottage, and went on to explain what he had in mind.

It was a nice enough evening to walk into the Village for dinner, and it gave them the opportunity to keep talking, and talk they did. They were very excited with Jake's plans. The cottage had been their parents' special place; it was their first home, and only Zoe had lived there. By the time Harry and Adam were born, they were living in the house in Pembridge Square.

Zoe's call to Jake the next day went unanswered. She tried his cell phone and it went right to voice mail. Throughout the morning she continued calling both phones to no avail. David suggested she ring up Adam to see if he possibly went flying and simply forgot his phone.

Adam hadn't seen him, but he said he would check. He left the office and went straight to the parking lot to his car. He was at the cottage in ten minutes. He tried the door, but it was locked. He lifted the knocker and rapped twice. There was no answer. He reached into the planter near the door and retrieved the key; opening the door, he called, "Dad, Dad are you here?"

He found him in his bed looking as though he were asleep. Adam felt for a pulse; there was none.

Once you have tasted flight
You will forever walk the earth with your eyes turned skyward
For there you have been,
and there you will always long to return.

Leonardo Da Vinci

He was laid to rest at Lyons Cottage beside his beloved Lexi on the third anniversary of her passing. As the Rabbi concluded the service, Zoe, Harry, and Adam stood hand-in-hand and repeated:

True Love is like a Diamond—precious, rare, and lasting forever!
Baruch Dayan ha'Emet—May they rest in Peace.

CHAPTER FORTY-FOUR

O ne day, a child asked his father, "Why is it always the best people who die?" The father answered, "My child, if you are in a meadow, which flowers do you pick? The worst ones or the best?"

It has been said that time heals all wounds, but to a fresh wound open and raw, time is but a distant future. Her Daddy was her Hero just as his Papa had been his. Her Mama's stories about him, the love they shared, and their love for her instilled in Zoe, as a mere toddler, her love for her Daddy even before she knew him.

Finishing her novel loomed large, but try as she may, she couldn't attain a mindset to return to it. More than a month had passed, and Zoe showed no signs of ending her mourning. The full-page obituary of Sir Jacob Lyons in the London Times resulted in a multitude of correspondence from around the world offering praise for his extraordinary life's journey and condolences to his family. Zoe did not read one; she continued to mourn.

David and her brothers grew more concerned with each passing day. This was not the wife and sister they knew—she was a realist, an optimist who faced things head on. David wanted his Zoe back, and he was determined to make that happen.

He prepared breakfast, and called for her to join him. He poured them each a cup of coffee and said, "I've made plans for us for the day. I'm determined to bring you back to the *land of the living*. I don't have to tell you what your father meant to me, and neither do Harry and Adam have to tell you what he meant to them. You are not the only one who loved him or misses him, and you can't possibly claim to have loved him more than anyone else.

"It is important to all of us that you get back to the novel; there is no better way you can honor him or prove your love for him. He entrusted you with that task because he knew that you, and only you, could tell his story the way he wanted it told. We both know you are not going to disappoint him."

They finished eating and she helped clean up. She went upstairs, showered, and dressed. When she came back down, she walked up to David and kissed him deeply. "I Love you David with every fiber of my being. You are right, absolutely right. Today is ours; tomorrow I get back to work. I have just one request; can we sandwich in a little flying to your plans?"

"I Love you too, but no sandwiching is needed. Flying was my plan, in fact my only plan."

Dare to dream, dare to fly, dare to touch the sky had been her Daddy's mantra, and she couldn't count the many times he told her that altitude cleared his thoughts. With David at the controls, Zoe allowed herself to lean back, close her eyes, and think. By the time they returned to the aerodrome, she was ready to move forward.

They stopped at the cottage, but didn't go in. They walked around the side and through the garden to the gravesite. "Daddy, I'm here to make you a promise; I will finish *A Diamond in the Rough* by yearend. The diamonds will be presented to their new owner per your wishes when the book is published."

They had dinner in the Village before driving back to London.

With Jake's passing, the family unanimously decided to forego their annual get-together over the holidays. They could always resume them next year or perhaps plan them impromptu throughout the year.

Zoe logged off the computer and exclaimed to David, "I have finished my novel." It was New Year's Eve.

David popped the cork and poured them each a glass of champagne. "Mazel Tov to the love of my life, my best friend, and my new favorite author. To a fabulous 2016—certain to be a year to remember."

She didn't recall agreeing to his suggestion, but before she knew what was happening, they were out the door and on their way to join the thousands of others, who braved the cold weather to experience the annual display of fireworks, centered around the London Eye on the capital's South Bank of the River Thames. Although temperatures hovered near freezing, the warmth that engulfed her came from within. Enfolded in David's arms, she gazed upward as burst after burst appeared in the sky. 2016 looked to be a very good year; she was sure of it.

Once her manuscript was in the hands of the publisher, she began orchestrating the event that would avail *A Diamond in the Rough* to the public, and present the diamond cache to whom her father deemed the rightful owner. She hoped to have everything in place when she received the date of the book's release from the publisher.

The family eagerly awaited the news that David finally texted to all—*It's a go!* The event was set for Sunday, 15 May 2016, and one thousand invitations were promptly posted.

The Grand Ballroom of the David InterContinental Hotel was decked out in its finest. From the eldest to the youngest, twenty-four members of the family were seated at two tables side-by-side for the dinner honoring their Patriarch Jacob Aaron Lyons. Preparations for the event had been ongoing for months and planned to coincide with the release of *A Diamond in the Rough* by Zoe Lyons Handler.

As they enjoyed dinner, the Lyons family relished feelings of elation. The room was abuzz with anticipation of what Zoe's book would reveal about diamonds—it was all about diamonds. A conclusion most reached based on the book's title and by recognizing the fact that his life's story was widely known.

They couldn't have been more wrong. Zoe penned the book from start to finish to include each and every aspect of her father's life, which in reality diamonds played a lesser role than aviation. In a unique and heartfelt way, she managed to deliver a cut and polished version of an extraordinary human being who lead an extraordinary life—her Daddy.

As dessert was being served, Zoe once again addressed the audience.

"Jacob Lyons lived his entire life rooted in love and family considering his close friends and employees an extension of that family. He was a *people* person who possessed an innate ability to *read* people, and never was that more apparent than to Harry, Adam, and me when we tried putting his feet to the fire. He was well aware that Adam and I pushed hardest.

"Although he sought neither fame nor fortune, they found him handily. At the age of seventeen he was trained to kill the enemy with a plane as his weapon. Agonizing over the loss of fellow pilots brought him face-to-face with the realization that each of his *kills* was somebody's husband, father, son. He confided in me that he carried that burden long after the War had ended. His decision to enter the world of aviation allowed him to cast that burden aside by using aircraft as a means for good instead of a weapon for evil.

"Although it was I who wrote the book, my brothers Harry and Adam are equally as dedicated to the story. In fact, it was Harry's idea to publish it after my father honored a promise he made to my mother to put pen to paper and write the Lyons story for our family. You will find their tribute to our father at the beginning of the book.

"Please welcome my brothers Harry and Adam."

As the applause died down, Harry stepped to the microphone. "When I received my advance copy of *A Diamond in the Rough*, for a few moments, I sat holding the book close to my heart without opening it. I held in my hands what few people are fortunate to ever realize, and for that Zoe, I thank you; your book is amazing. You have captured the true essence of Dad's lifelong journey as no one else could have.

"When I suggested to our father that we publish his story, he quickly agreed and just as quickly tasked Zoe, Adam, and me to write it. In turn, Adam and I quickly agreed that he really meant Zoe, and only included us in an effort not to hurt our feelings. Although I happen to know my sister was relieved when we opted out, she expected us to, and we didn't disappoint her.

"At times, it seemed our father knew his children better than we knew ourselves. His parenting style was by example, never seeking to influence our choices. He believed we are what we are today because of the choices we made yesterday, and he encouraged us to follow our hearts.

"This was never more evident to me than when I chose to become a physician, and showed no interest in learning to fly a plane. I am to this day his only child that is not a pilot, but I flew with him many times, just the two of us, and I treasure the advice and guidance he offered me on those flights.

"Now, I'd like to turn the microphone over to my brother Adam."

Adam approached the podium with a broad grin on his face. "There are certain advantages to being a twin, an identical twin, and Harry and I used those advantages many times growing up especially during our dating years.

"The story that our father couldn't tell us apart when we came home from the hospital has been circulating in the family for as long as I can remember. Exactly when he learned Harry was Harry and I was Adam, I can't tell you. What I can tell you is that though we were identical twins, he treated us each as one of a kind. He told us that just because we looked alike, it didn't mean we had the same dreams and goals.

"I'll never forget when I told him I wanted to learn to fly and become a pilot. I was fourteen years old. I knew I could take lessons at that age, but I also knew I had to be seventeen before I could get my license. Facing a three-year wait seemed daunting to me, and I told him how I felt. Never one to sugarcoat or defend any given situation, he asked that we revisit my feelings after my lessons had gotten underway.

"Of course, he was right. The euphoric feeling of being at the controls as the plane lifted off and climbed high above the ground below obliterated all thoughts of waiting. I could fly albeit with him sitting next to me, but all that mattered was I could fly. After that, waiting for a piece of paper was no big deal.

"Sis, my hat is off to you. I read my advance copy in one sitting; I didn't stop until I had read the last word on the last page. Excellent job."

The applause seemed to go on and on. Zoe stood waiting, but decided to begin speaking. "On behalf of the Lyons Family, I thank all of you for coming this evening, those of you who knew my father, as well as those who knew of him; those of you whose lives he touched, as well as those who touched his life.

"The Exhibit will remain on display in Tel Aviv for six months, at which time it will be moved to Jerusalem for an additional six months. I am pleased, honored, and incredibly proud to announce in accordance with my father's wishes, at that time, the chest and its cache of diamonds will become the property of the State of Israel.

"My ties to Israel began at birth. I am a *Sabra* having been born in the original Hadassah Hospital on Mount Scopus. The Pediatric Wing is dedicated to the memory of my grandfather—Dr. Emanuel Portman who served as Head of the Pediatric Department before the State of Israel was proclaimed. My mother was a pediatric nurse at the hospital when she gave birth to me, and later took classes at the University prior to returning to England and reuniting with my father after the War.

"Harry, Adam, and I will be available to answer any questions you may have, and I will be signing copies of my book that are available for purchase in the lobby—all proceeds of which will go to the Hadassah Hospital for research in memory of my mother--Alexandra Portman Lyons."

The excitement of the guests was infectious; no one seemed to want the evening to be over. The line entering the Exhibit was endless. Harry and Adam were besieged with questions as Zoe signed copy after copy of her book until she had signed the very last one.

As the woman who had purchased the last copy walked away, Zoe looked up to see a tall, distinguished black gentleman standing before her. "I'm so sorry, there are no copies left, but if you leave me your information, I will be happy to send you one."

He did not speak at first, but handed her a card that read, *Afram Botu Schiller, Professor Emeritus, Howard University, Washington, D.C.* "I was fortunate to receive an advance copy through my friends here at the University where I have been privileged to lecture throughout the years.

"Would you be kind enough to sign my copy to *Jamilia?*"

At the Westwood Nursing Home in upstate New York, the party they had assembled for his 95th Birthday was at long last over. To him, age was a number not a milestone; all it meant was that he had endured another year of mundane existence awaiting the end of his journey.

He had no family, no friends; no one came to visit him. He could find no cause for celebration with people who were incapacitated or mentally unstable that neither knew him nor he them.

He had been transferred to the State run facility upon his discharge from the hospital, after suffering a stroke while serving a life sentence at Attica for killing a guard during his fourth and final jewelry store robbery. He had simply traded a cell for a room.

Promising to return after she helped others to their rooms, the aide left him alone watching the big screen TV tuned into the evening news. As the anchor's voice blared to the empty room, a carved chest appeared on the screen causing him to move his wheelchair closer to the set to get a better look.

In Tel Aviv today, the family of Sir Jacob Lyons, the British billionaire philanthropist who passed away in 2015 bequeathed this intricately carved chest containing a cache of 100,000 carats of diamonds to the State of Israel. The Exhibit will . . . . .

The chest looked vaguely familiar. Again, he inched closer to the set until his wheelchair stopped. He closed and opened his eyes several times in total disbelief. It was the same chest; the very same chest that he had seen in his Uncle Franz's apartment. The realization that the diamonds had been there for his taking all along hit him like a ton of bricks.

The pain that spread across his chest was excruciating. As he gasped for breath, there was no one there to hear him or help him.

When the aide returned to take Rudy Schiller back to his room, she found him dead on the floor of a massive heart attack—the distortion of his facial features causing a look of horror on his face.

EPILOGUE

TEL AVIV, ISRAEL 2016

He invited Zoe, Harry, and Adam to be his guests for dinner the following evening. He was scheduled to fly back to Washington, DC in a couple of days, but offered to delay his return if another time would be more convenient. Zoe asked if David and her sisters-in-law could be included; he readily agreed. He made all of the arrangements.

For some reason she could not understand, Zoe had been drawn to Professor Afram Botu Schiller from the moment she looked up and saw him standing before her. When he extended an invitation to dinner, she accepted without hesitation on behalf of the others and without consulting them.

Messa's gourmet cuisine encapsulates Middle Eastern flavors and ingredients with Provencal cooking techniques served in a majestic white marble dining room featuring long walnut wooden tables adorned with festive wine glasses and candles.

Since its opening in 2004, it had become a favorite of Afram's reminding him of some of his mother's South African dishes; it was the first place that came to mind for this special occasion. He did, however, choose a more intimate and quieter seating option around the dining room's perimeter.

When his guests arrived, wine and hors d'oeuvres awaited them. He pre-ordered dinner but asked that it be held until he requested it be served. Thanking them for accepting an invitation from a total stranger broke the ice. He introduced himself and went around the table acknowledging each of them. Stopping at Zoe, he praised her novel adding that his children had often hinted that he do the same.

He began in South Africa when his father was killed trying to break up a fight; he was five years old. His black African mother left alone with a small boy, no means of support, and far from her native village was sitting on the side of the road cradling him in her arms as they carried his father's body away. That was where Franz Schiller found her.

They lived in a small shack down near the docks that his father bought when they first arrived in Cape Town. Franz set her up with a booth in the open market and for years she sold various items, many that he gave her from The General Store; they managed. His mother taught him to read, and when he wasn't seen with a book in his hand, he was carving pieces of wood and magically turning them into majestic animals and boxes as his father had taught him. Soon his mother's booth carried new items.

When Jewish immigrants from all over Europe began arriving in Cape Town, his mother was recruited to teach English to the children at the synagogue.

As he grew older, he did odd jobs and when Franz converted his store to The Smoker's Shop, he helped build the cases, paint, and supplied him with carved cigar boxes and humidors to sell.

His story told of the friendship between Franz, Ben, and Sidney adding his mother and him to the mix, confirming most of what they had pieced together in their search for the rightful owner of the cache. He recalled the brothers' trip to London and the party they threw welcoming them back to consoling them upon learning their brother Harry and his family had been killed in an air raid. They were there for one another throughout good times and bad.

His mother often referred to Sidney's death as the beginning of a downward spiral from which the three friends never recovered. Franz's death a year later was another terrible blow, but determined to fulfill his friend's final wishes, Ben summoned them to his cottage where he read the Will revealing that he and his mother were Franz's sole heirs. All funds resided in one account on deposit at the First National Bank of South Africa; The Smoker's Shop emptied of its contents was put up for sale, the proceeds of which would be deposited into their account.

The Bank acting as Executor of the Will was charged with carrying out its provisions and for a period of two years dispensed the funds on a monthly basis. There was an additional amount set aside for his education arranged by Franz before he died.

He and his mother were overwhelmed; they had not only inherited a princely sum that assured their wellbeing far into the future if not for a lifetime, but most importantly assured his education. While still digesting their newfound status, Ben told them about the Franz Schiller they did not know.

He began in 1882, the year Franz arrived in Cape Town—from Simon Abel's General Store to the farmhouse to finding the diamonds—the diamonds he felt he had stolen because he did not own the land on which he found them. He led them before the carved chest that once sat in Franz's apartment, lifting the lid, and revealing its contents—tray after tray of cut and polished diamonds.

Ben related how Franz had summoned him and Sidney to his home one evening, telling them where and how he had found and collected the diamonds over a period of twenty years. Seeking their advice and help, he opened an account at the Annex to have the rough stones cut and polished. Ben believed that although the diamonds had not been specifically mentioned in the Will, they were part of his estate and rightfully belonged to his heirs.

His mother would not hear of it. She questioned; what could a black African woman with a teenage son possibly do with them? They presented a liability she was unwilling to accept. Ben agreed. For the time being, the chest would remain on the table in his cottage; the chest he himself had carved and the table he had built to Franz's specifications.

Ben picked up where Franz left off on behalf of furthering his education. He approached a congregant at the synagogue who was a Professor at Cape Town University, and it was through his efforts and tutelage that he attended the South African Native College, earning degrees in Political Science and Economics. It was at this point in his life that he decided to honor Franz for all that he had done for him and his mother by assuming *Schiller* as his surname.

He was preparing to leave for college when Ben suddenly died—the very day he was due to return to the cottage that his mother had readied for his homecoming. During the many months he spent at the Sanatorium recovering from Tuberculosis, Ben wrote his own Will leaving everything to his nephew Jacob Lyons.

Further provisions instructed that he be cremated and that both his and Sidney's remains be shipped to London to be buried alongside their brother. The Bank held the Deed to his cottage; however, the Will stated his mother could live there as long as she wished.

He sealed his Will in an envelope and entrusted it to his closest friend, his mother. When Ben died, she opened the envelope, made note of his wishes, and presented it to the Bank to contact his nephew, his heir.

As he and his mother gathered the items from the cottage in an effort to determine how large a crate he would need to build, they came upon the chest of diamonds. His mother agonized for days knowing that the decision she was about to make had to be the right one; in the end, there was no decision to be made because the only person who came to mind was Jacob Lyons.

He carved a matching box to hold Ben's remains; they packed up the tools, and personal effects; and placing the chest in the crate, delivered it to the funeral home, nailed shut and ready for shipment.

He had already left for college when Jacob arrived in Cape Town. Apprehensive at first, his mother's fears soon dissipated when she met the young man whom she had chosen to entrust with the cache. They met over a period of days; the diamonds were never mentioned. He seemed more interested in learning about the uncles he never knew.

When it came time for him to return to London, he thanked her for taking the time to provide him the insight he sought. To his mother, Jacob's visit was a gift confirming that her choice had been the right one.

Upon graduating from the South African Native College, and having been accepted to Howard University in Washington, DC, he left with a heavy heart for the States, leaving his mother behind in Cape Town. Offered a professorship at the University upon receiving his doctorate, he convinced his mother to leave South Africa and move with him to America. She notified the Bank to sell the cottage, and arranged to have the proceeds go to the Great

Synagogue in return for three plaques on the Memorial Wall for Franz, Ben, and Sidney. She never looked back.

She told him many years later that it was not a hard decision to make. South Africa in the grips of Apartheid had nothing to offer black Africans, but more of the same she had experienced her entire life. She was not yet fifty and looked forward to a whole new world of experiences. She had a good life in America. She lived to see her only son marry, was a loving grandmother to six, and a loving great grandmother to eight; she died at the age of 100.

Through the years, they never stopped searching for news about Jacob Lyons or the diamonds. With the advent of the Internet, it became easier, and although they found an abundance of information about Jacob, no word of the diamonds ever surfaced.

On his last visit to Israel, he learned of the pending publication of Zoe's book and *by invitation only* dinner. Intrigued by the name of Zoe's novel, he convinced his good friend, Professor Levi Morris, to give him his advance copy along with his ticket to the Banquet.

He viewed Jacob's decision to bequeath the diamonds to the State of Israel as the perfect choice, the only choice because it connected everyone associated with them including Simon Abel on whose family's property they were found. The fact that Jacob made his decision without knowing the entire story, led him to believe that divine intervention had played a part.

How grand it would have been if Jacob and Jamilia had learned the outcome of their decisions; deep down, he believed they knew.

The hors d'oeuvres sat untouched; the wine bottles stood empty. He asked that dinner be served. After dinner they retired to the adjacent room, the all-black bar that stood in stark contrast to the majestic all-white marble dining room, extending their evening into the early hours of the morning.

Author's Notes

Each of us is born *a diamond in the rough* with the potential of becoming that perfect cut and polished stone. To that extent, the responsibility of the process rests entirely within each of us.

The actual process consists of five steps—
planning, cleaving, bruting, polishing, and inspecting.

Without question— *planning*—although time consuming, is the most important step as it determines the final value of the finished product.

The steps of *cleaving* and *bruting* encompass our years of youth through adulthood where nurturing our imagination enables our ingenuity to fuel our passion and establish our enterprise—as facet after facet we cut.

At mature adulthood we are ready for the *polishing*—
of our goals, our achievements, our benevolence.

Hate and malice purged from our hearts, we infuse the Scaif with a mixture of love and goodness making it possible to polish our facets symmetrically at angles that reflect us in the best light.

The ultimate step—*inspecting*—appraises the value of our finished product—that perfect cut and polished stone—for therein lies our *Legacy.*

Marilyn Land

DIAMONDS

Diamonds are more than aesthetically beautiful—they are enduring symbols of love, romance, and commitment. The stone's name is derived from the Greek word *adamas* meaning *unconquerable* and *indestructible* whose symbolic meaning lends itself aptly to its historic commemoration of eternal love.

Throughout history, diamonds have stood for wealth, power, and spirit, and worn by Royalty as symbols of strength, courage, and invincibility. Over the centuries, diamonds acquired a more unique status as the ultimate gift of love. It was said that cupid's arrows were tipped with diamonds that had a magic nothing else could equal. The Greeks believed the fire in the diamond reflected the constant flame of love.

The story of diamonds transcends cultures and localities. It is the oldest item that anyone can own; it is three billion years in age, a strategic and high tech super material that is formed in the earth's interior and shot to the surface by extraordinary volcanoes. It is carbon in its more concentrated form, the chemical element fundamental to all life; thus it is a native element. It is also extremely pure, containing only trace amounts of boron and nitrogen.

Diamonds are the hardest substance on earth, but their appeal goes far beyond durability. Adding to the mystery and aura of what makes diamonds so sought after, approximately 250 tons of ore must be mined and processed in order to produce a single, one-carat, polished, gem-quality stone.

Lodewyk van Bercken, a Flemish diamond polisher, invented the *Scaif* in the mid 15th century; this single invention transformed the diamond trade and is still in use today. His ingenious polishing wheel enabled him to quickly cut facets into diamonds with precision, and opened the door to the creation of complex diamond cuts which otherwise would have never been possible. He introduced the concept of absolute symmetry in the placement of facets on the stone. His meticulous and precisely studied advancements resulted in the first pear-shaped cut diamond.

Two years after the invention of the Scaif, when Archduke Maxmilian of Austria gave a diamond ring to Mary of Burgundy, the diamond engagement ring was introduced. Placing it upon the third finger of the left hand dates back to the early Egyptian belief that the vein of love runs directly from the heart to the tip of the third finger.

For millions of people around the world, a *DIAMOND*'s worth lies in the reason it was given and by whom it was given as the mystery and magic, the beauty and romance shining out from a simple solitaire says all the heart feels but words cannot express.

DIAMOND—just the mention of the name exemplifies wealth, prosperity, status, and exudes everlasting love.

The legacy of the *DIAMOND* will continue. It existed at the dawn of civilized man and will exist forever. It will be a part of love and prosperity, a part of intrigue and beauty, a part of weddings and celebrations, and a part of every woman's heart that keeps one on her finger. Men will always swear love by it, and love will always maintain the brilliance of earth's great gift—the *DIAMOND*.

THESE ARE A FEW OF MY FAVORITES

My happiness is to love you and be loved by you in return.

Jack Stewart Land

Diamonds are Forever!

Frances Gerety

There are in the end three things that last: Faith, Hope, and Love and the greatest of these is Love.

The engine is the heart of an aeroplane but the pilot is its soul.

Sir Walter Alexander Raleigh
Official Historian of the RAF

Aeronautics was neither an industry nor a science. It was a miracle.

Igor Sikorsky

Somewhere over the rainbow way up high,
There's a land that I heard of once in a lullaby,
Somewhere over the rainbow skies are blue,
And the dreams that you dare to dream really do come true.

Lyrics from Somewhere Over the Rainbow
By E.Y. "Yip" Harburg

Peace will come when the Arabs love their children
more than they hate us.

When Peace comes we will perhaps in time be able to forgive the
Arabs for killing our sons, but it will be harder for us to forgive them
for having forced us to kill their sons.

Israel exists as a fulfillment of a promise made by God Himself.
It would be ridiculous to ask it to account for its legitimacy.

Golda Meir

We must develop and maintain the capacity to forgive.
He who is devoid of the power to forgive is void of the power to love.
There is some good in the worst of us and some evil in the best of us.
When we discover this, we are less prone to hate our enemies.

Martin Luther King, Jr.

What lies behind you and what lies in front of you
pales in conjunction to what lies inside of you.

Ralph Waldo Emerson

In the end, it's not the years in your life that count.
It's the life in your years.

Abraham Lincoln

Above all else guard your heart
for everything you do flows from it.

Proverbs 4:23